I0684795

SHORES OF
K'ORGE

THRICE BORN

By Summer Hanford

Martin Sisters Publishing

SHORES OF K'ORGE
Martin Sisters Publishing Company

Publishing History
First edition published in 2017

Published by
Martin Sisters Publishing Company
Kentucky, USA

All rights reserved
Copyright © 2017 by Summer Hanford
Map art copyright © 2015 by Summer Hanford
The unauthorized reproduction or distribution of this copyrighted work is illegal. Criminal copyright infringement, including infringement without by monetary gain, is investigated by the Federal Bureau of Investigation and is punishable by up to 5 (five) years in federal prison and a fine of $250,000.

Names, characters and incidents depicted in this book are products of the author's imagination or are used fictitiously. Any resemblance to actual events, locales, organizations, or persons, living or dead, is entirely coincidental and beyond the intent of the author or publisher.

No part of this book may be reproduced or transmitted in any form or by any means, electronic or mechanical, including photocopying, recording, or by any information storage and retrieval system, without permission in writing from the publisher.

Martin Sisters Publishing Company
ISBN: 978-1-62553-980-9

Science Fiction/Fantasy/Young Adult
Printed in the United States of America

Visit our website at www. martinsisterspublishing.com

DEDICATION

To Joseph Guss, my 'Special Education Teacher,' as we called the position way back when. Thank you for your care and patience in working with a young person who couldn't tell a **3** from an **E**, a **b** from a **d** (or a **p**, for that matter), or a **g** from a **q**, and teaching her how to read and write. Thank you, as well, for putting my first fantasy book into my hands, so I could learn *why* I would want to read, and write. I am forever grateful.

THRICE BORN SERIES
MARTIN SISTERS PUBLISHING COMPANY

Gift of the Aluien
Hawks of Sorga
Throne of Wheylia
The Plains of Tybrunn
Shores of K'Orge

COMPANION SHORT STORIES
BY SUMMER HANFORD

The Forging of Cadwel
Hawk Trials for Mirimel
The Fall of Larkesong
The Sword of Three

ACKNOWLEDGEMENT

My gratitude, as always, to Martin Sisters Publishing for their continued confidence and support, and to Sycamore Hill Gardens for allowing me to participate in their events. I would like to acknowledge as well the wonderful Marcellus School District, a great place to get an education.

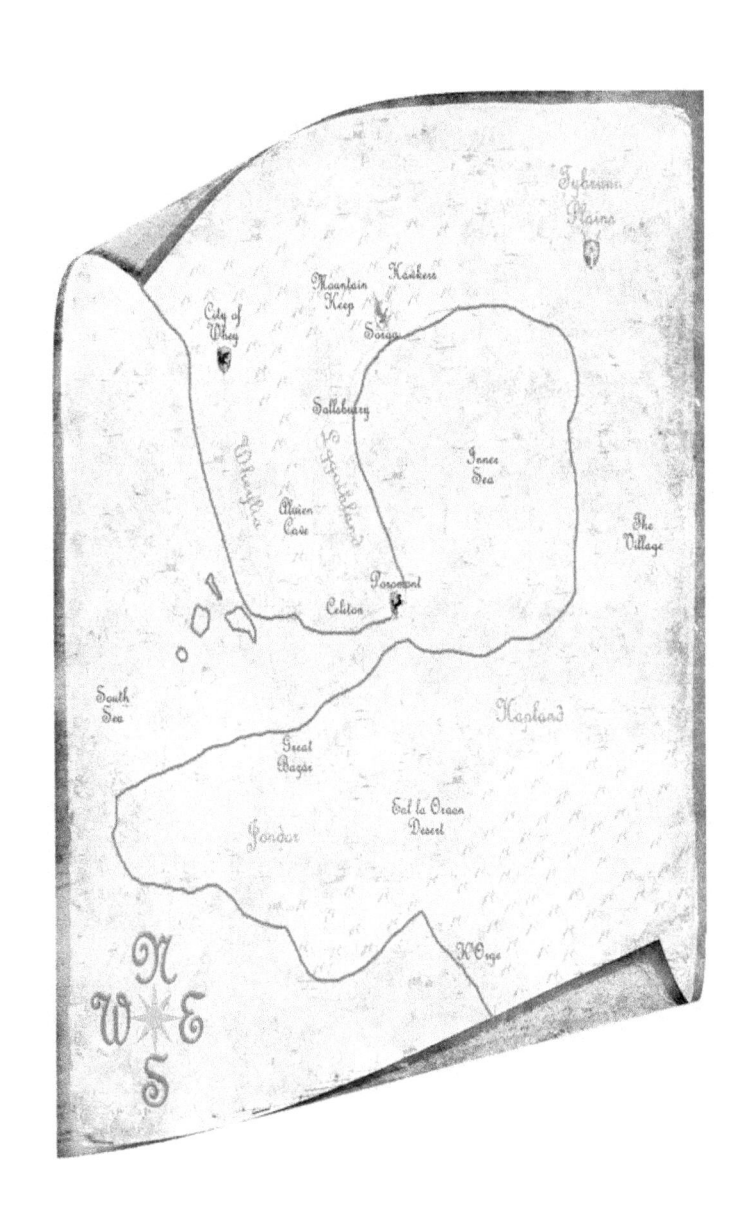

Chapter 1

Ari slammed his glass down on the low table between the couches in Sir Cadwel's study. Clear liquid sloshed free. He surged to his feet and headed for the door to the foyer, aware of footsteps following him. If he went straight to the stable, Stew might still be saddled. They could be in the capital in a matter of weeks if they rode hard, and Ari meant to.

"Ari, Mirimel." Sir Cadwel's voice stopped Ari as he reached the door. "Both of you, sit down."

Ari turned, pleased to find Hawk Guardian Mirimel behind him. He would need her to track the people who'd abducted Ispiria. He looked back at the couches, taking in the bard Larkesong's worried face, his mentor Sir Cadwel's familiar scowl and Chief Steward Natan's sympathetic mien. "I have to make all haste to the capital."

"You rode in only moments ago." Under Sir Cadwel's drooping gray mustache, his scowl gained force. "You need to rest, eat, bathe and hear what we know. A report on your last mission wouldn't go amiss, either."

"There's no time," Mirimel said, looking as anxious as Ari felt.

As well she should, Ari thought. Ispiria was Mirimel's cousin and one of the last remnants of her family. "I have to find Ispiria," he said. His fiancée was infinitely more important than a bath and something to eat.

"Princess Siara as well," Natan said.

Ari nodded. Of course they would rescue Princess Siara, too. It went without saying.

"Lad, Sir Cadwel is right. More so even than he knows." Larke's tone soothed. "This is too serious a crime for you to run off without a plan, or without availing yourself of his wisdom. In your mentor lies one of the keenest strategic minds of all time. I think we must acquaint him fully with the truths revealed on the Tybrunn Plain, so that mind of his may mull over what lies behind this kidnapping. I find the timing, and the bit about absconding across the ocean, to be suspect indeed."

That had been Ari's first thought upon learning of the abduction. Why take Siara and Ispiria across the sea? It coincided too perfectly with the Lady's wish for Ari to go there to seek the final part of a weapon he'd declined to pursue. A vision of the Lady's face, a once-loved visage, formed in his mind.

"It's no mystery," Natan said. He pulled a tightly rolled strip of paper from his doublet. It was the sort they used on birds sent from the capital. "The king's missive tells of a note saying Princess Siara is being taken to the holy land of the Overgod for conversion."

Ari ran a hand through his too-long brown hair. He recalled Prince Parrentine confiding there was pressure from some of the noble families to force Princess Siara to convert from her Wheylian faith to worship of the Overgod. Would someone really take that to such lengths, or was this an attempt by the Lady to force Ari to seek the final of three powerful magical stones? Ari looked about Sir Cadwel's study, his gaze skimming over book-lined shelves, weapons hung for decoration, the heavy leather furnishings and dark wood. For all the wisdom contained therein, he didn't see how there could be any answer to whether or not the Lady was behind the abductions. The only way to learn the truth was to find Ispiria and Siara.

"Sit down," Sir Cadwel repeated, his tone one Ari was accustomed to obeying. "You aren't leaving now, and you aren't going to the capital. King Ennentine has sent a ship, under Prince Parrentine's command. We will leave in two days' time and rendezvous with it on the coast. There's no reason to go running off. Arriving before the vessel will do no good. It shall take us directly to Jondor, as that's most likely where they headed."

"Us?" Ari repeated. "You're coming as well?" That was the first good news he'd heard from them.

"She's my grandniece. Of course I'm going." Sir Cadwel glowered around the room, as if daring anyone to say he ought not.

Ari crossed back to the couches and retook his place, though it took effort on his part not to dash from the room. It seemed wrong to sit about while Ispiria and Siara were in the hands of abductors. Mirimel remained by the door, arms folded across her chest. A scowl marred her pretty face. Though she was a little older than Ispiria and her curls more orange than Ispiria's red, Mirimel bore striking resemblance to Ari's fiancée. At least, when she smiled, which she rarely did.

"Cadwel, you can't go," Larke said. "Think of your vows."

"You're one to talk, bard."

"I, I'm afraid, am beyond redemption." Larke's tone was bitter. Still, he cast a look at Natan, indicating the conversation was moving to things the overly-handsome chief steward oughtn't to hear.

"I see." Natan stood. "This is the part where I'm asked to leave so you can discuss your secrets. Ones which, apparently, Hawk Guardian Mirimel and this wastrel of a bard are privy to, but not I, the man who runs your dukedom for you."

"Stay," Ari said. Four sets of eyes turned to him in surprise. "I am done keeping secrets from those I trust. My loyalty is to the king and to Sorga. Let the Aluiens safeguard themselves. This ridiculous web of half-truths brings only strife. If I discover Ispiria was taken as part of it, and I never even warned her she was in danger, I'll . . ."

He trailed off, his mind too numb to think of a suitable punishment or who to administer it to. Perhaps the real culprit was himself. He was the one who'd tried so desperately to uphold a hardly understood vow made when he was but fifteen, and under threat of death.

"Aluiens?" Natan's tone was tentative as he sat.

"It would be easiest to show you," Ari said, waving a hand at Larke.

Larke rose from the couch, visage troubled.

"You're going along with this?" Sir Cadwel asked. "You're going to reveal your nature simply because the lad is tired of secrets?"

"You don't know what happened on the plains." The bard's usually melodious tone was harsh. He closed his eyes for a moment, every muscle relaxing, though no one would have realized he was in such a state of tension before. A soft blue-white glow emanated from him, leeching color from his garish clothing and blond hair. When he opened his eyes, they were no longer the blue of the living, but infused instead with the shimmering of Orlenia, the magic substance flowing through his veins.

Natan breathed out a low oath and leaned away from Larke. His eyes on the bard, he blinked several times. Then he leaned forward, looking startled. "Larkesong?"

"The same." Larke issued an elegant bow.

"Larkesong?" Natan repeated, expression stunned.

"You can tone it down now, bard," Sir Cadwel said. "I think he gets the idea."

"You're Larkesong." Natan was no longer questioning. "You're the bard who was in love with Queen Parrella. The one who disappeared. I thought Cadwel had you killed."

The knight shot Natan a quelling glare. Ari winced, and glanced at Mirimel. Surprise made her blue eyes wide. Ari was relatively sure Larke would have preferred to tell Mirimel that story in his own time. Hearing the couch creak as Larke reseated himself, Ari turned back to find the bard appeared reassuringly human once more. Mirimel returned to her place. She scrutinized Larke's face, but he was looking at Natan. The chief steward still gaped at him.

"You haven't aged a day. How is this possible? How were you glowing?" Natan swiveled in his chair to level a hard look at Sir Cadwel. "How long have you known?"

"That Larkesong is alive and well, and still gallivanting about this world to torment me?" The knight gave a noncommittal grunt. "Some time now."

"And Larkesong is actually one of these Aluiens Ari spoke of? There are more, then."

13

"Yes," Ari said, impatient, though he had nowhere to ride off to in view of Sir Cadwel's news about the ship. "Many more. They all glow. Their veins are suffused with Orlenia, the source of their magic." He scrubbed his hands over his face. "I suppose I should start at the beginning."

For not the first time in recent months, Ari launched into the tale of how he'd been made more than human by the Aluiens and their magic. How they'd made him stronger, faster, better able to heal, and enhanced his ability to see in the dark, all in a convoluted effort to save his life. He broached the subject of Empty Ones, the evil opposite of Larke's people. He told of the Lady, of his distant relationship to her and of their family's ancient enemy. All this he did with as much brevity as he could, for Natan was the only one in the room not acquainted with the tale.

Ari decided to leave out that Sir Cadwel was also an Aluien. Mirimel didn't know, and telling Natan would likely lead to more confusion, and bitterness. Although Natan's own licentious conduct had gotten him expelled from the knighthood years ago, Ari was aware the chief steward harbored resentment for Sir Cadwel's accomplishments. There was no reason to add the fact that Sir Cadwel, the greatest knight the realm had ever seen, was now also a nearly immortal magical being.

When Ari was finished with the story of his past, he launched headlong into a summary of his doings since spring. He could hardly credit that it was only now just shy of fall. So much had happened during his time on the Tybrunn Plains, it seemed like a year must have passed.

He spoke of the Questri, a magical race of horses. Ari's horse Stew was one, as well as Mirimel's new mare, Larke's silver-gray steed, and Sir Cadwel's dun destrier, Goldwin. With more detail than he'd provided in the first half of his narration, Ari described his time among the Questri and the humans who served them.

As he spoke, he realized their other two companions, the only two in their party without Questri steeds, would arrive soon. The group had been outside Mirimel's home of Hawkers when they received Sir Cadwel's urgent summon to return. Their Questri mounts more fleet than normal horses, Ari, Larke and Mirimel had left the Wheylian swordmaster Cooro and the so-called cartographer, Lord Kenmar, to catch up as they could.

Ari wanted to get Kenmar's story out before he arrived. There were parts of the tale that would spur Sir Cadwel into attacking Kenmar. Ari's mentor needed to be in possession of the full story before Kenmar reached Sorga, so Sir Cadwel could understand Ari's inclination not to fight.

In as calm a manner as he could muster, Ari informed Sir Cadwel that Kenmar was secretly Ari's lifelong enemy, but had so far proved himself more of a friend. Ari spoke, choking slightly, of the Lady's betrayal and how it had nearly cost Mirimel her life. Taking a deep breath, he commenced to tell the vengeance and hate-filled tale that was Lord Kenmar's story.

"So, I've decided not to seek the final stone," Ari finally concluded. "Why turn myself into the weapon the Lady wishes me to be? I don't want to battle Kenmar. We have established a truce."

"You do not foresee the Lady accepting your inclination toward peace," Sir Cadwel said.

"No, I do not." Ari glanced at Larke. "We know the Lady believes the final piece, the final stone, to be somewhere across the ocean. She commanded me to go there, to seek it."

"Which is why you and Larke are suspicious of the timing of this abduction." Sir Cadwel leaned back in his armchair, his expression thoughtful.

"You believe this lady you speak of is pretending religious zealots took the princess and Ispiria?" Natan asked. He looked slightly dazed, as he had throughout Ari's monologue. "But, this could spark a war. Our princess, the future queen of Lggothland, has been abducted."

"If what Kenmar told us is at all true, it wouldn't be the first time the Lady has started a war as part of her feud," Larke said.

"You believe all of this?" Sir Cadwel asked the bard.

"She would have let Mirimel die, Cadwel. To prove a point." Larke shook his head. "I can't bring myself to see past that. I can't reconcile it with a person I can obey and love."

"How could I have forgotten about Lord Mrakenson?" Sir Cadwel mused. He narrowed his eyes at Larke. "Was it your doing? I'd every intention of riding up there and destroying that fiend at the first opportunity."

"It wasn't my doing. I would look to Kenmar. I'd wager spells to keep anyone from returning there are worked into the very stones of the keep."

Sir Cadwel nodded.

"I know I don't understand all of this." Natan spoke slowly, as if picking out each word. "I think, though, that you'll need this final stone. You need to complete the set and make your sword into the weapon it was fashioned to be."

Sir Cadwel nodded again. "Aye. There's no help for it."

"I don't understand." Ari looked between the two. "That would be playing into her hands. If she's behind this abduction, the purpose is to force me to go south to where the stone is, though how she'll make me search it out I can't imagine. If I

16

complete the set and become the weapon she wants me to be, won't she find even more ways to force me to do her will? She will make me battle Kenmar. If she'll harm Mirimel and Ispiria, she won't balk at any of you, or Lggothland itself."

"You have to find the last stone, lad." Sir Cadwel's voice was hard. "There may be only one way to end this."

Ari stared at him blankly. He turned to Larke for help, only to find a nauseated look on the bard's face. "How can we end this?"

"If this lady and Lord Kenmar are so evenly matched she can't best him without you to help her, armed with the completed sword, then you can't hope to best her without all three stones." Natan's tone was kind.

"Fight the Lady?" Ari realized, for all the anger and resentment he harbored toward her, even if she had Ispiria, he couldn't fight her. Could he? Attack the Lady, the ancient delicate Aluien who'd saved his life at least three times?

Yet, wasn't she the one who'd put him in danger to begin with? Had she not carefully crafted each of those moments, endangering and manipulating him to her ends? He shook his head, trying to clear it. "It won't come to that."

"We can hope not." Sir Cadwel's eyes didn't reflect any hope, though. "Larke, were you having any luck locating the stone, beyond the rumor it's to the south?"

"Rumor is all we followed. It did seem as if we drew nearer, though." Larke frowned. "If I could get to the scrying pool, I could summon the last images the Lady saw."

"If you return to the caves, will they allow you to leave again?" Sir Cadwel asked.

"Allow me to leave? My greater fear is they shall forever cast me out."

Sir Cadwel regarded Larke for a long moment, his fingers drumming on the arm of his chair. Finally, he turned back to Ari. "I will not be going with you after all. We don't know yet if these events are related. If they are, I believe you will need the third stone before this is through, and you can't seek it now. You must obey your king and track down those who abducted Princess Siara and Ispiria. Larke and I shall seek the stone."

"And Kenmar," the bard said. "He says he wants Ari to have it, and he's bound to be helpful."

"And we want to keep our eyes on him," Sir Cadwel added.

Larke answered that with a grim nod.

Sir Cadwel looked about, as if something might have changed within the study without his knowledge. "Speaking of which, you've been here some time. Swordmaster Cooro and Kenmar should have arrived by now."

Ari felt a new surge of anxiety. Sir Cadwel was correct. Cooro and Lord Kenmar should have joined them. Ari looked about the room at Sir Cadwel, Larke, Mirimel and Natan, wondering what had gone wrong now.

Chapter 2

As if in answer to the tension that filled the room on the heels of Sir Cadwel's observation, a knock sounded at the door.

"Enter," Sir Cadwel barked.

The thick wood swung open to reveal Swordmaster Cooro. He cast a quick glance about the room and came in, closing the door behind him before issuing a low bow.

"Where's Kenmar?" Mirimel demanded as Cooro opened his mouth to speak.

Ari was aware that, in spite of the fact he'd saved her life, Mirimel still didn't trust Lord Kenmar. She couldn't see past his involvement in the destruction of her home and the deaths of her family, or refused to. She blamed Kenmar because, long ago, he created the Empty One known as the Caller, who later burned her village and murdered her family. To Ari's mind, that was like blaming whoever had forged the ancient sword he wielded for any deaths he dealt with it.

"I see you are happy to find Cooro returned," the Wheylian swordmaster said, shooting Mirimel a smile. "He went to see his son. Rather, to check on him."

"He what?" Mirimel asked.

"You allowed this?" Sir Cadwel demanded.

"I couldn't prevent it." Cooro shrugged. Though there were other places to sit, the swordmaster crossed to seat himself on the couch across from Ari, right between Larke and Mirimel.

"Did he say anything more?" Ari asked. He wanted to believe Kenmar was on their side. Naive though Ari knew it to be, he trusted Lord Kenmar's overtures of peace. If they turned out to be false, it would cut.

"He said, I must ensure my runes remain strong. He can never be allowed out into the lands." Cooro shrugged again. "He said he was nervous, having been away for so long. I told him you wouldn't like it. He said he didn't care for it himself, but we would all like it less if his son escaped the keep. As I said, I had no way to prevent him."

Ari nodded. Though a brilliant fighter and acrobat, Cooro had no magic. There was no way he could challenge Lord Kenmar.

"We should go after him," Mirimel said. "We have Questri. We can easily overtake his gelding."

"No." Ari made his tone firm.

"No?" Mirimel repeated, looking defiant. "He's sure to be up to no good, Ari. Why didn't he mention he intended to visit his keep? It's awfully convenient he should decide to go there after we rode away."

"Maybe he would have said something when we reached the proper trail. We didn't give him any time to tell us when we left, after all. We proceeded with considerable haste."

"Why must you insist in seeing the best in that murderer?"

"Why must you insist on seeing the worst?"

Mirimel frowned at him. She was fingering the hilt of the broad-bladed hunting knife she wore at her waist. Ari didn't think she realized she was doing it.

"There's nothing to do about it now," Sir Cadwel said. "Without the third stone, perhaps even with, we can't stand against him."

"We would have some advantage," Ari said. "He doesn't want to kill us."

Across from him, Mirimel shook her head in disgust.

"Not to interrupt what is, every time, a stimulating argument between you both," Cooro broke in. "But may Cooro ask why the hasty summons and the many hawks?"

Everyone looked at Ari. He scowled, suddenly aware of why Sir Cadwel did so with such frequency. Why must it be him? They all knew what the trouble was, and were likely able to speak on it with less emotion than he. "Princess Siara and . . ." He cleared his throat. "That is, Ispiria and Siara have been abducted and taken away across the sea, to the holy land of the Overgod. His worshippers wish to convert the princess. That's about all we know at this point."

Cooro stared at him, mouth half open.

Ari nodded, agreeing with the sentiment. "Yes, it's bad."

"But, you must suspect this Lady--"

"We do," Mirimel put in. "We suspect the Lady. We need the third stone. It's all been worked out. We're going south in two days' time, to meet a ship, and you are going home to Wheylia."

Cooro, who had turned to her, whipped back around to face Ari, leaping to his feet. "You cannot order me gone. My queen said to aid you. I did little on the plains. She must have

21

meant for me to be by your side for this journey as well, as the princess is her granddaughter. You need me, Aridian. No man of the desert is as skilled a fighter as Cooro. I will help you recover your lost lady and the Princess of Wheylian blood, or I shall die in the attempt." This last was said in ringing tones, Cooro's face set in lines of defiance.

Ari raised his eyebrows. "Ah, I was going to ask you to come. I agree that Siara going missing must be the true reason Queen Reudi sent you. Mirimel was out of line in ordering you gone." Ari didn't look at her, but he could feel the glare Mirimel leveled at him for that statement.

"In that case, I vow to see this quest through at your side, Lord Aridian."

"Thank you," Ari said.

Before Cooro could retake his seat, Sir Cadwel stood. "I think we've accomplished what we can for now. You should all get cleaned up and ready for dinner." He turned to Ari. "You'll need to make a speech. Let the people know you'll return with Ispiria. Tell them that tomorrow we'll prepare and the following day, we'll head out. It will reassure them to know at least that much of our plans."

"Right," Ari said, standing along with everyone else. "Natan, could you arrange rooms for Cooro, Larke and Mirimel, and send me a valet, please?"

"Of course. If you'll all follow me," Natan said before leading swordmaster, bard and hawk guardian from the room.

"Ari."

Sir Cadwel's quiet voice called Ari back when he would have followed. Returning to the couches, he came to stand before the man who'd adopted him. To Ari's surprise and mild guilt, he realized he was slightly taller than Sir Cadwel now. He must have grown in the half year he was away on the Tybrunn

Plains. Not that he could stop himself from growing. He'd only that summer turned eighteen.

"Yes, sir?"

"We'll get them back. I won't see my family destroyed again, or this kingdom sunk into war."

Ari took in the deep lines on Sir Cadwel's face. His heavy brows drooped, the scar over his right eye adding additional harshness to a visage etched by countless sorrows. Though he didn't know everything about his mentor's past, Ari had some idea of how many sacrifices Sir Cadwel had made to bring peace to Lggothland. "Yes, we'll get them back," Ari said.

"Even if you must break vows? Even if it comes to confronting the Lady?" Sir Cadwel pinned Ari with his gaze. "That bard and I will find you the stone, but you must be ready to wield it."

"I will do whatever it takes to bring Ispiria and Siara home." Ari infused all the conviction he could into those words. "If there was ever a thing in this world to be certain of, you can believe that, sir."

"Good," Sir Cadwel said. "Go get cleaned up."

Ari nodded. Leaving Sir Cadwel and his two great shaggy hounds, who slept contentedly by the fireplace, Ari stepped into the foyer. He nodded to the guards standing to either side of the large double doors. He couldn't muster a smile, and didn't know that he ought to, but he did his best to look determined and sure. The lords of the keep might be gone for some time on this journey. Ari needed to instill confidence in the people of Sorga before he and Sir Cadwel departed. It was the least he could do for Natan, who would be left in charge in their absence.

Striding through the vaulted foyer, Ari followed the gray stone wall on his right to the steps leading to those chambers reserved for nobles. At the top, he walked down the corridor, passing all of the other doors, including Ispiria's, to the suite of rooms he and she would share once they were wed. Perhaps, Ari reflected, a bath and clean clothes would help in some way. He could only hope so, for at the moment his world seemed bleak and heaped with troubles.

Ari opened the door expecting to find a valet waiting within. Instead, standing in the middle of his sitting room was Lord Kenmar. Surprise stopped Ari in the doorway, and caution kept him there. The truth was, though, if Kenmar wanted to kill him, Ari had no defense. Dragging more of his friends into the fight would only lead to their demises as well.

He took in the worry in Kenmar's eyes and how the graying lord wrung his hands, the skin pulled thin and white. Reminding himself that he and Kenmar had declared a truce and were almost friends, Ari stepped into the room. He closed the door behind him. "Kenmar. We missed you when Cooro arrived."

"I only now reached Sorga. I'm sorry to sneak in. I didn't know what my reception would be from anyone but you."

From the apprehension on his face, Ari didn't think Kenmar was certain he was welcomed by Ari either. "I believe I've convinced everyone no fighting is called for at this time. Well, everyone but Mirimel."

Kenmar nodded, ignoring Ari's vague attempt to ease the tension thick in the room. "Thank you. I'd counted on you to tell my tale for me."

"We have a problem," Ari said, realizing Kenmar still didn't know the reason Sir Cadwel had summoned them to Sorga with such urgency.

"You know?" Kenmar looked shocked. "How?"

"Sir Cadwel told me. That's why he summoned us home."

"Because my son has escaped? But how did he know? I didn't see signs of anyone having been there but Suyla."

"Your son is not in the mountain keep?" Ari walked over and sank into one of the chairs beside the unlit fire. "That cannot be good." He raked his hands through his hair. "Wait, the Lady has been to your keep? Are you saying . . ." Ari could hardly fathom it.

Kenmar crossed to the chair opposite Ari, but didn't sit, electing instead to pace. "Yes, Suyla. She's been there. I could see the signs." He gestured wildly as he spoke. "She's unraveled my spells, and my son is gone." Kenmar stopped, turning in a tight circle, his eyes darting about the room.

Ari knew Kenmar had good reason to be wary. The Lady had warped the mind of Lord Kenmar's son until the young man became obsessed with murdering his father. "Mrakenson is a monster. Why would she free him?"

"I don't know, Ari. I just don't know." Kenmar finally sat, seeming to deflate like an empty water skin. "It can't be for any laudable reason, though."

Ari stared at him. No, it couldn't be. He'd thought his day couldn't grow any darker, but he hadn't expected this. Likely, the Lady sought an ally in her fight against Kenmar. Lord Mrakenson was powerful. In fact, Kenmar had asked Ari's aid in killing him, for he couldn't, or wouldn't, do it on his own. "You said he's most powerful inside the keep, wrapped in spells both to contain and augment him." Ari frowned. "Why did you give him spells to augment him?"

"Many of them were mine, from when it was my home and I worked magic there. Others he fashioned himself to try to thwart the prison I made for him." Kenmar closed his eyes. He looked thin, weary and utterly unintimidating. His clothing was rumpled, his gray-streaked brown hair limp with the grime

25

of travel. Ink still stained his fingers, for he'd kept up work on his maps even after he'd told them who he really was. "He will try to kill me. It's his only ambition. Suyla has driven all other thoughts from his wretched, twisted heart."

Ari didn't reply, his mind churning with the possibilities. Had the Lady merely let Mrakenson loose, or were they together? Did she do it to sow general strife, or to occupy Lord Kenmar so he couldn't help Ari? Worst of all, was Mrakenson anywhere near Ispiria and Siara? That thought sent fear and anger surging through Ari. That monster had no place being anywhere near his fiancée or Lggothland's future queen. The Lady wouldn't stoop so low.

"Did you have spells on the keep to stop people from returning there?" It wasn't important, Ari knew, but it was a question he could have settled, at least.

Kenmar opened his eyes. "I did. To keep them away, as well. When you tried to enter the keep, you were to have grown too afraid to go on and turned back. Most do."

Ari allowed a grim smile at that. He had been afraid. He now assumed Sir Cadwel had been as well, though it hadn't shown. "Fear wasn't the right motivation to discourage us."

"Yes, now knowing you, Stew and Lord Cadwel, I can see that."

"Your spells would have worked on Stew?" Ari hadn't thought of spells working on his Questri mount, though Stew was of a sentient race.

"Of course, though he's at least as fearless as you or Cadwel. I suppose the great brute of a horse Cadwel rides is as well." Kenmar drew in a deep breath. "I shall have to go after my son. Suyla knows that. I can't permit him free in the lands. He'll destroy all he touches."

"Do you think she meant to break our alliance? To stop you from helping me go after Ispiria?"

Kenmar jerked upright in his chair. "What? Go after Ispiria?"

Ari winced, realizing he hadn't imparted the information with any gentleness. "That's why Sir Cadwel summoned us back. Princess Siara and Ispiria have been abducted. There was a note saying they've been taken to the holy land of the Overgod for Siara's conversion."

"But you feel it has something to do with Suyla." Kenmar nodded, as if agreeing with his own statement.

"It seems too much of a coincidence they have been taken to where she wants me to go."

"She will stop at nothing to have her way." Kenmar's tone was filled with foreboding.

"We'll have to tell Sir Cadwel." Ari came to his feet. "First, I'm going to get cleaned up. You should as well. I'll send someone to ask Natan to have your old room readied." Ari looked about, realizing they were alone. "Where's my valet?"

Lord Kenmar coughed, looking down. "He's in the other room. He'll wake as soon as you enter."

"You enspelled my valet? Kenmar, we spoke of this."

"I know, no working magic on friends. Technically, as I don't know the lad, he's a stranger."

Ari leveled a hard look at him. He would never convince everyone Kenmar was on their side if he insisted on using magic on people.

"I apologize. Truly I do," Kenmar said. "I've done the lad no harm. I knew you would tell Cadwel all as soon as you arrived, and I wasn't sure what my reception would be. That's why I waited for you here."

"Well, no one wants to kill you right now, aside from Mirimel." Who was stubborn. Ari looked at Kenmar, curious. "Why did you come here at all? You could have gone after your son and not risked Sir Cadwel's ire."

"You mean, why didn't I give the appearance of betraying your trust the moment you let me out of your sight, and at the same time not warn you Suyla has released a villain far more dangerous than the Caller into the world?" It was Kenmar's turn to administer a rebuking look.

"Ah, right," Ari said. "Forget I asked."

"I must admit, I'm surprised at you, Ari." Kenmar's face was stern.

Ari rubbed the back of his neck, wondering if he even wanted to ask. "Why?"

"I'm inclined to run off after Ispiria, even knowing I must hunt down my son instead and even with hundreds of years of learning to be patient under my belt. You're quite calm. I'm not sure I even approve."

Ari dropped his hands to his sides, fists clenched. He drew in several deep breaths before he was able to formulate a polite enough response. "Believe me, I already tried that route. Sir Cadwel prevented me. We're to meet a ship along the coast and there's no point in leaving before the morning after tomorrow."

"Ah, I see. My apologies."

"Accepted," Ari said, though anger still coursed through him at the suggestion he didn't care about Ispiria enough.

"Truly, I didn't know. I can see I've offended you. I should have realized you would have the situation in hand. You're King's Champion of Lggothland. It was foolish of me to suggest you hadn't already formulated a plan of action. I let my own distress get the best of my tongue."

Ari raised a hand, halting Kenmar's rambling speech. "Yes, well, apology accepted. I didn't mean to become angry. I'm on edge."

"Understandably so."

Ari worked to relax the tension in his frame, forcing his anger down. Kenmar was correct. Ari was King's Champion. He was accustomed to pressure, to long periods of time under the shadow of strife. His experience and training didn't seem quite up to Ispiria being abducted, however. Anger, lurking and ready to escape his control, waited within him.

"Anyone would be angry," Kenmar said, once again displaying how easily he could guess Ari's thoughts. "Among other emotions."

"You're correct, though. I am not anyone. I am champion of Lggothland." Ari permitted the weight of that responsibility to settle more firmly on him. It was his, after all. He'd fought for the post. It carried one burden he was unsure he could bear, however. "Kenmar, do you believe it's fair of me to wed Ispiria?" If we recover her, his mind whispered. "When we find her. Am I dooming her to a life of danger, worry and sorrow?"

"Would you rather doom her to a life without the man she loves?" Kenmar asked. He looked at Ari with sad eyes. "It shouldn't always be like this. Once we put this trouble with Suyla and my son behind you, you will have only mortal enemies to deal with, and Lggothland has been at peace for some time."

"True," Ari said, trying to be reassured.

"More importantly, it isn't your decision."

Ari blinked at him. "Marrying Ispiria isn't my decision?"

"Whether you marry her is, but whether she weds you is her choice. Do you not respect her enough to permit her to make her own choice in this? What right do you have to decide

29

the life she's elected to pursue is too dangerous for her? What if Sir Cadwel hadn't permitted you to enter into tourneys because becoming King's Champion would be dangerous for you, the sole heir to Sorga?"

Ari couldn't fathom his misery if Sir Cadwel hadn't pressed the king to permit him into tourneys. Was that how Ispiria felt about becoming his wife? It must be, if she was willing to agree to it. She couldn't help but be aware of the life she was committing herself to, having grown up in a keep with Sir Cadwel as her great uncle. Ari had to admit, he didn't mind the idea she loved him so much that he was worth the trouble.

"I think it is a worry you should set aside," Kenmar said. "It won't aid you in the days to come. Once we have her back, then it may be addressed."

For the first time, Ari moved from the worry that he shouldn't permit Ispiria to be his wife to the idea that, after being abducted and dragged off across the ocean, she wouldn't want to marry him anymore.

"Oh dear," Kenmar said. "I've only made things worse."

Ari shook his head. "No, you've set me straight. Furthermore, you're correct. These aren't concerns for now. We must concentrate on finding Ispiria and Siara, and the final stone, and your son."

"Is that all?" Kenmar said with a wry twist of his lips, but the look in his eyes was bleak.

"I certainly hope so." Ari glanced toward his sleeping chamber. "You should know, I told Natan everything, so if he looks at you oddly, that will be why. I'll go wake up my valet and send him to ask Natan to have your old room readied. Then, if you'll excuse me, I'm going to get cleaned up. I need to appear at dinner tonight looking competent, not like someone who's been dragged behind a horse." He glanced down at his dirty, patched clothing.

"Yes, of course," Kenmar said. "Thank you, Lord Aridian."

Ari nodded, heading toward his sleeping chamber, frowning as he crossed into his room. The valet Natan had sent up stood like a statue, stilled by Kenmar's magic. Ari hoped he wasn't erring by trusting Kenmar. The older lord seemed genuine, but so had the Lady, and she'd left Mirimel to die. Yes, Kenmar had saved Mirimel's life, but that deed couldn't make up for all of the evil he'd done. Ari hoped, in taking Kenmar's redemption on faith, he wasn't making a mistake that would cost him Ispiria, and Lggothland its future queen.

Chapter 3

Before dinner, Ari warned Sir Cadwel, Larke, Cooro and Mirimel that Kenmar had returned. He didn't want any brawls breaking out when everyone arrived in the great hall for supper. The five of them, and Natan, flanked Ari at the head table, severe and silent as he addressed the people of Sorga. Hard as the faces gazing back at him were, Ari liked to think he'd given them hope.

He didn't permit Kenmar to tell the others his news until they convened in Sir Cadwel's study the following day. In the wake of learning Kenmar's son was free, agreement that only Mirimel and Cooro would accompany Ari south to seek Ispiria and Siara was quickly achieved. The rest of the day was spent pouring over maps of the southern lands and discussing how best to deal with the Lady, Mrakenson and the third stone.

Finally, it was resolved Larke would go alone to the lair of the Aluiens. There, he would seek knowledge of the Lady's plans and the third stone. He also intended, Ari gathered, to retrieve some personal items from his rooms, worried he wouldn't be welcome among the Aluiens any longer. Ari could see the sorrow in the bard over this, but also something akin to anticipation.

He knew Larke longed to be free of the rules of his people, but Ari feared what price the Aluiens would extract. The greatest punishment Larke's people could administer was to strip an Aluien of the glowing blue Orlenia flowing in his or her veins. They didn't return such a person to a mortal state, but left them empty and bereft, much like a monstrous Empty One. Larke once told Ari that the few times the punishment was enacted, the offenders went mad and took their own lives. Ari himself had briefly touched the Orlenia. Though his memories of that time were taken from him, he still felt the pull of longing its absence induced.

He didn't voice his fears, knowing Larke was aware of the potential consequences of his plan. Besides, there was no help for it. Someone must go to the Aluiens' lair, and Larke was the best choice.

For their part, Sir Cadwel and Lord Kenmar would set out to find Mrakenson. Kenmar hoped they would have success in containing him once more, until a more permanent solution could be found. Ari checked a grimace each time Kenmar used the phrase, aware the more permanent solution was for him to gather all three stones, affix the final one to his sword Fwellian, and kill Mrakenson. It was a terrible way for a father to speak of his son, but Kenmar had already spent hundreds of years trying to find a less dramatic resolution.

As their discussion drew to a close, Ari began putting away manuscripts and rolling up maps, though Mirimel still scrutinized several. He was tired from a day of talking, when what he wished to be doing was acting. He was also not looking forward to another evening at the head table, another reassuring speech, and a meal in a tense, silent hall.

"Kenmar and I will leave tonight, once the keep is sleeping," Sir Cadwel said.

"Sir?" Ari asked, looking up from the map he was tying closed.

"It will look odd if we ride out with you and turn aside to head north, and I won't spend the time to ride beyond sight of the keep and double back."

"It will look odd if you don't go with Ari at all," Natan said, frowning.

Sorga's chief steward had regained his composure from the day before and been very engaged in their plans. Over the course of the day, Ari had come to understand more forcibly the distance his vows to the Aluiens had put between him and Natan. He was pleased to see that breach closing.

Sir Cadwel looked to Larke. "Bard, can you make it appear as if we're with you?"

"Yes, easily enough. I can form illusions of you to ride with us, at least until we're out of sight of the keep."

"That's settled, then." Sir Cadwel's tone brooked no rebuttal. "Pack before dinner. You leave at first light."

They all looked at each other. Ari shrugged.

"Send word to me of any needs," Natan said, standing.

Mirimel held up a hand, staying anyone from leaving. "I know we've settled our plans, but won't Kenmar slow Sir Cadwel down? Goldwin is a Questri. Kenmar rides about on that unthinking gelding."

Ari was a bit surprised to hear Mirimel use the term unthinking. That was what the Questri called normal horses, and generally with derision. In truth, Ari didn't think of it as a polite thing to say.

"She makes a point," Natan said to Sir Cadwel.

"We are not reevaluating." Sir Cadwel's tone was firm.

"If I may?" Kenmar stood from the table. "If Sir Cadwel isn't opposed, I believe this form may help."

Kenmar's hands began to move, pulling glowing strands of color from the air, the majority of which were a gleaming green. He spoke in low tones in the same clipped language he'd used while healing Mirimel and her hawk on the Tybrunn Plains. Ari watched, fascinated, aware of the tension which sprang up in the room.

Mirimel's eyes were narrow, her hand on her knife hilt. Larke observed Kenmar intently, his fingers seeming almost to twitch as he studied the spell. Natan was looking from person to person, obviously unsure of the normalcy of what transpired. Cooro edged nearer to Mirimel. Sir Cadwel was the only one who didn't seem nervous, his expression unchanging.

Kenmar disappeared. It happened so swiftly, Ari gasped. In his shock, it took him a moment to realize a hawk, slightly larger than a Sorga Hawk, hovered above the spot where Kenmar had stood. It dropped down to perch on a chair back.

An expletive escaping Natan's mouth, he sank into a chair. Mirimel gaped at the hawk, an expression Ari was sure was mirrored on his own face. Cooro looked about the room, dropping low to peer under the table before coming back up to stare. Larke walked around the table, the hawk turning its head to follow him.

"That will do." Sir Cadwel's tone was even.

If Ari didn't know him as well as he did, he wouldn't have been able to pick out the telltale signs of shock in his mentor. There was tension in Sir Cadwel's frame, and a muscle twitched at the corner of his right eye. He rolled his shoulders back, another sure sign he was as startled as the rest of them.

"That's amazing," Larke said. He reached out a hand toward the hawk. "May I?" The hawk extended a wing. Larke lightly poked one of the feathers.

"It's a good thing your hawk's in the aerie, visiting," Larke said to Mirimel. "I don't know what he'd make of this." He ran his finger across the wing. "Remarkable."

"Impossible," Cooro said. "It must be a trick. An illusion. Kenmar is there. We merely perceive him as a hawk. An illusion will make him travel no more swiftly."

The hawk launched itself from the chair, flying in a circle about the room before landing again. Natan uttered another curse, ducking, as did Cooro. Mirimel still gaped at the hawk. Ari shut his mouth, not wanting to look as stunned as she did, and endeavored for something more like Sir Cadwel's calm. He wondered if Kenmar had selected a hawk to ingratiate himself to Mirimel, and if it would work.

"The high priestesses of Wheylia could transform themselves." Larke's voice was excited. "They say, in times of great need, a priestess can be metamorphosed into a dragon, but the price is high. Terribly high. Queen Reudi's house is the last known to pay it, during the first great war. Enough power to accomplish the feat was achieved by the sacrifice of a thousand male offspring." He looked about at them. "That's why the symbol of her house is a dragon, legend has it."

Ari was gaping again, but he couldn't help it. He'd never questioned why Queen Reudi's house had a black dragon on red as a herald. Now he knew the reason behind the dragon, and had a good idea what the red stood for as well. He recalled, a year ago in Wheylia, learning that the Witches of Whey long ago slew children for power. Each being had a spark of the Wellspring, the source of the witches' magic, within. Apparently, a quick way to get more power was to let that spark out of the being it inhabited. Why, though, would any house make a dragon formed from death into their symbol?

"Are you saying Kenmar killed a thousand babies?" Mirimel bit out, her awe transformed to rage.

"I should hope not," Larke said, looking shocked. "No, the women of Whey employ only the power of the Wellspring, as do the Aluiens. I'm not sure what Kenmar was doing, but it was different."

"It looked more like what he did when he healed Mirimel and her hawk," Ari put in, wanting to defend Kenmar. "With the colors and that strange language."

"Will this lady you all speak of transform herself into a dragon if Ari confronts her?" There was an edge of fear in Natan's tone. He cast Ari a worried look.

Ari turned to Larke. "Could she?" All three stones or no, Ari couldn't imagine facing an actual dragon. None of Sir Cadwel's books on strategy covered giant mythological fire breathing creatures.

"I believe the spell requires the thousand lives to be taken nearly at once." Larke shook his head. "I can't believe the Lady would do such a thing."

"But could she?" Sir Cadwel repeated Ari's question, his expression grim.

Larke frowned. "I don't see how, without considerable help. I don't know of any way she could harvest so many lives at once. To do so through magic would require nearly as much power as the spell of transformation is reputed to, and Aluiens do not have spells of death."

"I bet he does, though." Mirimel glared at Kenmar-the-hawk as she spoke.

Sir Cadwel waved a hand at Kenmar. "Are you changing back or do you plan to remain that way until we find your son?"

Kenmar appeared, his feet on the chair back. His arms flailing, he promptly toppled over. Larke and Cooro jumped to his aid, helping him up from the floor, but Mirimel backed away. Kenmar gasped for breath. Leaning on Larke, he reclaimed his other arm from Cooro's grasp and pulled out the chair, sinking into it.

"Thank you," he said, looking between Larke and Cooro. "I forgot that part. I should have flown down to the floor."

"Are you well?" Ari asked, for Kenmar looked exhausted and pale, sweat standing out on his forehead.

"You don't look like you could keep that up for much longer," Sir Cadwel said. "An interesting trick, but I fail to see how it helps us."

"How did you learn that?" As he spoke, Larke pulled out the chair next to Kenmar, sitting.

Kenmar held up a hand, laboring to catch his breath. He took out a kerchief and wiped his brow. "It's a very old trick," he said a moment later. He looked to Sir Cadwel. "I can maintain that form for days. It's changing that wearies me."

Sir Cadwel nodded, looking thoughtful, the twitch beside his eye stilled.

Natan cursed a third time. He cast Ari a dazed look. "This is the world you live in? How does it not take a toll on your sanity?"

"Who says it hasn't?" Mirimel muttered.

"You were truly a hawk?" Cooro asked, sitting on the other side of Kenmar. "It wasn't mere illusion, treachery to the eye? Can anyone do this thing? Must it be a hawk?"

"I'm afraid it takes years to master," Kenmar said. "For me, it must be a hawk, or one other form. Each form must be painstakingly memorized, the spell carefully crafted to fit it. That was one of the mountain hawks, common in my youth."

"Amazing," Larke said.

"I suppose you'll want to ride on my shoulder," Sir Cadwel said, scowling.

"I can't fly all day." Kenmar sounded slightly hurt.

Sir Cadwel gave a noncommittal grunt in reply.

"You're all mad to trust him," Mirimel said. "Can you not see how powerful he is? He toys with us. A being as ancient as Tal Mraken must devise very convoluted forms of amusement."

Kenmar flinched at the use of his true name.

Casting a glare about the room, Mirimel grabbed up two of the maps she'd been studying and stomped out.

Larke watched her go, shaking his head. "She is stubborn."

"She is young, and angry," Kenmar said. "And not wrong in her wariness. I know you all share it, to degrees. I can only hope to prove myself."

No one seemed to have a reply to that, for it was undeniable. Even Ari, though he felt a stab of remorse for the sorrow in Kenmar's voice, wouldn't claim he fully trusted the man. It would be foolish to, or to discount his ancient crimes, speaking of a different nature than the one Kenmar claimed now.

"Can this Aluien lady transform herself into a dragon, then?" Cooro's voice held a mixture of dread and anticipation.

Kenmar shook his head. "I believe Larkesong's assessment to be correct. She would need hundreds of followers ready to murder at her command. I cannot fathom that."

There was another stretch of silence. Ari didn't know if the other's thoughts paralleled his, though their faces were bleak. For his part, he was doing his best not to imagine a thousand simultaneous deaths.

"I believe I ordered you all to pack." Sir Cadwel's command broke into the quiet.

"Yes, sir," Ari said in automatic response to that tone from his mentor. Pivoting, he left the room, not really caring if the others followed. He didn't, however, head to his quarters to ready for his journey. First, he wanted to tell Stew and the other Questri how the day had gone.

Ari nodded to the guards in the foyer as he left the keep. Jogging down the steps and across the cobblestone yard toward the stable, he lifted his gaze to the autumn sky. It was dusted with clouds, rendering the world above the faded blue one often found marked the end of summer. The air was warm and still touched with humidity, but Ari knew soon it would grow crisp.

Early autumn, that of his fifteenth year, was when his and Sir Cadwel's paths first crossed. Ari had thought it coincidence then, good fortune, but in truth it had been the machinations of the Lady. He still counted it good fortune, however. If he'd never met Sir Cadwel and become his page, he would be working as a stablehand, not be a knight of the realm, King's Champion, Duke of Sorga and Ispiria's fiancé.

The stable doors were thrown wide, letting in fresh air, though they faced away from the afternoon sun. Ari's Aluien-enhanced vision didn't require notable time to adjust to the difference in lighting, and he strolled confidently toward Stew's stall. Goldwin, Sir Cadwel's giant dun destrier, occupied the stall to Stew's left, with Mirimel's black mare to his right. Larke's silver-toned steed, prince of the Questri, seemed to have disappeared as usual. He didn't take to being confined indoors as well as the others did.

"Stew, Goldwin, black mare," Ari greeted. The mare hadn't yet given permission for Ari to know her name. It wasn't a thing readily shared with humans. Ari knew Stew's true name, but it was long and he'd known his horse as Stew for years before learning it.

Stew and the mare both dipped their heads in greeting. Goldwin, as usual, affected indifference. The rangy old destrier was generally at least as grouchy as Sir Cadwel.

Ari looked about to make sure no one was near. He knew personal quirks were more tolerated in the nobility, but Mirimel had often pointed out how crazy it made him seem when he spoke to Stew as one would to another person. The people of Sorga didn't need worry over his sanity added to their troubles.

"I don't know how much you know, and you have no way to tell me, so please forgive me if I'm redundant," he told them once he was sure they were alone.

Stew dipped his head again in acknowledgment. Out of the corner of his eyes, Ari could see Goldwin's ears swivel toward him.

Taking a steadying breath, for it still hurt to acknowledge, he told them of the abduction. He could tell from the sympathy in Stew's and the mare's eyes they'd already heard. Likely, the stablehands spoke of it often enough. It was all anyone in Sorga seemed able to discuss.

As rapidly as he could, Ari summarized what had transpired inside the keep since they'd arrived the afternoon before. He told them of Mrakenson's escape, and the Lady's suspected involvement, causing them to exchange a worried look. The only time either evidenced surprise was when he described Lord Kenmar turning into a hawk. Ari concluded his monologue by detailing who was to embark on each part of the quest.

"So, I'll be taking a ship." He stopped, suddenly aware he hadn't asked if Stew and the mare were expected to go on the ship. Horses did, he knew, but only on large vessels. "I don't know if they will send a ship on which you can go south with us. I didn't think to ask, though I doubt the king's note specified."

Ari felt a mounting concern. He didn't want to go on a quest without Stew. The brief time he'd spent riding the packhorse on the plains had shown him how much he relied on Stew's intelligence, not to mention his endurance and speed. Stew would help insure their success.

It wasn't only the practicality of having Stew along, though. Stew had gone on every quest with Ari, starting with the one to bring home Prince Parrentine after he'd gone mad with grief over the decline of his first fiancée, Clorra, and run off. Ari hadn't traveled without Stew since Larke introduced them on the hill overlooking Poromont three years ago. Leaving Stew behind seemed the action of a fool.

"Maybe Sir Cadwel will know if you're to go on the ship." He looked from Stew to the mare and back again. "If you're meant to go, will you? I would have you with me on this journey. I need your help."

Goldwin snorted.

Ari ignored the dun destrier, watching Stew and the mare exchange a long look, communicating in the way Questri did among themselves. Ari wished he could understand them, the way Larke could and Mirimel was learning to, but it took magic. Though altered by magic, Ari didn't seem to possess any of his own.

Stew turned back to him and dipped his head, ears forward.

"I'll take that as a yes until proven otherwise," Ari said, smiling. "Thank you. I'll see you in the morning."

Ari left the stable, his eyes on the keep of Sorga. The ancient structure was carved from the range that sheltered it, built half against the tall mountains and half inside it. The blue and white, brown-hawk-adorned flag of Sorga snapped in the breeze atop each tower. The gray stone castle was massive, weathered and ancient, yet to Ari it held the warmth of home.

Tinted rose by the setting sun as the keep was, his eyes still caught an even brighter splash of color. Mirimel stood in the aerie cut into the side of the mountain, hawks perched about her. Her orange curls blew in wayward swirls in the wind. Ari couldn't see her eyes from where he stood, but he knew they were more blue than the sky above, and more judgmental than the gods. He only hoped her judgment of Kenmar would prove false, and her tracking skills true, for he was relying on her to help him hunt for Ispiria.

As Ari returned to his chambers to pack for the journey, something he could do in a matter of moments, he assured himself they must be sending a ship that could transport horses. The king had many ships, of all sizes. He wouldn't separate Ari from his destrier. Half of being a good knight, after all, was having a good horse. Or in Stew's case, a great one.

Satisfied with that line of reasoning by the time he'd made ready to leave, Ari set his saddlebags on the floor, near where his sword, Fwellian, leaned against the wall. The two milky-white stones set into the hilt seemed almost to glow in the dim light in his bedchamber. The third facet, the one nearest the blade, remained a dull, empty pit.

Larke had told him the stones, once assembled, would meld body, mind and purpose. Ari didn't know what that meant, but it would reputedly give him the power to stand against even Lord Kenmar. Or, though he still couldn't bring himself to imagine it in spite of all he knew, the Lady.

Chapter 4

Ari made another speech at dinner, assuring the people of Sorga their lords would find Ispiria and Princess Siara. He promised to bring Ispiria home to them, and wed her. He also promised, as he'd heard the whispers about the keep, to return the princess to the capital and stave off war. All knew, in the event Ari's mission wasn't successful, Prince Parrentine would take the southern lands apart to find his bride, or avenge her. Nor would Sorga shirk in aiding him. The people of Lggothland would not see the crime of abducting their princess go unpunished.

Late that night, once the keep was for the most part abed, Ari snuck down to the foyer. He found Sir Cadwel, Natan, Kenmar and Larke waiting, along with the two guards, one on either side of the closed keep doors. The guards were asleep on their feet, likely Larke's work, but the other four turned at Ari's approach. Sir Cadwel had saddlebags slung over his shoulder and wore no armor. His garb was nondescript, though he wore his greatsword with the crest of Sorga embossed on the pommel.

"Ari," the knight rumbled in as close to a whisper as his voice ever came.

"Sir." Ari stood awkwardly, not sure how to say good bye. In the forefront of his thoughts was that Sir Cadwel and Kenmar were going after a being powerful enough that it had taken both Larke and the Lady combined to ward him off during their first confrontation. Sir Cadwel was strong, an Aluien, and had Kenmar with him, but Mrakenson might have the Lady on his side. To make matters worse, Kenmar was still not to be completely trusted, especially where his son was concerned. The odds stacked against Sir Cadwel's mission gave Ari the unsettling feeling he could be looking on his mentor for the very last time.

Ari glanced at Kenmar, weighed down by the knowledge it was on his word that Sir Cadwel trusted the man. Kenmar stepped forward, holding out a hand for Ari to clasp. Ari did, certain his face conveyed his fears.

"Farewell, Aridian, and be assured, I will lay down my life to protect Lord Cadwel, if it comes to it," Kenmar said in a quiet voice.

Sir Cadwel snorted. "More likely to be the other way around."

"Were Cadwel easy to kill, someone would have done it long ago," Natan said, but his tone was subdued.

Casting Ari a worried look, Larke moved to the door. At his gesture, the guards unbarred and opened it, their movements slow and their eyes closed. Cool night air swirled in as Larke slipped out on silent feet.

"Sir," Ari said again, turning back to his mentor. Behind Sir Cadwel, Ari could see Larke going about the courtyard, enspelling the outer guards as well.

"If we finish our task before you find the princess and Ispiria, we'll catch up to you," Sir Cadwel said.

"Yes, sir." Ari pushed the words out past the tightness in his throat.

Sir Cadwel scrutinized him through narrow eyes. Reaching out, he clasped Ari on the shoulder. "Lad, Natan is right. If I were easy to kill, I'd long since be dead. Before a year has passed, this will all be settled, and before two years go by, I expect to be playing with my great grandniece or nephew in the courtyard behind me."

Ari blinked rapidly, his thoughts scattered by the idea of his and Ispiria's children. Though he knew Sorga would need an heir, he hadn't thought much beyond the marrying Ispiria part. Sir Cadwel smiled slightly as he turned away.

As Sir Cadwel and Kenmar made their way down the castle steps, Ari moved to stand under the arch of the doorway, beside Natan. Larke, enveloped in a faint blue-white glow, led Goldwin from the stable. Settling his saddlebags, the knight mounted. Kenmar cast Ari one more reassuring look, then began his spell. In moments, the graying lord was replaced by a hawk. Oddly silent for a raptor, he winged upward into the star-specked sky.

Sir Cadwel waved and Goldwin set out toward the gate, which swung silently open at a gesture from Larke. Natan beside him, Ari watched bard, knight and Questri move through the killing zone toward the outer gates where, no doubt, Larke would repeat the process of enspelling the guards and unbarring the way.

"You said the plague wasn't a plague," Natan said softly, referring to a time, two years ago, when most of Sorga thought their dukedom struck by disease. "Is that what they did, these Aluiens? Walk in here, glowing, and put us all to sleep with magic?"

"Yes," Ari said. They'd repaired the keep as well, and the village of Hawkers, replacing memories of the sacking of Hawkers and siege of Sorga with the falsehood of a plague.

"So I saw Sorga besieged by monstrous, magical wolves and don't recall any of it?"

"Pretty much," Ari said. He'd neglected to go into detail about how Natan had missed the battle, having been hit over the head before it began.

"And you plan to defy beings like that?" Natan gestured toward the glowing form that was Larkesong. "What if they get ahold of you and change your mind about who you are, or what you want?"

Ari glanced at the steward, seeing his face creased with worry. "They can't. Not really. I'm fairly immune to their magic now. I've had practice warring with its hold."

"I hope you're right." Natan shook his head, his expression still tense.

"Was I right to tell you the truth? Would you prefer ignorance? Larke can take the knowledge from you."

Natan cast him a startled look. "No, don't ask him to do that. I . . . I prefer it this way, strange though it all is." He looked down. "I want to apologize again for what I did, the stealing. I was, well, I suppose I was resentful, and jealous. I've dedicated the past twenty-five years to running this keep, and all those years, I've been Cadwel's confidant. The one person in Sorga who could speak to him as a friend. Then you appeared from nowhere to become like a son to him, and he handed you the dukedom."

"You didn't think I was worthy."

"No, nor did I think you cared. Not about Sorga, and not about me and all I've done, and do."

"I love Sorga," Ari said, infusing into that declaration as much fervor as their hushed tones permitted. "And I appreciate you. Sorga would be a shambles without you."

"Yes, of course it would." Natan flashed him a quick smile. "You were handed the dukedom, but you're never here. Cadwel cast away his title like a leprous blanket and can't be bothered with the keep. Obviously, the place would be a disaster without me."

"I know, and I didn't mean--"

Natan cut him off with a gesture. "I understand now. You and Cadwel got embroiled in something and I wasn't a part of it. You protected Sorga, and saw it rebuilt by these Aluiens. I understand now that you both love this place, and why I've been excluded. That's why I'm apologizing again. When I did so before, I was sorry. I'd behaved in an unbefitting manner and I was remorseful for that. Now that I fully understand, I'm sorry for more, for betraying your trust. I hope I haven't lost it."

Ari shook his head. "You have not. I trust you with my life. More importantly, Sir Cadwel and I both trust you with Sorga and the lives of everyone in it. I'm sorry we're both leaving, again."

"At least now I understand why. I hope, this time, you can settle things once and for all."

"As do I," Ari said, though the idea of settling things left him feeling grim.

"Larkesong will set this all back in order?" Natan's gesture included the sleeping guards and open gates.

"He will."

"I'm going to retire then. All watching this will do is give me strange dreams. Sleep well, my lord," Natan said, turning away.

"Sleep well," Ari whispered after Natan's retreating form. Alone now under the archway, he returned to watching Larke moving about the far outer wall. Ari kept watching as the outer gates opened and Sir Cadwel rode through, Kenmar somewhere high above in the night sky. Though he knew he should sleep, and trusted Larke to restore the fortifications and guards to rights, Ari stayed where he was.

When Larke finally returned, he looked tired, but he smiled at Ari. "I was hoping you would be here still."

"What is it?" Ari asked, suddenly leery.

"Nothing troubling. Merely that Cadwel and I decided no Kenmar illusion will travel with us on the morrow."

Ari waited, sure the bard would expound.

"You were never before so stoic," Larke murmured, his eyes sad. He watched Ari for a long moment, then shrugged. "There's no reason Kenmar should go with us. It will be simpler to give the keep the feel that Lord Kenmar is about than to work enough spells to ensure the stablemen care for his gelding properly while not realizing it's odd to find it in the stable when he rode away on it."

Ari nodded. "Actually, that makes good sense."

"Actually?" Larke gave him a slightly injured look. "Actually? As if I don't generally make good sense?"

"I'm going to sleep," Ari said. "Unlike you, I need rest."

"Actually," the bard muttered to himself, his tone indignant.

Ari headed for the stone steps leading to the nobles' quarters.

"Actually indeed."

"Don't forget to close the door and wake up the guards," Ari called back down the steps in a whisper he knew the bard's keen hearing could make out.

Larke's outraged muttering increased, but Ari was sure it was mostly for show.

The next morning, in spite of the early hour, Ari found most of the keep assembled on the castle steps when he came out. Stew was saddled and waiting for him. Larke, Cooro and Mirimel were already mounted. Beside them stood an illusion of Sir Cadwel astride Goldwin, scowling fiercely. Ari could tell it was an illusion, could see right through knight and destrier if he made the effort, but no one else seemed to notice anything awry. A faint cry high above drew his eye. He looked up to see Mirimel's hawk executing a slow spiral against the brightening sky.

As Ari descended the steps, the Cadwel illusion turned toward him, scowl deepening. Ari shot Larke an amused look.

"My lord," Natan said, coming forward to help Ari mount, though the assistance wasn't necessary even for show. Ari wasn't wearing his plate, or taking it. They were going to a land warmer than their own and were fitted out more for speed than battle. As they would reach the ship in a matter of days, journeying through moderately populated terrain, they weren't even bringing a packhorse.

After clasping Ari's hand, Natan stepped back. Ari turned Stew to face the broad steps leading up to the keep, where the people of Sorga were gathered in the morning shadows. Though the sun wasn't yet high enough to reach over the eastern arm of the mountains and into the courtyard, the sky above was already a promising blue.

"Someone has wronged Lggothland, and Sorga," Ari called, raising his voice to be heard throughout the yard. "Someone has taken both the princess of our land and the lady of our keep." He felt his countenance harden into hard lines to match the anger dwelling within him. "I will find Lady Ispiria and Princess Siara. I will find who took them. I will make this right for Lggothland and Sorga. You have my word."

Ari would have added the traditional vow, that he would complete his quest or give his life in the attempt, but the people of Sorga started cheering and he decided to let them. Why remind them of the harsher half of a knight's vow? They didn't need to think of their lord dying while trying to bring the future lady of the keep home. Let them send him off imagining only success. After all, should he fail, they would have time enough to think on it then.

With a final wave to the people of Sorga and a nod to Natan, Ari wheeled Stew away. He was aware of the others following him through the first gate, the illusion of Sir Cadwel waving as well. He wondered if Larke could make the illusion speak and elected not to, or if it must stay silent. He supposed if it could speak, they were all lucky the bard hadn't chosen to wax eloquent.

Once out from under the deep shadows of the inner keep, Ari urged Stew into a run. Stew's strides lengthening, they sped across the killing zone, the wind of their passing whipping at Ari's face. He leaned lower in the saddle.

There was no reason to run. The ship was unlikely to arrive much sooner than the king's note suggested. Running wouldn't get them to Ispiria any quicker. Still, it eased Ari's heart. A shadow flickered along the ground to his right and a glance over his shoulder revealed Mirimel's hawk keeping pace above.

Flying across the killing zone, Ari drank in the exhilaration of the run. Stew's powerful strides made the arms of the mountains to either side of them a blur. To gallop on Stew was freedom, almost akin to how Ari imagined flight. He and Stew were strong, fast and determined. He meant every word he'd spoken to the people of Sorga. They would bring Ispiria home.

They galloped through the second gate and out onto the plain. Ari knew Stew would run forever, but he tugged lightly on the reins, reminding his horse to slow. Cooro, at least, wouldn't be able to keep up with them. His piebald mare was a light, swift steed but she wasn't Questri.

It didn't take the others long to catch up and they headed south at a more sedate pace. Larke stayed with them for the several days it took to reach the coast, even though the journey took them southeast and his destination, the Aluien caves, lay to the southwest. Ari didn't comment on the bard's presence, enjoying having him there. Where Mirimel was often a bit gloomy, Larke and Cooro were both more buoyant. Though Ari knew there was some tension between the two, with Larke seeming to care for Mirimel and Cooro having vowed to win her love, they got along well and made fine travel companions. When at last they drew near the small coastal town that was their goal, Ari felt a touch of sorrow, knowing the bard would leave them soon.

The smell of the sea was Ari's first hint they were almost to their destination. It reached him long before the tall trees shrouding the roadway gave way to the shabby wood and thatch buildings of the town. From his readings, Ari knew the village had once prospered, being Sorga's only deep water port, but since peace had settled on the kingdom and there was no longer a reason to avoid large swaths of it, sea commerce there had dwindled. Now, it was a fishing town, though the people who stopped to watch Ari and his friends ride toward the docks looked well fed and well clothed enough.

The dirt streets sloped sharply toward the bay and Ari imagined they'd be quite treacherous in spring. He remembered to smile and nod, acknowledging those they passed in case he was recognized, but his eyes were on the slender piers extending out into the ocean, and the enormous sailing ship gliding in to dock at one. The ship looked to be well over a hundred feet in length and had four towering masts, multiple sails furled along them. From the tips of the masts flew the king's blue and silver flags, the rearing black horse adorning each seeming to jump about in the breeze.

As Ari and his companions made their way through town, the ship eased up to the dock and was made fast. A broad ramp was extended from the side of the slightly rocking vessel. The dark wood of the vast hull gleamed as if lacquered and polished, and the entirety was trimmed out in blue. From where they were, Ari could make out that the bowsprit was adorned by an elegantly carved white bird.

The water below the vessel was so dark as to be black. Ari imagined it was quite deep. At first, he couldn't fathom how they'd built the piers, but he soon discerned they, too, were floating. The calm waters of the bay moved the great ship and the dock it was moored at almost in harmony. To the south, a second pier was surrounded by a scattering of smaller vessels, others tying up to it two deep. It occurred to Ari the villagers had been forced to move their boats to accommodate the king's.

By the time they reached the waterfront, a small crowd had amassed both behind and before them. About the docks, which smelled rather strongly of fish, people had stopped in their work to stare, first at the ship and then at Ari's approach. As Ari watched, many of them flocked to the top of the pier, barring his way, their faces curious. Ari held up a hand, halting the others as he tugged lightly on the reins to let Stew know he wanted to stop.

"Are you Sir Aridian, my lord?" one of the dock workers called.

"I am," Ari replied.

A murmur went up through the crowd. People began bowing, peering up at him as they did so. Ari made sure to keep his face composed as he looked about, aware he was these people's lord. This village, where he'd never before been, was part of Sorga. He took their taxes and they were under his care.

He cast a look back up the dusty, rutted street. Natan was correct. Ari had been so busy as Sir Cadwel's page, and now as king's champion, he hadn't had time for Sorga. Yes, he knew the ducal keep and the people there, but what of the rest of the dukedom? For that matter, he'd never once set foot in the Northlands, his protectorate. He vowed that once he had Ispiria and Siara safe, he would make a tour of his dukedom, as Sir Cadwel's father used to do. It was Ari's duty to know all of Sorga.

"Please rise," he said to the bowing populace, raising his voice to carry. "It wasn't our intention to interrupt your work, or displace your ships."

"We're honored to have the king's ship in our harbor, and to help any way we can, my lord," one of the men said, moving to the front of the assemblage as they straightened. He doffed his hat, holding it in his hands, revealing gray hair that stood on end. "And we'd plenty of warning. They sent in a smaller vessel first so we'd know to clear the dock for the Albatross. We heard from them what's happened. It's not right, someone taking our princess and Lady Ispiria. We'll all go with you and fight by your side, my lord, if you ask."

Ari looked about at the grave faces, swallowing his first reaction to that offer. A glance behind him showed Larke looked worried, Mirimel speculative, and Cooro to be grinning. Ari didn't know if the swordmaster was amused by the idea of these people fighting, or the idea of attacking the kingdoms to the south, but he wouldn't permit either.

"As I'm sure the king's men told you, we believe this treachery was carried out by a small group of people." Ari kept his tone and face serious, for he knew their offer to be. "Therefore, I feel myself and my companions will be able to retrieve those wrongly taken from Lggothland." He saw the people shift, looking at each other. "If we prove insufficient, and this abduction proves to be the work of one of the southern kingdoms, I will return to take you up on your offer. I know the people of Sorga are proud, and you won't let one of your own be carried off without retribution."

His words were met with steely-eyed nods and calls of affirmation, and Ari relaxed slightly, pleased his speech was well received. These were his people. He wanted them to think highly of their lord. It didn't matter to their daily lives if they respected the man they were beholden to, but he thought it only right to try to seem worthy.

"We know you can't linger, my lord," the gray haired man said. He turned, gesturing, and the others began to move aside, forming a walkway between them. "You may as well walk your horses right out onto the pier. That there's the biggest ship I ever laid eyes on. They already got a ramp out for the horses."

"Thank you," Ari said, urging Stew forward once more.

"She's called the Albatross, you said?" Larke said behind Ari.

"Aye. The king's own ship. She's a beauty."

"That she is," the bard replied. "A ship like that, on a voyage like this, needs a ballad. A suitably grand ballad." Larke's tone was dreamy, and a bit wistful.

"No ballads," Mirimel said in a low voice Ari didn't think he was supposed to overhear. "Keep your scattered brain on getting to that pool, gathering your possessions, and getting back out of there in one piece."

"My dear girl, the Aluiens are peaceable. They aren't going to harm me."

"Do as I say, Larkesong. Humor me."

Ari agreed with Mirimel. He would have said so, but he was sure he was eavesdropping. Not that he could help his enhanced hearing. He urged Stew toward the base of the pier, wishing they had some other choice than to send Larkesong into the lair of the Aluiens alone.

Chapter 5

When they reached the base of the pier, Ari turned Stew back toward the others before dismounting to await them. Following suit as they reached him, Ari, Larke, Mirimel, Cooro and their horses soon formed a loose circle. Looking about, Ari could see curious eyes on them, but no one moved to intrude. A glance skyward revealed Mirimel's hawk spiraling overhead, almost like a lookout.

Ari turned to Larke. "Are you going to greet the prince?"

"I think not." The bard shook his head. "'T'would be cruel."

"Cruel?" Cooro repeated, his look questioning.

"I think it would give him undue hope for aid I cannot, at this moment, provide," Larke said.

"Won't they already have seen you?" Cooro nodded toward the Albatross. "It's a long pier, I grant, but not so long as that."

A sly grin turned up the corners of Larke's mouth. "You see me, of course, but those on the ship do not. I've taken precautions."

Cooro blinked rapidly. "Though from a kingdom where magic is no stranger, Cooro will never accustom himself to your subtleties, bard."

Larke raised an eyebrow.

Ari agreed with the bard's reaction, unsure what Cooro meant by the statement. "Thank you for that," Ari said to Larke before the conversation could veer. "I agree the sight of you would give Parrentine false hope. You've never had the most amiable relationship. There's no reason to strain it further."

"So this is goodbye then," Cooro said, his tone neutral.

"Aye, but there is one final thing I must do, I think," Larke replied, contemplating the Wheylian swordmaster.

Cooro's eyes narrowed slightly. Larke stepped forward, moving to stand before the Whey. Ari tensed, unsure what the bard intended.

"If you would step aside?" Larke said to Cooro. "I believe I must bespell your mare. She won't board the Albatross willingly. It will save all involved considerable grief if I do something to stave off her natural reaction."

Cooro looked to Ari, who nodded. He was pleased Larke had thought of it. Stew and the black mare would walk up the ramp without prompting, but Cooro's mare, only a horse, may not be as willing.

Larke glanced over his shoulder at the black mare. "I'm going to bind her to you. She'll follow you onboard, and off. It will be up to you to guide her."

The black mare huffed.

Larke turned back to Cooro's horse. Murmuring, his voice so low Ari couldn't make out the flowing Aluien words, Larke

62

wove his long fingers through the air. Shimmering blue runes materialized, settling onto the piebald mare's forehead and disappearing.

Ari watched with the same awe he always felt. His fingers twitched, longing to reach out and gather up the runes before they could vanish. What would it be like to control the Orlenia the way Larkesong could?

Larke's display lasted only a few moments before he dropped his hands to his sides, stepping back. Cooro's horse looked about, her eyes quickly settling on the black mare. Adoration radiated from her gaze. The black mare leveled an unamused look on Larke.

"There." Larke dusted his hands together. "Now you won't have any trouble with her."

"Thank you," Cooro said.

"Travel safe, Larke," Ari said, extending his hand.

"I shall and fear not, lad, we'll put all to right," the bard said, clasping Ari's proffered hand.

Ari nodded, wanting to believe that was true.

Larke gave him an encouraging smile before turning and clasping hands with Cooro. "Try to keep them out of trouble," the bard said.

"Him?" Mirimel shook her head. "He's more like to be the one getting us into trouble."

Larke turned to her. He held out both hands. Mirimel reached to take them, the sea air tumbling her orange curls about her face. Ari looked down, trying not to intrude.

"Try not to let your temper get the best of you," the bard said, his voice soft.

"Try not to let your assumption people are good get the best of you," Mirimel said.

"But they are." Larke's tone was earnest. "I've lived far longer than you, my dear girl. More people will surprise you with their goodness than their evil."

"Yet one evil person can undo so much good."

Ari recognized the cynical edge in Mirimel's tone. It almost never left, no matter what she spoke of. He wondered if it had always been there, or was a product of her family being murdered and her home burned. He wished he'd known her before that dire day. He gave a gentle tug on Stew's reins, deciding he and Cooro should head out onto the dock to give the two more privacy.

"Keep up on your lessons," Larke said. "I shall miss you, you . . ."

To Ari's relief, whatever else the two said was lost to the brisk sea breeze. He felt an odd tightness in his chest. Larke's life had always mattered to Ari, for the bard was his most steadfast friend, but it did so doubly now. Ari wasn't certain Mirimel could lose another person and not be embittered beyond repair. He hoped the flighty bard realized that and would take extra care.

"Ari," a strong voice called.

Ari looked up, and smiled in spite of dire thoughts and circumstances. Prince Parrentine stood near the bow of the massive ship, waving. His blond hair was tangled and his skin ruddy from wind and sun, a good change for the prince was often too pale. Ari waved back, and Parrentine left his post, hurrying toward the center of the ship. He reached the bottom of the wide ramp only moments before Ari and Stew. The Albatross looked even larger up close.

Parrentine clasped Ari in a rough embrace before stepping back to look at him. "Well met, Lord Aridian."

"Your highness," Ari said, bowing. At Ari's shoulder, Stew dipped his head in greeting.

"Stew," Parrentine said, nodding in turn. "We've set up a paddock on the deck. It's not the way we normally go about it, but it's a short journey by sea, the weather is calm this time of year, and I thought Stew and Goldwin would prefer it."

The prince's eyes slid past Ari. Parrentine frowned, turning back with a question on his face.

"Sir Cadwel and Goldwin will not be joining us yet," Ari said. He turned, waving Cooro forward. "This is Swordmaster Cooro, of the Wheylian court. I mentioned him in my reports of our time there. Queen Reudi sent him to aid us in this quest."

Parrentine's handsome face gave clear view of his surprise, but he nodded in response to Cooro's elaborate bow.

"Your highness," the swordmaster said. "While unable to replace Sir Cadwel, Cooro shall do all in his power to assist in bringing your princess home. None shall prevail against Lord Aridian and Cooro."

"I can believe that, Swordmaster, for your reputation precedes you."

Cooro grinned at that, never one to shirk a compliment.

"I also have Hawk Guardian Mirimel with me," Ari said. "She's the best tracker I know, and a deadly shot."

"And she is Lady Ispiria's cousin, is she not?" Parrentine asked, his gaze sliding past Ari to travel down the dock.

Ari looked back to see Mirimel approaching. Cooro's horse angled away from him, trying to go to the black mare, who followed Mirimel down the pier. In the town above, Ari could see Larke and his gray making their way up the hill, moving away from the sea. The bard shimmered like a heat mirage. Ari could tell by the way people moved around Larke without looking at him that no one else could see him.

"She is," Ari said. He gave Mirimel what he hoped was an encouraging smile as she drew abreast of them. "Prince Parrentine, may I present Hawk Guardian Mirimel."

"Your highness," Mirimel said, bowing from the waist as a man would.

"Hawk Guardian," the prince replied, inclining his head. "I have heard many praiseworthy things of you."

"And I of you, my lord," Mirimel replied.

Parrentine's face settled into a contemplative look. As his smile faded, Ari could more easily discern the tension in the prince. There was a tightness about his mouth, a grim cast to eyes ringed from lack of sleep, that bespoke of the façade his easy greetings were. Following Parrentine's gaze, Ari took in Cooro and Mirimel, trying to see them as the prince must.

The swordmaster was not a tall man, though of average height for a Whey. His black hair was cropped short around a face Ari knew women found it difficult to resist. The lines at the corners of his eyes and mouth showed him to be a man who smiled often and the smattering of gray in his hair gave indication of the fact that he was at least twice Ari's age. In truth, the Whey looked older than Larke, who appeared only about ten years Ari's senior, though the bard was actually older than Sir Cadwel. Overall, though Ari knew Cooro to be one of the best warriors to walk their lands, his serviceable gray attire and easy manner provided little on which to judge him.

Outside their northern home, Mirimel was an oddity. Dressed in green and brown hunting pants and tunic, she wore both a broad-bladed knife and a quiver of short arrows at her waist. Her bow was slung across her back and Ari knew she carried at least one small blade in a boot. For many of those not from Sorga, Mirimel was the first woman they'd seen who didn't don skirts, and some found it unsettling. If Parrentine did, he gave no indication of such.

"This is a fine vessel, your highness," Ari said, breaking into the silence that had fallen over their small group. Above, gulls circled, glinting white against the sky. Ari cast about, but didn't see Mirimel's hawk. "You command her?"

"Yes, and sadly I will only be going with you as far as she does," Parrentine said, a bitter edge to his tone. "Why don't you board and we can convene in the great cabin to discuss our plans. The tide will turn soon. We barely beat it on the way into the harbor."

Ari nodded. Taking up Stew's reins, he realized part of what he saw in Parrentine's eyes as he scrutinized Mirimel and Cooro, was jealousy. Ari didn't envy Parrentine his duties. Whereas Ari's role as King's Champion obligated him to go after Siara and Ispiria, Parrentine's place as sole heir to the throne of Lggothland prohibited him from doing the same. Ari was glad he only had to imagine how terrible it would be to not be able to act, but to wait instead while others sought Ispiria.

Ari lifted his eyes to the deck as he led Stew up the ramp, and nearly stopped. Waiting on the ship were two young nobles, looking to be brother and sister. Both appeared shy of Ari's eighteen years, and both were blond. What struck him, though, was the girl's face. Though he'd only one portrait of his mother and a few briefly seen images conjured by magic to go by, the girl waiting above bore her a striking resemblance. Ari cast a questioning glance at the prince, but Parrentine's abstract gaze wasn't on him.

"Lord Aridian," the young man said, bowing as Ari and his companions came aboard.

The girl curtsied and Ari finally noticed a man in the king's colors, his uniform marking him as the captain, stood beside her. A sailor hurried forward to take Stew's reins. Ari gave his horse a parting pat. He couldn't pull his eyes from the girl's face, though he was peripherally aware Cooro and Mirimel were leading their horses after Stew. Cooro's mare, showing no signs of fear, ambled after Mirimel's Questri mount, as Larke had promised she would.

"Your highness, Lord Aridian," the captain said, bowing. "You've arrived in good time, my lord, to catch the tide. Shall we cast off, your highness?"

Beside Ari, Parrentine gave a slight nod. "Yes, immediately, Captain."

The captain saluted. He strolled off across the deck, barking orders. With a quick glance, Ari took in sailors rushing about in some form of organized chaos he couldn't yet comprehend. Turning back, he found the blonde girl smiling at him encouragingly. The young man stood up straighter.

Parrentine gestured to them, a forced smile on his face. "Lord Aridian, may I present Lord Danton and Lady Cyanna, your cousins."

Ari bowed, trying to contain his shock at hearing his mother's name. "Lady Cyanna?" he repeated, his tone questioning.

"Yes, my lord," she said. "I'm named after your mother."

"Did you know her?" Ari asked, though the girl looked too young. In truth, she looked younger than his mother did in her portrait.

"No, my lord. She disappeared before I was born. I'm fifteen," she added helpfully.

Ari nodded. His mother had died a little over eighteen years ago, on the night of his birth. "You look like her."

"Do I?" She smiled, her blue eyes bright with interest. "I look like my mother, everyone says."

Ari swallowed the familiar tightness in his throat. Why hadn't the Lady taken him to his aunt? He would have grown up with his cousins and a woman who looked like his mother. Not that he didn't care for his adopted aunt, uncle and cousins, but it wasn't truly the same. He supposed he was lucky the Lady had saved him at all, for her true goal had been to kill Lord Kenmar.

"Our mother is your mother's younger sister," Lord Danton said.

"Your cousins are here to repeat for you what they know," Parrentine said. "They were near when the abduction took place." He cast his brittle smile across them. "When you're ready, I'd like to speak to you in the great cabin, Lord Aridian. Now, if you'll excuse me?"

Parrentine turned, striding aft. Ari bowed to the prince's retreating form before sweeping his gaze across the ship. Two narrow corrals had been set up on the deck outside the cabin Parrentine entered. Stew stood in one, the black mare and Cooro's piebald horse in the other. There seemed hardly enough space for them, but Ari couldn't see anywhere else the horses could go. For all its massive size, the deck seemed to be full of masts and ropes, the latter forming a complicated looking pattern of rigging.

The breeze was stronger on deck, whipping Mirimel's orange curls about her head as she and Cooro walked back toward Ari and his cousins. Under his feet, Ari was aware of the gentle, almost soothing sway of the Albatross. He could feel his muscles automatically compensating for it. The sailors who moved about the deck, and Cooro and Mirimel, didn't seem to be troubled by it at all.

"Lord Danton, Lady Cyanna," Ari said as Mirimel and Cooro came abreast them. "These are my companions in arms, Hawk Guardian Mirimel of Sorga and Swordmaster Cooro of Wheylia." Ari turned to his friends. "These are my cousins. Ispiria was staying with them."

Bows and a curtsy were exchanged.

"Cooro is honored to meet you, my lady, my lord," Cooro said.

"You're Ispiria's cousin, aren't you?" Lady Cyanna asked Mirimel. "You look just as she described you." She smiled, but her lips trembled. She shot a worried glance at her brother.

"My lord, we are filled with remorse we didn't take better care of Lady Ispiria," Lord Danton said. "Our family was honored by your recognition of our connection, and that you entrusted Lady Ispiria to us, and we have failed you."

He dropped to his knees, much to Ari's chagrin. "Really, there's--"

"Please, my lord, my father has instructed me to offer up my services, to be your bondsman, until such time as Lady Ispiria is restored to you. I am already seventeen, too old, I know, but it would be my honor to serve as a page to you."

"Lord Danton, stand up," Ari said, aware half the ship was watching. "You're a lord and past the age to be indentured, and this is not necessary. Your family was charged with chaperoning Ispiria, not keeping her safe from such unforeseeable actions as took place."

"My lord, my father insisted. It is for our family's honor. We won't have our newfound relations look down on us. I am as brave as any man alive. It is my duty to make amends."

A glance at Cyanna showed her to be no help. The eyes she leveled on her brother shone with pride. Ari looked from Cooro to Mirimel, beseeching.

"What skills do you have?" Mirimel asked.

"Your pardon, Hawk Guardian?" Lord Danton looked up, frowning slightly.

"Skills. Lord Aridian is the greatest knight in two lands. I am a tracker and can shoot an apple out of a tree from farther away than you can likely see it. Swordmaster Cooro is nearly as skilled with a blade as Lord Aridian, and an accomplished acrobat. What are you offering us?"

Danton cast about, his frown deepening.

"He's been trained in all the gentlemanly arts," Cyanna said, tipping her chin up. "He can ride and fence."

"I see," Mirimel said, her tone condemning.

Danton surged to his feet. "I am a skilled huntsman and duelist. I, too, can track, fight and shoot."

Ari cast Mirimel a warning look. He didn't want to start off his relationship with his cousins in an argument. She opened her mouth, likely not to say anything soothing. Cooro held up a hand, forestalling her. She glared at him, but her jaws snapped closed.

"There is some room on this deck, is there not?" the swordmaster said.

Ari turned to him, glimpsing the confusion he felt reflected in his cousins' faces. "Not much. Not with the horses."

"Enough, though," Cooro said. "Cooro thinks, fleet as this vessel likely is, we shall still have several days of travel before we reach the southern lands."

"We'll be there in a matter of days, if the weather holds," Lord Danton said.

Ari took in that prediction with surprise. The king was correct. A ship was quite a bit faster than riding the length of Lggothland. Ari had ridden it often enough, at varying speeds, to know.

"Well then, there is time for friendly bouts." Cooro grinned.

"Friendly bouts?" Ari repeated, wondering where the swordmaster was going.

The look Mirimel turned on Cooro was inscrutable. "A splendid idea. Bouts, and stakes."

Ari wasn't sure he trusted the smugness in her tone.

"Exactly." Cooro aimed his grin at Lord Danton. "If you can best Cooro or Lord Aridian in fighting, or Hawk Guardian Mirimel with a bow, you are welcome to join us on this journey. Not as a page, for that truly would be beneath a fine Lggothian lord, but as our companion."

Danton looked to Ari, his excitement clear. "Do you agree to this, my lord?"

Ari suppressed a sigh. Trouncing his cousin likely wouldn't get their relationship off to a good start, but he supposed it was better than refusing him out of hand. "It sounds like a fine idea."

"Perhaps some of the crew, or the prince, would care to test themselves as well?" Cooro said.

Ari shrugged. They hadn't spent time on dueling for days. He knew Cooro was eager for a bout or two. It would likely do them all good, and there was no sense getting out of practice. "You arrange it. I must go meet with the prince. I've kept him waiting long enough." He bowed to his cousins. "It is good to finally meet you. I'm sure we shall talk more anon."

They bowed back, Danton appearing eager and Cyanna worried. Ari hoped his cousin wasn't too averse to losing. Leaving them, he headed aft to discover what his prince wished to tell him. From Parrentine's mien when he'd left them, Ari could already guess it was nothing good.

72

Chapter 6

At Ari's knock, the door to the large cabin on the aft of the ship opened. The page who greeted him was distinct, with amber eyes and burnished skin, and vaguely familiar. Searching back to the day he'd defeated all rivals and taken his place as King's Champion, Ari thought he remembered him. The young man in Parrentine's livery must be the boy who'd been holding the sword Ari now wore, Fwellian. On that day, nearly two years ago, Ari hadn't had the presence of mind to wonder at the obvious foreignness of Parrentine's page, though he did now.

The page bowed, backing into the room. "My lord, the prince is expecting you," he said in soft tones, his words betraying an accent.

"Thank you." Ari entered the large, comfortable looking cabin. As the door closed behind him, he could hear the captain calling out orders and was a bit disappointed he wouldn't see the massive sails unfurl. The cabin he stood in had windows on three sides and was fitted out with cushioned benches, tables, and other comforts. Obviously, the room was meant as a gathering place, though only Parrentine and his page occupied it now.

The prince sat at the largest table. His elbows rested on it, framing an untouched goblet of wine. A nearly full carafe stood on a sideboard, along with a selection of bread, fruits, cured meat and cheese. Parrentine sat with his face pressed into his palms, but he lifted his head as Ari approached.

All pretense at normalcy was gone now. Pain radiated from the prince's eyes, the blue of his irises dark with it. His mouth was squeezed into a thin line, tension evident in every muscle. He let out a sigh, pushing himself upright in his chair. "Ari."

"Your highness, were you waiting on me to begin eating?" Ari asked. Parrentine had turned to drinking when Clorra died. Surely it would be best if Ari encouraged the prince to take food.

"Eat?" Parrentine stared at him blankly.

"Yes, your highness," the prince's page said, hurrying forward. "You should eat."

Parrentine shook his head. "Later, Mattah."

The page, Mattah, cast Ari a beseeching look. For the first time, Ari realized Parrentine was thinner than he should be. He recalled as well how the prince had given up eating when Clorra was ill. Then, Parrentine had sunk into madness, forcing Ari and Sir Cadwel to intervene. Ari didn't want to see the prince return to that state.

"Perhaps we should have the food here in case we want it. Let me move this out of the way." Ari pushed the wine glass across the table. Behind him, he could hear Mattah gathering the tray of food.

"I suppose Cadwel wasn't the right choice if we wanted you educated in subtlety," Parrentine said, his lips turning up in a hollow rendition of a smile. "Don't worry. I wasn't going to drink it."

Mattah set the tray down between them, the nearly imperceptible nod he gave Ari seeming to confirm the prince's claim.

"Take a seat, Ari, and I'll tell you what little I know." Parrentine didn't so much as glance at the food.

The chair beside Ari scraped back as Mattah pulled it out. "Thank you," Ari said, sitting. Parrentine's page retreated to stand unobtrusively by the door. He placed a carefully blank expression on his face, but Ari was sure he would be able to hear them from where he stood.

"Siara--" The prince's voice cracked. He cleared his throat.

Ari turned back to face his sovereign, searching his mind for some comfort he could give. Muted by the wooden walls about them, Ari could hear sailors calling to one another and the rigging creaking. The ship rocked beneath them. Parrentine opened and closed his mouth again, obviously struggling to begin. He didn't look at Ari, training his eyes on the windows across from him instead. Outside, the horizon bobbed with the movement of the ship.

"Siara and Ispiria, along with your cousins and several other young people, were on a picnic." The prince's voice was rough. "You know how diverting the ladies seem to find those little jaunts. I suppose it's nice for them to be out of doors."

Ari nodded.

"I didn't attend. I never do, though Siara always asks." Parrentine scrubbed a hand over his face. "They were well guarded. We're never lax."

"I know," Ari said. The picnics generally included not only guards but a legion of servants. Still, a field or glade must be considered less secure than the castle. Of course, there was no reason for a nation so long at peace to worry overmuch about the safety of ladies picnicking within sight of the capital.

"Your cousins can tell you the details of what happened, but the long and short of it is a search was put on for a croquet ball that had entered the forest. It's unclear how Siara and Ispiria ended up unguarded. Lord Danton claims he told the guards to accompany them while he searched with his sister, but the men who were with them say the opposite." Parrentine glanced at Ari. "When questioned on the matter, Lady Cyanna routinely resorts to tears."

Ari drummed his fingers on the table. "You believe my cousin is lying."

"Someone is. The guards in question are not green."

Ari stilled his hand. He'd finally met his family, and they were somehow complicit in the abduction of the princess and Ispiria? "I will endeavor to learn more from them both."

Parrentine nodded. "Once the lieutenant in charge realized Siara was missing, he immediately sent riders back to the castle for reinforcements and commenced to search. It didn't take long for him to realize Lady Ispiria was also missing, or to locate their trail." Parrentine frowned. "I don't know how they were so much swifter than we were. By the time my men followed their trail to a deserted beach, the ship we assume they were put on was a speck on the horizon." Reaching into his doublet, Parrentine pulled out a parchment and offered it to Ari. "This was tied to a staff driven into the sand."

The rolled parchment was flattened and tattered at the edges. It was secured with a familiar green ribbon, one of Ispiria's favorites. Ari untied the strand of silk, swallowing against the surge of pain he felt at the sight of the ribbon Ispiria must have been wearing the day she was taken. Setting it carefully aside, he uncoiled the parchment, using both hands to hold it open on the table.

Dear Noble Sirs,

Though it pains us to take such steps, we cannot permit a Wheylian heathen to defile the Lggothian throne, nor to perpetuate her vile lack of faith through the royal line. It is unfair to ask the fine nation of Lggothland to suffer such disgrace.

Our concerns have been raised before both King Ennentine and Prince Parrentine of the royal line of Lggothland, but have not been addressed. Princess Siara has not denounced her heathen ways, but instead dwelled for a year in the heart of paganism alongside the sorceress queen of Wheylia.

We see no recourse but to remove the princess to the holiest of places, the first temple of the Overgod, to cleanse her soul and guide her onto the righteous path. At such time as she denounces her pagan faith and kneels to the Overgod, we shall return her. Be assured, in the time between now and then, no harm will befall her.

Faithful Servants of the Overgod

Ari reread the short note several times. Nowhere did it mention Ispiria. Had her abduction been an accident of circumstance? He released the note, letting it fold closed. "Siara will never kneel to their god."

"I know." The prince's voice was soft. The ship creaked about them. The scenery without shifted as the Albatross left the dock.

"This was almost certainly written by a noble," Ari said, for peasants generally had little, if any, skill with reading and writing. "And hiring a ship points to wealth."

"We thought the same. We have riders out. We're attempting to confirm the location of every noble in

Lggothland, which will take some time." Parrentine took up the parchment, unrolling it, though Ari suspected the prince had the words it contained memorized.

"A noble could have hired the work done, not dirtying his own hands. Even if your men can locate every one, it still won't necessarily lead us to who has done this," Ari said.

"I'd like to believe the expedition won't be fruitful even if fulfilled, that it's not any of our own. It could be someone from another land altogether, though I can't imagine to what end." Parrentine dropped the worn parchment to the tabletop. "There are too many options, and we've too little information."

"My cousins may know more." Ari was aware of the hard edge to his tone. Could Lord Danton wish to accompany Ari for a different reason than to restore his family's honor? Did he plan to sabotage their venture? "Before I question them, I have information for you. I'm not sure if it's relevant. In truth, I have no reason to think it is, except that my heart tells me so, and Sir Cadwel agrees."

Parrentine's expression flickered with hope. "What do you know?"

"It's of a very discreet nature," Ari said, lowering his voice. He nodded toward where Mattah stood by the door.

"I trust Mattah as I trust you," Parrentine said.

A glance revealed a slight reddening of the young man's face, visible even with his dark skin, confirming Ari's suspicion Mattah could hear them, though the page kept his gaze forward and his expression blank. Ari turned back to Parrentine. If Ari could tell Natan about the Aluiens and his family, he supposed the prince could elect to tell his page.

While the Albatross set sail, Ari launched into his tale again. He was relieved that this time he only had to recount the events that had transpired since his return from Wheylia. The prince knew all that had happened before then, having lived through portions of it alongside Ari. Trying to be as succinct as possible, Ari told Parrentine of the Lady's revelations that spring, and his subsequent journey to the Tybrunn Plains. He described the Lady's half-truths and her willingness to sacrifice Mirimel's life to pit Ari against Kenmar. He also told Lord Kenmar's story. He felt a bit awkward doing so, for it was less his tale to tell, but knew he couldn't leave it out or Parrentine wouldn't truly understand. When Ari was done, the prince sat staring at him for a long while.

"You feel the Lady, that little old Aluien who tried to prevent us from making Clorra go mad, the one who convinced the other Aluiens to save your life and give you your powers, has stolen Siara and Ispiria to force you to complete the sword and slay Lord Kenmar, who you say is the first Empty One?"

Ari coughed. It sounded a bit ridiculous summed up like that. "She did say the final stone is across the sea and urged me to go there searching for it."

Parrentine shook his head. "Siara never liked her, or trusted her."

"She doesn't like or trust Larkesong either, but I know him to be my ally." In truth, there were far fewer people Princess Siara did like or trust than didn't.

"Do you trust Lord Kenmar?"

Ari shrugged. "I can't say yes. I don't think it would be wise to trust him completely. He's admitted to sending the Caller to kill my parents."

"But you've traveled with him. Even now, Sir Cadwel and Lord Kenmar travel together."

"Right now, I trust him more than I trust the Lady, and we may need his help to stand against her." As Ari said it, he realized he still didn't believe they would have to fight the Lady.

Surely, were she behind Siara's and Ispiria's abduction, he would be able to reason with her once he found them.

"Something about this does not sit right with me." Parrentine frowned, his gaze abstract once more. "You feel she may be behind the abduction. First, she tried to order you to travel across the sea to seek the third stone, and now you think she tries to lure you. How would she know you'd elected not to seek it? Do you think one of your companions informed her?"

Ari hadn't considered that, and didn't really wish to. That would mean either Larke, Mirimel or Cooro was the informant, for certainly Kenmar was not. "I think she was watching us in her scrying pool. I spoke my decision aloud. That likely sealed Siara's and Ispiria's fate. We'll know for sure once Larke returns, for he can conjure up what she was last seeking."

"Unless he is the traitor, in which case he will lie."

Ari shook his head. "Larkesong is loyal."

Parrentine's face remained skeptical. "Still, if she doesn't know where the final stone is, it seems a lot of trouble to go to in order to lure you somewhere."

"Maybe she's found it." Ari couldn't deny the prince's logic, but he knew in his gut the Lady had taken Siara and Ispiria. Maybe he was wrong about why, but he wasn't wrong about who.

Parrentine leaned toward Ari. "Do you truly believe there is no way for anyone to find these stones? No magical means of locating them?"

"Yes, I believe that. If we seek them, we'll be forced to follow rumor and conjecture. It will take research and diligence. That's why Sir Cadwel, Larke and Kenmar will attempt the task."

A slight smile flickered across Parrentine's face. "I'm not sure that will be necessary, but I am sure the stone isn't in any of the southern kingdoms. Reading your report of what Queen Reudi said about the sword I gave you seemed to confirm a suspicion of mine." Parrentine turned toward his page. "Mattah, do you have the stone?"

"Yes, my lord." Mattah crossed to them, pulling a small pouch from his doublet.

"Stone?" Ari's mouth went dry. Parrentine couldn't mean. . .

Mattah proffered the pouch. Ari stared at it, making no move to take it. Casting him a frown, Parrentine reached for it. He untied the strings, dumping a small glimmering white stone onto the table between them. Mattah retreated to his position beside the door.

Ari eyed the stone where it lay near the tray of food. It was milky white and opaque, yet seemed to glow slightly from within. It was unremarkable looking, save for the smooth finish and an odd attraction it held. Ari knew, should he pick it up, it would be heavier than it appeared and warm to the touch.

He lifted his eyes to meet Parrentine's. "I . . . how . . . where . . ." he stammered before clamping his mouth closed over his swirling thoughts.

"I take it this is the stone?" Parrentine poked it where it lay. "It doesn't look worth razing Hawkers and laying siege to Sorga for. May I see the others?"

Nodding, Ari stood to unsheathe his sword. He lay it on the table, pommel toward Parrentine. The other two stones glimmered on the hilt, above the empty socket. Ari stared down at the third, still stunned. He'd never truly thought to see it. He hadn't even decided if he wanted it. Though he didn't really understand what having all three accomplished, he knew they were dangerous. Having them all made him dangerous.

"Shall I see if anyone has the skill to set it into the hilt? Do you know what will happen if we do?"

Ari shook his head. "I don't, and we can't. It takes magic. The Lady affixed the first one, and Larke the second."

"You'd best keep it until you find someone who can set it for you, then." Parrentine picked up the stone and put it back in the pouch, offering it to Ari.

Ari eyed it reluctantly. "I don't know what sort of weapon it will turn the sword into. Or me."

Again, a weary smile momentarily lessened the pain on the prince's face. "I believe we've had this discussion before, Ari. Someone has to have the power to defeat the evil loose in our world. I know it's a weighty burden, but there's no one whose honor and integrity I know to be more suited to the task than you." Parrentine's expression hardened. "And as your prince, I order you to take this stone. You swore to do all in your power to keep Lggothland and my family safe."

Ari sighed, taking the pouch. Aware his hands shook slightly, he tucked it into his doublet. "Yes, your highness."

"Hopefully, once that stone is added to the set, no matter who is behind the abduction, nothing will stand between you and rescuing Siara and your fiancée."

Ari swallowed, nodding, still hardly able to comprehend he now had all three stones. "How do you come to have the last stone, your highness?"

"It was given to me along with the sword." Parrentine nodded toward Mattah where he stood beside the door. "Mattah's mother lives in Jondor. It was she who led me to the man I purchased your sword from, and she gave me the pouch with the stone. Where she got it from, I do not know, but I think you should ask her. If this plot is all one and the same, knowing may help us."

Ari scrutinized Parrentine's page more closely. His skin was darker than usually seen in Lggothland. His hair, a deep brown, was streaked with blond. Ari had read that the deeper one traveled into the southern lands, the darker in complexion people became, their skin better adapted to a harsher sun. Though pages for the upper ranks of the nobility were routinely supplied from the bevy of younger sons each house boasted, it was obvious Mattah's mother wasn't a typical Lggothian noble. Nor should she be, if she dwelled in Jondor.

"Mattah's already written to her, telling her what happened. I'd hoped she might discover if the ship docked there, or some information about those on board. She hadn't written back before I left to meet you, but you can ask her what she's learned when we arrive."

Ari raised his eyebrows. Obviously, the prince trusted not only Mattah, but his mother as well. By Ari's estimation, the woman's involvement made her suspicious, something Parrentine clearly didn't believe.

"When we dock in Jondor, he'll take you to her. I have been ordered by my father to remain with the ship, but he issued Mattah no such command. We will remain in port while Mattah gives you what aid he is able."

"Sir Cadwel said we would sail for Jondor, but I'm unsure why. What makes that land our destination?"

"The ship we dispatched, though it lost the one that took Siara, last saw it headed for Jondor. That's all we have to go on, save that Jondor had a large port. Now, with your talk of the stone being involved, I have more confidence we head to the correct city."

Ari nodded. "Can you tell me anything of the man who sold the sword to you?"

"He was old, and blind. We met in an abandoned dwelling and he charged me one silver for the sword. I thought it fairly odd at the time, but didn't dwell on it. I counted myself lucky to have been led to such a fine weapon and returned home. To Siara." The pain returned to Parrentine's face in full force.

"I will return her to you." Ari infused as much determination into his tone as he could, for he would get Siara and Ispiria back. He would not permit any other outcome. He had Cooro, Mirimel, Larkesong, Kenmar, Sir Cadwel and their Questri on his side. No one, nothing, would stop them.

"I know you will." The prince sank back in his chair, looking miserable. "I have faith in you, Ari. You should know one other thing, though. Something I've told no one else."

Ari cast a glance at Mattah, but the young man's face was like stone. "Yes, your highness?"

"You're not only searching for my wife, Lggothland's future queen. You're also searching for the heir to the throne. Siara is with child."

Chapter 7

After Ari's meeting with Parrentine, Mattah led him to a small room below deck, where his possessions had been stowed. There was little more than a bed, which was too short for Ari, and enough space for him to stand facing it. Mattah departed immediately and Ari only lingered long enough to mark the room's location. Returning to deck, he checked with Stew to ensure he was comfortable and then took up a position on the rail, where he hoped to be out of the way. Where Mirimel, Cooro and his cousins were, he didn't know.

Nor, in that moment, did he precisely care. He leaned against the rail, watching the coast of Lggothland rush by to the west. The Albatross cut through the water, her square white sails billowing against the deep blue of the sky. Though the angle of the sails told a different tale, the momentum of their passage created enough breeze to press Ari's sun-streaked brown hair back from his face. Light glinted off the swells, making the ocean between him and Lggothland sparkle like a treasure trove.

As the king's ship sped south, the tang of salt air enveloping them, Ari reflected that the experience didn't disappoint. Being aboard the Albatross captured all of his dreams about what travel by ship would be. The great vessel bore them south with all haste and Ari found the sensation almost as invigorating as galloping with Stew. He'd never be able to soar like one of Mirimel's hawks, but if he closed his eyes and turned his face into the wind and sun, he could imagine he was.

Ari kept his eyes shut when a familiar, nearly undiscernible tread drew near. Fabric slid across the lacquered rail as Mirimel settled against it beside him. "Your cousins are hiding something."

"I know." Ari didn't turn to her, clinging to the illusion of freedom the Albatross granted.

"You do?"

Ari smiled slightly at the surprise in her tone. Opening his eyes to the lowering sun, he glanced at Mirimel, but any emotion that may have been on her face was already gone. "You expected me to argue."

"I did. I was prepared for a speech about how I always see the worst in people, followed by some sort of naive nonsense about waiting to condemn them until we know the truth."

"Parrentine already told me they haven't been honest about what happened."

"You and the prince are close."

It was a statement. Ari realized he hadn't included any form of honorific. Was he truly so comfortable with the future ruler of Lggothland now? He recalled a time he'd been nearly too awed to speak to royalty. "We've traveled together," he offered, though he knew it was an understatement of what he and Parrentine had endured in their doomed quest to save the prince's first wife.

"What are we going to do about your cousins?" Mirimel asked.

"Firstly, we won't condemn them until we know the truth."

Mirimel muttered something.

Fortunately, the wind carried her words away from Ari's ears. He didn't ask her to repeat them, relatively sure they weren't complimentary. "I think we'll hold a few exhibition matches before these bouts you have planned to test Lord Danton's worth. We'll make sure he knows how easily things could go poorly for him. Then we can see if he's up for a duel with me or would rather discuss what happened."

Mirimel smiled, but there was no mirth in it. "An excellent idea. Do you wish to shoot with me and spar with the Whey?"

Ari shrugged, unconcerned with the details. "However you care to arrange the matches suits me."

Mirimel cocked her head to the side, eyes narrowing. "You're very calm."

"Why shouldn't I be? Do you have any reason to think you, me, Cooro, the prince and a ship full of men loyal to the crown can't deal with two nobles who are hardly more than children?"

She frowned, a line appearing on her brow. "I do not, but not worrying isn't like you. You always worry, more than you should." She gestured toward the large cabin Ari had left Parrentine in. "Take the prince. He may have smiled when he met us, and gone through introductions pleasantly enough, but any fool can see he's clinging to sanity. He's bereft, nearly terrified. As well he should be, with his wife spirited off to who knows where."

Ari glanced about, but no one stood near. The sailors he could see appeared well occupied with the rigging or high in the crow's nest. "I am worried about him. When his first wife was ill, he was overwrought. He truly did go mad."

"Why aren't you in a similar state? Ispiria is missing, Ari. This isn't like when the Caller took her and we could track her down in a matter of days. Someone put her on a ship and sailed away with her. When we found out you seemed agitated enough, but ever since you've been disconcertingly calm. Ispiria is gone. How are you standing here taking in the view?"

"Because nothing will happen to her." Ari shrugged. "The Lady took them to force me to go where she wants me to go, and do what she wants me to do. She'll keep them safe, and when we catch up to them, I'll find a way to reason with her."

Mirimel's frown only deepened. Her orange hair tumbled about in the breeze. "We don't know for certain that's what happened, or will happen."

"When we pressure him, I'm sure the reason my cousin's story contradicts the guards' will turn out to be because he doesn't know what happened." Ari leaned against the rail. Shadowed with the lowering sun, a town was slipping past. "When I question him closely, he'll get that dazed look on his face that people who have been manipulated by the Aluiens get. He'll stammer and try to change the topic. It was the Lady who took Ispiria and Siara, I'm sure of it, and they are perfectly safe in her care." He glanced at Mirimel, reading the skepticism in her expression.

She swept her hair back from her face, glaring at him. "You mean the same lady who was willing to let me die to prove you can't trust Kenmar? They're safe in that lady's care?"

"I'm sure of it," Ari reiterated, wishing Mirimel didn't always have to take the worst view.

"You can say that as many times as you like, Ari, but it doesn't change the truth. We don't know what is happening to Ispiria, or what will. If the worst should happen, you need to be ready. You won't have time for shock, or grief. We will likely only get one chance at retaliation." Mirimel's expression softened. "This is no time for your pristine ideals. I can't let you walk around like this, Ari."

Ari stared down into the water for a long moment, watching the ripples the Albatross made. The water looked darker now, the sun too low to lend it life. Slowly, he eased his grip on the railing, displeased to see he'd dented the lacquered wood. "Why not?"

"Pardon?"

Out of the corner of his eye, Ari was aware of her scrutiny. "Why can't you let me walk around this way? Would you rather I be like the prince, holding onto my sanity by a slender cord?"

"No, of course not. That's not--"

"I know you're trying to protect me, Mirimel, and it's . . . nice." Searching back, Ari realized someone protecting him was rare, though Larke always had. He turned to face her again, pushing a hand through his tangled hair. "I can't let myself doubt like you can. I can't go through my days that way. This, how I am, is what will let me find them and bring them back. To be any other way will court fear, and madness."

Her blue eyes searched his hazel ones. She pressed her lips into a thin line of discontent, but nodded. "Have it your way."

"Thank you." Ari looked about. "Where is Cooro? For that matter, where is your hawk?"

"Who knows where that Whey is? Likely scouring the ship for women, though the only one about is your cousin and I already made it clear to him that she's too young for his games."

Ari raised his eyebrows. "Surely he didn't need you to tell him that."

"Lggothian noblewomen are more sheltered than Wheylian women, of any rank. I thought it advisable to point that out to him."

"What did you threaten to do to him?" Ari didn't try to hide his amusement.

"Toss him overboard to use as a target when I challenge your cousin to a shooting match."

Ari nodded. "Fair enough. You do realize he'll misconstrue your threats as jealousy?"

"He's a fool."

Ari knew better than to argue. "And your hawk?"

"She'll catch up to us before we lose sight of Lggothland, I should think."

"She?" Ari had thought, all that time, that the hawk who traveled with them was male. "She's small for a female."

Mirimel gave him a pitying look. "You spent months on the Tybrunn plains with that hawk as your companion and you don't even know if he's a he or she? Telling the difference is easier to learn than Ancient Wheylian, yet somehow you managed that. Can't you apply yourself to anything not related to the martial arts?"

"So he is a he?" Ari asked, chagrined. After the sacking of Hawkers, he'd taken the time to learn more about the Sorga Hawks, the sentient raptors who dwelled in the mountains around his home and who'd carried messages for the lords of Sorga for centuries, giving them a tactical advantage in times of war. He'd been sure the little hawk who traveled with them was male, until Mirimel confused him.

"He is, and I sent him to keep an eye on Larkesong. The gods only know what trouble that fool will get himself into. Whatever it is, I'll want to know."

"You sent him with Larke? But we need him. He's supposed to help us find Ispiria." Ari pushed down a surge of panic, reminding himself that he was calm. Ispiria would be safe with the Lady.

"Which is why I asked for a volunteer to accompany us to the southern lands."

"From the dock? From how far away can you speak to the hawks?" Ari wondered if Larke had a similar ability with the hawks and the Questri, or if the skill was indeed part of a true Hawk Guardian's special magic.

"It's not exactly like that."

To Ari's surprise, Mirimel blushed. It was only a hint of color, touching her cheeks but not spreading across her face. Ari supposed Mirimel's skin wouldn't dare a full blush. Not with her temper. "I'm sorry. We don't need to speak of it."

"No, we can." She peered toward the setting sun. "There is no real rule against speaking of it, only my father's. He ordered me to never admit to my abilities."

Her dead father. Another topic they never spoke on. Ari realized he'd best tread carefully. "He did?"

Her lips curled at the corners in one of her mirthless smiles. "He said having magic was dangerous. He said it brought trouble, and I should never tell anyone. If only he'd extrapolated his theory to that stupid stone and cast it from the aerie."

Ari's hand went to the hilt of his sword, where the stone the Sorga Hawks had guarded was set into the hilt. The hawks had kept it safe, removing it from the village when the Caller attacked Hawkers to claim it. They'd brought it to Ari, who'd ridden out to the village. He hadn't comprehended the extent of the danger until it was far too late for Mirimel's kin.

It was over two years since the sacking of Hawkers, but Ari didn't imagine two years was long enough for Mirimel to come to terms with losing her family. Taking in Mirimel's perfect profile, so reminiscent of Ispiria's, he wondered if he should put an arm about her. When Ispiria was upset, she sought that comfort.

"I can't speak to the hawks across distances, but I can project emotions." Mirimel's tone was hard. "I had the idea about a day out from Sorga. I don't know if I could call them from any farther than that. It would be difficult. Either way, another hawk will catch up to us."

Movement caught Ari's eyes and he took in the way she restlessly tapped a finger on the hilt of her broad-bladed hunting knife. No, he shouldn't touch her. This was Mirimel, not Ispiria. Mirimel didn't seek comfort from anyone. She kept her anger in easy reach, ready to call on the fierceness of it to aid her. It was part of what made her such a good warrior, though Ari sometimes wondered at what cost.

"I see," Ari said, aware a response was required but leery of provoking her.

Mirimel turned from the rail. "We'll begin the exhibition matches in the morning. I'll work out the details with that Whey. I believe we're all to dine with the prince in the aft cabin, shortly after sunset."

"Right." He bowed to her back as she turned and walked away.

Ari returned to the sunset. Mirimel had mentioned open water. He hoped he would get to see the sun rise and set from it, and the ocean under the moon and stars. He didn't know how many opportunities his life would afford for a sea voyage.

Certainly, it was a rare privilege to be aboard the king's greatest ship.

Trying to press the dreariness Mirimel left in her wake from his thoughts, Ari fixed his eyes on the darkening coastline. He drew out the moment, for dinner promised to be stilted and overshadowed by grief, suspicion and anger. He wasn't looking forward to it. Still, come morning, Ari would have the joy of dueling Cooro, and the satisfaction of making Lord Danton talk.

Chapter 8

The smooth motion of the Albatross as it cut through the ocean overcame the discomfort of the truncated bunk. Ari couldn't recall when he'd last slept so well. He woke before dawn, dressing quickly and hurrying to the deck. While the dark coast of Lggothland still sped by to the west, the sun would rise that morning from the unbroken expanse of ocean to the east, and Ari meant to see it.

He stood at the rail, aware of sailors moving about in the predawn light. Sooner than he expected, the sky transformed from deep blue to layers of bright color. To his eye, the deepest red was reminiscent of Ispiria's hair. Ari watched, transfixed, as the sun finally crested the horizon, a glowing ball of fire resting far out in the sea.

He wondered if Ispiria liked sailing. Had she gotten to see the sun rise? He hoped so. He hoped she and Siara were being well cared for. He wouldn't let himself think of them locked away and afraid. If that turned out to be the case, he—

Ari exhaled, trying to let go of the anger threatening to wash over him. Ispiria and Siara were well. He knew that. They were well, and a level head was called for.

The sunrise having lost its appeal, he turned his back on it, leaning against the rail. To the fore of the ship, a young sailor was using a piece of charcoal to mark off a square, and Ari realized he was readying for the bouts. More men than were normally idle already loitered near where the young man worked. Glancing up, Ari could see the sailor in the crow's nest fastening ropes to the mast, likely affixing some sort of targets for Mirimel.

On the opposite end of the deck from where the matches were to take place, Parrentine's page, Mattah, entered the great cabin carrying a large tray. Ari's stomach growled and he left the rail, heading for what he trusted was breakfast. He didn't know what was served aboard a ship, but hoped it wasn't the typical fair of last evenings roast cut into cold strips. Ever since his brief, unremembered time as an Aluien, Ari had lost his taste for meat. Unbidden and unwanted, the image of a deranged Princess Clorra nibbling on raw flesh skittered through his mind.

Ari shook his head, trying to shake the memory away. It seemed unfair the Aluiens should take away his blissful recollections of his summer as one of them, yet he must live with memories like Clorra's lips covered in Parrentine's blood and the burned out shell of Hawkers. Though, for all they seemed benevolent, the Aluiens never claimed to exist for good. Rather, when looked at objectively, their goal of harvesting the best mankind had to offer to swell their ranks could be seen as selfish. Especially since, once a human became an Aluien, they were prohibited from interfering with other humans ever again.

Ari paused when he reached the door Mattah had passed through. His thoughts had only grown darker as he crossed the deck, not a good temperament to begin his day with. Firmly turning up his mouth in what he hoped looked more like a smile than a wince, he pushed open the cabin door.

Mattah looked over from where he was setting out trays of food on the sideboard. His intelligent amber eyes met Ari's briefly before he bowed. "Good morning, my lord. I was told you're an early riser, so I took the liberty of bringing up some food."

"Thank you, Mattah, and all that really isn't necessary." Having grown up believing he was the nephew of innkeepers, Ari was still uncomfortable with the fuss his titles evoked.

"I didn't feel you would eat it all, my lord. I simply wasn't sure what you wished for."

"Not the food." Ari closed the door, crossing the room. "The honorifics and bowing."

"You do not wish me to address you properly, my lord?"

"Well, I could do without it, especially from someone I'm traveling with and who's in the prince's trust."

"Sir Aridian then?"

Ari caught an amused glint in Mattah's eyes. "How about you call me Ari, and tell me what's humorous about my request." He turned to the sideboard, noticing a small pot of porridge with relief. "Have you eaten?"

"Pages usually eat after--"

"I'm aware." Ari realized he sounded like Sir Cadwel and again attempted a smile. He wished the sunrise hadn't put him so poignantly in mind of Ispiria, dredging up the worries Mirimel didn't seem to think he had and spoiling his mood. "Why don't you have a seat and break your fast with me? I insist we're doing away with formalities."

Mattah eyed him for a moment before nodding. Ari served himself a bowl of porridge, taking some fruit as well. Mattah, after looking over the food he'd set out, took fruit, bread, preserves and cheese.

"I didn't mean to be amused at your expense," Mattah said once they were seated. He pulled his piece of bread in half, dunking it in the preserves before taking a bite.

"Was it at my expense?" Ari had thought so, but couldn't fathom what was funny about his request.

Mattah shrugged. "I was . . . that is, his highness told me you would say as much. In truth, he bet me a silver it would be less than a day before you requested I call you by name. I'm pleasantly surprised to find him correct."

"The prince knows me well, it seems," Ari said between mouthfuls of porridge.

"Everyone in the capital speaks of you, often. I didn't doubt his highness, but it's difficult to always know fact from fable."

"They speak of me often?" Ari grimaced. He knew, as King's Champion and duke of the second most important holding in the land, he would be spoken of. He didn't like the idea, though.

"Yes, especially since Lady Ispiria arrived."

"Oh?" Ari asked, immediately on guard.

"Well, at least half the young men are in love with her, so they spend hours boasting about how they'll best you and win her heart and hours more regaling each other with tales of your great deeds, in seeming contradiction of having any chance of beating you."

"I see." Ari supposed the gossip about him could be worse.

"And for their part, half of the ladies hate her, though half love her, likely because she's kind to everyone. Even lowly pages."

Ari didn't miss the embarrassed way Mattah muttered the last bit, but was more concerned with what he'd said about the ladies of the court. "Hate her?"

"For being your betrothed." Mattah looked up from his plate. "You're the most marriageable man in the kingdom. Even more so than the prince's cousin, Lord Janvis. They all complain that they never had a chance, as you're rarely in the capital, and say Lady Ispiria cheated by being born in Sorga."

"How deep do you think this hatred runs?" Deep enough for someone to plot against Ispiria?

"Oh." Understanding cleared the hint of red from Mattah's face. "You mean, would someone have the princess kidnapped as part of a plan to remove Lady Ispiria?" He frowned. "It seems farfetched, doesn't it?"

Ari relaxed back into his chair. "Yes, it does. I'm leaping at shadows, and that's not my role."

"Ladies don't usually have access to much money," Mattah said, his tone thoughtful.

"True, and you are correct, what was done obviously took a fair amount of coin."

Mattah nodded. "Even if the ship was stolen, the sailors and abductors must be paid."

Ari raised his eyebrows. For a young man of what Ari guessed to be about fourteen, Mattah seemed rather adult. "May I ask how you came to be Parrentine's page? Usually, the noble families would vie for the position for their sons."

Mattah winced, tearing the bread into smaller bits. "Yes, so I've often been reminded. I have stolen the place of a loyal citizen."

"I take it the reminders aren't friendly."

"I should not complain. It would be worse where I'm from. That's why my mother gave me to the prince, so I would have a better life." He dropped the bread, retrieving a piece of fruit.

"What would be worse?"

"The name calling. The dislike. The exclusion."

"Because you're the prince's page?" Ari would have expected the position to infer a certain level of deference. He recalled meeting the king's personal valet and how respected the man had seemed.

Mattah gave him a bemused look. "Because my skin is dark, my eyes are yellow like a cat's, and I speak with an accent, letting all know I am not from your land."

Ari considered that, trying to reorganize his thoughts. "When my first valet, my friend Peine, went north with me, the young ladies of Sorga were smitten with him. People in Sorga are mostly blond with light colored eyes, and of taller, heavier build. Peine is a Whey. He's nowhere near my height, dark haired and has brown eyes. I think the girls in Sorga thought he was exotic."

"I didn't say the girls in the capital don't like me." Mattah shot Ari a slightly devilish smile, though he was turning a bit red again, discernable even under his darker skin.

Ari decided not to pursue that topic. "Yet, it would be worse for you to have stayed in Jondor with your mother?" He wondered if Mattah had a father, for neither he nor Parrentine had mentioned one.

"Much worse."

"I've read about the Great Bazar in Jondor. They say people there are very diverse, with all different skin tones, hair and eye colors, languages and styles of dress. People from all of the kingdoms of the southern lands congregate there, as well as Lggothians and Wheys. Wouldn't so many peoples living in relative peace foster tolerance?"

"You may have read accounts carried back by adventurous Lggothian lords, but you do not understand the place. Yes, there are people from many lands, but they guard their ways jealously. I am a mixed race, my mother from one people and my father from another. To most in Jondor, that makes me an abomination. At best, it leaves me with no place, no people of my own. If I'd known I was to go there, I would have hidden from the sun as my mother used to teach me. When I am very pale, I can almost pass for one of her people."

Ari stared at him, dumbfounded. "That's absurd," he said as the door to the cabin opened.

He and Mattah both turned to find Mirimel and Cooro entering. Mattah jumped up. He cast a guilty look at his plate, dropping his napkin over it.

"Swordmaster, Hawk Guardian," Mattah said, bowing. "I beg your pardon me for dining before you. I shall remove myself immediately."

"Don't be daft," Mirimel said. "Sit down and eat. Ari, what sort of nonsense have you been putting in his head, and what is so absurd?"

"Judging Mattah based on the tone of his skin is what's absurd." Ari elected to ignore the accusation he was putting nonsense in anyone's head.

"Yes, it is, but people are fools. I've told you as much." With that, Mirimel headed for the sideboard.

"In this, the fair Mirimel is correct," Cooro said, following her.

"I've asked you not to call me fair."

"Beautiful, then."

101

"Don't make me have to stab you before breakfast."

Cooro chuckled, but may have taken her seriously, for he said no more.

Ari turned back to Mattah to find a defiant look on his face. "I have offended you?"

"Only with your blindness, my lord."

"You're making him call you my lord?" Mirimel asked. She set her plate on the table, glaring at Cooro when he reached to pull out her chair before yanking it back herself. "That isn't like you, Ari. Sit down, Mattah. Finish your food."

Ari decided to ignore that comment from Mirimel as well, concentrating on Mattah instead. "My blindness?"

Mattah retook his seat across from Ari. "You say it is absurd, and I agree, but you act as if it is something found only in my homeland." Mattah nodded toward Cooro as he took a place beside Mirimel. "In Lggothland, there is distrust of Wheys. You cannot deny this."

"That's because people think their women are witches." While Ari didn't agree with mistrusting Wheys because of that, it also happened to be true that most Wheylian women had some measure of mysticism, though usually so little as not to matter. "It's not because of their skin."

"Believe me, if your Wheylian neighbors had skin different from that of Lggothians, it would be."

Ari shook his head, unsure how to argue against that and aware they'd drifted far from anything that would help him find Ispiria.

"He's likely right," Cooro said. "Even among my people, the wealthy endeavor to keep out from under the sun's rays, lest they brown themselves like common workers."

Mattah nodded, his mouth full of the last of his food. Looking down, Ari realized he'd finished his porridge as well. Mattah stood again, gathering up his plate and Ari's bowl.

"Philosophy at breakfast is all well, I suppose, but before your cousins arrive I'd rather discuss--"

What Mirimel wished to discuss went unsaid, for the door opened again. Parrentine entered, awarding them all his hollow smile. Mattah deposited the used dishes on the sideboard, hurrying forward to help the prince with his chair. It worried Ari that the prince didn't wave his page away, seeming hardly to notice the assistance. Were Parrentine well, he wouldn't have permitted the coddling.

Before they were done exchanging greetings with the prince, Ari's cousins arrived. The talk about the table grew just as stilted as the evening before. Mattah retreated into his role of proper servant, making him essentially unnoticeable to Ari's cousins. Mirimel ate stoically. Cooro dined with the enthusiasm he generally employed in all things. Ari remained at the table, attempting to encourage normalcy, though he didn't think he was very apt at it. Mattah brought Parrentine an artfully arranged selection, but the prince ate nothing at all.

Finally, talk at the table ceased altogether. Mirimel stood up. "I think it's time for today's entertainment, don't you all?"

"Aye," Cooro said, rising. "The crew is looking forward to it. They long to see the great Sir Aridian in his element."

Ari pushed back his chair, standing. "I don't suppose you thought to find me a weapon to use in our bout, Swordmaster?" While Ari was strong enough to duel with his greatsword, something most were not, to do so would give him an unfair advantage over Cooro's estoc and ruin the fun of the match.

"I'll loan you mine," Parrentine said. He tossed his napkin over his untouched food.

"Thank you, your highness." Ari sketched a brief bow.

"You'll fight for show with sharpened blades?" Lord Danton asked.

"Cooro and Lord Aridian live life on the cusp," Cooro declared.

"We'll be in little danger." Ari endeavored to sound slightly bored, so his cousin would begin to understand the futility of challenging him. "Swordmaster Cooro and I are in complete control of our weapons."

Mirimel rolled her eyes, muttering something unflattering about male hubris that Ari hoped only his enhanced hearing could make out.

Parrentine came to his feet. "If we are all done here, I see no reason not to begin." That was met with a chorus of agreement. "Leave the clearing up for later, Mattah. There's no reason you should miss any of the matches."

"Yes, your highness," Mattah said, looking pleased.

Ari was pleased as well, both for Mattah and because the prince's consideration meant he hadn't fallen into too desperate a state yet. Ari smiled slightly, his mood lightening, cheered by the prince's presence of mind and anticipation of the matches. Parrentine led the way from the cabin, onto a deck now awash in sunlight.

Chapter 9

Ari hadn't had the opportunity to ask Mirimel or Cooro precisely what they had planned, so he was reassured when Parrentine and Mattah took a place on the quarterdeck beside the captain. Ari and the prince sometimes sparred, but Parrentine looked in no shape to do so. Nor would it be advisable to emphasize the prince's state.

Looking around as he followed Cooro, Ari saw sailors gathered about the deck and hanging from the rigging. Though more people than he'd realized were onboard had converged on the deck, he assumed, and hoped, someone was still minding their course. Ari supposed, even as quickly as the Albatross sped south, she wouldn't veer easily. So long as Lggothland was starboard, they were headed in the correct direction.

Cooro and Mirimel came to stand before the quarterdeck, so Ari joined them. Moments later, his cousin appeared beside him. Lord Danton wore a light blade, his hand clutching the hilt hard enough to turn his knuckles white. His blond hair was tied back, presumably to keep it out of his face. There was a shifting in the crowd, and the men parted to permit Cyanna to pass through. She climbed the steps to stand near Parrentine and the captain. The ribbons on her hat fluttered about her face, but didn't obscure the worried look there.

Parrentine stepped up to the railing at the edge of the raised quarterdeck. The sailors fell silent, though the ship did not. Somewhere behind Ari, sailcloth snapped. Everywhere, ropes and pulleys creaked and the wind whipped against the rigging. The ocean swells kept up a steady, though muted, rhythm against the hull. The prince cleared his throat.

"We are about to have the good fortune of watching a display of the finest swordsmanship and marksmanship Lggothland, and Wheylia, have to offer."

Many of the men cheered. Beside Parrentine, Mattah's expression betrayed his excitement.

Parrentine held up a hand to still them. "First, we shall have a bout between Sir Aridian and Swordmaster Cooro. This will be followed by Sir Aridian's demonstration of the greatsword and then an archery competition between our champion and Hawk Guardian Mirimel."

There were pleased murmurs in the crowd.

"We will then invite anyone who wishes to challenge Hawk Guardian Mirimel in an archery competition to do so. Similarly, any who wish to Challenge Swordmaster Cooro or Sir Aridian with blades may do so. Let it be known, Lord Danton has already issued a challenge to all three combatants."

Next to Ari, his cousin shifted, the rustle of his garments a nervous murmur against the sounds of the sea. Ari didn't look at him, steeling himself. Though the first relation by blood Ari had ever met, Lord Danton almost certainly knew something more than he was telling. Ari had to cow his cousin into confessing, for he knew he didn't have the heart to do more. Of course, if he became angry enough, he could possibly see his way to accidentally leaving Mirimel alone with the young lord. She would carve the truth from him.

Ari winced, unsettled by the thought. He couldn't do that, he realized. Permitting the hardhearted hawk guardian to extract the truth would still be wrong. The guilt and shame would still be Ari's, for allowing it to happen. How could he be the man Ispiria loved if he was party to something like that?

"Are you ready, Sir Aridian?" Cooro's voice broke into Ari's dark thoughts.

A quick glance told Ari everyone else had cleared away. "My sword?"

Mattah moved to the steps leading up to the quarterdeck, carrying the prince's sword. A cabin boy ran forward to collect it, bringing it to Ari. The boy proffered the prince's sword, the crest of the royal house embossed on the hilt. Ari glanced up at Parrentine, who nodded.

"A moment," Ari said, not reaching for the offered weapon. He unbuckled his sword belt. Knowing the boy wouldn't be able to carry his greatsword, he handed it to Cooro with a murmur of thanks. Ari turned back to the boy, aware of Cooro crossing to leave Fwellian with Mirimel.

Making his movements slow and careful to show his respect, Ari accepted the prince's sword. He unsheathed it, handing the leather casing back to the boy, who dipped an awkward bow and scuttled backward out of the marked square.

"Take your places, sirs," Parrentine said.

Ari and Cooro moved to the center of the square. They bowed to the prince, and then to each other. Rising from his bow, Ari caught Cooro's grin.

Ari grinned back. As usual when he sparred, his cares seeped from his mind. His world grew focused. Sword work was a singular joy to Ari, and there were few opponents he'd met who reached Cooro's skill.

"Begin."

As if released from a trebuchet, Cooro leapt forward at the prince's command. Ari was ready for him, spinning aside rather than blocking. He knew if he blocked, Cooro's feet would collide with his midsection. The Whey was an excellent acrobat.

Ari didn't halt his spin, coming all the way around. As he expected, Cooro's blade was whipping toward the back of his head. Again, Ari didn't block. Instead, he ducked low. Cooro's estoc whistled over him. Ari attempted to sweep the Whey's feet from under him with the flat of his blade, but Cooro was in the air.

The estoc came down in a slashing motion, aimed for Ari's neck. Ari brought his sword up to meet it, surging to his full height. Cooro flew backward as their blades met, propelled by the force of Ari's parry.

Most opponents would have landed hard, sprawled on their back on the deck. Somehow, while one hand still held his sword, the dexterous weapons master got the other to the deck. In what seemed to Ari a superhuman effort even he wouldn't be able to mimic, Cooro pivoted, pushed off the planks of the Albatross and landed back on his feet.

All about them, the sailors cheered and yelled. Cooro grinned, dropping into a defensive crouch. Again, Ari matched the Whey's expression. This time, he leapt forward, the prince's sword aimed at Cooro's gut.

Cooro was apparently done with acrobatics for now. He met Ari's charge head on. What ensued was a display of swordsmanship nearly too fast for the eye to follow. Ari and

Cooro struck, dodged and parried, dancing about the marked off square.

Ari made sure to rein in his Aluien-given strength. To unleash it would likely shatter at least one of their blades, and could harm Cooro. He didn't have to restrain his speed, however, for Cooro was as quick as he. Though twice Ari's age and a head shorter, the Whey had the skill and diligent training to face Ari as an equal.

As their bout wore on, Ari began to wonder how long Parrentine would let them spar. On the heels of that thought, Cooro executed an unexpected move involving launching himself from the deck and using the rigging to spin himself over Ari's head. Ari was quick, though, and accustomed to Cooro's tricks. He got himself turned about just in time to parry.

"Hold." Prince Parrentine's voice rose above the cheering as the sound of Ari's and Cooro's blades meeting echoed across the water.

Ari lowered his sword, turning to face his prince. He glanced at the sun, realizing it was significantly higher in the sky. He also realized he was dripping sweat. At no signal that he could see, the cabin boy rushed forward, offering Ari and Cooro both damp cloths.

"Thank you, Sir Aridian, Swordmaster Cooro, for that amazing display," Parrentine said. "I imagine few have seen its like. We are all honored to have stood witness." Here, Parrentine paused for the cheer that rose from the onlookers. "Sir Aridian, do you find yourself ready for your display with the greatsword?"

A glance at Ari's cousin showed Lord Danton's face was whiter than the cloth the cabin boy had brought. "I am, your highness. I thank you for the loan of your sword." He bowed to the prince.

"It was our pleasure," Parrentine said. "Never has it been put to finer use."

At a wave from Ari, the cabin boy hurriedly brought the sheath. Ari wasn't sure if the awe on the boy's face was for him or for being permitted to carry the prince's sword. Ari sheathed it and returned it to the boy, who brought it to Mattah. As Ari crossed to retrieve Fwellian from where Mirimel stood, he wondered if he should offer to sharpen out the numerous nicks he'd put in the prince's blade.

"Good show," Mirimel said.

"Thank you."

"Of course, when I go up against you, I won't go easy on you to protect your reputation."

Ari shook his head, amused by her barb. "That's alright. I can win without your help." Knowing it would aggravate her, he proffered the cloth he still held.

She raised an eyebrow, but took it. "You should likely keep it. Not that it will help with the smell."

Mirimel wrinkled her nose and Ari felt a wave of anger wash through him. When Mirimel acted as if she didn't hate the world and everything in it, she looked too much like Ispiria. His Ispiria, who was funny and loving and didn't deserve to be carried off to who knew where or to what end.

Mirimel cocked her head to the side, her hand dropping to her knife hilt. "It was a joke."

"I know. I was thinking of Ispiria." He took up his greatsword, handing the sheath and belt to Mirimel. "Sorry," he added, for her face retook its usual glower.

She shrugged. "Don't be sorry. Be impressive." Her eyes slid past him, narrowing to flashing blue slits, and he knew she was looking at his cousin.

Ari nodded, taking himself back to the marked off square. After another round of bows and brief speeches, Parrentine gave the signal to begin. Ari stood for a moment in the center of the square, Fwellian held loosely in one hand. Casting Lord Danton a hard look, he commenced his display.

Ari had no target or opponent. He'd decided merely to go through offensive and defensive combinations. He began with the simplest, letting the clarity of swordsmanship subdue his anger and still his spirit.

His every movement was precise. His sword cut through the warm salt air at a speed only attained by the best swordsmen. Each combination was flawless.

He knew that wasn't what drew gasps from the crowd. Excellent swordsmen were few, but not unknown. What made Ari stand apart, and what he hoped would drive home to his cousin the futility of attempting to evade him, was that Ari wielded his greatsword in one hand. The combinations he displayed weren't meant for such a heavy weapon. They were reserved for swords like Parrentine's. Yet, with his strength, Ari could wield Fwellian as if the massive blade had been forged for dueling.

When he finished, Ari bowed to the prince, but his eyes once again sought his cousin's. Lord Danton's face was tinged with green now, his blue eyes wide with fear. Ari felt sure he could ask his cousin anything at this point and be assured of an eager, truthful confession. Still, he'd promised Mirimel a bout of archery and he knew she liked to show off.

They took a break then, men scurrying about to check on Mirimel's targets while Ari reclaimed his sword belt and sheathed Fwellian. An open lane was cleared from the quarterdeck to the great cabin. It took Ari a moment, but he identified the round targets, rings drawn on them in charcoal, as the lids off barrels. When all was ready, he and Mirimel stood through another brief speech by the prince before turning to the first target.

"You have the honor, Sir Aridian," Mirimel said, offering her bow and quiver. "And don't you dare lose any of my arrows in the ocean, Ari," she added in an undertone.

Ari accepted the bow and quiver. He glanced about at the targets, set various distances away about the gently swaying deck. Given they were aboard a ship, none of the targets were far, but all rocked in time with the waves below. The farthest was affixed to the great cabin, perhaps fifty feet away. The most difficult to hit, however, was the one she'd ordered placed on the outside of the crow's nest on the tallest mast. It was a shot Ari doubted he could make, but knew from experience Mirimel could.

Setting the quiver at his feet, Ari selected an arrow. He was acutely aware of the sway of the ship. The breeze of their passage would speed the arrows along, but a strong wind blew from the northeast as well. Sighting up the first target he released an arrow, praying he didn't embarrass himself.

The sailors cheered as the arrow sank into the ring encircling the center. With a glance at Mirimel, whose face bore a slight smile, he took the second shot. This time, adjusting for how the first arrow had flown, he managed the outer edge of the center ring.

Ari made a good showing of the others, doing well enough to impress the audience until it came to the final shot. The steep vertical angle, coupled with the wind swirling about the crow's nest, was too much for Ari's skill. His arrow went wide of the target, sailing past the crow's nest altogether to plummet into the deck above the great cabin. Ari exhaled in relief, glad he hadn't lost an arrow.

He turned to Mirimel with a bow.

"An excellent showing, my lord," she said.

The ship of onlookers must have agreed for, in spite of his solitary miss, they cheered him.

"Thank you." Ari proffered the bow.

"A moment." Reaching down, she took up her quiver, fastening it to her belt as she would if tracking or hunting. "Please reclaim the arrows," she called, raising her voice.

At that signal, sailors scrambled about, collecting arrows. They brought them to Mirimel, each face revealing anticipation. Glancing about, Ari could see even his cousins seemed eager to learn if Mirimel could best him. Only Cooro's expression was different, holding the same mild amusement Mirimel's did. The three of them knew the truth. The day would never come when Ari could outshoot her.

Mirimel carefully arranged her arrows before taking her bow from Ari. She bowed to the prince, who indicated she should proceed. Ari stepped back as she turned to face the first target.

With awe inspiring swiftness, Mirimel let loose one arrow for each target. She hardly seemed to sight up in between shots, her hands moving nearly as quickly as Ari's did when holding a sword. He barely had time to see where she hit the other targets before she was leaning back, brow furrowed in concentration. There was a loud twang as she released the bowstring. Ari gasped along with everyone else when her arrow sank into the center of the target affixed to the crow's nest.

For a moment, the only sounds on deck were of ship and sea. Then, everyone began to cheer. Even Parrentine, who had read reports of Mirimel's skill, wore a suitably impressed expression.

The prince raised his hand as the cheering dwindled. No one ran to collect Mirimel's arrows, all positioned within inches of the center of each target. All eyes moved from Parrentine to Lord Danton and back again.

"Thank you for that truly amazing display, Hawk Guardian Mirimel," Parrentine said. "Never did I think to see the day our champion would be so thoroughly bested in a martial matter."

Ari thought that was going a bit far. Over the years, he'd worked especially hard with a bow, which didn't come as naturally to him as other weapons did. He wasn't as good with it as he wished to be, and was sure everyone in the capital could recollect his poor skill with the weapon. It had nearly cost Ari his place in the first joust he'd attended. Still, he'd shot well. He caught the satisfied look on Mirimel's face and schooled all peevishness from his own.

"The time for challengers has now come," Parrentine continued. "Are there any aside from Lord Danton ready to meet our three combatants?" Silence answered that question. "It is settled, then. Lord Danton, come forward."

Ari felt a pang for Cyanna, who looked stricken as her brother walked slowly across the deck to stand before Parrentine. As Lord Danton was between him and the prince, Ari couldn't see his cousin's face. He was sure he detected a faint tremble in the hand squeezed around Danton's sword hilt, though.

Lord Danton bowed very low to Parrentine. He dropped his hand from the hilt of his sword. "Your highness, I revoke my challenges."

Ari felt another pang of conscience, for this was met with murmurs and a smattering of mockery. No one spoke loudly enough to be identified, though. A wise choice, as Danton was still of noble birth.

Parrentine raised his gaze to where Ari and Mirimel stood. Cooro appeared to Ari's left.

"Do you, Hawk Guardian Mirimel, accept Lord Danton's withdrawal?"

Ari kept his gaze forward, wishing they'd discussed this eventuality. They had his cousin cowed. It would do no good to push him back toward defiance by humiliating him. Mirimel didn't like to back down from a competition, though.

"I do, your highness," Mirimel said, to Ari's relief.

"Swordmaster Cooro, do you accept Lord Danton's withdrawal?"

"I do, your highness."

Parrentine brought his gaze to Ari. "And you, Sir Aridian, champion of our fair realm, do you assent to your cousin revoking his challenge?"

Everyone looked at Ari, as if considering for the first time that he might force Lord Danton to fight him. His younger cousin, Cyanna, clutched the rail, appearing to be on the precipice of tears. Between Ari and the prince, Lord Danton stood at rigid attention.

"I do, your highness, on the condition that he and I meet in the great cabin within the hour, to come to an understanding over his reasons for issuing a challenge."

Lord Danton's flinch was visible even from behind.

"Then you are released from fighting this day, Lord Danton," Parrentine said. "Our champion has offered you a generous reprieve. Be thankful."

Ari worked to keep a hard smile from his face. Generous, maybe, but not a true reprieve. Before the day was out, he would have the truth from his cousin.

115

Chapter 10

When Ari entered the aft cabin nearly an hour later, he was surprised to find Lord Danton wasn't the only one waiting. Mattah stood to one side of the door, doing his best to look invisible, while Parrentine sat on a bench at the back of the cabin, his gaze trained out the window. The large central table was occupied by Lord Danton, Lady Cyanna, Cooro and Mirimel. Ari shut his mouth firmly over his annoyance. After all, he hadn't asked them to stay away.

Lord Danton pushed to his feet, bowing. He wore a sickly version of a smile. "Cousin Aridian."

"Lord Danton," Ari replied, nodding.

"You said you wish to discuss my reason for challenging you, my lord." Danton glanced at his sister nervously. "As you know, it was my attempt to join your party. I erroneously felt I had something to offer."

Ari crossed to stand before his cousin. Danton wasn't a short man, but he didn't reach Ari's height. Likely, in time, he would grow into a man of heavier stature, but he was still half boy. His slender build, coupled with a perceptible tremble, gave the impression that Ari could reach out and topple him backward with one finger. "Yes, I recall."

"Well, then, you know why I challenged you. I wished to amend my family honor." He swayed away from Ari. "Now, I can see you shall do that well enough without me."

"Well enough?" Mirimel's low words reached Ari. "I should say much better."

Over Lord Danton's shoulder, Ari could see the grin on Cooro's face, and Lady Cyanna's flush.

"Thank you, Lord Danton." Ari regarded his cousin with what he hoped was a calm expression. "I understand all of that. What I would like to hear about is the source of your guilt in this matter."

Danton cast another look over his shoulder at his sister. "You placed Lady Ispiria in our care and we failed."

"No one has blamed you."

"I blame myself."

"Why?" In spite of Ari's best efforts, the question rang through the cabin like an accusation.

"I . . . that is," Lord Danton stammered.

Ari readied himself for the look of confusion sure to come over his cousin's face. Lord Danton wouldn't be able to formulate a response, Ari was sure, for the Lady had taken Ispiria and Siara and would have enspelled him to still him and then buried his memories on the incident deep in his mind. It was that sort of magic which led to inconsistent tales such as his cousin had told. Ari had seen the effects more times than he could wish. "Yes?" he prompted.

"I feel the guilt is mine for searching with my sister. I should have remained with Lady Ispiria and the princess, not sent incompetent and corruptible guards with them. I didn't do my duty to you or the realm."

Ari stared at his cousin, too surprised to answer. He cast a look to the back of the room to find Parrentine frowning at him. Nearer, Lady Cyanna had her face turned toward the table, but Ari could see her pallor.

"Incompetent and corruptible?" Ari was aware of a tendril of anger wending its way out of a place deep inside him. "You are maintaining that you did not accompany Ispiria and Princess Siara?"

"I did not." Lord Danton had firmed his stance, a note of belligerence entering his tone. "Are you calling me a liar, my lord?"

Behind Ari's cousin, Mirimel snorted. "If he is, are you going to challenge him?"

Lord Danton didn't turn. The only indication he'd heard Mirimel was the ripple of muscles in his jaw as he clenched his teeth together.

"What do you say to your brother's claim, Lady Cyanna?" Mirimel's voice was even, for which Ari had to give her credit, but her blue eyes may as well have been sculpted ice.

Lady Cyanna raised her head. Trembling, she looked across the table at Mirimel, then past her brother to Ari. Raising a clenched hand to her mouth, Lady Cyanna started to sob.

Ari caught the flicker of relief in Lord Danton's eyes. His cousin's posture relaxed slightly. He looked over his shoulder at his sister. "You've upset Cyanna."

"Not nearly enough." Mirimel stood, leaning across the table. "I don't need you to be able to talk, my lady. Just nod or shake your head. Did your brother stay with you?"

Cyanna squeezed her eyes shut, crying harder. Mirimel glared at her. Hiccups began to wrack Cyanna's frame. Ari pushed a hand through his hair, anger leaving him. They were torturing his young cousin. It wouldn't do. He would have to excuse her.

Mirimel's hand shot out, slapping Cyanna with a force that brought her eyes flying open. She stopped mid hiccup, her hand dropping from a mouth round with surprise. Ari could see the red mark Mirimel's hand left on Cyanna's cheek.

"Feeling better?" Mirimel asked.

Cyanna nodded.

"Was your brother with you?"

Lord Danton turned. He made to step toward his sister. Ari clamped a hand down on his cousin's shoulder.

Her stunned eyes fixed on Mirimel, Cyanna shook her head.

Nodding, a satisfied look on her face, Mirimel sat. Everyone's eyes moved to Lord Danton. Ari couldn't see his face, only the back of his head, but his cousin started trembling again.

"But I'm sure he had nothing to do with this," Cyanna blurted. She swiveled in her chair to look at Ari. Her nose was running. One cheek was bright red, the other white. "He's ever so lazy. He probably let them go into the woods alone and doesn't wish to admit it." Her eyes darted to her brother, their look pleading.

Ari turned Lord Danton to face him. "Is that the source of your guilt? You let them go alone?"

His cousin flinched, his glance skittering to where Ari still held him by the shoulder. "Yes."

Mirimel surged to her feet, the heavy wooden chair toppling with a crash. "I'll use your lying carcass for target practice."

Peripherally aware of Cooro grabbing Mirimel's arm, Ari squeezed his cousin's shoulder tighter, to regain his attention. "The guards said you told them you were going with the princess and Ispiria. Why would they say that if you intended to remain behind?"

"I don't know," Lord Danton mumbled.

Ari sighed, loosening his grip. Though he could see guilt in Lord Danton's every trembling limb, Ari wouldn't hurt his cousin. He had another ploy, though. He looked passed Lord Danton, to the back of the cabin. "Your majesty, I will not blame you if you wish to leave the room. I am going to tie Lord Danton up and let Hawk Guardian Mirimel use him for target practice."

"Finally," Mirimel said.

Ari was a bit taken aback by the mirthless smile on her face. Did she imagine he meant it?

"I'll ask the crew for rope," Cooro said, heading for the door.

"No." Cyanna's cry stopped the swordmaster. "Just tell them, Danton. Please, tell them. They'll see you did it for the good of Lggothland, and Lord Aridian will understand you didn't mean for Ispiria to be taken."

Lord Danton's face turned white. He swayed and likely would have fallen if Ari didn't have him by the shoulder.

Fear stabbed into the heart of Ari's anger. He still didn't know what had happened, but it didn't sound like his cousins were innocent pawns caught up in the Lady's machinations. What if he'd been wrong? What if the abduction had nothing to do with the Lady? If what they strove for was to convert Siara, could Ari be certain the abductors would even keep Ispiria alive? "Cooro, the rope."

"No, I'll tell you. Please, don't let her shoot him." Tears coursed down Cyanna's cheeks again.

"Cyanna, stop," Lord Danton bit out.

"Get extra, Whey." Mirimel's voice was stony. "Lady Cyanna will make a fine target as well."

"You can't," Lord Danton cried, pulling away from Ari to face Mirimel. "She's a lady."

"She won't be once I have your house stripped of its titles." The prince's voice was quiet, but carried easily to the front of the cabin. Parrentine stood, coming forward at a slow pace.

"But, what of Mother and Father, and our brothers and sister?" Cyanna wailed.

"If you are forthcoming, I shall be inclined to judge each member of your family separately, instead of visiting ruin upon your house." The prince's face was composed into hard lines of anger. "Mattah, fetch the rope. I want the traitors bound."

Behind him, Ari heard the door to the cabin open and close.

"We aren't traitors." Lord Danton lifted his hands, beseeching Parrentine. "We all know how horrible the hundred years of war were. We've all grown up with the stories from our fathers and grandfathers. The followers of the Overgod are trying to save Lggothland from succumbing once more to battle and the horrors of famine, pestilence and destruction that accompany them. Princess Siara must convert. The people won't stand for a heathen queen. They'll rise up and revolt, like in Hapland."

"The people?" Parrentine's voice was low, the edges rough. "I doubt you've ever journeyed more than half a day's ride from Poromont. The people of Lggothland follow the old religion, as do at least half of the noble families. This stain of

122

the Overgod hasn't spread throughout the kingdom. It's contained within the capital. When I return, I shall see it scoured from there as well."

Ari wasn't sure that would be a wise course, but now wasn't the time to debate the matter with his prince. The skin about Parrentine's mouth was white. His bloodshot blue eyes were ringed by flesh tinged gray with fatigue. Ari had seen his prince in the grasp of madness. He could tell Parrentine was fighting a war with it now. "Perhaps we should sit," Ari ventured.

Parrentine nodded stiffly. The door behind Ari opened. He watched his cousin turn toward it, a frantic look on his face. Ari turned too, taking in a glimpse of glorious blue sky, white sail and a web of rigging. Mattah closed the door behind him. He carried a large bundle of rope.

"Sit down, Lord Danton." Ari strove for a reasonable tone. The last thing he wanted was to chase his cousin about the ship. Danton might fall overboard or be injured. Then how would Ari find out what he knew?

With a jerky nod, Lord Danton sat beside his sister. Righting the chair, Ari took Mirimel's vacated seat across from her, Parrentine beside him. Mattah came forward, his expression worried. Mirimel and Cooro took the rope from him and Mattah returned to his place by the door. To Ari's relief, Cooro bound Cyanna. He could tell by the way Danton winced that Mirimel was in no mood to be gentle.

Cooro and Mirimel moved to the other end of the table when they were finished. Lord Danton, his arms bound to his sides by rope that wrapped about him and the chair, kept his face downturned. Cyanna still cried, but her tears were a slow seep.

"Tell us what happened." Parrentine's voice was calm again, and hollow.

The eyes Ari's cousin raised reflected his defeat. "I knocked Princess Siara's croquet ball into the woods. I'd noticed, on other picnics, that she would go after her own, instead of summoning a servant. I offered to help look, of course. It hadn't occurred to me Ispiria would help as well, though it should have." He cast Ari a pleading look.

Ari didn't try to hide the loathing he felt for his cousin in that moment. Did Danton think that excused him in some way? Did he expect Ari to forgive him for luring Siara into the forest simply because he hadn't meant for Ispiria to go along?

"I tried to separate them. I knew what was coming. Lady Ispiria wouldn't be drawn from the princess' side."

"What was coming?" Parrentine's tone was cold enough that Ari almost winced.

"We had a plan. A ship was waiting. It's just as the note says. She's being taken to the holy land, for conversion."

"Where was the ship bound?"

"Your guess is right." Danton cleared his throat. "The men who followed the ship were right as well. They went to Jondor."

"And from there?"

Ari added a glower to the prince's question.

"I don't know." Danton's look became pleading. "I've never been to the holy land. I was told I could go, once the princess converted. It was to be a part of my reward, to see the holy land and enter the most sacred shrine."

"You expect us to believe you have no idea where they are taking my wife?" Parrentine leaned forward, his palms on the table.

"I swear it, your highness."

"On your sister's life?"

"You wouldn't," Danton gasped.

Ari could see fear on the faces of both of his cousins. He wished he didn't share it. A part of him didn't believe Parrentine would kill Cyanna, but he truly wasn't sure. Once already, Parrentine had not only lost the woman he loved, but suffered greatly in doing so. Then, Ari had worried his prince would never recover, but somehow Siara's love had saved Parrentine. With returned madness lurking in the prince's eyes, Ari wasn't sure to what lengths Parrentine would go to rescue a second bride.

Cyanna started sobbing again, tears she couldn't wipe away flowing down her cheeks. The redness rimming her eyes couldn't hide the guilt, though, and Ari wondered how much she'd known of her brother's plans. Had she been a bystander, or was she an accomplice? Had she called away any guards who'd tried to follow Siara? Ari decided not to voice that suspicion, worried it was true.

The silence drew out, making Ari uncomfortable. He kept his expression hard, though, and didn't look at his prince. Parrentine would speak when he wished to do so.

"In truth, I very well may order the death of your sister." Parrentine's voice was quiet, and weary. "She will be tried for treason, as will you. Any lenience I or my father may muster will be decided by how successful Sir Aridian's mission is."

Ari tried to hide his dismay as he realized the truth in Parrentine's words. What his cousins had done was treason, and treason to the crown usually had only one punishment. Even if he intervened, exerting all of his influence, the best he could hope to win for his cousins was exile.

"I swear I've told you everything," Lord Danton said. "My part was a small one. I needed only to ensure Princess Siara went into the woods. It didn't even matter if there were guards with her, so long as they were few."

"You must know something more." Parrentine shook his head. "I'm finding it very difficult to think of any reason I might spare your life, or offer clemency to your house. As I cannot prove you acted alone, I shall be forced to strip your family of their lands and titles, and confer them on someone more worthy."

"We do know more," Lady Cyanna said in a rush.

"Cyanna," Danton hissed, shaking his head.

"Danton and I were brought into the circle by our great aunt," Lady Cyanna said. "I didn't even know we had a great aunt until she came to us one day at court. There were others, as well. I can give you a list."

"Cyanna." Lord Danton's voice was angry and, oddly, sharp with fear.

"We had meetings. We all pledged to do our part to keep Lggothland from war." Cyanna's face was pale and puffy, robbing her of her beauty and dulling her resemblance to Ari's mother.

"Who orchestrated the meetings? Who funded the abduction?" Parrentine asked, leaning forward, his face intent.

"Our aunt," Cyanna said. "She paid the men to take Princess Siara, and for the ship, and said it would be too fast for any to catch."

Danton turned to his sister, a look of terror on his face. "Stop it, Cyanna. She said if we spoke of her we would die."

Cyanna cast her brother a sorrowful look. "We're traitors. We're going to die anyway. Besides, you can't believe that. How would she kill us? We're on a ship in the middle of--" She broke off, surprise making her eyes go round. She made a sucking, gasping sound.

126

"Cyanna?" Danton cried.

Still looking surprised, Cyanna fell forward. Her face hit the table with a jarring bang. Cooro jumped up, but Ari knew it was too late. He stared at his cousin, fear that the Lady had cast whatever spell attacked Cyanna like lead clogging his veins.

Moving to Cyanna's side, Cooro reached out, touching her neck. He shook his head slightly, dropping his hand. His eyes met Ari's across the table. The regret in them confirmed what Ari already knew.

"Is she dead?" Danton whispered.

"Aye, she's gone." The swordmaster's tone wasn't gentle as he turned to Lord Danton.

Tears sliding down his cheeks, Danton stared at his sister's still form. Ari knew how he felt. It seemed incomprehensible that his young cousin, whom he'd met only the day before, sat dead and bound across from him. He hadn't even had a chance to save her. Anger twisted in his gut.

"I guess we have our answer." Ari hardly recognized the growl as his voice. "Princess Siara and Ispiria were taken by the Lady." And he would do whatever he must to find them, and her.

Chapter 11

As he had done every day of the voyage, Ari leaned against the rail alone. Today was different from the days before, though. Today, he could contemplate the ever-nearing coastline of Jondor. As the sun rose higher, the land before him grew until it filled the horizon and he could begin to distinguish details.

Straight ahead was a sprawling ant's nest of sand colored buildings, low and capped with flat roofs. Set among them were large swaths of green. Ari could count eight from where he stood on the gently swaying deck of the Albatross. Each splash of color appeared to be surrounded by thick walls. He couldn't tell yet if they were manned, but he suspected so. In the center of the city was a vast open area populated by hutches and tents, which he could only assume was the famed Great Bazar.

Outside the city rose rolling brown hills, semblances of roads snaking away across the scrubby desert. Ari's eyes went to the one heading toward Hapland, though he didn't think he would need to follow it. The religion of the Overgod was nearly as new there as in Lggothland. Wherever this holiest of places in the faith of the Overgod was, it likely wasn't to their east.

As they drew nearer, white winged gulls swooped about them, seeking the small fish that cavorted in their wake. High above, on the edge of the crow's nest, Mirimel's new hawk let out a warning cry. The gulls scattered in a cacophony of reproachful squawks.

Ari heard his prince's footsteps long before Parrentine came to lean against the rail beside him. A glance showed the prince looking as worn as ever, though he had better color from his time spent on deck in the southern sun. The ruddiness Ari had noted when they met in Sorga was replaced by tan. Ari wished Parrentine's worries were as easily scorched away as the pallor of his skin.

Though they'd spent the trip amiably enough, mostly in discussion of the southern lands and peoples, the mood onboard the Albatross had taken a gloomy turn after Cyanna's passing and that ill tenor still clung to the ship. Unable to hide her death, Parrentine had told the crew her heart stopped in shame the moment she heard her brother's confession. The prince's story gave Cyanna a noble, almost romantic legacy very at odds with the truth. Ari didn't refute it, however. It wasn't his place to gainsay his prince, and he thought the tale might help the rest of his mother's family, who didn't appear to be involved. It certainly bolstered the crew's lack of sympathy for Danton, who was spending the remainder of the voyage locked in his small cabin.

"The conclaves of the water barons," Parrentine said, pointing toward one of the circles of green.

"Water barons? Do you mean, the green is grass?" Ari asked.

"Grass, fruit trees and the like," Parrentine said. "That's why there is a city here. Water wells up in eight spots, from deep below the earth. The water barons use it to control the populace. If you must leave the city on your search, you will need to purchase water from one of them."

"Is one water baron better than another?"

"They should all be the same," Parrentine said. "If they could ever agree, they'd have the ability to squeeze the life from the region. Fortunately, they're never in accord and so must always work to undersell each other. No single one ever seems to come out ahead, so we have no alliances with them."

Ari hadn't considered that. He was often lax about keeping in mind that, as King's Champion and Duke of Sorga, he was more than just another Lggothian. He was obligated to consider the politics of his homeland, Hapland, Wheylia and, it seemed, of Jondor as well.

"When we dock, Mattah will take you to his mother," Parrentine said.

Ari nodded. Behind them, sailors moved with increasing rapidity, readying the Albatross to dock.

"You're sure you're taking enough coin?" Parrentine asked.

"You've given me enough to buy a small kingdom." Ari hardly had room to carry it all.

"Because you've my permission to do so if needed. Don't forget the extra, for Quinless."

"I'll have Mattah take it," Ari said. "He won't forget a gift from you to his mother."

Beside Ari, Parrentine shook his head. "Mattah can't carry any coin, unless you are with him at all times, which you should try to be. It's dangerous for him here."

"Dangerous? Did he not grow up here?" Ari rather felt he, Cooro and, especially, Mirimel would draw significantly more attention than Mattah.

Parrentine shot him a pitying look. "For all the evil you've faced, Ari, you still don't see the failings of man, do you?"

"You sound like Mirimel." Ari wished they had Larke with them, though perhaps not even the bard could lighten the mood of their mission.

"Though she looks like Ispiria, Hawk Guardian Mirimel isn't very much like your fiancée, is she?"

"Not really," Ari said. "Is Mattah in danger because of the color of his skin, then?"

"It's more what it signifies." Parrentine's tone was thoughtful. "He's of mixed race. To the people here, that is irrefutable evidence that he has no house, no standing, no place in their world. Without a place among a people, he has no rights under the law. Anyone may rob him, or beat him, or what have you. It will be your presence that keeps him safe. They will assume he is your property and will treat him accordingly, like they would Stew."

The comparison was a confusing one for Ari. Mattah was more than a possession, and more than a horse. Then, Stew was more than a possession or a horse. Ari frowned across the dwindling gap of water between the Albatross and Jondor. "Maybe Mirimel is correct. Maybe people are fools."

Parrentine chuckled. "She is not correct, but I can appreciate the sentiment." He shook his head again. "People are the product of their world. Remember when you and I first met?"

Ari nodded. It wasn't something he was likely to forget, his prince half dead and more than half mad, alone and starving in the Wheylian mountains.

132

"I had lived in a very small world. You and Cadwel helped me enter a broader one, though I'm afraid I fought you ever step of the journey. Changing the world I lived in changed me. I'm lucky Cadwel is so stubborn, and that you are forgiving."

Ari thought about that for a long moment. He and Parrentine rarely spoke of those dark days. The prince had been rather difficult, even disappointing, for a time. It wasn't only Ari and Sir Cadwel, though, but Siara who had changed him. Parrentine sighed, and Ari knew the prince's thoughts paralleled his own. "I will bring them back," he promised.

"I know you will," Parrentine said, his voice quiet but filled with conviction. He looked about. "We should go stand with the captain. We'll be too much in the way soon."

Ari followed Parrentine as he left the rail. They climbed the short stair to the upper deck, from which the captain supervised the steersman and the rest of the crew. Ari wasn't surprised to find Mirimel there, answering her nod of greeting with one of his own. It took him several long moments to locate Cooro, who was high above in the crow's nest.

The crew scurried about while the captain barked orders. Ari couldn't tell if anyone was listening to him, or obeying, but supposed they must be. With a smoothness that belied the chaos on the deck, the Albatross sidled up to the dock. Buoys and ropes were thrown and the ship secured. While it wasn't as interesting to watch the sails be furled as Ari imagined it would be to see them unfurled, the mechanics of it still fascinated him. Last of all, a section of the rail was removed and the wide plank put in place, so man and beast could walk from the deck.

At that signal, relative calm settled over the Albatross. Ari, Parrentine and Mirimel climbed down from the upper deck to find Mattah bringing up the last of their gear. From within his paddock, Stew watched Ari with interest, while the black mare seemed nearly ready to jump the low fencing and race for freedom. Ari wasn't sure if it was the ship she wanted to escape, or her constant shadow, Cooro's piebald mount.

Ari picked up Stew's tack and his saddlebags from the pile Mattah had assembled and crossed to the paddocks. "It was a pleasant enough crossing, was it not?" he asked Stew, opening the gate of his enclosure.

Stew dipped his head.

"I've never been on a ship before. Have you?"

Stew regarded Ari without expression. He pawed at the deck once, indication he wasn't as patient with the wait as he seemed.

"I'll take that as a maybe." Ari settled Stew's tack in place before reaching for the saddle bags. "These are rather heavy. The prince has them full of coin."

Stew snorted, turning his head to cast Ari a haughty look over his shoulder.

"Yes," Ari said, smiling slightly. "I'm aware you're very strong."

"Are you done making a spectacle of yourself yet?" Mirimel asked, leading the black mare over.

"No one can hear me but Stew. Most people talk to their horses."

The black mare nodded, shaking her mane.

Mirimel frowned at her. "We'll wait for you on the dock."

"Don't go far," Ari said. "From what I hear, this isn't the safest place."

Mirimel raised her eyebrows, but apparently didn't elect to take too much offense because she turned away. While Ari was rechecking Stew's tack and his possessions, nervous to be carrying so much coin, Cooro passed by with his piebald mare.

Ari hadn't seen him climb down, though Cooro has likely made quick work of it.

Parrentine, the captain and Mattah stood at the top of the ramp, the former two waiting to see him off, Mirimel and Cooro already heading down the ramp. Ari stopped before his prince with a bow, adding another for the captain. Mattah wasn't watching Ari and Stew, but rather had eager eyes fixed on the city.

Parrentine squinted up at the sun. "By the time you speak with Mattah's mother, it will be late. Even with a full crew onboard, the docks here aren't safe at night. We'll have to pull up the plank until morning."

Ari nodded, wondering if he should return to ensure Parrentine's safety.

"Take rooms at the Equestrian," the prince continued. "Anyone can tell you the way."

"I remember the way," Mattah said.

"Good," Parrentine said. He turned back to Ari. "We'll leave with the morning tide. Bring Mattah back, and anything you learn, before then. Once I return to Poromont, the Albatross will come back for you. If you need her to meet you at another port, send word here."

Though he knew it wasn't protocol, Ari extended an arm to his prince. They briefly clasped hands. "I will not rest until I find them."

"I know." Parrentine's expression was grim.

Stepping back, Ari turned to the captain. "Thank you for a safe and swift journey."

"It was an honor to have you aboard, Sir Aridian."

Gesturing to Mattah to join him, Ari led Stew down the ramp. Behind him, he could hear the captain saying something to Parrentine about how well behaved their horses were. Ari didn't care. He was through exerting himself to keep meaningless secrets. Besides, no one would likely even believe him if he admitted Stew and the black mare were Questri and Cooro's piebald steed enspelled to behave well. Ari had long since learned that one of the greatest forms of magic was peoples' inherent resolve to see what they expected to see.

As he, Stew and Mattah reached the dock, Mirimel held up her arm. She angled her face toward the crow's nest. "Come, it's time."

Ari looked over his shoulder to see the female hawk who had joined them wing down. She didn't land on Mirimel's upheld wrist, flapping past it to alight on Cooro's shoulder. Mirimel's look of shock was comical, but Ari knew better than to laugh.

Apparently, Cooro did not know better. He turned to her with a smug grin. "We've grown close, spending our days together high above the deck."

Mirimel's eyes narrowed. Ari could practically see her plotting the swordmaster's demise.

Clearing his throat, Ari turned to Mattah. "Lead on."

"This way," Mattah said, setting a swift pace down the dock.

Parrentine's warnings in the forefront of his mind, Ari kept close to Mattah as they plunged into the quayside chaos. All about them people shouted, selling, transporting goods and cursing indiscriminately. Items of every type were being hauled bodily, with mules and horses, wagons, carts and wheelbarrows. There were towers of bales and barrels piled with precarious haphazardness.

People of every skin tone swarmed about, though few were fair like Ari and his companions and nearly all were dressed in unfamiliar styles. Of these, Ari saw little that made sense in view of the scorching sun above, but didn't feel his tunic and breeches to be any more comfortable than the other clothing he saw. He thought some of the more flowing garments might be best, but worried they would entangle him in a fight.

Mattah halted as a string of giant beasts, taller than horses, with long necks and humps, was led past by bare chested, dark skinned men. Holding Stew's reins loosely, Ari came up beside Mattah. He tried not to gape. A memory came to him of Kenmar speaking of one day seeing these fantastic creatures.

"Camels," Mattah said, glancing at Ari.

"Camels?" Ari repeated the word slowly.

"They can travel the deep desert for days without being given water."

Ari nodded. "Where are we going?" he asked. "Rather, I know we go to see your mother, but where is she?"

"She has a shop. I've never seen it, actually. She bought it after I left, with the money Prince Parrentine sent her to thank her for finding your sword. It's on the near side of the bazaar, one street removed from it."

Mattah rocked up on his toes as he spoke, peering down the line of camels. Behind them, Ari could hear Cooro smugly telling Mirimel he'd told her there were such creatures and that she needed to trust his word better. She growled something in reply.

"How long has it been since you've seen your mother?" Ari asked Mattah. Would it be worse, he wondered, to have a mother and not be able to do more than write her for years at a time, or not to have one at all, like him?

"I came to your land with the prince the winter before Princess Tiana was born."

A year and a half, then, Ari thought. Perhaps a bit longer. He judged Mattah to have fourteen years. It wasn't unusual for a young man to leave his home and enter the service of another. Still, it must be an easier feeling to know your family was somewhere you could ride to than to have them across an ocean.

"Do you know anything about the sword?" Ari asked as the last camel walked by.

Mattah shook his head, setting out again at a quick pace.

The only cities Ari had spent any time in were Poromont and The City of Whey, and always he'd resided in a castle. The experience of riding in procession through either northern capital bore very little similarity to wending their way through the crowds in Jondor. The air was hot and dusty, and Stew had to keep nipping at would be pickpockets.

By the time Mattah came to a halt outside one of the many squat stone buildings, Ari was moderately disoriented. With the region so flat, he couldn't even pick out the direction of the sea any longer, though he could judge it based on the angle of the sun. Even so, the way back lay through a warren of streets, none seeming to lead where it first appeared to.

As far as Ari could tell, there was nothing to set their destination apart from the structures surrounding it, save a sign in a language he couldn't read. Looking back over his shoulder once, his expression eager, Mattah led them toward the alley running between the building and its neighbor. He disappeared into the darkness of it, flittering from sight.

Ari followed more slowly. He knew Parrentine trusted the boy, and had no reason not to agree with that assessment, but they were in a strange place, far from any aid. Behind him, he heard Mirimel give a sharp command, and the swish of feathers through air as her hawk sped skyward. The sound reassured

138

Ari. Mirimel and the hawk could guide them with surety if, for any reason, they were forced to run.

Taking Stew with him, Ari stepped from the blazing sunlight into the deep shadow of the alley. It took his Aluien-enhanced eyes only a moment to adjust. The space between the two buildings was empty. Mattah's footprints were clear in the sandy street, though, leading to the back of the alley.

Dropping Stew's reins, Ari crept forward, one hand resting lightly on the hilt of his sword. He could see shifting sunlight at the other end of the alley and assumed there must be a courtyard. Reaching the end of the building, he took a settling breath and stepped around the corner.

Chapter 12

A large dark-skinned man, shirtless like the ones leading the camels, spun to face Ari. At the man's side, a bright-colored silk sash held an unsheathed sword. It was wide-bladed and curved, giving it a wicked look. Ari's hand tightened on Fwellian's hilt, the two stones warm against his palm.

"Lord Aridian," Mattah said, stepping around the man.

Behind him, Ari could hear Stew approaching. "Mattah."

"Meet my father, Kanja."

Ari dropped his hand from his sword hilt, bowing to hide his surprise. "It is an honor to meet you, sir." He straightened to see Kanja watching him through dark eyes. After a moment, he nodded.

"That is the normal greeting with his people," Mattah said, hurrying around his father, his face flushed.

Ari realized Mattah was worried his father had given offence and offered a smile. If Mattah knew him better, he would realize Ari wasn't so easy to offend. Stew walked up behind him, sticking his nose over Ari's shoulder to take in the courtyard.

The yard wasn't overly large, but it held a squat, broad canopied tree. The leaves were small and thin. They danced in the nearly imperceptible breeze, creating an ever-moving tapestry of light and shadow on the hard packed earth. It was noticeably cooler in the courtyard than on the roadway, a pleasant change. To Ari's right was a rail for tying mounts, an empty trough before it. To his left a gate rested open, obviously used to secure the courtyard. Past the rail a dark doorway loomed, leading into the shop.

Kanja eyed Stew for a long moment, a line marring his brow. He gestured toward the rail.

"My father will give Stew water if he will go to the trough," Mattah said.

"Can your father speak?" Ari asked. He grimaced, belatedly realizing that someone being unable to speak didn't make them unable to hear. He turned to face Kanja. "My apologizes."

Kanja shrugged. He gestured to Stew again. "Come," he said in a voice as rich as Larkesong's, but infinitely deeper.

Stew started forward. Ari wasn't sure if he was more surprised by Kanja or his horse.

"He prefers not to speak," Mattah said, coming to stand beside Ari.

"Is everything well in there?" Mirimel's voice hissed from around the corner. "My hawk can't see through the tree."

"Perfectly well," Ari called. "Come meet Mattah's father."

Mirimel came around the corner with her bow half drawn, the black mare following her. Stew looked over from where Kanja was pouring water into the trough and snorted. The mare crossed to join him. Mirimel lowered her bow.

"Mattah," a warm, feminine voice called.

Ari turned toward the shop doorway and went still. The woman who emerged was tall, with long, graceful bronze limbs and hair that looked like molasses and honey swirled together. Her eyes were a bright yellow, seeming nearly to glow, and tilted up at the corners under dark lashes. She held her arms open and Mattah ran to her.

"Close your mouth before drool starts leaking out," Mirimel hissed, jabbing Ari with an elbow.

Ari snapped his mouth shut.

"She is a goddess come to earth," Cooro breathed from somewhere to Ari's right.

Blinking, Ari realized Cooro's mare was crossing the courtyard to push her way up to the trough. Kanja was still adding water, but his dark eyes were on Ari and his friends, and bright with amusement. Ari could only assume the man was accustomed to the reaction his wife evoked.

Mattah and the woman, who Ari guessed was Quinless, were speaking rapidly in a tongue Ari wasn't familiar with. Mattah stepped from her embrace but kept her hand, pulling her toward them. Ari could make out his own name as well as Parrentine's, Mirimel's and Cooro's.

"Lord Aridian, this is my mother, Quinless," Mattah said.

Ari bowed.

"Mother, this is Parrentine's champion, Lord Aridian of Sorga, and his companions Hawk Guardian Mirimel and Swordmaster Cooro."

Mirimel bowed with easy grace, Cooro with elaborate flourish.

"I am honored to meet Prince Parrentine's champion, and you, Hawk Guardian and Swordmaster," Quinless said. She released Mattah's hand, putting her arm about his shoulders. "And for this chance to see my son."

"You could visit Poromont," Mattah said. "I've told you so. Prince Parrentine would send a ship."

Quinless shook her head as he spoke. "We have a shop which will not run itself. You must visit us, and tell me of the many great things you do in the northland with the prince."

Mattah made a face. "I don't do great things. I fetch and carry."

"For a prince," Quinless said, sternness touching her tone. "And, for all your words, here you are, having crossed the ocean again and part of a great quest."

Her words brought Ari's cares cascading back. "Yes, he is part of a quest. One we hope you can assist us with."

Quinless nodded. "Come inside. I shall close the shop early so we may speak without interruption. Kanja will lock the gate, so fear not for your mounts and possessions." She paused, looking toward Mattah's father.

Following her gaze, Ari could see Kanja chuckling to himself, though no sound emerged. Ari looked back to Quinless in confusion.

"Kanja seems to think the idea someone could steal your mounts is amusing." Quinless shrugged in an elaborate ripple of silk. "Sometimes he is an odd man."

Ari watched the still laughing Kanja, wondering what magic, if any, the man possessed.

Kanja winked.

"Come," Quinless said. Her arm still about Mattah, she turned, steering him toward the shop door.

Ari watched her go, somewhat mesmerized by the fluid grace of her movements.

"By all that's sacred, you two are dolts," Mirimel muttered, shoving Ari toward the door. "If you don't start thinking about red curls and milkmaid complexions, Lord Aridian, I'm going to put an arrow in you."

Ari winced, moving to follow Mattah and his mother.

"I didn't say stare at me instead, Whey," Mirimel said, behind Ari.

"I am but fixing an image of your bright curls, your skin the color of fresh cream, and your luminous blue eyes in my heart, oh fair one."

"It's Ari I'm concerned with. You can go back to ogling Mattah's mother," Mirimel said, her tone offhanded to the point of complete unconcern.

Entering the dark interior of the shop, Ari grinned. Mirimel's tactics were improving. If there was one thing Cooro hated, it was being ignored.

Making his way past shelves populated by what looked to be various medicinal herbs, Ari stepped into the slightly brighter room at the front of the shop. It, too, was shelf filled. Flasks and jars were stacked about. Herbs, dried and fresh, hung everywhere. Quinless stood at a long counter, which created a barrier to the rest of the room. Nodding to her, Ari walked around it to stand on the side a customer would use. Mattah was moving about the space, closing the door and shutters, and lighting lamps. Mirimel emerged from the back of the shop next, followed closely by Cooro, who didn't even glance at Quinless as they moved to stand with Ari.

Silence fell. Mattah returned to his mother's side. Everyone looked to Ari expectantly.

Remembering the smaller sack of coins Parrentine had given him for Quinless, Ari drew it from his tunic, sliding it across the counter. "The prince asked me to give you this."

Quinless hefted it, arching an eyebrow. "I had already decided to help you."

"Uh, I don't think he meant for it to buy your assistance," Ari said, hoping he hadn't insulted her.

She laughed. "I am sure not, and I spoke in jest. Your prince enjoys sending me gifts." Her smile grew. "And I have no compunction about taking them." The coins disappeared beneath the counter. "Do you wish for water?"

Ari shook his head. "No, thank you. Prince Parrentine said Mattah wrote to you, telling you what happened."

"He did." Her face turned grave. "Someone has stolen your princess, and one of her ladies."

Ari didn't need to look to see Mirimel's scowl. "Yes, Lady Ispiria. My fiancée and Hawk Guardian Mirimel's cousin."

Quinless turned her golden eyes on Mirimel, her expression compassionate. "She is your younger cousin. I can tell from the fierceness in your eyes. Like a sister to you." She leaned across the counter, embracing Mirimel, who must have been as surprised as Ari, for she didn't pull away. "You and your companions will retrieve her. You must have faith."

Quinless released her and, as Ari expected, Mirimel did look stunned. On her other side, Cooro did as well. Mirimel's mouth twisted into a scowled. "I do have faith."

"Good, for now I shall tell you something hard." Quinless sighed, turning back to Ari. "I discovered that the ship Mattah described came to these docks, but I can find no one who remembers any leaving it. It remained for one night, from sunset to sunrise, then sailed out into the bay and sank. No one swam from the wreckage."

"There was a crew onboard?" Ari asked, the horror of that idea warring with his inability to believe the Lady would do such a thing.

146

"They say no crew was seen. The boat simply floated in and came to rest against the dock. None dared board it. Most would not even look at it, lest it somehow visit vile sorcery upon them."

Her tone was filled with sorrow, but to Ari her words brought relief. The more they learned, the more he was sure powerful magic was involved. Likely no crew had ever been aboard, and where there was magic, the suspects were few. Knowing that didn't help him hunt for them, but it reassured him that Siara and Ispiria were safe. If the Lady had them, or even Mrakenson, they would be well enough until Ari reached them. They hadn't been taken for reasons which placed them in direct danger, but rather as lures.

"You do not seem alarmed." Quinless looked between them. "Not even my son. I do not know the whole of it, I see."

"It's a long tale," Ari said. In spite of how Parrentine trusted her, Ari still wasn't sure he should tell her all he knew.

"It involves sorcery, mother, as you and those who saw the ship suspected," Mattah said. "The prince and Lord Aridian believe a magus has taken Princess Siara."

Ari was taken aback by Mattah's bluntness, for in Lggothland most people scoffed at the idea of magic.

"A foolish creature, to anger both a prince and a great knight," Quinless said with no trace of skepticism.

"Indeed, madam, and my queen as well, for Princess Siara is her granddaughter," Cooro said.

Quinless turned to him. "You are a Whey, I think? I have heard your kingdom is ruled by a mighty witch. This perhaps makes you well suited to hunt your enemy here. In the southern lands, we have as many types of sorcery as we do peoples. I hope the magi you seek is not too mighty to cross."

147

"We have some hope of finding a way to best whoever it is," Ari said, seeking to turn the conversation to learning what she knew, rather than telling their tale. "Prince Parrentine suggested I might ask you about my sword. You helped him find it, I believe?"

"So it is a magi blade?" Her tone held satisfaction. "I thought as much."

"She knows something about your sword?" Mirimel asked Ari. "How is this?"

Ari grimaced, realizing he should have mentioned that part to Mirimel and Cooro sooner. He'd permitted himself to dwell in a calm haze of nearly silent meals and the lull of the open ocean after Cyanna died. Looking back, he realized his friends must have been permitting him space for his thoughts. That was kind of them, but in that space, he should have found time to tell his companions Parrentine's revelations about his sword.

"Mattah's mother led Prince Parrentine to the sword, and gave him a small white stone."

"A stone?" Mirimel repeated.

"The stone?" Cooro asked, his eyes flickering from Ari to Quinless and back.

Ari nodded, further regretting his lack of foresight. They'd revealed more to Quinless than he wished. He could only hope Parrentine was right to trust her.

"I think you must hear the whole tale," Quinless said. "Mattah will make tea."

"He needn't go to the trouble." Ari was too on edge for tea.

"In our culture, the offer of drink is one of friendship," Mattah said, looking between Ari and Quinless. "If you are not friends, you must pay my mother to tell you what she knows, but to do so now would be a grave insult, for she has offered both water and tea. If you don't accept one, and pay her instead, she is within her right to invent a false tale."

"What about the money Ari gave you when we came in?" Mirimel asked Quinless.

"That was a gift from your prince." Quinless smiled. "It is between him and me. In truth, the prince and I have never taken drink together."

"I would be honored to accept your invitation, madam," Cooro said, stepping back from the counter to bow.

"Ah, yes, let's have tea, or water," Ari said, chafing at the delay. "Thank you for the offer. Do you need any help, Mattah?"

Mattah shook his head vigorously. "I'll manage," he said, but he gave his mother a quizzical look.

"Your father will show you where to find drinking water and glasses." Quinless turned back to Ari, still appearing amused. "I think tea shall take more time than Lord Aridian has patience for."

Ari pushed a hand through his hair, aware he wasn't being diplomatic. Trying to smooth his features, he sought about in his mind for an apology.

"Do not fret, my lord," Quinless said. "It is clear to me you care deeply for both ladies, and for your prince, and this drives you to impatience." She looked him up and down. "In truth, you seem as one who takes many cares onto his shoulders. It is good they are so broad."

Ari felt his face heat under her gaze.

"Mattah doesn't know where to find water?" Mirimel asked, her tone sharp.

Ari didn't know if she was angry or suspicious, or who with. Probably both, and everyone.

"We came to this shop after Mattah left us," Quinless said. "He has never lived above it with Kanja and me. In truth, I thought I would work many more years before we could afford a shop of our own." The look she cast about the room was one of contentment.

"You would work?" Cooro asked, leaning his elbows on the counter. "Is this land like mine, then, where women hold many more jobs than men?"

Quinless shook her head, but her eyes danced. "No. I think not. I employed myself at one of the few occupations where women can make ready money."

There was a clattering of feet. They all turned toward the sound, coming from the back of the shop.

"I have water," Mattah said, appearing in the doorway behind the counter. He was out of breath, giving the impression he'd been hurrying.

"Oi, Mattah, you've spilled some," Quinless said in the first truly unhappy tones Ari had heard from her. "You lose your way, living in the northlands with their endless lakes and rivers."

"Sorry, Mother." Mattah hung his head, sliding the tray onto the counter.

The tray held a glass carafe, wrapped in intricate copper filigree. Likewise, the five glasses were encased in copper spirals and leaves, some reaching outward to form handles. Ari had never seen their like. He thought Ispiria would find them very pretty. As he studied the workmanship, it took him a long moment to notice the few drops of water that had bounced from the carafe onto the copper tray.

Quinless put an arm about Mattah, pulling him close. "No, it is I who am sorry. I should not expect that your new home would not change you."

150

She released him, her expression clearing, and deftly poured water into the glasses. Setting the carafe aside, she held out the tray, permitting each of them to select a glass. Ari could tell by the laughter in Quinless' eyes he wasn't the only one who noticed that Mirimel reached across the others to take the water nearest their hostess.

"To friendship," Quinless said, raising the final glass to them. Once they'd all sipped their water, which tasted of copper, she set her glass aside, placing her hands flat on the counter. "My part in the sword's tale is small, but I spoke to the old man, after your prince left, and learned his story. I am glad I did, for now he is dead, I am told."

"Dead?" Mirimel repeated. "How?"

Quinless shrugged. "He was very old. I assume in some usual way, though I did not ask. His daughter spoke of it, here in my shop."

"You did not know this old man and his daughter well, then?" Ari asked, feeling a bit less hopeful.

"I know her, not him at all. She is the laundress for Jondor's finest brothel."

Mattah choked on his water, sputtering. Ari agreed with the sentiment, unsure what relevance that detail held.

"Brothel?" Cooro asked, his eyes lighting up with interest.

"We're here for a reason, Whey," Mirimel snapped. She eyed Quinless.

"Yes, you have come for a reason, though not the one I thought from reading Mattah's last letter," Quinless said. "I am glad, for I know much more about the sword's story than I do of the ship. I had felt I was giving your prince meager service for his patronage, but this story I can tell. It all began when I found a small pouch containing a white stone, accompanied by a note, both hidden in my laundry. The note spoke of where I must stand, who to look for, and to find a means to be by his side come morning, to give him the stone."

Chapter 13

Ari turned the filigreed glass in his hand, watching Mattah's mother tell her tale. He couldn't help but notice how her skin gleamed like burnished gold in the flickering lamplight that filled the shop. Cooro was wrong, though. She wasn't a goddess among them, for she was too earthly. Her nature exuded too much warmth to be ethereal.

"The note also said I was to assure your prince I could guide him to the sword he sought, though I did not know how to find such a weapon," Quinless continued. "I did as I was bade, for the note promised I should be rewarded well. More than that, it bore the mark of the magi, a mark not lightly traced or lightly ignored." She took a sip of her water. "I stood where the note advised to stand, and captured your prince's attention."

Ari didn't know how to interpret Quinless' smile any more than he could Mirimel's frown. Cooro listened with obvious interest, Mattah with downturned eyes.

"To my surprise, this first attempt to stay by your prince's side until morning was unsuccessful," Quinless said. "I was forced to bribe men to find where he had gone, and set out in search of him."

Mattah pressed his lips in a tight line, making Ari wonder what Quinless was leaving out. He didn't really care, though, so long as the missing information didn't have to do with the sword or who had taken Ispiria and Siara.

"They located him easily enough, and Kanja and I managed to find our way into his retinue, so to speak. Your prince even provided us a room. Imagine our surprise, perhaps even fear, when hidden in the sheets of our bed we found a second note. It was for Kanja, telling him where we must take your prince in the morning and that he must be made to pay one Lggothian silver for the sword we would find there, and pay by his own hand."

"You led Parrentine somewhere because you found a note?" Ari asked, anger stirring in him. "What if it had been a trap of some sort? Anything could have been waiting for him."

"I see you think me irresponsible, Lord Aridian, but I assure you Kanja and I did not do this thing lightly," Quinless said. "Even for the little time I'd known him, I was fond of your prince."

"Then why do it?" Mirimel asked, looking between Quinless and Mattah, though Ari knew none of the decisions had been the young man's.

"The mark of the magi was upon it." Quinless watched them for a moment, as if gauging their reaction to her words. "To ignore it would have been to bring ruin on us and our kin."

Mirimel scowled, and this time Ari understood why and agreed with the sentiment.

"So you would have led Prince Parrentine anywhere to avoid bringing trouble down on yourself?" Mirimel asked. "I hardly find that honorable."

"I see the fire in your soul matches your locks," Quinless said, her easy smile the antithesis of Mirimel's demeanor. "I do not think I can make you understand, Hawk Guardian Mirimel. I may have liked your prince, but I hardly knew him. Would you ask me to risk my house, and Kanja's, for some foreign man?" She shook her head. "Besides, I did not think I betrayed your prince. There was about the notes a sense of peace. I was sure what we did was for his good as well, not only our own."

"How convenient for your conscience that these suspicious notes came with a feeling of peace," Mirimel said, her tone hard.

"Do all of the laundresses congregate in one place?" Ari asked, as much to know as to prevent an argument. While he agreed with Mirimel, it was long since done. Casting blame did no one any good.

At least he could see now why Quinless had mentioned the employment of the old man's daughter. She was a laundress, and a note had appeared with Quinless' wash and in the clean sheets at the inn.

Quinless gave an elegant shrug. "They do, but I do not believe them truly relevant."

"Undoubtedly not," Cooro said.

Ari wasn't as sure, but was happy to hear more of the tale before deciding. "Please, continue."

"In the morning, we led your prince into an old part of the city, where buildings are abandoned and lean close, making tunnels of the streets. It was there we found the old man." She frowned, her gaze growing abstract, and Ari knew she looked into the past. "He was blind, and seated alone on the floor of an abandoned home, holding a dirty, ancient looking blade."

Ari closed his hand over Fwellian's hilt. He could feel the warmth of the two gems there, and the empty socket where the third would sit. He was very much aware of the stone hidden in his tunic. He still wasn't certain he wished it set into the sword, but having it on his person, where it could be snatched away, made him worry.

"All proceeded to the notes' instructions," Quinless said. "Your prince took the sword, and the small stone, and paid with one silver. Then, he was back on his ship and taking Mattah away." She stopped speaking, turning toward Mattah with pain-touched eyes.

"Did the note tell you to do that as well, Mother?" Mattah asked, looking up from the counter's top.

"No." She shook her head. "Your father and I spoke of it in the night, after we met the prince. Your fate we decided on our own."

Mattah frowned, looking down again.

"We want only to give you a good life," Quinless said.

Mattah shrugged. "I know," he said, but he didn't meet her amber-eyed gaze.

Quinless sighed, turning back to Ari. "I was curious about what Kanja and I had done. I could never find who placed the second note, but knew who must have borne the first, and both were in the same learned hand. When I questioned my laundress, she directed me to her father as both the source of the note she left me and as the old man waiting with the sword."

"Your laundress was the same as the one serving the brothel?" Ari asked. "What about the inn? Did she launder there as well?"

Mirimel exchanged a look with Cooro that Ari couldn't interpret. Both remained silent, though the weapons master grinned.

"She did not," Quinless said with a smile at least as inscrutable as his companions' expressions. "As I said, I could not discover who had placed the second note, though I did try. No one should have known Kanja and I would be given that bed. We did not know ourselves."

"Yet the note was addressed to Kanja?" Mirimel asked, her gaze intent.

"It was. Not to me, as the first, though it was in the same hand, nor to your prince or any of his people, though it seems reasonable one of them may have discovered it. It was very odd. As I said, it struck no little fear in us, finding it there, marked by the magi."

"And you still led Prince Parrentine where it told you to," Mirimel muttered.

"Did your laundress' father know where the notes were from?" Ari asked, trying to keep the conversation on the details they needed to learn.

Quinless watched Mirimel for a long moment, her expression kind, before turning back to Ari. "He knew of the one left for me. The same woman who brought the sword to him gave him the note for his daughter, with instructions to leave it for me. Of the other note, he knew nothing."

"Perhaps she placed it herself?" Cooro suggested.

Ari felt that was the least important part of what Quinless said. "A woman gave him the sword? What woman?"

Cooro shot him a sharp glance, as if understanding the suspicion behind Ari's question.

"When I met the old man, he was pleased to tell me his story, so I shall pass it on to you," Quinless said. "Years ago, he was given the sword and told to watch over it. He was advised that all he must do was keep it until the day he was told who to trade it to, and for what amount. Then, he was to give the coin he received for the sword to the woman who first brought him the blade, and his offspring would become wealthy, his family would prosper. He waited until nearly the end of his life, but he did accomplish this thing."

"So he met her three times?" Ari asked, his heart thudding hard in his chest. "Once years ago, once when she brought the note, and once when he gave her the prince's coin. Did he say any more about this woman? What did she look like?"

Quinless shook her head, honey-colored streaks rippling in the candlelight. "He said little. He never saw her, even the first time, for he was always blind. He said she spoke with a foreign cast to her words, lilting like Kanja's people, but rounder." She looked at Cooro. "Maybe he meant like your Whey friend. That is what I thought, though we will never know the truth of it."

"No one else ever met this lady?" Ari pressed, exchanging worried looks with Cooro and Mirimel. "Not his daughter, or anyone?"

"Only he," Quinless said. "For years, his family thought him mad. They toiled, working diligently every day, always with hardly enough to eat, yet he kept a sword given to him by a mysterious woman, never selling it." She smiled. "Now, though, they have learned he was wise. He is gone, but my former laundress is a wealthy woman. She comes and buys expensive herbs from my shop and pays another to do her wash."

Ari put his elbows on the counter, resting his chin in his hands. "A mysterious lady."

"A woman." Quinless issued another elegant shrug. "He did not call her a lady. I think there is a difference in your tongue, as in ours."

"Did he say anything else about her voice?" Mirimel asked. "Did it sound young, or old?"

"I am sorry, Hawk Guardian, I did not think to ask," Quinless said. "I was not expecting to learn much from a blind man whose family thought him mad. At the time, I as well thought he was, and me with him, to follow the instructions found in mysterious letters, magi marked or no."

"It must be the Lady, Ari," Mirimel said. "She is playing some game with you."

"It makes no sense." Ari frowned down at his water glass. "If she had the sword and a stone, why not give them to me herself? Why break my trust and force me to seek them?"

"Who knows why?" Mirimel tapped a finger on the brightly lacquered wood. "As with Kenmar, these ancient beings have convoluted amusements."

"Cooro must side with Ari in this, fair one," Cooro said.

"Fair one?" Mirimel muttered, narrowing her eyes.

"From all we know, it seems impossible that the Lady would give up the sword and stone only to have them returned now," Cooro continued, ignoring Mirimel's look. "She must not know Ari has--"

Ari held up a hand, recalling his conversation with Parrentine. "It may be too late, but I'm unsure we should speak of such things."

Quinless raised her eyebrows, looking affronted.

"Not out of mistrust for any in this room," Ari said. "When speaking with the prince, he asked me how the Lady we speak of could have discovered I'd decided not to do her bidding. He suggested someone with me was a spy."

159

"Kenmar," Mirimel muttered, interrupting.

Cooro shook his head.

"I do not believe anyone who was there the moment I made my decision is a spy for the Lady." Ari gave Mirimel a quelling look. "I think she was using magic to watch me. I think I gave her the knowledge the moment I spoke the words aloud."

"But you told Prince Parrentine everything," Mattah blurted. "And spoke of the . . . of many things."

Ari straightened, running a hand through his unruly brown hair. "I know. It is likely already too late. If she is watching, then she has seen."

"This magic she uses to watch, this pool you and the bard spoke of, I assume it doesn't move?" Cooro asked.

"No, definitely not." Ari could picture the low stone wall, forming a circle and filled with dark water. It was in a cavern deep in the Aluien caves, under the Wheylian mountains. It was unmovable.

"If the Lady is innocent, she is at the pool and watching, and it does not matter, for if she is innocent, she is forgiving and kind." Cooro spoke slowly, as if working out the thought as he voiced it. "If she is the one who abducted the princess and your Ispiria, she is not at the pool any longer, for she is taking them to the holiest land of the Overgod, and so cannot see us."

"A lady took the princess and your love?" Quinless asked. "Now I see your worry, for I spoke of a woman ensuring you have the blade you wear." She looked thoughtful. "I wish I knew more to tell you about the sword, Lord Aridian. I am sorry."

"I am as well, though you have given me much to think about, and I thank you."

"We know the Lady and Kenmar are playing games with you," Mirimel said. "We also know a woman, most likely a Wheylian woman, made sure you got that sword and . . ." She looked about, as if she would be able to see magic spying on them. "Well, the sword, and other things anyone spying on us almost certainly already knows about. My point is, it's no leap to guess the Lady and the Wheylian woman manipulating you into having the sword are the same."

"No." Cooro shook his head. "It makes no sense."

"Does it make less sense than two Wheylian women, both likely with magic, both trying to get Ari that sword and the pieces missing from it?"

Ari mulled that over, watching Cooro and Mattah do the same. Quinless looked from face to face, seeming to take in every detail. Ari realized he was tapping his fingers on the counter and stopped.

"There are many women in this world, fair one," Cooro said. "Many of them are Wheylian, and many of those have magic. Cooro cannot take your assumption on faith."

"You won't have to." Mirimel's tone was confident. "It will bear itself out as truth before we are done unraveling this."

"Either way," Ari said, leaning his elbows on the counter once more. "We're at a dead end. The ship sank. No one saw anyone leave it, though I am sure they did." He turned to Quinless. "How long ago did the ship sink, after docking for one night?"

"That was half a moon ago and more, Lord Aridian."

Ari frowned. "Even for you, there will be no tracks to follow from the dock," he said to Mirimel.

"They say the water barons have vast libraries," Mattah said. "In them must be books on the holy places of the Overgod, and my father will know. His people worship the

161

Overgod, though not in the way the people in Lggothland or in Hapland have come to. In the old ways, with offerings and fire."

"You do not need to go to the water barons and pay for their knowledge," Quinless said. Four pairs of eyes turned to look at her. "I know nothing more of the ship, or sword, or of one lady or another, but I know the holiest land of the Overgod."

Hope made Ari stand up straighter. "You do?"

"As Mattah said, the Overgod was once known only to Kanja's people. He was born in the heart of their lands, far to the south, past the Eal la Oraan Desert. Mattah knows only little, for Kanja does not speak of his home. It is a city of smoke and salt, of the quaking earth and fire shooting into the sky. The god of which you speak first came to our world in K'Orge, the day the city was shaken free of its mountain home and sent down the slopes and into the waves below. In that place, ruined and rebuilt, you shall find the holiest temple of the Overgod."

Chapter 14

Ari stared at Quinless, hardly able to believe they'd been handed the answer. It seemed too fortuitous.

"K'Orge," Cooro murmured. "Why does that sound familiar?"

"Kenmar." Mirimel's tone was clipped, and Ari could tell her suspicions were further stoked. "He spoke of it the day we met the Questri. A city in the southlands that fell from the top of a mountain into the sea, when the ground quaked."

"More than quaked, Kanja's people would tell you," Quinless said. "They say fire exploded into the sky, shooting from the peak on which the city was built. The world shook, and the heavens with it."

She spoke with the passion of a practiced teller of the tale. Her slender arms gestured, seeming to draw images in the air. Ari wasn't sure if it was the topic she loved, or the art of telling it. Quinless, he realized, was accustomed to being observed.

"K'Orge fell from its mighty perch, from its seat of arrogance, and plunged toward the ocean below," Quinless continued. "It was halfway into the sea when it stopped sliding and then it only did so because Kanja's people, the Dinji, fell to the ground and begged a god, any god, to come forth and save them."

"And one did?" Cooro asked.

"One did." Quinless awarded Cooro a smile. "A man stumbled down the mountain into the broken, half-submerged city. He said the worst of the city had been taken by the sea, stilling the god's anger for a time. Indeed, the wealthiest part had fallen, for the rich lived on the seaward side, gazing out over the beauties of the world. The poor dwelled pressed against the mountain peak. Still, many of the poor lived on the back side of the mountain, and it was later found they had been taken as well, buried alive by stone."

Looking at them each in turn, Quinless shrugged off the inconsistencies of gods and men. "The Dinji took the man's words as truth, though, and cast from them all but their trousers, belts and swords, for all else is a trapping of wealth. They rebuilt their city where it lay, and their women and children stay there to guard it and honor the god. The men travel, craft and trade, but never keep what they bargain for or create. Coin is shared for the good of the city, or used to purchase gifts for the god. Those, they take to the mountain peak to throw in, for a great hole gapes there. Anything given to the god burns to ash within, taken in smoke and flame."

Quinless fell silent, a slight smile curving her lips. Around the shop, lamps sputtered, their flames casting dancing shadows. The room smelled of herbs, both harsh and sweet. Ari blinked, wondering what hour it was. They would need to find the inn Parrentine spoke of, and form a plan, and send

Mattah back with word of what that plan was, though not alone.

"So, you think we should go racing off to this K'Orge place?" Mirimel asked.

Quinless shrugged. "It is not for me to decide, but that is the holiest place of the Overgod."

"Forgive me if I don't want to take one person's word for it."

"I do forgive you, Hawk Guardian, for I can see that inside you there is endless pain and sorrow. Trust is hard won in a heart such as yours. I can only hope there are those who will fight for it. You have too much life ahead of you to live as you do." Quinless reached out, resting a long-fingered hand against Mirimel's cheek.

To Ari's surprise, a shimmer of tears formed in Mirimel's eyes, making glittering sapphires of her irises. She yanked her head away from Quinless' hand. Turning on her heels, she stomped through the door at the back of the shop.

Quinless dropped her arm. "I spoke too much."

"No," Cooro said, his voice touched with sorrow. "You spoke too truly." He pushed away from the counter. "Cooro will go after her."

"She'll only find a reason to yell at you," Ari said.

Cooro flashed him a grin. "I know." Whistling softly, the Whey mirrored Mirimel's path.

"He does not love her," Quinless said.

Ari whipped his head back around to look at her. "I beg your pardon? Do you mean, she does not love him?"

Quinless had her full lips pressed into a firm line. "I mean what I said, Lord Aridian."

"Please, call me Ari." Out of the corner of his eye, Ari saw Mattah smile at his words. "Why do you say Cooro doesn't love her? He's been pursuing her since they met, even though she endlessly refutes him."

"He loves to chase," Quinless said. "I can see it in him. I recognize it. He loves knowing he cannot catch her. This brings him great joy, which he confuses with love for her. Were he to catch her, his love would disappear, leaving them both without happiness."

"I'm pretty sure Mirimel hates him, so there's no danger of that."

"There is great danger. She is balanced on a knife's edge. The line between anger and love is, for some, a very fine one." She gave Ari a warm smile. "You are not one such. It will be difficult for you to understand, I think. You know only one way to love."

"Ah . . ." Ari had no idea what to say to that. He wondered if he should ask her about the time Siara kissed him and he liked it, making him worry he didn't love Ispiria as much as he thought he did. He shook his head, disregarding the idea as ludicrous. What was it about Quinless that made her so appealing to talk to?

"Your hawk guardian is broken inside," Quinless continued. "When the pieces of her heart rebind, they will be shaped by faith. Don't let that faith be misplaced, Lord Aridian, or she will be lost."

"I, um, I'll do my best?" Ari had little idea what they spoke of.

"I know you will." She glanced at Mattah. "I would offer you a place to stay this night, for my heart would be made happier by time spent with my son, but there is no room in the shop for all four of you."

That Ari could understand. "Parrentine told us to stay at the Equestrian. If you can give us directions, we'll go there.

Mattah should stay here, if you both want, and return to the ship in the morning. He'll need to make a report to Parrentine."

Quinless rewarded Ari's offer with a dazzling smile. "You are very kind. I can see why your prince values you."

"I think it's because Ari can chop a man right in half with his sword," Mattah said. "Or so people say." He looked to Ari, as if for confirmation.

"Is that true?" Quinless asked, looking surprised for the first time.

Ari shrugged. "I suppose it is. I wouldn't, though. I mean, not unless I had a very good reason."

To Ari's relief, her smile returned. "That, I think, is why the prince values him," she said to Mattah. "Will you stay here with your father and me this night? Must you return so soon? Will we see your prince?"

"Parrentine promised the king he wouldn't leave the ship," Mattah said. "The king is worried he'll run off after Princess Siara. I have to go back with him tomorrow, but I can stay here tonight."

Quinless pulled Mattah into a hug.

"I'll let Mirimel and Cooro know it's time to find the inn," Ari said, feeling like an intruder.

Mattah wriggled from of his mother's embrace, turning to face Ari. "It has been my honor to journey with you, Lord Aridian."

"It's Ari," Ari said. Reaching across the counter, he held out his hand.

Mattah blinked once, then clasped hands with Ari. "It's been my honor, Ari, both to journey with you and to see your feats of arms with Swordmaster Cooro and Hawk Guardian Mirimel."

"You can tell them that yourself, if you don't mind. I was hoping you would give us instructions on how to find the Equestrian."

"Of course." Mattah nodded.

"Also, tomorrow, please tell Parrentine what we've learned, and that I have the hunt in hand. Will you have any trouble returning to the ship before the tide?"

"Kanja and I shall take him," Quinless said.

"I can travel the city on my own." Mattah stood up straighter as he spoke, giving his mother a beseeching look.

"You can, yes," Quinless said. "But you attract much attention in the clothing of your foreign lord, and I should like to give my thanks to Prince Parrentine, for all the good he has done us."

Mattah turned back to Ari, appearing mollified.

A smile ghosted across Quinless' lips. "It was Kanja's and my honor to meet you as well, Ari. We wish you good fortune in your hunt."

"Thank you." Ari bowed.

"I'll point out the way," Mattah said, heading toward the back of the shop.

Walking around the counter, Ari followed him through the door. They made their way past the crowded shelves, and out into the afternoon light. Mirimel and Cooro were already mounted, Mirimel's hawk perched on her shoulder this time. Stew was standing beside Kanja, waiting for them.

They said their farewells, though Kanja did not speak aloud, and set out. Mattah's directions proved sound, making the Equestrian simple to find. Ari balked a bit at the lavishness of the inn and the price of the suite, but did as Parrentine had advised and took rooms for them.

They spent the remainder of the evening arguing about what to do next. Cooro was ready to take Quinless' word and ride out to K'Orge. Mirimel was adamantly against such an act. Ari had the feeling Quinless was right, but with nothing more to go on, he wasn't ready to leave Jondor. He wanted to try Mattah's idea and visit a water baron's library. Surely, scholarly works of the region would tell them what they wanted to know. Of course, the one thing Mirimel and Cooro did agree on was that would be boring and a waste of time.

In the wake of their late evening of endless discussion, Ari was mildly groggy the following morning. Knowing there would be more talk at breakfast, he had food brought up to the sitting room of the suite instead of going down to the common room to dine. That way, at least they would have only magical spying to worry over.

To Ari's delight, breakfast consisted of dried fruit, water, preserves, flat bread and a pungent hard cheese. There was also a bitter, dark, sludgy liquid he couldn't name. It came with sour tasting cream and a bowl of sweetener, but no amount of either made it drinkable by Ari's estimation.

"Have you settled on a plan yet, champion of your king?" Cooro asked around a mouthful of bread and preserves.

"I think I shall attempt a library," Ari replied.

Mirimel groaned.

Before she could speak, Ari held up a hand. "Meanwhile, you two will canvas the city. Ask about the ship. Ask about red headed strangers. I think Ispiria would stand out here, even with all of the different peoples I've seen. Also, see if anyone else agrees with Quinless about where this most holy place of the Overgod is."

Mirimel frowned, but she nodded, popping a piece of dried fruit into her mouth.

"A sound plan. We shall reconvene here this afternoon?" Cooro asked.

"Yes. If anyone isn't back by dinner, the others should form a search. "

"Why wouldn't we be back?" Mirimel asked. "Do you have reason to believe we'll be interfered with?"

Ari shook his head. "I'm just trying to be cautious."

Cooro took a sip of the bitter drink and grimaced, frowning down at it. "A day spent in your lovely company, Hawk Guardian. Cooro has been granted a gift."

"We are not spending the day together." Mirimel's words were clipped.

"But of course we are. Canvasing the city, as Lord Aridian suggests."

"I can search alone, thank you."

Cooro shook his head. "You can, but you should not. This is a strange land, with customs we do not know. Trouble may lurk here and, as the mighty Aridian pointed out, your bright locks will draw undue attention."

"You're more likely to get into trouble than I am." Mirimel crossed her arms in front of her. "Knowing you, you'll be distracted by the first pretty smile you see and end up being chased out of another man's home before the day is out."

"Both are possible," Ari said. "Which is why you should ask around together. Consider it that you're looking out for one another."

"Fine," Mirimel snapped, grabbing up another piece of fruit. "But who will look out for you?"

Ari suppressed a scowl, wondering why everything was an argument with Mirimel. "I shall look out for myself. I'm not saying I'm more capable than either of you. Just more durable."

"He makes a worthy point," Cooro said cheerfully. "And we cannot split up if we actually stay together."

To Ari's relief, Mirimel shrugged, returning her attention to her food. Soon enough, they'd finished their meal. Mirimel and Cooro left the inn immediately. Ari went down into the common area, seeking the innkeeper.

He was a whip-thin man with dark hair and a pointed beard. He cheerfully answered Ari's questions about which water baron had the greatest library and how to get there. Ari slid a coin across the ornately inlaid desk before heading from the inn.

As he followed the directions given him, he frequently stopped those he passed, plying thcm with the same two questions. There seemed to be a general agreement on whose library was greatest, though not on the precise path to reach the enclave. Still, the sun was several hours from its zenith when Ari reached the walled keep of one of Jondor's eight water barons.

Men at arms walked the top of the wall, which was covered in a thick plaster like many of the other clay-brick buildings of Jondor. The water baron's soldiers strutted back and forth, not bothering to look down. The closed gate Ari stood before was both massive and ornate. It was made of metal, bands of iron, copper and bronze interwoven in patterns that appeared designed to be both decorative and strong. His eyes tracing the geometric design, it occurred to Ari how rare wood must be in Jondor, a land where few trees ever grew.

Having no idea what else to do, Ari walked up to the gate and knocked. The sound of his closed fist hitting the gate echoed around him. A small window, hardly more than the size of Ari's hand, slid open in the gate. To his surprise, the giant metal doors weren't as thick as he'd supposed.

Two dark eyes appeared in the opening. A man's voice, hardly intelligible through the small opening in the door, said something Ari didn't understand.

"I cannot tell what you're saying," Ari said, leaning closer and speaking loudly, to be sure he was heard.

"I said, delivery time is over," the man repeated, this time in accented Lggothian. "Come back in the morning." The small window slid shut.

Ari pounded again. When the window opened, he didn't wait for the speaker. "I'm not here for a delivery."

"Here to buy?" The man sounded more pleased with that prospect. "Buying begins an hour before sunset. Come back then." The window snapped shut.

Ari pounded a third time. A glance upward showed the guards atop the wall had stopped in their rounds to peer over the ramparts at him. The window slid open again.

"I'm not here to buy or to sell." Ari got the words out quickly. "I'm here to use the library."

"The master's library?" The man's face pressed against the gate, his eyes looking Ari up and down. "You do not look as if you can read."

"I assure you, I can read," Ari said.

"How many tongues? We don't have many works in your barbarian words."

"Three." Ari didn't think it would help his cause to offer that the other two, aside from Lggothian, were Wheylian and Ancient Wheylian.

The eyes stared at him for a long moment, unblinking. "No." The window snapped closed.

Ari frowned at the gate, anger stirring inside him. He pounded again. When the window opened, he decided to attempt a different tactic. "I am Lord Aridian, Duke of Sorga,

172

Protector of the Northlands, and Champion to Ennentine, King of Lggothland. I wish to visit your library."

The eyes narrowed. "You are not."

Ari blinked. "I assure you, I am. On my honor. I would not lie."

"Lord Aridian we have heard of. He is ten feet in height, and as broad as three men. He has eyes made of fire for scorching his foes, and a voice like thunder. His strength is such he could open our gate with his hands alone. Lord Aridian would not lie. I think you are a vagrant." The window closed.

Ari gaped at it a moment in surprise. His anger was quick to return, though. He eyed the gate, wondering if he could open it with his bare hands. It seemed likely.

"All you needed to do was bribe him." The voice was soft, lyrical and feminine, and coming from over Ari's right shoulder.

He spun, finding a small figure covered head to toe in black, with only deep brown, angled eyes visible. "Excuse me?"

"He was waiting for a bribe. When you told him the number of languages you speak, my lord, you were to offer him a like number of coins. If they shone brightly enough, he would have let you inside."

"Oh." Ari frowned, trying to place her accent. It seemed Wheylian, but mixed with that of Kanja's people. "What do I do now?"

"He will not open to your knock again. Give me three coins, and I shall buy us passage." She held out a slender hand. Her skin was light, but darkened by the sun.

Ari scrutinized the diminutive form, unable to tell much, covered as she was. He glanced back at the closed door, and upward, to the mass of armed men watching them. Finally, he nodded, reaching inside his doublet for three silver coins. "Fine, you get us in."

Chapter 15

Ari held out the three silver coins to the woman.

She shook her head. The robes that covered her from head to toe rippled. "You must pay in gold. You have agitated him, and there are two of us."

Ari closed his fingers, looking around. There was an empty space around the water baron's walls, and the roadway was broad. No one could be hiding near, or brazen enough to ambush him, and there was nowhere for the woman to disappear if her offer was false. He returned the silver coins to their pouch and brought out gold ones, dropping them into her small palm.

"I am Kiala," she said, closing her hand around the coins.

"I'm Ari," Ari replied, his mind more on the fact that it was a Wheylian name, and vaguely familiar, than on his words.

"Are you sure you do not mean Lord Aridian, Duke of Sorga, Protector of the Northlands, and Champion to Ennentine, King of Lggothland?" she asked as she walked passed him to the door, her voice bright with amusement. She knocked lightly.

Ari saw no reason to reply to that as the window in the gate slid open once more. Kiala held out her hand. The three gold coins sparkled in her palm. The eyes framed in the small window went wide.

"May I assist you, fairest one?" the man asked.

Ari snorted at the compliment. For one, there was no way to know what Kiala looked like under her all-encompassing robes. For another, his eyes weren't even on hers, which were pretty enough, but instead fixed on the coins.

"We should like to visit your master's library."

"Of course, fairest one, but weapons must be left with me, and I must search you."

Kiala looked over her shoulder at Ari. "Well?"

Wincing at the frivolity of it, he brought out two more coins. He reached over her shoulder and dropped them to rest with the others. "One for my sword, and one for no searching."

The eyes in the window flickered to him before returning to the coins. If drooling made a sound, Ari was sure they would be able to hear it. A glance upward showed the guardsmen on the wall crowded into the space above the gate, watching with avaricious eyes. Ari wondered how long the gatekeeper would keep his gold.

"If the great Lord Aridian swears you come to view the master's tomes and do no harm, I see no reason to doubt his word of honor."

"I do," Ari said.

The window closed again, but this time Ari could hear orders being called out. He couldn't understand the words, thought whether that was because of the gate between him and the speaker or the tongue in which they were uttered, he was unsure. He turned to Kiala as the door creaked. "Thank you for your assistance."

"And thank you, my lord, for paying my way in," she said.

Ari mulled that over, belatedly wondering why she was there. He frowned.

"My business is with the camel trader, supplier and water merchant," she said, as if understanding his frown. "I sought entrance early in the hopes of procuring the best provisions and beasts. I am readying for a long journey. Later, they will hold the evening auction. I would have to pay more than what is fair, as many of the men will not stand for a woman outbidding them."

The massive door swung open. Ari forgot about camel merchants and a handful of gold coins. Before him was an oasis of green. Grass carpeted the ground. Fruit and nut trees stood in loose clusters, their branches decked in brightly colored birds. Camels, horses and ponies grazed beside a sparkling blue pond. Geese paraded about, honking and squawking. Across the compound was a low desert-colored building, larger than most in Jondor, but still constructed of clay. Palm trees flanked it, casting long, fringe-topped shadows.

"Come, Lord Aridian," Kiala called, striding forward. "They do not like to keep the gate open for long."

Ari followed after her, pausing to wait while she approached a scrawny dark-haired man whose eyes labeled him the gatekeeper. Ari looked back, hearing the gate begin to swing shut behind them. Outside the compound, the world was still yellow, sand-choked and dry. The land inside seemed one of impossible vibrancy by comparison.

The gate closed with a thud. Ari stifled a wince. Scrutinizing the compound with a more critical eye, he was

177

relieved to see many brick staircases ascending the outer wall. If needed, it would be easy enough to fight his way to the top and slither down the outside, though he would risk breaking something when he hit the ground. His eyes scoured the enclosure for a rope, real or makeshift.

Her business with the gatekeeper apparently concluded, Kiala strolled back to Ari. "My business takes me that way." She pointed toward a cluster of smaller buildings and paddocks, near the pond. "The library is in the baron's home. If you go round to the south side, there is another entrance. You may need more coin to be admitted, but there will be less expense and fuss at the side door than if you try to enter through the front."

"Thank you," Ari said, bowing.

"Here." Kiala held out her hand. A flat, dark, rune covered stone with a coin-sized hole through the center rested in her palm. "It's what I trade in. Magi stones. If you look through this one, you will be able to read words written in those languages you do not know."

"Really?" Ari reached for it, but stopped. "How much is it?" He'd only brought so much coin with him.

"It is a gift." He couldn't see her expression beneath her robe, but her voice sounded as if she smiled. "To thank you for paying my way."

"Surely it's worth more than I paid," Ari said, taking it. It was smooth, save for the runes scoring it, and light.

"It's worth is for me to judge," she said. She bowed, as Mirimel might. "Until we meet again."

Ari bowed back, watching for a moment as she walked off toward the pond. He wondered if she really was a Whey, and what she was doing there. It wouldn't be too odd, he supposed, for a Wheylian woman to trade magic stones in the southlands.

After all, in Wheylia, the women often had magic and were the heads of the households. Still, it seemed a bit odd to find her with no servants or husband following her. After a moment he shrugged, setting off across the rich lawn.

After a bit more questioning and another bribe, Ari found himself in the water baron's library. It was a low-ceilinged, musty, little-used seeming room. There were many books, scrolls, maps and ledgers, but they weren't well-kept and seemed devoid of organization. The baron might have the largest library, but it was clear he took pride in his collection for the size alone.

Crossing the room, Ari moved from window to window, opening the shutters. Far from illuminating, the light which streamed in seemed only to emphasize the layers of dust his presence was stirring. Shrugging, Ari picked a corner to start in. He held up the stone Kiala gave him, closing one eye to peer through it with the other.

Each title scrawled on the spine of a book or penned at the top of a scroll appeared to be in perfect Lggothian. Ari lowered the stone. Readable words changed to a gibberish of symbols, some of them bearing no resemblance to what he even knew as letters. Amazed, he raised the stone again, then held it away from his face so he could look at it.

Ari knew about magic. He had no choice but to believe in it. Still, Aluien spells seemed designed to manipulate humans, as did Empty One magic. Much of what both did was illusion and trickery. Kenmar's sorcery, though Ari had seen little of it, seemed more practical. The stone, however, was another thing entirely. This was usable magic. This was something Ari could keep, employ, and gain from. A grand gift indeed.

Putting it back to his eye, he set a slow pace along the shelves. He wasn't truly sure what he sought, but several hours

179

of looking found two books and one scroll on the history of K'Orge, as well as a scroll claiming to hold the original teachings of the Overgod. These four Ari took to a table, sitting down in a puff of dust to peruse them in more detail.

He started with the ancient looking, splintering scroll telling of the Overgod. It was a bit tricky, carefully unrolling the scroll and wedging it open with books so he could read sections through the stone. He winced each time it cracked, trying hard not to crumble the edges and lose words.

The scroll spoke of the teachings of the first prophet of the Overgod. It did not name K'Orge, but did speak frequently about how the temple was built during the rebuilding of the city, which had been struck from the mountaintop and flung into the sea by the Overgod. As Ari didn't know of any other city with the same history, and didn't think it likely there were many that had both been tumbled and survived, he felt relatively sure the city in the scroll was K'Orge.

What was more interesting were the teachings. They weren't very similar to what the priests of the Overgod preached in Lggothland. The scroll spoke of the evil of amassing too much wealth. It talked of sharing good fortune, and raising up the lowest among men to the benefit of all. It seemed very clear on the notion that it was the wealthy few who'd angered the god, and because of them the city had been cast down and so many killed. Ari wondered what had happened, in the thousands of years and miles, to turn what the scroll contained into the religion the wealthiest in Hapland and Lggothland embraced.

As that was a mystery for another day, Ari carefully rolled the scroll and returned it to where he'd found it, though he was still sure there was no reason to the placement. He turned his attention to the other scroll, and then the two books, in turn.

180

All three told much the same story, one that mirrored the origins of the Overgod.

The oldest book, its pages thick and leathery with terribly faded ink, held an additional detail about the destruction of K'Orge that caught at Ari's memory. It spoke of a race of sea creatures known to dwell in the water at the foot of the mountain. There seemed to be a relationship, not defined in the book, between a sect, or perhaps even cult, of men and women in K'Orge and the sea creatures. It was not said, but was implied, that the humans somehow communicated with them to learn of storms, or where to fish, and the like.

When the city fell, it landed atop the home of these creatures, killing many. The survivors came to help, attempting to save those drowning in the angry sea. Something seemed to poison them, to the best Ari could tell from the faded pages. The author thought it was the gold in the wealthy homes, leaching into the water and bringing death. Ari didn't think gold melted into water at all. He wasn't sure if he was interpreting the fragmented words incorrectly, or if the author's prejudice against the wealthy colored how he interpreted the events. To make matters worse, the tale was recounted as having been handed down from his great grandfather, who was living in the city when it fell.

Finally closing the second book, Ari slid the stone into his doublet and rubbed his eyes. He realized one was sore from reading, and the other from being squeezed shut for hours. His shoulders ached as well and he stretched. A glance out the window showed the afternoon nearly gone. He realized he needed to leave if he wanted to return to the Equestrian soon enough to prevent Cooro and Mirimel from worrying.

He stood, carefully returning books and scroll to the shelves, the fragmented story of sea creatures playing out in his mind. Once, just after the sacking of Hawkers, Larke told Ari the three stones had been placed with three magical races for safekeeping. The Sorga Hawks, or Sorrecia, were given one to keep safe in the sky. The Questri, Stew's race, were given one to safeguard on land. The last stone, Larke said, was hidden with a race that dwelled in the sea, and was lost along with them.

Though Ari had found only the one garbled reference to this race of sea creatures who could communicate with man, he felt in his gut that, true or not, it was the final piece of the puzzle. If the Lady had found similar references, she would conclude the third stone was lost in the sea, in the ruins of the ancient city of K'Orge. Ari didn't know how much of the first city still lingered below the waves, but he was sure the Lady believed the stone to be there. She was likely in K'Orge, even now, searching the waters for it while Ispiria and Siara were locked somewhere in the rebuilt city, her prisoners.

All signs pointed to K'Orge. Few were mysterious, and why should they be? The Lady wanted to be found. She wanted Ari to have the completed sword and to take it up, stand at her side, and kill Kenmar with it. More than ever, he was sure that was her plan, and why Ispiria and Siara had been taken.

The talk of converting Siara was a ruse, an easy way to use Lggothian pawns, like Ari's cousins, to help her. She could have manipulated them with magic, but why go to the trouble when they were more easily led by lies. The only truth in the note she'd left was that Ispiria and Siara were being taken to the birthplace of the Overgod.

Leaving the library and the water baron's home, Ari made his way back across the vibrant enclave. He looked about as he crossed the grounds, but didn't see Kiala and her camels. He supposed she'd finished her negotiations long since, for he'd been reading for hours. When he reached the gate, no bribes were required to return to the dusty streets.

It didn't take him as long to return to the inn as it had taken to find the water baron's enclave. With a nod to the innkeeper, Ari made his way above stairs and down the cool, dark hallway to their suite. He could hear Mirimel and Cooro arguing before he even reached the door.

". . .me ten piece of gold," Cooro said, sounding testier than usual. "Cooro is not so rich as your prince and lord, that he can spare such funds. Nor does Cooro have a wife to keep him, like most men."

"That I can understand," Mirimel said. "Who would want to keep you?"

"Must you always be ungrateful? How many times must Cooro save you from your temper?" Cooro asked.

"I would have figured some way out."

"So you say, but there was no other and you know this. If Ari will not repay me with the prince's coin, you must swear to pay me with ten kisses."

"A kiss from me is worth more than one piece of gold," Mirimel said, but there was an odd note in her voice. She didn't sound as angry as Ari would have thought. She sounded, almost, teasing. Quinless' warning rang in Ari's ears.

Not stopping when he reached the door, he flung it open. He used perhaps a bit more force than intended, wincing when it bounced off the wall and swung back toward him. Catching it, he entered the room, closing the door behind him with more care. "Hello."

Mirimel and Cooro sat at the dining table, across from each other. Mirimel's face was touched with red, but Cooro appeared his usual self, smiling broadly. He gestured to the chair beside him with one arm, the food on the table with the other.

"Ari, we were soon to worry. Come, dine with us."

"I was reading for longer than I thought I would be," Ari said, taking the chair. The food on the table smelled good, the thick fragrant yellow sauce making it difficult to identify.

"Give this Whey ten gold crowns," Mirimel snapped, pushing her plate away. "We have word of Ispiria."

"And Princess Siara," Cooro added, frowning at Mirimel.

"What word?" Ari asked, his mind no longer on food.

"We found a merchant who passed an old lady and two young women on the road," Mirimel said, excitement in her voice. "He thought the one woman was the granddaughter of the first, who was in charge, by his estimation. The other woman he called an exotic redheaded slave." She grimaced, shooting a glance at Cooro.

"It seems the man tried to purchase the redheaded slave," Cooro said, taking up the tale. "He was told she was not for sale." He shot a grin at Mirimel. "After telling us this, he tried to purchase Mirimel. Cooro had quite the negotiation going, until the fair Mirimel stabbed our generous informant in the arm."

"I didn't hurt him," Mirimel muttered.

"He squealed like a stuck boar," Cooro said.

"I mean, I didn't hit anything vital. I wasn't trying to kill him, just let him know what I thought of his attempts to test the stock. I am not a milk cow."

Ari raised his eyebrows. That was what he got for letting the two of them wander the city unsupervised. "What happened? Did you at least find out which way they were headed?" Although he knew. South, to K'Orge. Still, excitement thrummed through him at their news.

"They were going south," Mirimel said. "Nothing much happened. He cried like a child, guards came. There was shouting."

"Then, the little hawk swooped down from above and entered the fray, which provoked calls of witchcraft." Cooro sighed. "Cooro was forced to spend all of his coin on bribes to keep us from the gaol." He threw up his hands. "Your prince owes me for this."

Ari nodded, reaching inside his doublet for the coins. "That confirms what I read." Handing Cooro his money, Ari gave them a quick summary of his day, focused on his readings. When he was done, having reassured Mirimel that the tradeswoman he'd met wasn't trying to do them harm, he concluded with, "It's decided. Tomorrow, we shall find a guide to take us south to K'Orge."

Chapter 16

Ari woke early, impatience and excitement thrumming through him. He'd seen maps of the southlands. He knew reaching K'Orge wasn't the work of a day, or even a week. Still, he was eager to start. His world seemed brighter. The time for indecision was ended. Now that he knew where to go, he could act.

He dressed quickly, entering the common room of their suite to find Mirimel already at the table eating. With a nod, he took the seat across from her. "Good morning."

"It is." She looked up, actually smiling. "When we're done here, you'll settle up with the innkeeper while I see to the Questri? Cooro is already out."

Ari nodded, wondering when he'd become responsible for paying for everything. Of course, he had their coin, so it was only natural. He didn't even know if Mirimel had money. Apparently Cooro did. "Wait," he asked, his mind registering all of her words. "Cooro?"

"Yes." She frowned at Ari. "You do remember him? He travels with us."

"Usually, you call him that Whey, or that fool Whey, or something more along those lines."

Mirimel shrugged. "I'm in a charitable mood. He did keep me from being tossed in a cell."

"Are you admitting to needing help?" Ari didn't know what to think. Quinless' warning came back to him.

"I didn't need help, but since he's too great a fool to see that, it was kind of him to offer it," Mirimel said, but her tone lacked its usual bite.

"If you say so." Ari wondered how much stock he should put in Quinless' words, and if there was anything he could even do.

"Are you sure you want to hire a guide?" Mirimel asked, tapping the table with one finger. "I can find our way. We'd do better to buy a map. Maps don't betray you."

"I am confident you can find our way." Ari felt it best to begin with a compliment. There was no need to ruin Mirimel's peaceable temper. "We do not know these lands or the dangers in crossing them, though, and a map can't tell us that."

"We have my hawk to scout, and all three of us to face down any danger, not to mention the black mare and Stew."

Ari started assembling food on his plate to give himself a moment to phrase a reply. He didn't want to begin his day with an argument. "I would still prefer a guide." He grinned. "How's this, if he does betray us, you can kill him."

Mirimel smiled. "Fair enough."

"Where is your hawk, anyhow?" he asked, realizing for the first time that the little raptor hadn't been coming into the inn with them.

"While you were speaking with Quinless, Kanja told us some of the peoples here are superstitious about birds. He recommended she stay out of sight as much as possible. She's on the roof." Mirimel's eyes took on an abstract look and her hand paused, a piece of dried fruit halfway to her mouth. "She says the sun has appeared and we should begin our hunt."

"She is correct." Ari looked around, though Cooro could hardly have entered the room unseen. "Where did you say Cooro went?"

"He took his mare to Kanja." Mirimel poured herself water, offering Ari some. "Kanja said she would not survive in the desert and that he would look after her if our journey took us to K'Orge. Cooro left very early. I think he hoped, as well, to give Mattah our news of yesterday, for the prince."

"What will he ride, then?" Ari asked, for Cooro couldn't mean to go on foot.

"I suppose one of those camel creatures."

"Does he know how?" Ari's mind conjured up an image of Cooro atop one of the large humpbacked animals.

"It will be entertaining to find out." Mirimel's smile was more vicious this time.

Cooro still hadn't returned by the time they finished eating. Both impatient to leave, Ari and Mirimel gathered their scant possessions, taking them down to the stable. Stew agreed to carry Cooro's saddlebags along with Ari's, at least until a camel could be found. Leaving Mirimel with the Questri, Ari went to settle up with the innkeeper.

The thin man seemed sorrowful at their departure, beseeching them to return soon. Ari didn't doubt his honesty, in view of how much coin he was making off them staying there. Asking for directions on where to find a guide, Ari left the man with an extra silver piece, bidding him to pass the information along to Cooro.

Leading Stew and the black mare, Ari and Mirimel set off for the bazaar. They found it buzzing with people even at the early hour. Ari paused for a moment on the outskirts, then took a deep breath, plunging into the crowd. His senses were instantly bombarded by colors, sounds and smells. Everything cried for attention, and everyone moved constantly. Ari didn't know how people could think amidst the melee of offerings, let alone make decisions on what to purchase.

Bolstered by the innkeepers advice, they made their way to the northeast corner, where trade caravans unloaded and guides could be found. Ari approached the loose ring of men, many crouched in the sandy street throwing dice, with mild apprehension. He considered that Mirimel might be correct about the map, for the men didn't look like a reliable lot.

"Lord Aridian," a woman's voice, touched by a Wheylian accent, called.

Ari turned to see a diminutive black-robe shrouded figure. Though he'd never seen more than her eyes, he identified them and the voice as belonging to Kiala. Angling in her direction, he strode toward her.

She bowed as they drew near. "What brings you to the bazaar so early today, my lord?" Her eyes swept over Mirimel and the Questri.

"Good morning, Kiala," he said, ignoring Mirimel's questioning look. "We're seeking a guide. Can you recommend a reliable one?"

"I may. Who is your friend?" She turned to Mirimel, repeating her bow. "I am Kiala."

"Hawk Guardian Mirimel," Mirimel supplied, bowing in return. "You must be the tradeswoman who helped Ari gain

190

entrance to the library, and gave him that stone." Ari could hear the suspicion in Mirimel's voice. "Where did you come by such an artifact? Are you Wheylian?"

Kiala chuckled. "You must be the orange-haired northern witch who created such a stir here yesterday. I should have known you were a companion to this one. He smells of trouble. Didn't you have a Whey with you then?" Kiala looked about. "You should ask him of my accent."

"Or you could answer my questions." Mirimel's voice was flat.

"What sport would there be in that?" Kiala turned back to Ari. "Where do you need a guide to, my lord?"

"We're headed to K'Orge." Ari was aware Mirimel was attempting to glare him into silence as he spoke.

Kiala's eyes crinkled at the edges. "Why, fortune of fortunes. That is where I am headed. I have come today to hire a guard to accompany me. Do you use that sword well?" Not waiting for Ari to respond, she looked to Mirimel. "And what of you, northern witch, do you shoot the bow you bear, or is it merely decoration?" Ari wished he could see her face, to know if she smiled. Her voice sounded amused.

"Why don't you go stand over there and I'll show you?" Mirimel asked.

Kiala laughed again. "Perfect. What of your Whey?"

"He isn't my Whey," Mirimel said, too quickly for Ari's comfort. She blushed slightly.

Kiala's eyes narrowed. "I see."

"Are you truly journeying to K'Orge?" Ari asked, heading off what he was sure would be a perilous line of conversation.

"I truly am, and I would be pleased to take you on as guards." She looked from them to Stew and the black mare. "I can see these mounts are up to the task. What of your Whey?"

"He needs a camel, I think," Ari said.

"I have one for him. My mounts and supplies wait at the edge of the city for me to return. I did not want to negotiate the bazaar with a train in tow." Kiala gestured southward. "We shall go there. I will send a boy to find your friend."

"A moment," Mirimel said, glaring at Kiala with unconcealed suspicion.

"Certainly." Kiala bowed, backing away. "I shall permit you to discuss my offer." She moved a few paces off, presenting them with her shrouded profile.

Ari was sure Kiala would still be able to hear them if they spoke above a whisper, so he used one when he turned to Mirimel. "I think we should take her offer."

"Of course you do." Mirimel didn't bother to lower her voice, or hide her exasperation. "You trust everyone. Your arch enemy could walk up and ask you to make friends with him, and you would probably say yes . . . no, wait, you definitely would."

It would take someone less astute than Ari not to hear the sarcasm overlaying Mirimel's words. "Just because I am more trusting than you are doesn't mean there aren't people who can be trusted."

"Why would we go with her? Doesn't it seem rather convenient she appeared here, now, when we're looking for a guide, and is going where we want to go?"

Ari shrugged. In truth, it did seem suspicious. He didn't care. If Kiala was part of this, then he would have her by his side where he could keep his eyes on her. "No one is trying to keep us from K'Orge. If anything, the Lady would have left those who could help us reach it."

Mirimel's annoyance softened with surprise and he knew he'd made a good argument. She looked toward Kiala, her expression assessing. "She is only one woman. I doubt we would have trouble subduing her if needed."

Ari nodded, though he didn't think it mattered. Friend or foe, Kiala wasn't there to fight them. Besides, he rather thought she was a friend. Again, her name nagged at him, trying to shake something loose in his memory.

"How many others will travel with us?" Mirimel raised her voice, aiming the words at Kiala.

She turned back to face them. "No others."

"If we're your guards, will you pay us?" Mirimel asked.

"You will be my guards, but I will be your guide." Kiala spread her hands wide. "The two equal one another."

"She can't be any less reliable than one of that lot," Ari muttered, nodding toward the lounging guides, many of whom had stopped their game to watch the three converse.

"I suppose you're right," Mirimel said. She crossed to Kiala, holding out a hand. "We'd be pleased to take you on as our guide, and safeguard your passage."

Kiala clasped Mirimel's hand, nodding. "And I am pleased to be your guide, and have you as my guards." She stepped back, gesturing south again. "Come. I will take you to my caravan. We can send word to your Whey to join us there."

As Ari and Mirimel followed Kiala, some of the watching guides grumbled. Most returned to their dice games. None interfered.

When they reached the edge of the bazaar, Kiala caught a small ragged-looking boy by the arm. She spoke to him rapidly in a tongue Ari didn't know, earning another suspicious glare from Mirimel, and put a coin in his hand. "He will find your friend," Kiala said, watching the boy scurry away.

Ari had little faith in that, but shrugged away Mirimel's muttering. It wasn't as if Kiala could force them to depart without Cooro. No matter the boy's success, many people had seen them standing near the guides in the bazaar and many would have overheard their conversation with Kiala. Ari wasn't worried about Cooro finding them.

The route Kiala led them and the Questri on through the city at first seemed circuitous, but soon Ari realized it was the most direct way. Based on the sun, she led them south and did so with easy precision, expertly navigating the twisting and branching streets. They crossed wider streets with lead-windowed shop fronts, and narrow ones where the buildings nearly touched above. Water baron conclaves came and went, and homes both palatial and small. Finally, they joined a wide boulevard. After nearly an hour of walking, they found themselves on the southern outskirts of the city.

Leaving the sprawl behind, Ari looked out on the vast barrenness of the desert. He'd never seen a land that appeared so devoid of life. Even the road, though awash in people, carts, camels and horses, dwindled into obscurity within eyesight. It was as if nothing could prevail against the emptiness. Any attempt at permanence was scoured clear by the sand. The midmorning sun made long shadows of the rippling dunes. To Ari, it was an unfathomable landscape. He was glad they had a guide.

Kiala led them toward an open area dotted with piles of stone. Several of the piles were encircled by camels and horses, and those were attended. As they drew near one, Ari realized the small pyres of rocks were piled atop reins, creating the quadruped rings. He supposed it was the best they could do, having only rock and sand to work with.

They stopped at the farthest circle, Kiala handing the two men waiting there some coin. Both bowed, hurrying away after a brief exchange of words in one of the many languages spoken in Jondor. Ari didn't think it was the same one she used when addressing the street urchin earlier.

Kiala's circle was made up of six camels, two with riding saddles and four piled high with supplies. Ari didn't see much that looked as if it might be merchandise, but if she traded in objects like the rock she'd given them, she may not have many and the space they took up would be small. Still, the extra riding camel made him suspicious. It was almost as if she'd planned to journey with them, and knew Cooro would need a mount.

The camels were large, bigger than even large horses, like Stew. The black mare, fine boned and sleek, seemed small beside them. She eyed them with disdain, though they looked back with placid enough expressions. Stew, for his part, appeared interested, his ears forward and his eyes bright.

Ari looked about, taking in the wide spacing between groups, creating a moderate amount of privacy. People could see each other, but no one could sneak near enough to hear conversations unobserved. He turned back toward the city, for Cooro would be easy to spot when he came out.

"Yours?" Kiala asked. She was pointing upward, at a barely visible speck circling high above. Her question was aimed at Mirimel, not him.

"I don't own her," Mirimel said in a truthful, yet evasive reply.

Kiala chuckled again. Ari didn't know if she did it because she was amused, or because it was obvious how much it annoyed Mirimel. A shrug made her black robes ripple. "You are a hawk guardian. She is a Sorga Hawk. I think my assumption stands."

"You know of Sorga Hawks?" Mirimel asked sharply.

"I am well read." Kiala turned to Ari. "You may put the Whey's things on the camel with the green saddle."

Ignoring Mirimel's glare, Ari retrieved the extra set of saddlebags from Stew. The two Questri following him, he carried Cooro's packs over to the camels, moving slowly. Ari had no idea what to expect from the large, humped beasts. They looked silly and powerful in turn. He moved slowly to stand between the two saddled ones, keenly aware that the rocks holding down their reins wouldn't keep them from bolting if they wished to. They watched him with curious, calm eyes.

Ari was glad he was tall, and wondered how Cooro would mount, or how Kiala did. He didn't see any sort of mounting block and the stone piles didn't look stable enough to climb. Perhaps Cooro could engage in some sort of acrobatics, but that would still leave the little tradeswoman on the ground. Ari supposed he could always lift her into the saddle.

The green saddle had empty saddlebags of its own, so Ari fitted Cooro's inside, pleased he didn't have to figure out how to adapt horse tack to so large a mount. When he was done, the camel standing sedately the entire time, he reached out a tentative hand to it. It eyed his offering with an unchanging expression, so Ari patted it on the nose. It blinked once.

On the opposite side of the pile of stones, Stew approached one of the other camels, his eyes bright with interest, and extended his nose. The black mare looked on with a disapproving expression. It so mirrored the one Mirimel often wore, Ari had to suppress a grin.

"I think I see him," Mirimel called.

Ari extracted himself from between the camels, crossing to stand next to her. Kiala came up on his other side. Her diminutive form fit almost entirely into his shadow, her black robes making her strangely invisible. She clenched her hands before her, her knuckles white. Ari wondered if she'd met Cooro before, for she seemed oddly nervous as she watched the swordmaster stride across the sand toward them.

"Here you are," Cooro called as he neared, eyeing Kiala with interest. "Cooro has been but moments behind you all morning. You've led a merry chase, and I see you have a new lovely companion for Cooro." He came to a halt before Kiala, offering a sweeping bow.

"Swordmaster Cooro," Ari said, gesturing toward her. "This is our guide to K'Orge."

Kiala held up a hand, halting Ari before he could continue. "I will introduce myself to this one."

Ari frowned, but nodded. He exchanged a glance with Mirimel, who looked as interested as he. Were they to have their suspicions about their fortuitous guide answered so soon?

Cooro frowned, looking back and forth between them. "May I know your name, my lady? It is Wheylian I hear in your voice, but I think colored by many years far from our land."

"Yes, quite a few years." Kiala tugged at her headdress, pulling it free.

Chapter 17

Ari watched, holding his breath, as Kiala pulled off her obscuring headdress. She revealed herself to be a Whey, which didn't surprise him. She looked a touch younger than Cooro, who was twice Ari's age, though it was always difficult to tell with Wheylian women. If they had magic, they seemed to hold onto youth longer than those who didn't.

She was fair, like all Wheys, though her skin was tanned and freckles crossed her nose, something Ari had never seen before in her people. Her black hair was untouched by gray, and her smile matched the amused glint in her dark eyes. There was a calm candor in those brown depths that hinted she was somewhat older than she appeared.

What struck Ari dumb, though, was how familiar she looked. To his eye, and not just because they were of the same people, she looked amazingly like Princess Siara and, for that matter, Queen Reudi. Unsure what the resemblance could mean, he turned to Cooro.

The swordmaster gaped at Kiala in unfettered shock. To Ari's surprise, Cooro sank to his knees in the sand. "Princess Kiala," he breathed.

"Princess?" Mirimel snapped.

The name snapped as well, fitting into place in Ari's mind. Siara's lost aunt. The middle daughter. When Queen Reudi sent her younger two daughters out into the world beyond her borders, Siara's mother met her father, a Lggothian noble, and bore her. Siara's Aunt Kiala disappeared. If Ari recalled correctly, it was said she'd gone across the sea to the south, never to be seen again.

"Until now," Ari muttered, unsure if he was more surprised or amused to find Princess Kiala alive and, apparently, waiting for them. The more he learned of the world, the more he realized the seeds of his fate had been sown long before his birth. He bowed. "Princess Kiala, it is my honor to meet you."

"Princess?" Mirimel said again. "This is foolishness. How do we know this woman is Princess Kiala? Just because she is a Whey doesn't make her story true. Didn't Princess Kiala of Wheylia disappear twenty years ago?"

"I think Cooro recognizes her." Ari gestured to the swordmaster, who still knelt, looking up at Kiala in awe.

"She's a witch. She likely enspelled him. What else could make him stop talking?"

Ari wasn't sure if Mirimel's denial was born of shock or mistrust, but he was sure this was Siara's aunt. Mirimel had never met the princess, or any of the royal family of Wheylia. Ari had, and the resemblance was unmistakable.

"Stand, Swordmaster," Kiala said. "While I enjoy appropriate subservience in a man, it doesn't do for Wheylia's future king to grovel in the dust."

Cooro, halfway to his feet, stumbled, pitching forward.

Kiala reached out, grabbing his shoulders to steady him. "In my sight, you always move with the grace of a great hunting cat," she said, frowning.

"Future king?" Mirimel's voice was little more than a squeak.

Cooro pulled away from Kiala, straightening. His face was white as chalk, sweat dampening his brow. "Your sight?" he whispered.

"What madness have you gotten us into now?" Mirimel cried, turning on Ari.

Ari held up his hands, taking a half step back from her anger. "You can't blame me for this."

"In your sight, you saw me as king?" Cooro's whispered words were addressed to Kiala.

"We shall wed, you and I." Her slow smile was made all the more chilling by the strange calm that came over her. "Though I grow old for bearing, my magic sustains me. I shall birth two children, a daughter and a son. A meager showing, but it shall be enough to carry on my house."

Cooro made a strangled sound, staring at Kiala with wide eyes.

Mirimel swung back around to watch them.

"You shall have the rearing of our son and he will be frivolous, as most men are. Our daughter will grow strong and powerful, and bear many fine daughters of her own. All of this I have seen come to pass, if we can but survive the challenge before us now."

"This is ridiculous," Mirimel said. "Cooro, you can't believe this. Even if she really is Princess Kiala of Wheylia, she's obviously been driven mad by the hot southland sun."

201

Cooro shook his head slowly. "All queens of Wheylia have the sight." His voice was awed.

"No sane person would make you a king," Mirimel said, almost beseeching.

"If I might interrupt, what do you mean, if we survive the challenge before us now?" Ari asked, far more concerned with the immediate future. He rather thought Cooro would make a good king, if he could be serious enough when required. Besides, in Wheylia the queen was the real power. Cooro wouldn't be put in charge of anything very important. All in all, Ari was happy for his friend.

Kiala turned to face him, the chill leaving her smile. She seemed to grow a bit smaller, almost as if she consolidated and became more real. In moments, she was again the laughing, bright-eyed tradeswoman he'd met the day before. Ari decided he liked her better that way than as an all-seeing Wheylian royal.

"For years, starting even before my mother sent me from her, I have been plagued by the sight like few others before me. It brought me here. It tormented me, beyond reason or magic, driving me to find both the stone you carry and the sword."

"You," Ari said, interrupting her. "You gave them to the old man. Why not give them to Parrentine yourself? Why the secrecy?"

"Every path I looked down ended in disaster," she said.

"What does that mean?" Mirimel snapped. She was eyeing Princess Kiala with no little mistrust.

"Mirimel," Cooro said, his expression serious. "You must address the princess with more respect. She is my future queen."

"Yes, and wife, if you want to believe her." Mirimel accompanied her words with a glower.

"Enough," Ari said. He didn't raise his voice, but he did infuse it with command. He glanced around, taking in the ever-increasing height of the sun. "We can't stand here arguing. We risk being overheard, and the desert sun grows ever hotter. Let's go somewhere more sheltered to discuss this."

Kiala considered him for a moment, then nodded. "Yes, let us remove our beasts and ourselves from this sun. We all, save you, Thrice Born, will burn. Even the camels and your Questri will not enjoy the harshness of the noon light."

Ari decided there was no point in being surprised Kiala knew about the Questri, or called him the Thrice Born. As a Wheylian sorceress, he supposed she had knowledge of such things. "You have somewhere in mind?"

"There's a tavern, facing out from city." She pointed north across the picket area. "They will stable and water our mounts while we speak on these things. I would advise a private room, for we shouldn't set out until near sunset. It will be better to travel the open desert at night."

Mirimel folder her arms across her chest, glaring between Ari and Kiala.

Kiala's lips quirked in a smile. "Come. I will tell you my story so you may satisfy your curiosity and set aside your fears."

"Who said anyone is afraid?" Mirimel asked.

Cooro shot her a stern look.

"To the tavern," Ari ordered, gesturing toward the city. "We can speak there, and take a meal. If we're to set out across the desert, this may be the last good food we have for some time. I can't speak to your skills, your highness," he added, turning back to Kiala. "All three of us are terrible cooks." The very thought of eating his own cooking dulled Ari's appetite.

"You cannot ask the heir to the Wheylian throne to cook." Cooro's tone was offended.

Mirimel rolled her eyes, turning on her heels to walk toward the horses and camels, where Stew and the black mare still lingered.

"By that thinking, you also cannot stop the heir to the Wheylian throne from cooking if she chooses to," Kiala said. "I'll ready the camels."

"Please, your highness, permit Cooro to do it," Cooro said, jumping in front of her as she turned toward them. "You should not be asked to perform such menial tasks."

Kiala sighed. "I was not asked, and I will do as I like, Swordmaster. If we are to have a happy union, you must learn to obey me. Besides, I warrant you don't know the first thing about camels." She stepped around him.

Cooro looked at Ari, blinked several times, and then hurried after Kiala.

Mirimel led the black mare over, Stew following, and they watched as Kiala tied the camels in a line. Cooro bustled about her like a bee bumbling through a flower garden. He took ropes from her hands and tied them for her, after which she redid each one. He tried to lead camels to the back of the line she was forming, though he couldn't get them to move. Mostly, as far as Ari could tell, he was in the way and undoubtedly making the process take twice as long as it could have.

"He's acting like a fool," Mirimel said.

"You've gone soft on him." Ari grinned when she shot him an annoyed, questioning look. "In the past, you would have said he is a fool, not just acting like one."

"Fine, he is a fool, and he's in good company with you. Why are you trusting this woman? Do you actually believe she's a princess?"

"I'm sure of it," Ari said, his tone serious. "You forget, I know Siara, and I've spent time with Queen Reudi. She is definitely their kinswoman." He shook his head. "It fits too well not to be true. Queen Reudi's line has been embroiled in this from the start. Her daughters were sent away to avoid catastrophe later. This is Queen Reudi's sacrifice of twenty years ago coming to fruition."

"You weren't even alive twenty years ago."

"I don't think that matters to them."

Mirimel made no reply as Kiala led the string of camels closer, repeatedly brushing off Cooro's attempt to take the lead beast's reins. As they drew near she adjusted her path, angling toward the tavern she'd pointed out earlier.

"Lord Aridian, walk with me," she called, gesturing to him.

Looking hurt, Cooro dropped back, letting Ari take his place beside Kiala. Stew trailed behind him, still eyeing the camels with interest. Kiala gave Ari a bemused grin, shaking her head.

"He's not what I expected, from my visions of our future," she said.

"He's not been himself since realizing who you are," Ari offered by way of reassurance.

"Hopefully he will become himself again soon, before he drives me mad."

"You cannot speak to the princess of Cooro's people as you did earlier." Cooro's whispered words reached Ari's Aluien-enhanced hearing almost as clearly as if they stood side by side, not walked several camel lengths apart.

"If Kiala doesn't like the way I talk to her, I'm sure she'll tell me so," Mirimel replied.

"You should say her highness. You must refer to her more respectfully," Cooro whispered back.

"I wager she'll order you to be less subservient long before she orders me to be more so." There was challenge in Mirimel's voice.

"A wager?" Interest lightened Cooro's tone, making him sound more normal than he had since seeing Kiala's face. "What shall you wager Cooro? Perhaps a kiss?"

"Don't be daft. I'm not kissing the Witch Queen's husband. No woman in her right mind would."

Cooro groaned. "You speak truly. No woman will dare kiss Cooro again. My days of unfettered happiness are ended."

"They are, aren't they?" Mirimel sounded smug. "What a shame."

"Is it an interesting conversation?" Kiala asked, drawing Ari's attention back to her.

He blushed as he hadn't in years. "Ah . . ."

"I rather thought it must be, looking at your face." A glance showed her to be frowning. "Will Mirimel be a problem for me?"

"She's slow to trust, but she won't do more than grumble."

"That's not what I mean, Aridian."

Ari pondered that for a moment. "With your plans for Cooro?"

"Yes, though they aren't my plans, but rather fate's. So far, I am unimpressed."

"He's not usually quite so mule brained." Ari hastened to defend his friend. "And no, Mirimel isn't . . . that is, I rather think her affections lie elsewhere, though I starting to worry a bit. It's lucky you joined us."

From the corner of his eye, he could see her shake her head. "If only it were luck."

The tavern proved to be efficient, and expensive. Ari was glad he had the prince's coin, though he knew he was wealthy in his own right, if he ever chose to be. Seeing how easy it was to spend what he had, he was rather pleased he didn't, as a general rule, carry much coin with him. He felt the tithes the people of Sorga paid should be used to better the duchy, not spread lavishly about a foreign land. He supposed the same could be said for the prince's coin, but then, Parrentine had provided it to help them on their quest to save Siara, which seemed like a good use.

Unlike an inn, the tavern didn't have sleeping chambers for rent. It also, as far as Ari could see, didn't have chairs. Even in the private dining room they took, there were only low tables and even lower divans, covered in thick, brightly upholstered pillows. Ari was forced to unbuckle his sword belt and lay Fwellian beside him in order to sit. He was doubly glad not to be wearing armor. He thought that, even with his strength, getting up and down from the piles of cushions would be a chore in plate and mail. Besides, the enclosed lamp-lit space was quite warm.

They settled into the cushions while water, flat bread, dried fruit and an earthenware pot of thick stew were brought. Kiala also asked for something called Karkadeh which, when it arrived, turned out to be some form of warm tea. Ari didn't understand the logic behind drinking something warm when he was already too hot, but he liked the mild sweet flavor a good deal more than the thick brown sludge that had accompanied breakfast. The Karkadeh smelled better, too.

Once they were alone they began serving themselves, though Cooro attempted to serve Kiala. She waved him off with an abrupt gesture. He settled into a somewhat sullen silence. The look he angled at Kiala was a strange mixture of awe and annoyance. Ignoring him, she leaned back in the cushions, loosely cradling a glass-and-copper cup of Karkadeh. She took a sip, looking around at them.

Her gaze finally settled on Ari. "Starting quite young, I was plagued by visions of the stone you carry, and the sword. It didn't take me long to find images of them in my mother's books, for they are well known to my people. We crafted them. Our heroes, of so long ago as to be myth, wielded them."

Ari nodded. In Wheylia, Queen Reudi has shown him one such image.

"As I'm sure you know, the stones cannot be sought by means of magic." Kiala smiled. "The sword, without them, can be. When I left Wheylia to seek the objects of my visions, I knew already where the sword lay." She grimaced. "It took years of searching to find the stone."

"You didn't seek the other two?" Ari asked. He realized his hand rested on Fwellian's hilt, the two stones there warm against his palm.

Kiala shook her head. "It took comparatively little seeking to discover where they were, for the dividing of the stones and sword is recorded in our ancient tomes, ones only the high priestess may read." Her smiled widened slightly. "The high priestess and, perhaps, her irreverent and stealthy daughter."

Ari raised his eyebrows at that, wondering what it would be like to raise daughters who could wield magic. He suspected he was fortunate Lggothians didn't possess such talents.

"Also, as I'm sure you know, one was with the Sorrecia, another with the Questri. I deemed neither to be the one from my visions, for it always rested in a muddy and rusted chest under the sea."

"You didn't think you should find all three?" Mirimel asked, her tone bitter.

Ari could only imagine she was thinking that, if Kiala had come twenty years ago and taken the stone, the Caller wouldn't have burned Mirimel's home to get it.

"I am sorry for your village, and your family," Kiala said to Mirimel. "I did not know why I must seek even one stone, and saw nothing to be gained in having all three. The sight is not that clear. I was unsure if I was meant to bring them together or ensure stones and sword would never meet again. I did not know enough then."

"Do you know for certain, then, that the Lady has gone to K'Orge?" Ari asked. "She wants me to complete the sword and use it to help her slay Kenmar. I guessed she went to K'Orge thinking I would arrive and find the stone there, but now we know it's not in K'Orge. Was it ever?"

"It was." Kiala took another sip of tea. "I found it there, in the sunken part of the city. I do not think Suyla knows I took it. I believe her research will mirror mine, leading her there to seek it. Further, my visions of the confrontation we must win, though darkened by your presence, Thrice Born, take place in K'Orge."

"What confrontation?" Mirimel asked, leaning forward. "Will Ari kill Lord Kenmar?"

Kiala shook her head. "I do not know. I have seen a great, sweeping darkness overshadow the half-sunken city of K'Orge. I can feel death there, and great suffering. I do not know whose."

"Not Ispiria's," Mirimel snapped.

"No, not Ispiria's, or Siara's," Ari said. "Not while there is life in my limbs."

"Nor while Cooro may prevent it." Cooro's tone was brash. "I have vowed as much, and Cooro always keeps his vows."

Ari nodded, returning his gaze to Kiala. "So you found the stone, and the sword. Why did you have the old man sell them to Parrentine?"

Kiala sipped her tea. "Because you are outside fate."

"I've been told as much," Ari said, though he'd never been very sure what the words meant. "What does that have to do with selling them to my prince?"

"The sight of the Witch Queens of Whey cannot fathom your fate any more clearly than other magic can, Aridian." She leaned forward, refilling her cup. "I tried many ways to discover what was to become of the stone, why I was plagued by visions of it. I can see the fate of others, and could learn from them, but all who come near you are plunged into a fog of uncertainty."

Mirimel snorted.

"Once I determined you would have need of the sword, I wished to better track the path of your life." Kiala shrugged. "I had your prince pay my servant so I could spy on him, to learn more of you. It was the best way to accomplish it, and get the sword to you, without setting foot on Wheylian or Lggothian soil, which I dared not do."

Chapter 18

Ari stared at Kiala, startled she'd just admitted to spying on Parrentine. "You must know I am sworn to protect the royal line."

Kiala settled back against the pillows once more. "I'm not harming your prince, simply watching him."

"I told you she couldn't be trusted," Mirimel said.

Cooro turned outraged eyes on her. "Do you impugn the honor of the crown?"

"Cooro, enough," Kiala snapped. "If you don't begin treating me as a person instead of some sort of vaunted object, I shall put out your eyes."

"My eyes?" Cooro gasped. "What is Cooro without his vision? A swordmaster no more."

Kiala shrugged. "You may need them, but I don't. They aren't the part of you Wheylia requires in service to the crown."

Cooro stared at his future queen, his features slack with surprise. Mirimel covered her mouth with her hand, coughing.

She made no other sound, but her bright blue eyes told Ari she was concealing mirth. He rather felt they were getting off topic.

"Still, I must ask you to cease spying on Prince Parrentine," Ari said.

"I should have known you would feel this way." Kiala set her tea down, reaching inside her robe. She pulled out a silver coin and proffered it to Ari.

Taking it, he found it to be a Lggothian silver crown. Parrentine's image was molded on one side, the horse crest of the royal house on the other. Etched all over it were runes nearly too small to see. Ari had no idea how lines so fine had even been made. "What do the runes mean?"

"They are the spell. That is the coin your prince paid my servant with. When you cross a witch's palm, or in this case her servant's, with silver, you give her power over you. I used that power to create a keyhole into the prince's life."

"How does it work?" he asked, intrigued in spite of himself.

"Hold it up to your eye, as you did with the reading stone."

Ari held it up. Instead of the coin blocking his vision, he could see through it. He brought it closer, peering into what really did seem similar to a keyhole.

Parrentine sat at the large table in the aft cabin of the Albatross. His elbows rested on either side of an untouched plate of food. He looked much older than his four and twenty years. Over his shoulder, Ari could see Mattah hovering, looking anxious. As Ari watched, Parrentine pushed the plate away, returned his elbows to the table, and buried his face in his hands. Mattah's expression clouded with even greater worry.

Then, the prince lifted his head. For a moment, he seemed to stare directly at Ari. Parrentine's expression was resolute. He stood, striding from the cabin. The vision followed the prince as he sought out the captain, pointing south.

As they began speaking about their course, Ari jerked the coin away from his eye, startled into motion by the sound of Parrentine's voice. "No one should have this. How can we unmake it?"

Kiala shrugged. "Easily enough. Next time we have a fire, throw it in the flames. The runes will burn off. Are you sure you don't want it? Could you not protect him better?"

Ari shook his head. "I cannot protect him if I am not with him." Unable to put into words how wrong he found her method of gathering information, he turned to the nearest lamp. There was no way to drop the coin in the dancing flame without smothering it, so Ari held the silver there. He gritted his teeth as his skin burned along with the runes.

"Ari," Mirimel cried, lunging across a pile of cushions to grab his arm, though she wasn't strong enough to move it. "Stop that."

The outside of the coin shimmered, the runes dissolving. Ari dropped the silver piece into the lamp, yanking his fingers back, wrinkling his nose at the smell of scorched flesh. Mirimel let go. She slid back into her seat. The look she gave him was murderous. Ari shook his hand, trying to alleviate the pain. It was already dissipating as his skin started to heal. Cooro looked nearly as shocked as he'd been by Kiala's threat. Kiala, for her part, wore a slightly exasperated expression.

"Done making a spectacle of yourself?" she asked.

"I found the coin offensive," Ari said, sitting back against the cushions. "I have the feeling I've been spied on for much of my life. I take exception to it."

Kiala shrugged, her eyes going to his hand. The black blistering was gone, but it was still red and stung. "I'll have to remember not to give you cause to take exception to me."

"Why didn't you come forward sooner?" Ari asked, uncomfortable with her implication. "Why were you afraid to return?"

"As I said earlier, I can see a bright, prosperous future for Wheylia," Kiala said, taking back up her tea. "Every time I made plans to reveal myself, or return home, that prospect was replaced by a chaos of smoke and war. Even when I sent the stone with your prince, I felt danger to that beautiful future. The danger battled with the need I'd come to feel for you to possess all three stones. I could not see your path, but I know there was something that had to come to pass before you could be allowed to have the stone. Some action that must drive events forward on the journey toward peace. Likewise, revealing myself too soon would have thwarted this narrow path toward hope on which we tread."

Ari took up a piece of bread, chewing on it while he thought. What would be different if he'd had all three stones sooner? Would he have tried to kill Kenmar? Would Kenmar have tried to kill him instead of befriending him? He didn't like to think either could be true.

"Ispiria wouldn't have been taken," Mirimel said, her voice dripping vitriol. "If Ari hadn't refused to seek the final stone, Ispiria, and Princess Siara, would be safe in Poromont even now."

"We cannot know for certain," Cooro said. His tone was normal but his eyes were on Ari's hand, which was no longer even red.

"I can know," Mirimel said. "The scheming of these people destroyed my village, and now Ispiria has been taken because of them."

"Not because of me." Kiala shook her head. "I am as much a pawn as you. I seek only to keep Suyla from wreaking destruction on Wheylia."

"The Lady will destroy Wheylia?" Ari shook his head. "That makes no sense. She is a Whey, and an Aluien."

"I know what I have seen, and the vision cannot lie." Kiala spoke with assurance. "I saw Suyla conquering Wheylia, and taking your lands. I believe this to be the goal of her youth. The Empty Ones, her death, even being an Aluien, are merely unforeseen obstructions to it."

"Ispiria and Siara being taken is part of the Lady's plan to rule all of Wheylia and Lggothland?" Ari didn't bother to hide his skepticism.

Kiala pressed her lips into a firm line. "I can see you doubt me, so answer me this, what was Suyla before she became an Aluien? What path did she walk?" She looked to each of them in turn.

When she came back to Ari, he shrugged. "She was a general. She fought in the war between your people and the race that used to live in Lggothland, long ago."

"Not just a general. Suyla is the greatest general Wheylia has ever known. She also perpetuated so many evils in her quest to suppress the rebellion of our menfolk and bend those who dwelled in Lggothland to her will that her name has been all but scoured from our histories. Only the highest ranking among us still know it."

Ari frowned, trying to reconcile the Lady with the picture of a general Kiala drew. He'd had the same trouble when listening to Kenmar's tale of the Lady's deeds. Yes, she was mysterious, and dedicated to destroying the Empty Ones, but she had saved Ari's life, more than once. He glanced at Mirimel. The Lady had also left Mirimel to die.

"So she wishes to wage war?" Mirimel said, her tone holding only a hint of question.

Cooro frowned, his expression speculative.

"Aluiens don't make war," Ari said. "Even if what you say is true, they would stop her."

"Have they ever done ought before save reprimand her once the deed is through?"

Ari blinked. He didn't know for sure, but the stories did make it sound like that. As with the sacking of Hawkers and siege of Sorga, the Aluiens seemed to come sweeping in after the destruction was wrought, mending walls but unable to restore lives.

"Let us set the stories and niceties aside, and look only at statements of truth," Kiala said, directing her words at Ari. "There are different kinds of magic, but the kind the Aluiens use, and Wheylian priestesses, is that of the wellspring. Here, in the southern lands, some types of magi may touch the wellspring, as did the race dwelling in Lggothland before your people, but none use solely it, as Aluiens and the Witches of Whey do." She paused. "Now think on this, all beings containing life carry some small spark of the wellspring's power within them."

Ari nodded. He was relatively sure what Kiala said was true, except he knew nothing of the magi of the land they were in. He'd spent so much of his time learning about fighting and war, and Wheylia, Lggothland and the Tybrunn Plains, he hadn't had time to read about the southern lands yet.

"It is also true that, as humans grew in number, those who wielded the magic of the wellspring saw their power diminish, for they could not harness vast amounts of it as they once did. It became divided among the many, the spark for an ever-growing number of lives."

"Which is why the women of Wheylia turned to deeds of great evil," Cooro said. "We are taught as much, in explanation for the curse our women bear. It is in my mind that you, Ari, have been told this, so let Cooro assure you of its truth."

"What you're saying is that, the more people and other living things there are, the less power Wheylian sorceresses wield?" Mirimel asked, frowning.

"Not only Wheylian sorceresses," Kiala said. "All who use the magic of the wellspring."

"I don't understand," Ari said, his mind shying away from the implications of her words.

"Suyla wishes to eliminate her enemies, yes, but she also loves to make war. The Khan Dar knew this when he took her in. It seems to me he does not mind it. He is willing to permit her to visit vast swaths of death now and again, to cull the herd, as it were," Kiala said. "I am convinced this is what the Khan Dar hoped for when he chose her. What other skills has she but plotting and death? Each time thousands of humans die, the wellspring is reconsolidated and the power of the Aluiens renewed."

"Aluiens aren't like that," Ari protested. "They're scholarly and kind."

"Are they? How many of them do you know well? What balance of them are kind?"

"Maybe she has a point, Ari," Mirimel said.

"She doesn't. You know Larke. Can you see him waging war?" Even as he said it, Ari realized the other Aluien he knew well, Sir Cadwel, was indeed warlike. Mirimel and Cooro didn't know his mentor was no longer human, though. He wondered if Kiala did.

Mirimel shook her head. "Larke would not wage war, no, but he's constantly at odds with them over their ways. Not to mention, he lived in a time of great war and rode with Sir Cadwel's army, encouraging them with ballads of valorous deeds of arms. To one who didn't know him well, he would seem to love war, wouldn't he? And who else do we know? The Lady." The look on Mirimel's face when she said Lady spoke plainly enough that she believed the tale Kiala told.

"But the wellspring is used most by our people, my lady," Cooro said, watching Kiala intently. "You cannot be saying that one of our own generals would turn on us?"

"Suyla is responsible for the deaths of thousands of our people." Kiala's dark eyes were as flat as her tone. "She's never balked from our deaths before."

Ari rubbed at his forehead, his skull aching. "You're trying to convince us that the Khan Dar chose the Lady, and permits her feud with Kenmar, because it pleases him each time she, or he, kills hundreds of people?"

"Could he not have stopped their fight long ere now if he wished? Could not the might of the Khan Dar have slain every Empty One, preventing the death visited on the people of Sorga? Was restoring your walls and town only to keep their secret, or to assuage their guilt?"

Ari stared at her, unsure what to think.

Kiala shrugged. "I do not know your path, Thrice Born. I cannot see what you must do to ensure Wheylia's safety. I can only see we still walk it, and I will do all in my power to keep us following it."

Ari frowned. Lady Kiala had a hard look to her. It wasn't just the seriousness in her brown eyes. She had the same air of

218

ability that marked Mirimel. That assurance that spoke loudly of not needing anyone. Whereas Mirimel wielded that trait, using it to keep others as far from her as possible, Lady Kiala bore it almost carelessly. Her self-reliance was so well worn as to be taken for granted.

"No," Ari said.

She frowned. "No?"

"I don't believe you. I have listened to the Lady. I have listened to Kenmar. Now, I've listened to you." He shook his head. "I don't believe the world is that evil. I won't. I can make myself see the battle between Kenmar and the Lady. I can understand that Ispiria and Siara have become involved as a plot to influence me. I refuse, though, to believe that the Aluiens are willfully permitting the death and destruction of mankind."

Kiala shrugged. "I doubt they wish it to be all mankind. I'm sure eradicating my people would be enough for them."

Ari shook his head again, more vigorously. He'd had enough of stories, histories and talk of strange magic. "All I need to know is if you are sure about where Ispiria and Siara are and if you can guide us there."

"I am sure, and I can," Kiala said, nodding.

"I believe her," Mirimel said, folding her arms across her chest.

"Of course you do." Ari didn't try to keep annoyance from his tone. "Her tale paints a whole race as evil, or at best opportunistic, and you like to believe the worst of everyone."

"That's not true." Mirimel's tone was surprisingly soft. "I don't like to. I find I usually must. What do you think, Whey?" she asked Cooro.

"I think the princess speaks the truth," he said, agony in his voice. "It pains me to say as much, but our people have

219

visited much evil on themselves in the past. It is easy to see them doing so again. We are a broken race. War is ingrained deeply in us."

Cooro's words brought to Ari's mind the war games the Wheys had put on display for him during his time in their land. He also recalled his first impression of their city. The design had obviously been created with war in mind, and been startling in its inherent practicality and cold-heartedness. He rubbed his forehead again, wondering if he was wrong not to try to see the worst of things. Perhaps it would be better to be prepared for the worst, instead of being surprised by it.

"I do not ask you to believe me, Lord Aridian." Kiala's voice broke into Ari's thoughts. "Whatever this thing was that needed to come to pass to give us the chance to stave off the destruction of Wheylia, it has happened. We walk the only path that offers a hope for peace. At least, I greatly hope that we do, for that is the last my vision showed me before I met you outside the water baron's conclave. By mingling myself into your fate, I have hidden the future from my sight. I am now a part of your story. I walk by your side, outside the realm of certainty."

"What if I refuse your help and set off for K'Orge without you?" Ari asked.

"Then you refuse Cooro as well," Cooro said. "A paltry payment for my loyalty."

"I thought I told you to stay out of my battles?" Kiala said to Cooro, her tone less than patient. "Lord Aridian will not decline my help." She turned back to Ari. "There's no reason not to take the aid I offer. I have provisions, and transport. I am familiar with the route to K'Orge. Even if you don't believe me, you must at least acknowledge that I have every reason to wish for your success."

"Success at what, exactly?" Ari asked, narrowing his eyes.

"At killing Suyla. Was that not clear?"

He blinked once. "I won't do that."

Her look of unconcern was grating. "We shall see what you will and will not do once we reach K'Orge." Her dark eyes were steady on his. "You can, of course, cross the desert without me, or secure another guide. I will simply meet you there." Cooro opened his mouth, but she held up a hand, stopping him from speaking.

"I trust her to get us there, for she has her own reason to do so," Mirimel said.

"Do you trust that K'Orge is where they are?" Ari asked.

Mirimel nodded. "The note said the most sacred temple of the Overgod. Quinless and Kanja believe it to be K'Orge. The books you read, though read through Kiala's magic and therefore suspect, seem to confirm that. Cooro and I spoke to a man who met them on the south road. All things point south, where K'Orge lies." Mirimel placed her palms on the table, spreading her hands wide. "Besides, we don't have any better ideas."

Ari looked to Cooro, receiving the nod of affirmation he expected. It was Ari's turn to shrug. "To K'Orge we go, then, so long as everyone is comfortable with my skepticism, and my lack of agreement to kill anyone when I get there."

Mirimel's lips turned downward. "Someone took Ispiria, Ari. When we find her, someone will die for it."

Ari considered that for a moment. "True enough, but promise me you'll give me time to figure out who before you start killing people."

Mirimel shrugged.

Ari knew better than to press her for an answer. He pushed back his plate. "I guess I'll do as suggested and try to rest until we leave."

Kiala tipped the last of her tea into her mouth. "A good plan. We reconvene an hour before sunset." Standing, which caused Cooro to leap to his feet and bow, she headed toward the door.

Ari watched as Princess Kiala of Wheylia left. His worries stayed in the room with him.

Chapter 19

The desert night was cool and moonless, but brilliant with stars. Though Ari's first impression had been a world devoid of life, the sands shifted and moved around them, various small creatures going about the timeless pursuits of their lives. As they rode, Ari's keen eyes picked out lizards, rodents, insects and even small owls which seemed to nest in burrows in the ground.

He soon learned camels could travel greater distances without rest than horses could. Because he and Mirimel rode tireless Questri, this permitted a better pace than Ari had expected. Odd looking though they were, the camels were able to carry a large quantity of supplies, including water for themselves, the humans, Mirimel's hawk and the Questri. They were also quite calm, the three pack camels walking in a peaceful line behind the one Kiala rode.

Most surprising, however, was that they could kneel. Ari supposed Stew could too, if he really wanted to, but it seemed a much less natural thing to ask a horse to do. The camels would kneel on command, making it easier to pack and unpack things they carried, and to mount and dismount.

They took several breaks during the night's ride, to rest themselves and their mounts, but Kiala didn't call a halt until the sun was low in the sky the following morning. Ari could admit he was tired, but did his part setting up tents. Cooro, who'd been made to learn the difference between riding a camel and a horse first-hand, looked even more tired than Ari felt, lacking his usual vigor. Mirimel and Kiala both seemed virtually unaffected, though Ari suspected stubbornness was the heart of that in Mirimel's case. Kiala, he thought, was likely accustomed to the hours they kept.

After setting up his tent, Ari joined Cooro in erecting a tarp to shade the camels and Questri. Mirimel's hawk, who'd slept in front of her saddle most of the night, took to the sky, circling high above. Kiala and Mirimel watered the mounts before coming over to Ari and Cooro.

"Drink it all," Kiala commanded, handing Cooro a copper cup. She looked at Ari, who accepted the cup Mirimel held out to him. "You too. Thrice Born or not, the desert will leech the life from you if you don't take care."

Ari gulped down the warm metallic-tasting water, handing the cup back to Mirimel. "Thank you."

"There's dried fruit and nuts in a pack on one of the camels," she said, nodding toward where they stood passively. "You should be pleased, since that's about all you eat anyhow."

Ari could guess which camel, as Kiala was leading Cooro over to one, giving him much the same information. He caught Mirimel's arm when she would have followed. "You studied Sir Cadwel's maps."

She cocked her head to the side, nodding.

"And you know your stars, though we're farther south than I've ever seen them from."

She nodded again.

"Do you think we're headed toward K'Orge?" he asked in a low voice. "There is a road going southeast, after all, but we veered from it almost immediately."

Mirimel pressed her lips into a firm line. She glanced upward, though to seek the sun or her hawk, Ari didn't know. "We're headed almost due south, as I'm sure you can tell. K'Orge should be to the south and east." She shrugged. "I don't know the best route. We've a desert and mountains to cross. It could be there are few passes, though I should think the road would take us to one. It seems a bit odd not to follow it."

Ari nodded. He'd been thinking much the same thing. "You'll keep an eye on our path?"

She raised her eyebrows. "Would you expect otherwise?"

Ari couldn't help but smile. "Not really."

Mirimel gave him an answering smile before turning back to the others. "My hawk will watch while we sleep," she said, raising her voice.

Kiala looked upward, squinting. "We should likely post a guard as well."

Mirimel shrugged. "You guard if you like. I trust my hawk." Pivoting away from the camels, she headed toward one of the low tents they'd set out.

"Don't close up your tent for long, front or back," Kiala called after her. "It will be too hot inside and few creatures dare the sun to trouble you."

Mirimel made no response, though it was impossible she couldn't have heard. Ari wondered if he should have held his tongue. He'd likely encouraged her mistrust in Kiala by asking about their direction.

Shrugging, for words could never be unspoken, he walked over to Kiala and Cooro, joining them. They stood quietly, chewing on nuts and dried fruit. Ari helped himself to both. He was particularly fond of the figs, something they didn't have in Lggothland.

After a short while, Cooro stretched, wincing. "Cooro shall take advantage of the hawk and stretch out his bones. The camel, it bounces."

"You both feel safe being guarded only by a raptor?" Kiala asked, looking between them.

"If Mirimel says the hawk will watch, she will watch, my lady," Cooro said.

Ari nodded his agreement. He'd couldn't help but notice that, since learning of his fate, Cooro had stopped calling Mirimel silly things like most beautiful one and begun referring to her by name. Ari hoped that meant the peril of unhappiness Quinless had warned against was ended.

Kiala shrugged. "We aren't in a dangerous region. In truth, we're unlikely to be stumbled upon by anyone. I suppose I must become accustomed to taking the word of others again. I will agree that we shall all rest."

"She is a Sorga Hawk," Ari pointed out. It wasn't as if Mirimel was suggesting they put their safety in the care of a random bird, but rather a creature who was as intelligent as any human.

Cooro dusted his hands off on his trousers, then bowed. "Ari, my lady, Cooro bids you good rest."

Ari returned his bow with a nod, reaching for another fig. Kiala squinted up at the sky. Reassured by her trust in Mirimel's hawk, Ari decided to take the direct approach to assuage his fears about their course. "What route do we travel? As far as I can judge, we've headed due south. We left the road shortly after setting out."

Kiala lowered her gaze to him, nodding, her slightly amused expression suggesting she read his unease. "Our aim is to spend as little time in the desert as possible. It's not so bad here as it is deeper south, but it's not a forgiving place. We will enter the mountains, where the air is cooler and there is more water and greenery to be found, and wend our way through them to the coast."

Ari conjured up an image of the southlands in his mind, as seen on Sir Cadwel's maps. "Won't that take longer?"

"A bit, but the dangers are much less."

"How dangerous is the more direct route?" In his mind, he could picture Ispiria and Siara locked away somewhere, waiting for him. Each day he didn't appear, would they grow more forlorn? They must know he was coming for them. It was impossible to think otherwise.

Kiala grimaced, looking tired for the first time. "I'd hoped to avoid this discussion for several days, in view of your skepticism of the truths I shared." Her voice was low, her eyes straying to the tents.

Ari tried to tamp down the anger that surged in him. "So we aren't going to Ispiria and Siara as quickly as possible?"

She shook her head. "No, we are not. For the reason I said, but another as well."

"And that is?" he pressed when she broke off, regarding him with worried eyes.

"We must stop somewhere first."

"Where could we possibly need to go? You realize my fiancée and your niece are being held captive, and I must save them, and as quickly as possible." He didn't add, unsure if

Kiala's magic would have revealed it to her, that Siara was with child. Assuming it in his power to prevent it, there was no chance he was going to allow Siara's baby to be born in the Southland. She and Parrentine had suffered enough heartache. They'd already been forced to send their first child away, to be raised as heir to the Wheylian throne.

"Yes, I do realize--"

"You will be able to send Tiana home," Ari broke in, excitement over the idea causing the thought to spill out as it came to him. "If you go back to Wheylia to be queen, and to have a daughter, Siara's baby can return to Lggothland. She and Parrentine can have their daughter back." Ari grabbed Kiala by the shoulders, pulling her into a quick embrace.

He set her back on her feet. She blinked up at him, looking truly startled. Ari cleared his throat, a bit embarrassed by his enthusiasm. He'd spent a year in Wheylia with Siara and Princess Tiana, before traveling to the Tybrunn Plains that past spring. He knew how much Siara loved her daughter, and how much pain it caused her to leave Tiana in Wheylia and return to Lggothland without her.

Kiala smiled. It was a real smile, warm and joyful. "Yes, Princess Tiana can return home. If we come out of this alive, I promise you, Aridian, she will be back in Lggothland with her mother and father before her second birthday."

Ari felt a lightness in himself that hadn't existed since the last time he and Ispiria had been together and happy, not weighed down by the cares of their world. He grinned, having difficulty affecting the level of sternness he felt was required for his next question. "So, where are you secretly leading us and why?"

"The where is as I said, into the mountains as quickly as possible. The why is also as I said." She held up a hand when he opened his mouth to critique that answer. "The additional where is to Aluiens."

That damped Ari's mood, throwing him into confusion. "Yesterday afternoon you said the Aluiens are deliberately permitting the deaths of hundreds so they can hoard the power of the wellspring. Why would you lead us to them?"

"I was speaking then of the Aluiens who remain in their cavernous home in the Wheylian mountain range. We are going to the ones who left. The ones who would not make the Khan Dar's pact."

"The ones who went across the sea because they wouldn't agree to become like Aluiens I know? Why does everyone who won't conform end up across the sea?" That was also where the Whey's once sent any young woman who showed an affinity for magic, during the long-ago time when the practice of magic was forbidden.

"I went across the sea." Kiala's tone was dry.

"My question stands," Ari said.

Kiala's mouth was turned down with annoyance, heightening her resemblance to Siara, but she shrugged. "My people used to send those who didn't or wouldn't conform across the sea because it was an easy way to all but assure their death without having the blood on our hands, or forcing people to agree to actual murder."

"Really?" Ari hadn't expected that answer. "I always thought the girls who were sent away ended up living in the southern lands."

She shook her head. "They were placed in small crafts with no shelter and only enough food and water for a day. It was tantamount to a death sentence."

"Weren't they hardly more than children?" he asked, struggling to rearrange his thoughts.

"Wheylian women usually manifest the gift of magic before the age of fifteen. Sometimes as young as eleven or twelve."

"But that's cruel."

"We have a history of harshness in Wheylia." She regarded him with calm, dark eyes. "How is it you are so resistant to accepting this?"

Ari didn't have an answer to that. All he knew was he didn't want to go through life like Mirimel or Sir Cadwel. He wanted to be more like Larke and Cooro. They seemed happier. "Alright, then. Why are we going to see these Aluiens?"

"Because, no matter what you plan right now, or how you feel about it, I think you need the final stone set into the sword," Kiala said, watching him intently.

Ari recalled how the other two had been affixed to the hilt. The Lady had used a drop of the Orlenia flowing through her veins to set one, and Larke had done the same for the second. "Wheys use Orlenia. Can't you gather enough to set the stone?" He made a grasping sort of gesture as he spoke, the hunger to touch the raw power of the wellspring clawing at the edges of his mind.

She shook her head again. "I can't do it. I work with runes because I can't call enough raw Orlenia to myself to work enchantments with it alone. It takes a drop of pure magic to set each stone. If I killed someone, or perhaps several animals, I could attempt to gather the sparks of life before they escape back into the wellspring, but short of that I don't have a means." Her eyes strayed to the camels.

Ari turned to look at the shaggy humped creatures as well. "Ah, no, that's not necessary. We can go to the Aluiens." Even if Ispiria and Siara were waiting for him to rescue them, he couldn't justify murdering people, or animals, to save time. "It isn't far out of our way, I gather?"

"No. Not far at all. Some might argue it the better route to travel, though it will take a few days more."

"Good. I'll tell Mirimel and Cooro about the detour before we set out tonight."

"So you are resolved to complete the sword?" Kiala asked.

Ari drew in a long breath. "Yes. I am. It would be foolish not to. Between the Lady, Kenmar and you, someone is lying. I don't want to kill anyone, but if it comes to trying to do so, I want to make sure I win." He looked down at her, a harsh weight settling on him. "Nothing is going to stop me from bringing Ispiria and Siara home."

Chapter 20

To Ari's surprise, Mirimel didn't protest the delay. She instead showed a slightly disturbing enthusiasm for completing the sword. She wanted Ari to be capable of killing Kenmar, the Lady, and anyone else she decided needed to die.

Their trek across the desert landscape remained uneventful, though Ari found it strangely tiring. He felt weighed down by his worries, wondering if going to the Aluiens was a mistake. Traveling at night didn't help, for the night world was washed out and bleak after each day's vivid sunset. Fortunately, it wasn't long before mountain peaks began to rise from the desert, and Ari's spirits with them.

The land became hillier and dotted with shrubs, and the air cooler and more fragrant, less filled with dust. To Ari's relief, they started to travel in daylight. As the range loomed near, Kiala didn't lead them upward, but rather entered a series of valleys, each with steeper sides than the previous. At first, Ari was worried the camels, so steady on sand, wouldn't fare well, but they soon proved just as surefooted on rocky valley floors. The remains of old campfires bespoke of a known pass, but they had yet to meet any other travelers.

On their tenth day in the mountains, nearly through the range by Ari's estimation, Kiala brought them to a halt well before when they usually broke for their midday meal. She'd shed her black robes and headdress when they left the desert and now wore loose fitting sand-colored breaches tucked into tall boots. These she topped with a white tunic of some sort of light, billowing fabric and a leather vest. The wide belt encircling her waist secured both a knife and a slender curved sword.

From where he rode behind her, Ari could see nothing of her expression, only her black hair, which fell in a single braid. Looking back as Stew halted, he took in the appreciative expression that had lingered on Cooro's face ever since Kiala's change of attire. For her part, Mirimel was peering upward at the ribbon of blue sky high above the steep canyon walls. Ari knew her hawk was above, though he couldn't see her.

Kiala turned in her saddle, her profile coming into view. "We're nearly to the village of the Aluiens."

"Can we expect a reasonable welcome?" Ari asked, recalling how difficult it had been to convince the Aluiens in the Wheylian mountains to even speak to him, let alone permit Ari and his companions into their lair.

"Of course. All else aside, I am known to them."

Ari nodded and she set out again, leading the way forward.

The valley walls continued to converge on the trail, playing on Ari's nerves in spite of Kiala's assurance. At the narrowest point, one of the camels had to be pushed through, scraping the sides of the packs he bore. Ari succumbed many times to the urge to glance upward. It was too perfect a location for an ambush for him to feel safe.

The trail opened up after that, though, and two more twists brought them into a verdant valley. Water trickled down the mountainside in chattering rivulets, converging to form multiple small streams that crisscrossed the valley floor seemingly at random. The steepness went out of the slopes, their gentler sides permitting intervals of green, leaving the walls dotted with small trees and festooned with trailing vines.

Though the mountains were a luxury of temperateness and life after the desert, the valley they entered put the rocky gorges behind them to shame. It was the most lushly alive place Ari had ever visited. Birds moved from tree to tree in chattering acrobatic masses. Scruffy, truncated deer peered at them from the shade of mountain ash, chewing placidly. Ari could feel their calm, as if man had never visited pain or fear on them in all their days.

Looking up the path, Ari realized there were buildings worked into the flora before them, and bridges spanning the streams. He blinked several times, for the structures were so perfectly blended by material and color as to be almost one with the trees, rocks and shrubs. It was only a slight elevation in orderliness, rocks piled more neatly or a wall made plumb, that gave away their roles as dwellings and shops. Here and there, a garden could be seen, though they were more unruly than any gardens Ari had known.

Kiala looked back again, grinning. "The valley of the Aluiens."

Ari let Stew follow her down the path, stunned into silence. He'd assumed they were headed to a cave entrance. He couldn't quite wrap his mind about the idea of Aluiens living in a valley, in the open, under the sky. It was green, alive, and exposed for all to see. It bore no resemblance to the secret, hidden caverns of the Aluiens he knew. Their lair, while beautiful with its runes of light and deep sparkling veins of quartz, was cold, hard and aloof when juxtaposed against where he found himself now.

He twisted, peering back the way they'd come, seeking some sign they'd passed through a magical veil. There must, he thought, be an illusion to keep people out, and Kiala had circumvented it. He reached inside his tunic, touching the amulet the Lady had given him, realizing he was so accustomed to wearing it, he hardly noticed its presence anymore. It was the same temperature as his skin, giving no indication magic had been used.

Urging Stew forward, Ari came abreast Kiala. She sat higher than him on her camel, but Stew was a large horse and Ari was much taller than the diminutive Wheylian princess, bringing them nearly to eye level. "Aluiens live here?"

She nodded, her expression amused. "Not what you expected."

"How do they keep people out? Was it back where the camel got stuck?" he asked, realizing that would have been the best place for a magical blockade.

"Was what back where the camel nearly got stuck?" She cast him a questioning look.

"The illusion, or whatever they use to keep people from finding them," Ari clarified.

"They don't do anything to keep people from finding them. How would we trade with them, then?"

Ari let Stew fall back as they approached the first of the many bridges he could see, for they were too narrow for two. His mind worked over her statement as first Kiala and then he and Stew crossed. The bridge was stone, piled so carefully as to meld seamlessly with the road, an arched opening permitting the clear water below to pass unhindered. Up close, he could see each rock was bedecked in thick moss, giving the bridge an ancient, fuzzy appearance.

The Aluiens Ari knew kept a strict policy of isolation. They maintained that knowing humans would lead to helping them, which in turn would make man rely on their help. This, they felt, would someday result in man's distrust and eventual disdain. When Ari heard the argument, years ago, he'd accepted it. Now, colored by Kiala's theory about the Khan Dar's desire for man to suffer times of mass death, Ari wondered if the Aluiens' isolation had a more dire root.

What if, instead of remaining aloof to protect mankind from disaster, the Khan Dar did it to remove his followers from caring for man? New Aluiens were required to give up all contact with those from their former life. They had to remain in the Aluien cave for years, keeping themselves apart while those they once loved grew old and died. The only exceptions Ari knew of were Sir Cadwel, who had all but tricked the Aluiens into waving the rule for him, and Larke. Larke's disobedience to the rules had been at the Lady's command and had, ultimately, proven him still too attached to humans, something he'd been punished for.

Mirimel rode up beside Ari on the black mare, pulling his thoughts back to the present. Her hawk was perched on the pommel of the mare's saddle, though Ari hadn't heard Mirimel call her in. She appeared unusually at ease as she rode, a slight smile on her face.

Mirimel fit in the valley, Ari realized. With her green and brown hawk guardian garb, she blended into the world around them as naturally as the moss covered stones. It was more than that, though. There was an ease to her as she rode. He could all but see her ears twitching, taking in the sounds of animals, birds and insects. Her blue eyes had a soft look to them, as if she gazed on a beloved friend. Only her hair stood out, the bright orange like a spring flower or the first leaves of what should prove to be an exuberant autumn display.

He suppressed a sigh, turning his gaze ahead. Had Ispiria been brought this way? Had she seen this place and all its beauty? In his travels, Ari had seen sights he would love to show her, but none so much as this. She would be radiant, like Mirimel was. He could all but picture her in her favorite green gown, walking the valley floor, trying to tempt the odd, dappled little deer to eat from her palm. When would they have a life like that, rather than one of constant turmoil?

"How can you look so sad here?" Mirimel asked. Her eyes were slightly awed, reflecting the verdant world around them.

He shook his head, not wanting to rob Mirimel of a rare moment of happiness. "I'm not sad. I'm confused. This is nothing like the home of the Aluiens in Wheylia."

"Larke said it's a cave."

She stated it, but Ari sensed the question. Mirimel had never seen the rune-lit caverns Larke had called home for nearly half his life. "It's a secret place. It's beautiful, but not like this. It's like the difference between the queen when she's in state and when she smiles." Parrentine's mother had a countenance a sculptor would weep over, and was terribly imposing for it, until she smiled and brought marble to life.

"I've never met our queen," Mirimel said, shrugging. "I wonder if these Aluiens will be smiling to see us."

With that, in spite of Ari's efforts, the glimmer went out of Mirimel's eyes. Her gaze no longer reflected the glory of the valley around them. Leeriness and mistrust shown out in its place. She nodded to her hawk, sending the little brown raptor spiraling upward to keep watch.

Ari supposed it was for the best. As alluring as their surroundings were, they had no real idea what they were walking into. "Let me know if she sees anything of note."

Mirimel nodded. "I best remind that Whey to keep his wits about him. He's easily distracted." Reining the black mare in, she dropped back to ride with Cooro.

They crossed several more bridges before reaching what seemed to be the central and largest uninterrupted patch of valley floor. Homes and, to Ari's ongoing surprise, shops, cropped up in small clusters on all of the larger stretches of stream-free land. He could smell wood smoke and cooking, his grumbling stomach reminding him it was near lunch time. This was another oddity, for the Aluiens he was familiar with didn't need to eat. The Orlenia in their veins sustained them.

They passed people as well, many of whom stopped in their tasks to wave, all of whom watched Ari and his companions with curiosity. Oddly, he wasn't the focus of their attention, or even Kiala, or Cooro. They seemed most interested in Mirimel. A glance at her dark expression revealed she'd noticed as much. Though Ari couldn't understand the murmur of their lyrical speech, he realized the reason for their interest when he noted more than one of the women reach up to touch her hair.

The people, Aluiens he supposed, in the valley were more than pale. They were white to the point of appearing almost gray. Their skin was nearly devoid of color, their eyes a crystalline white with the barest tint of blue. Their hair, too, was white. The curious and envious looks Mirimel was receiving spoke of the allure her bright locks held.

Indeed, some of the Aluiens had streaks of color in their hair, the reds and purples ranging in levels of brightness like new and faded dye. Here and there, younger ones had their locks completely colored, the berry-tones strikingly unnatural. Of these, many wore their hair short and sticking up, a direct contrast to the flowing locks of their elders.

It was then Ari realized fully how different the people before him were from the Aluiens he knew. Half-remembered words surfaced in his mind. The Aluiens who stayed in Wheylia and partook of the Orlenia, they were nearly immortal, but could bear no offspring. That was the sacrifice they'd made to have Orlenia flow in their very veins in place of mortal blood.

These Aluiens were different. They were a race apart from men, yes, but they were mortal. Their pallor made him unsure they would bleed red if cut, but they wouldn't bleed magic. They would bleed life. They lived, loved, had families and died, just like members of any other race.

The knowledge comforted him. Not only because it meant he could defend himself and his companions from them, but because it made them seem more real. Ari wasn't the best at it, but he could deal with people. They were much more approachable than glowing semi-immortal beings.

About the time he decided this, they came to a halt before the only completely free-standing building Ari had seen so far. The others, built of rock and wood, all seemed half-formed about the bases of large trees or rock outcroppings. Some, he'd noted, definitely had streams flowing in one side and out the other. This building was different.

Made completely of moss covered stone, it stood taller than the rest, alone in a cleared space. It wasn't very imposing. Anywhere else, it would have seemed a slightly larger than normal sized dwelling for a family. It was the largest building in the valley, though, as far as Ari could see. It stood two stories, the vines covering the roof making it impossible to guess its material. It had a large, doorless arched opening and smaller arched windows. Inside, Ari could see a long table surrounded by numerous chairs.

In front of the building was one of the willowy Aluiens. His undyed rough-spun trousers and tunic marked him as no different from the others, many of whom trailed along behind them, but his posture was rigid. He stood framed in the doorway of the stone building, hands clasped before him. Around his neck was a silver chain and from it hung a swirled green stone.

He seemed to be waiting for them, and Kiala rode right up, veering aside when they drew near. She dismounted and wrapped the reins of her camel, the pack camels in a line behind it, around a tree limb, gesturing for Ari, Mirimel and Cooro to do the same. Patting at her hair and straightening her tunic, she crossed the mossy ground toward the waiting Aluien. Ari caught up to her as she bowed, adding his own obeisance. He was aware of Mirimel and Cooro coming up behind them.

The Aluien held out his arms. "Princess Kiala, it is a pleasure to have you among us once more." His words were thickly accented, to the point it took Ari a moment to interpret them.

"Master Castin, as always, the honor is mine," Kiala said. Though her words and demeanor were civil, Ari had spent enough time with her to hear an undertone or worry. She stepped forward and Master Castin placed his hands on her shoulders, kissing her once on each cheek.

Cooro issued a low growl but, surprising though the gesture was, Ari didn't think it anything more than custom.

Kiala stepped back, half turning to Ari. "May I present Lord Aridian, Duke of Sorga? I am sure you've heard of him."

Ari thought that was asking a lot, as Sorga was halfway around the world from where they were. He bowed again, for good measure. It was obvious Master Castin was an important person in the village, if not the leader of these Aluiens. Ari didn't wish to begin his time among them by offending. He was aware many others had gathered in a loose semicircle, watching them.

Master Castin held out his arms. Ari didn't need Kiala's meaningful nod toward the Aluien to tell him he was supposed to step forward. He did, receiving two perfunctory kisses as well. The odor of old parchment reached Ari's nostrils.

"Thrice Born," Master Castin said, dropping his arms as Ari stepped back. "We are both honored and dismayed to have you among us. Of you we have heard, for your footfalls shake the core of this world."

"I am honored to be among you, and dismayed to dismay you," Ari said, after taking a moment to sort out the words. He could all but feel Mirimel and Cooro wince at his clumsy phrasing. He ignored them, hoping the Aluien's dismay was nothing he needed to worry over.

A smile touched Master Castin's pale face. "Please, make your friends known to me."

Ari waved Cooro and Mirimel forward. "This is Hawk Guardian Mirimel, of Sorga."

After she bowed to him, Master Castin bestowed a kiss on each of Mirimel's cheeks, which she endured expressionlessly. "We have heard of the Sorga Hawk, of course, and their close relationship with man." He raised his gaze skyward for a moment. "She says you are a kind friend, though sometimes violent of temper. We beseech you to contain that side of your nature while among us."

Mirimel's shoulders stiffened. "Of course."

Master Castin eyed her thoughtfully. "I think your temper is what causes your hair to grow full of fire."

Mirimel raised her eyebrows, casting Ari a resigned look.

Ari gestured Cooro forward, hoping to head off further discussion of Mirimel's temperament and looks. "And this is Swordmaster Cooro of Wheylia."

Mirimel stepped back to make room, looking relieved.

Master Castin bestowed his odd form of greeting in response to Cooro's bow. "Your highness, we are honored. It is not often we receive both a Princess of Wheylia and her royal consort."

"Ah . . ." Cooro shot Ari a look even more pleading than the one Mirimel had given moments ago.

To Ari's right, Kiala chuckled. "That hasn't come to pass yet, Master." She winked at the Aluien. "You're going to scare him off."

"My deepest apologies. I intend no such discord."

"I'm jesting. We spoke of how humans make light of things, remember?"

Master Castin smiled. "Ah, yes, I remember this thing." His warm expression was fleeting, however, as he looked around at them. "Now, tell me if it is a jest as well, that you have brought these instruments of war to our people? If so, I am afraid you must explain to me how it is amusing, for I see it as nothing of the sort."

Kiala winced. "No, not a jest, I'm afraid."

Ari stepped forward once more. "We've come seeking your help. It is a small matter. We do not intend to disrupt your valley for long."

243

Master Castin turned an unreadable look on Ari. "I see. You are here then to test us, Thrice Born."

Chapter 21

Ari regarded Master Castin for a long moment. His eyes strayed to the Aluien's amulet, noting the way the swirled green stone seemed to writhe, creating an oddly serpent-like impression. It reminded him of how the tangled pattern engraved on his silver amulet sometimes seemed to move before his eyes. "I am not here to test anyone. At least, not to my knowledge."

"You are an instrument of strife. No boon you have come to ask will be acceptable to us." Master Castin's expression remained neutral, but his tone was condemning.

"Master Castin." Kiala stepped forward. "You know I am a friend to your people. I wouldn't bring you a man capable only of strife."

"It may be you would, as one of your jests."

"I told you--"

"She said she does not jest." The voice, belonging to a woman, was even more heavily accented than Master Castin's.

Ari turned to see the crowd parting respectfully, a woman coming through. Though she would have appeared normal among Ari's people, compared to her own she lacked height, making up for it in curves. Her hair was chopped short and died a bright raspberry. She was the first grown Aluien Ari had seen without long white locks.

"Dyne," Kiala greeted, her tone warm.

"Princess Kiala," Dyne said, kissing her on both cheeks.

Releasing Kiala, Dyne turned in a slow circle, words in a language Ari didn't know bubbling off her tongue. Much of the whispering about them ceased. Ari realized the bulk of it must have been translating, for it was obvious the Aluiens didn't speak the language of Lggothland. When Dyne completed her circle, she was facing Master Castin. He frowned at her, an expression she returned.

"Dyne," Kiala said, touching her lightly on the shoulder. "May I present Lord Aridian?"

Dyne turned to him and Ari bowed. When he straightened, she planted kisses on his cheeks, standing on her toes to do so. Unlike Master Castin, Dyne smelled of crisp herbs.

Releasing Ari, Dyne turned back to Kiala. "For a bringer of strife, he is very handsome."

Behind them, Master Castin snapped something in the Aluiens' language.

Kiala shrugged. "I suppose he is, for a Lggothian," she said. Neither woman gave any indication they'd heard Castin. "Though he's terribly young."

Ari raised his eyebrows. Had they forgotten they were speaking one of the few languages he could understand?

"Ah, you like your Wheylian man here, your swordsman prince." Dyne turned her scrutiny on Cooro, who bowed.

"That I do. May I present Swordmaster Cooro, future king of Wheylia?"

Words burst forth from Master Castin, causing Dyne to turn from Cooro without finishing the ritual greeting. "No, it will be decided in council this night," she said, answering him in Lggothian.

"What is to decide? What question they have is meaningless. We shall decline," Master Castin replied in the same tongue. He gestured toward Ari, Cooro and Mirimel. "Look on them."

"I was trying to, but you interrupted."

"They surely seek to increase strife." Castin's eyes lingered on Ari as he spoke.

"Whatever they seek, they will ask before the council. You have become master in my place, but the laws are the same. They will ask. Council will discuss. Only after do you answer." Castin glowered at her, but Dyne appeared wholly unmoved. "You are sowing strife by this arguing. All can see this."

He looked about, taking in the ever-increasing audience. Ari guessed half of the village was there now, watching the exchange. Castin pressed his lips together in a firm line. Turning on his heels, he passed through the doorway behind him, disappearing into the stone building.

Dyne shook her head. "Come, we shall rest in my home. Bring your camels." She turned to Stew and the black mare. "You may go as you like. Our village is open to you, though all frown on the tree at the heart of your lands."

Ari cast Stew a surprised look, which his horse returned. Apparently, Stew was as caught off guard as Ari by Dyne's reference to the Orate Tree, the cruel secret of Stew's homeland.

247

"Come, come," Dyne said, gesturing to Ari and his friends. "The council is long from now. You will want rest."

"A long time from now," Kiala murmured in gentle correction. "And thank you."

Ari and Mirimel divested Stew and the black mare of their tack while Kiala and Cooro gathered the camels. As they followed Dyne, Ari could hear her murmuring the phrase 'a long time from now' under her breath, as if practicing. Again, the crowd parted easily for her, though the Aluiens about them looked on with clear interest. Ari wondered if the easy passage was a sign of respect for Dyne, or the usual behavior of what he was coming to realize were a peaceful people. Glancing back through the tunnel of willowy forms, he glimpsed Stew and the black mare heading down a different trail than the one Dyne led them on.

Her home wasn't far. It seemed to consist of several loosely defined, wall-less spaces with vine covered roofs. There was also at least one closed in area, build over a stream and against a large rock. The area she brought them into contained a cooking station of sorts, shelves of food goods and dishes, and a set of rough wooden chairs and table.

After exchanging formal greetings with Cooro and Mirimel, Dyne showed them where to tie the camels. They were settled quickly, Mirimel's hawk winging down to watch before launching herself skyward once more. Dyne bustled about, heating water from the stream and crushing herbs into earthenware cups. Soon, they were all seated with mugs of a warm fragrant drink and a plate of dried fruit. As there were no figs and he'd had his fill of leathery fruit during their journey, Ari ignored the offering.

"I take it this Castin fellow is going to be a problem?" Mirimel said, making no move toward her cup or the plate. "You didn't expect to find him in charge."

Kiala shook her head. "I did not. Dyne, how is it you are displaced?"

"Displaced?" Dyne's confusion was obvious.

"Why are you no longer council head?"

"Ah. Yes, this is bad for your plans, I see. I offer apologies."

Ari hoped apologies wouldn't really be needed. He'd given up the fastest route to Ispiria and Siara to come to the Aluiens.

"And I accept your apologies, but how did Castin end up in charge?" Kiala asked.

Beside her, Cooro took a tentative sip of his drink, raising his eyebrows at the taste. Ari wondered if that meant it was good or bad. It smelled good.

"I was made to give up my place." Dyne let out a long sigh. "I was found to have sown strife."

"Dyne," Kiala said, her tone long-suffering. "What did you do this time?"

A surprisingly wicked smile flittered across Dyne's pale face. "I lay with a younger man. His mother had a match she wished for him. He did not want it. We had more fun together than this match would have been."

It was Ari's turn to raise his eyebrows, wondering if he'd heard the thickly accented words correctly. Mirimel looked similarly shocked.

Cooro set his mug aside and leaned forward. "I think Cooro will need to hear of this in great detail in order to understand."

"That won't be necessary," Kiala said as Dyne opened her mouth to speak. Far from angry, the look Kiala gave Cooro was amused. "You'll just have to use your imagination, Swordmaster. I'm sure it's quite vivid." She picked up her drink, taking a sip. When she lowered her mug, her expression was serious. "This is not good for us."

"So you have come to sow strife?" Dyne asked, looking leery for the first time.

"What do you mean, sow strife?" Ari cut in. The way they kept using the word, he felt he was missing some of the meaning behind it.

"We know only peace. It is a difference between us and our once-kin," Dyne said.

Ari shook his head. "The Aluiens in Wheylia are peaceful. They don't kill for meat or wage war."

Kiala gave him a pitying look. "They don't eat meat because the flesh taints the soul. For many of them, doing this is merely a selfish act. Living as long as they do, they cannot afford to take in so much pain and suffering as they would if they consumed once-living creatures the whole of their existence. As is your nature, you ascribe too much good to them."

"I hadn't thought of it that way," Ari admitted. He'd been told of the risk inherent in eating animals, or humans as some Empty Ones did, but it hadn't occurred to him that not eating flesh was simply a means of survival for the Aluiens in the north. "Do you call yourselves Aluiens?"

Kiala reached for some fruit, her distant expression giving Ari the feeling she already knew the answer to his question and had her mind elsewhere.

"We do name ourselves Aluien," Dyne said. "Many also call ourselves Luienalle, what means True Ones in your tongue, for we stay as we were."

"I thought you said the ones who wouldn't join with the Khan Dar were doomed to fade away and die, or some such thing," Mirimel said, looking at Ari.

"That's what the Aluiens told me." Ari was no longer sure how much of what he'd been told was true.

"We are passed down that the Khan Dar made this threat to us," Dyne said. The way she said Khan Dar revealed the True Ones had no great love of the leader of the Aluiens in the north. "Yet we are here. We have babies, when they have none. We have magic less strong, but we have enough to live as we do."

"How do you live?" Mirimel asked. "What do you mean when you say you know only peace?"

Dyne smiled. "I think you would like to know only peace, fire-hair."

Instead of bristling, Mirimel's expression turned wistful. "Tell me what it's like."

"We do not hunt. We do not kill." Dyne turned to Ari. "We do no thing that will add strife into the world. Strife is making the world have more harm, chaos and destruction."

Ari winced, knowing that would be trouble. "How, ah, strict are the True Ones on that?"

"It is our law."

"Right," Ari muttered. "Why do magical beings always feel the need for laws, especially ones that hamper my goals?"

Kiala blinked, her eyes refocusing. "Would you really want magical beings not to have laws? We had that once in Wheylia, during Suyla's time."

"It was not a good time," Cooro added. "Not for any but the witches, begging your pardon, my glorious future queen. Cooro believes they found it a grand way of behaving."

"I see your point," Ari assured them, before either Whey could elaborate, and he did. It wasn't that he wanted powerful beings to behave with unfettered avarice. He'd simply hoped for an easy path, for once. "The council will meet this evening?"

"Yes. At the building where Castin was waiting for you," Dyne said.

"What time?"

"When the sun no longer shines down into the valley. You will know it. A bell will ring."

Ari nodded. He leaned back in his chair, feeling the strain of inactivity. While they were sitting in this pleasant valley, waiting for the sun to cross the sky, Ispiria and Siara were imprisoned somewhere, hoping he would appear.

Kiala looked at the half-eaten dried fruit in her hand. She turned and tossed it toward the camels. "Well, if we have to stay here, how about some real food, Dyne? We've had nothing but dried fruit and nut-meat for days. I'll trade you some figs for whatever you're cooking, if Lord Aridian hasn't eaten them all."

Dyne's pale eyes brightened. "I have a stew. You fetch your figs. We shall have a nice meal, and you shall show me what others you have to trade with me. Tonight, you will speak at the council, to Castin."

Chapter 22

More in depth exploration of the True Ones' valley revealed it to be every bit as beautiful as their first look promised. There were trickling waterfalls, which Dyne explained gurgled year round, for the snow on the mountaintops melted where it touched the warmer air of the valley nestled among the foot of the peaks. These waterfalls, as Ari noted when they rode in, created a myriad of brooks and streams, dividing the valley floor hundreds of times over.

Ari didn't really know what to call the land between the streams. The word island seemed too monumental to apply to them, for the water surrounding most was something he could jump across, or even step over. No true separation was created, only delineation. After several hours of exploring the valley, Cooro and Kiala returned with Dyne to her abode. Ari and Mirimel walked on, more interested in exploring than rest.

They took in island after island, of all shapes and sizes. The largest continuous land seemed to be the area where the council building stood and most of the businesses were clustered. The smallest he and Mirimel found wasn't large enough for Ari to lay on without head or toes in the water. Not that he could test that, for on it stood a single oak tree, cloaked in nearly as much moss as bark.

The tree's massive roots all but engulfed the small parcel of earth on which it stood, winding their way through the surrounding streams. Gnarled as they were, the massive appendages could be used as bridges to reach the trunk, though there was nowhere to stand save on the tree. Small creatures scurried here and there and birds came and went, revealing that the oak teamed with life.

Ari stood for a long while in the waning afternoon light, taking in the tree that was a whole world to so many living things. Mirimel was silent beside him. Her hawk winged down, alighting on one of the top branches. Even that didn't seem to strike fear into the creatures scurrying below. It was obvious they truly didn't know strife.

Mirimel let out a long sigh.

"We'll be on our way soon, to find them," Ari said, to reassure her.

She shook her head. "For once, that wasn't what I was thinking about."

Ari lifted his gaze to Mirimel's hawk, who was preening herself. "She won't eat any of them, will she?" He gestured to the tree, and those living in it. "I have the feeling it would be frowned upon." It also didn't seem fair. The creatures in the tree had no idea of the danger the hawk posed.

"No, she won't. She appreciates this place."

Ari nodded, relieved.

"It would be nice to live this way, wouldn't it?" Mirimel's tone was wistful.

"You could. When all of this is over, you can live any way you like."

She turned a frown on him. "No, I can't. This is . . . wonderful. It's pleasing to know this valley exists, but I couldn't live this way."

"You don't have to be so angry. You don't have to find reasons to fight." He put as much conviction into his words as he could muster. He would be happy to see Mirimel give up the burdens of anger and sorrow she carried.

"I'm not looking for reasons to fight. You don't have to look. They're all around us. How could I live here, or like this, knowing there are things out there like the Orate Tree, or Empty Ones, or even the people who would beat and rob Mattah for not belonging to one race?"

Ari winced, for her tone was strident. "Don't you think it sort of evens out? Yes, those things are out there, but this valley is here. There's balance."

"Ask Mattah if it evens out for him."

"Why do you always draw me into these arguments?" Ari knew he sounded plaintive, perhaps even beseeching, but he truly wanted to know. Mirimel was capable of being pleasant. Why did she always turn their talks into censures on his character?

To Ari's surprise, she smiled. "You're a great man, Ari, even if you don't quite know it. You're also a very important man. You are duke of the largest dukedom in Lggothland and the justice of our king. I just want to make sure your head is on right, that's all."

"My head would be a sight better if you wouldn't constantly make it hurt."

"Not to mention," she continued over his words. "You are going to marry my little cousin. I won't let that happen if you don't intend to be the best of men."

Ari suppressed the urge to tell her she couldn't stop him from marrying Ispiria if she tired. Saying it would make him sound childish, and Mirimel would take it as a challenge. "You know I place Ispiria's happiness above all else."

"No, I don't know that. Nor, I think, can you, for you are a servant to the king." She leveled a contemplative look on him. "I think you will do your best, though, and I was pleased with the prince when I met him. He will be a good king. I do not see you being asked to do terrible things, or kept always far from Sorga, and Ispiria, waging wars for him." She nodded, as if satisfied with her assessment of Ari's future. "You've taken the most telling step, coming here to have the final stone set into the sword. Now let's just hope they'll agree to do it."

"That's the most telling step?" He rather thought his quest to rescue Ispiria the most important step. He worried taking time away from it to enter the valley they stood in was an error.

"Yes. Arming yourself properly means you can do what is called for. Leaving the sword unfinished would be a coward's way out of difficult decisions."

Ari's lips twitched as he suppressed a smile. "Now you're a seer, too?"

"Not by means of magic, but I am someone who can see the truth in things, uncolored by your tendency to ascribe goodness. Either the Lady or Kenmar is a liar, or both. Someone is going to have to die before this is through."

All inclination to smile fled Ari. "I hope it won't come to that."

"Do you know what? I hope the same. I really do."

In the distance, a bell rang out, three clear bright notes echoing through the valley. Ari looked about, realizing most of the creatures had stilled, settling for the evening as those of the night woke. It must have grown dark while he and Mirimel spoke. His Aluien-enhanced sight often caused him not to notice the transition from day to night. If he wasn't paying close enough attention, he wouldn't realize the sun was low until all light was gone, robbing even his sight of the ability to see color. "We should go back."

Mirimel nodded. She walked forward, though, toward the tree. Kneeling, she placed a hand on one of its massive roots, murmuring something too low for Ari to hear.

"Talking to trees?" he asked, keeping his tone light. Mirimel was quick to take offense.

"Just wishing it, and this valley, well." She stood, dusting her hands on her breeches. Her hawk left the branches above, angling toward the center of the valley.

Ari looked about as they headed back, a wave of melancholy overtaking him. "I suppose this will be another place we never see again."

"Another?"

"Like the Tybrunn Plains. What could possibly ever call us back there?"

"Speak for yourself. When this is over, I'm returning to those plains. I have unfinished business with the Orate Tree."

Ari didn't want to know what that meant. He supposed it was fortunate Lggothians didn't realize they dwelled beside another sentient race. If Lggothland had diplomatic relations with the Questri, Ari would probably be called on to stop whatever it was Mirimel was planning. Knowing her, whatever it was, it was sure to qualify as an act of war.

As night fell more fully, lights began to glimmer in the treetops and on rooftops, and along the streams and bridges. In spite of how anxious he was to receive an answer to his request, Ari's steps slowed as he gazed about in wonder. He couldn't tell if it was magic, or some form of nature he'd never encountered before. It reminded him of the Aluien caves, but while their light was organized into carefully drawn runes, these lights twinkled, scattered and moved, floating in the air about them.

As they neared the larger central building, Ari saw Cooro, Kiala and Dyne waiting for them in the gathered crowd. Ari didn't know if a crowd was normal, but suspected it wasn't. Castin stood before the open doorway, looking peevish. Ari caught sight of Stew and the black mare, standing outside the semicircle of True Ones, their gazes alert.

Ari could make out Mirimel's hawk perched on the roof of the stone building. As he watched, she darted her beak toward one of the lights, which flittered away. Mirimel cast a sharp glance upward. The hawk ruffled her feathers and settled down.

"They're fireflies," Mirimel whispered as they walked through the quickly parting crowd.

"Fireflies?" Ari looked about in disbelief. "But there are so many. Everywhere."

Mirimel shrugged.

"You are slow, Thrice Born," Castin said, his tone as annoyed as his expression suggested. "We have delayed starting our council for your question. We know you will ask something of strife, and wish to make an answer for you and send you on your way so we may discuss our matters of peace."

This brought a murmur from the crowd, though if they agreed or disagreed, Ari couldn't tell. Aside from a hiss of annoyance from Dyne's direction, the bubbling speech of the True Ones was indecipherable to him.

Ari bowed, hoping it hid the annoyance he was working to remove from his face. "I beg your pardon for our slowness. We were entranced with your valley and lost track of time."

Castin watched him through narrowed eyes, making Ari worry he'd somehow given offense. After a long moment, Castin whirled away, turning to stomp into the building. "Of his people, only the Thrice Born may enter," he said over his shoulder before disappearing into the darkness within.

"What about of my people?" Kiala called, appearing at Ari's side with Cooro and Dyne.

No answer came. The crowd rustled and other True Ones came forward to enter the building. They cast Ari worried glances as they passed. He didn't know if they were concerned for him, or for themselves. As they crossed under the opening in the wall, each was swallowed by the lack of light within.

Dyne touched Ari's arm. "You go in now."

"I'm going too," Kiala said.

Dyne caught the princess's arm as she started forward. "He called the Thrice Born only. Do not begin in strife."

Kiala pressed her mouth into a firm line, but nodded. Beside her, Cooro peered toward the dark opening in the building, looking worried.

"Why can't I see inside there?" Mirimel asked, on Ari's other side. "When someone steps inside, it's like they're swallowed by darkness."

Ari didn't need to look to know Mirimel had a hand on her knife hilt. If anyone was going to sow strife, it would be her. "It's probably just dark in there, compared to out here."

"Can you see inside? Can't you see no matter how dark it is?" she asked.

Ari could see as well in almost no light as he could standing under the noon sun, yet he could see nothing inside the building. He agreed with Mirimel. It was ominous.

"You go in," Dyne said, giving him a light push forward.

Ari looked back at Kiala, trying to gage how well she knew these people. Though she looked worried, she offered a slight nod. Scanning Mirimel's and Cooro's concerned faces, Ari turned back toward the building. It wasn't as if he would give up now. He'd come for their help, and he would ask for it. Squaring his shoulders, he walked through the door.

Inside was light. It wasn't the light of flames or fireflies, but rather runes etched into the stone of the walls and ceiling. Aluien magic Ari recognized. Castin sat at the head of the long table Ari had glimpsed earlier, four other True Ones on each side. There was nothing else in the room. As there was no chair at the end of the table near the door, Ari came to stand there, opposite Castin and his disapproving visage.

"You are slow again," the council head stated.

"And I apologize again. I was unsure about the wall of darkness I had to pass through." Ari still wasn't sure about it.

"The wall?" Castin frowned. One of the other members murmured a word and his face cleared. "Ah, the blinding. This is to keep council matters within until the meeting ends. It is not a wall. Any may pass through, but only do if asked."

"So, it's a spell to make it so no one can see or hear what you're doing?" Ari thought someone could have told him as much. Obviously, they were so accustomed to it, they didn't realize how daunting it was.

"Sometimes, in the council, there is strife. We must contain this, so the valley is not polluted."

Ari nodded, understanding better now. It wasn't just to be secretive. They didn't want the people they presided over to see them argue. It was like how his aunt would always call his uncle into the kitchen when she wanted to voice her displeasure, instead of doing it before the guests or Ari and his cousins.

"You are slow. Ask your question." Castin's tone had found a new level of annoyance.

"Now?" Ari blinked. Usually, councils stood on ceremony.

"Is it not why you have come?"

"Ah, yes, it is." He reached about in his mind, gathering his thoughts. "It's a small thing. I was hoping you could use Orlenia to set a stone I have." He decided it was best to ease into the idea of the stone being added to a sword.

Several of the council members murmured in their bubbling tongue. Many looked relieved, giving Ari hope. It wasn't such a great thing to ask, after all.

Castin held up a hand. "What stone?"

Ari retrieved the pouch from inside his tunic. "This one. I can show it to you if you like?" Castin nodded, so Ari dumped the stone into his palm, then held it up for them to see.

That created a stir among the council members. Pale eyes went wide. Several gasps could be heard. One of the male True Ones made a sign before himself, as if to ward off the stone.

"That stone was lost outside of magic," Castin said.

"Yes. Princess Kiala found it. She said I need it to prevent great strife in Wheylia," he added, hoping that might sway them toward his cause.

"Do not think to make tricked of us, Thrice Born," Castin barked. "Such a stone is for the sword, the Witches' sword. What use has a sword save for strife?"

Ari looked about, assessing the faces of the others. Though he couldn't understand their murmured words, he could sense agreement. Many nodded, their eyes still round and worried. Several more made warding signs, drawing them in the

261

air before their chests. If Ari was any judge of tone, soon they would all be in agreement with Castin, though he was the only one who wasn't speaking. Instead, his mouth remained fixed in a thin line, his eyes on Ari.

"This stone is for the sword, Fwellian," he said, breaking into their talk. "But it is not for strife. I am not for strife. I'm sworn to uphold the peace of Lggothland. If I use Fwellian, which I hope not to, I will do so to end strife."

"Creating strife can never end strife," Castin said, coming to his feet. "This is blasphemy to us. Ending strife through violence is an illusion."

The other council members gaped up at him. Castin looked around, breathing hard with anger. Casting Ari a look of blame for his volatile behavior, the council head reseated himself.

Ari tucked the stone away, rearranging his thoughts. "If there is one person, one being, who is planning to visit great evil on the world, wouldn't using the sword on that one being be justified by the strife it would prevent?" Ari asked, though he wasn't sure who that might be. Did he mean the Lady, and he would be preventing her from wreaking havoc on Wheylia, or did he mean he would use it on Lord Kenmar, to broker peace with the Lady? Maybe he would only be called to use the sword on Lord Mrakenson, the single most vile Empty One he'd ever encountered. That eventuality didn't seem bad at all.

Several of the council members were shaking their heads. "You do not understand our ways," one said, her voice thickly accented. "We will not do any form of strife."

Castin gazed down the table at Ari, his expression smug.

"You won't be doing any form of strife. All I ask is for a drop of Orlenia to set the stone. That is an act of creating only."

262

This set off another round of arguing. Ari wished he had some idea what words they spoke. It appeared as if some, at least, agreed with him, or there would be no debate. Voices rose and arms gesticulated. Castin raised his hand. He barked something into the silence that fell. The council members looked about, nodding.

Not looking at Ari, Castin turned to the council member on his right. "Do you wish to set the stone for the Thrice Born?"

"No."

Castin turned to the next member, repeating the question. She said yes, adding a defiant look to her reply. Thus, it went around the table, Castin passing over Ari without looking at him. When the final council member was reached, the tally was four yes and four no.

A slow smile spread across Castin's face as he finally deigned to acknowledge Ari again. "I am the breaker of the tie. I vote no."

Ari let out his breath in a long sigh, searching his mind for anything he'd left unsaid. Should he beseech them on behalf of Ispiria and Siara? Could he truly say he believed the stone must be set to win their freedom? He could tell by their expressions they wouldn't care, but he couldn't give up now.

"I make a new motion now," Castin said, still speaking Lggothian, before Ari could martial a new argument. "I motion we keep the Thrice Born here in our valley for all time, to stop the strife he makes in the world."

Ari narrowed his eyes, dropping a hand to Fwellian's hilt. That, he hadn't expected.

Chapter 23

Though Ari could think of several responses to the suggestion of imprisoning him in the valley of the True Ones, he decided to go with the simplest. "No," he said, his tone firm.

One of the council members who'd voted against him said something in their tongue. Castin nodded. Standing again, he fluttered rapidly moving fingers through the air, more unintelligible words leaving his mouth as runes of Orlenia appeared. Ari frowned, wishing he could capture them. A drop of Orlenia and a few words of magic were all he needed from them. The woman who first voted in his favor began speaking in earnest, but Castin ignored her. Ari braced himself for whatever spell the master of the council was weaving.

"I think you shall stay here as long as we desire, Thrice Born," Castin said, releasing the runes toward Ari.

The amulet he wore grew ice cold against his chest, not that Ari needed its warning to know a spell had been cast on him. His arms and legs, even his eyelids, suddenly felt too heavy to move. He stood up straighter, shrugging the spell off. He had plenty of practice breaking through both Empty One and Aluien magic. Castin's spell was weak compared to those employed by most of Ari's foes. Still, the attempt annoyed him. "Try anything like that again and you won't believe how much strife I will loose," he growled.

Castin wasn't the only True One to gape at him in surprise. The council leader took his seat once more, all but falling into it. The others exchanged fearful looks, even those who had supported him.

Ari leaned forward, planting both hands on the table. "I came here seeking a simple boon, which you have denied. That is your right. Preventing me, or any of my companions, from leaving this valley is not." He looked around the table, taking in how scared they were, and sighed. "You may not choose to believe me, but I do not like war. I have no intention of fighting with or killing anyone if I don't have to. I will do what I must to prevent death and to recover those who were taken from us, but I am not seeking violence."

Silence filled the room once more.

"We offer apologies, Thrice Born," the female council member to Castin's right said. "It is not our way to imprison. Our way is to avoid strife. Some among us take this too far, forgetting that to force a way on another is an act of strife."

Castin looked down at the table, shrinking in on himself a little.

Ari felt the weariness of defeat settle on him. He knew there was no chance the council would side with him now. He was already creating the strife they feared, simply by being there. "May my companions and I rest here tonight, or must we leave now to avoid any trouble, for us or you?" Ari addressed

266

himself to the female council member, as she seemed to be championing him.

"You may stay this night." Her tone was slightly defiant as she looked about the table. "We will attempt no spells on you or your people. You will promise to visit no strife on us?"

"I promise," Ari said. "You have my word of honor as a knight."

Castin made a derogatory sound.

The woman snapped something at him in their tongue before turning back to Ari. "Please leave the council chamber, Lord Aridian. Your question has been answered. We have our questions to speak on now. One will be the choosing of a new master for this council."

Castin's head snapped up, his eyes wide. The woman turned a glare on him, as if daring him to speak. Around the table, the other faces were similarly unsympathetic. Only the man who, as far as Ari could tell, had recommended Castin work the spell, wasn't glaring. Instead, he looked down at the table, his arms pulled in to his sides as if he endeavored to be small enough not to attract notice.

"Thank you," Ari said. He stepped back from the table, bowing.

"Lord Aridian," the woman said before he could turn away. "Ask Dyne to enter here."

Castin's face twisted into a grimace, but he didn't protest.

"I will," Ari said, nodding. Bowing again for good measure, he walked back through the doorway, which framed a muted view of the outside world.

Most of the crowd had already dispersed. Stew and the black mare still stood off to the side, watching. Mirimel, Cooro, Kiala and Dyne were in a loose cluster near the entrance to the council chamber. Six sets of eyes turned on Ari when he walked out, and he imagined he could feel the gaze of Mirimel's hawk as well. He shook his head, watching the hope on their faces fade as he crossed the open space to them.

"They said no?" Mirimel asked.

"They voted no," Ari said. "Four to five."

"Dyne," Kiala groaned.

Dyne cocked her head to one side. "What did you ask of them?"

Ari retrieved the stone from his tunic, pouring it out into his palm. He knew he was supposed to tell Dyne the council wished to see her, but perhaps he could have an answer first. If Dyne would help them, with or without the council's agreement, the stone could still be set. "I asked them to set this stone into the hilt of my sword."

Dyne stared at the stone in his palm, her wide clear eyes sparkling with a myriad of reflected firefly lights. She leaned away from him, shaking her head. "It is a weapon. A thing for killing."

"Will you set it into the sword for me?" Ari asked, though he already sensed her answer in the horror of her expression. "It will help me save my fiancée, and the princess of Lggothland."

She was still shaking her head. "I will not do this thing." She lifted her eyes from the stone to meet Ari's. "And I will not go against the council."

Kiala frowned. "You won't help us?"

Cooro let out a low whistle, taking a half step back as if he feared the hard edge in Kiala's tone.

"What if you were on the council and they took another vote?" Ari asked, clinging to hope. "One vote would turn the outcome."

"No, it would be the same." Dyne's voice was quiet. "I cannot say I would vote yes to this."

Kiala's frown deepened, mirroring the one on Mirimel's face.

"So the council would still be tied," Ari said, his half-formed plan, that Dyne rejoin the council and he ask again, slipping away.

"It is a surprise, this vote. None should vote yes. It is disliking Castin which made them vote as they did," Dyne said. "On the council, only conscience guides me. I would vote no to setting the stone."

Ari rocked back on his heels. "You're saying he actually helped me nearly get a yes?"

Dyne nodded.

"Why didn't you tell me I didn't have a chance?" Ari asked, putting the stone away once more. "We wasted half a day in this valley."

"You did not tell what you would ask, only a boon."

Beside Ari, Mirimel let out a curse. "She's right. We didn't tell her."

Dyne blinked at Mirimel, her brow creased with worry. "You are full of strife, fire-hair."

Cooro chuckled.

"I am." Mirimel glared at Dyne through narrowed blue eyes. "But don't let it worry you. I'm going to take this strife out of your valley as soon as I can and apply it to saving my cousin, and killing anyone who tries to stop me."

Ari caught Kiala's wince, even as Dyne's face grew cold. She turned to Kiala. "I cannot have one such as this in my home. She must sleep elsewhere this night."

"I understand," Kiala said, her voice calm. Skimming past Cooro's surprised expression, she turned to Mirimel. "Will you

269

be well enough on your own?" She cast a quick look back at Dyne. "She may still remain in the valley?"

Dyne studied Mirimel for a long moment. She nodded. "Fire-hair may remain."

The head of the True One who'd championed Ari appeared, sticking out of the darkness shrouding the doorway. Ari felt a pang of guilt, knowing he should have sent Dyne to them immediately. Keeping her outside hadn't helped.

The True One council member spoke to Dyne in their tongue. She replied, casting an annoyed look at Ari. He shrugged. Still talking, Dyne headed for the doorway. The entirety of both women disappeared inside.

"We should get some rest," Kiala said. "They might still decide to turn us out."

"They told me, in there, that they wouldn't," Ari said.

"That was before fire-hair's speech." Kiala cast Mirimel a look of reprimand. "And, I think, before you didn't carry out their wish of sending Dyne to them."

"I was hoping to convince her to help us." Ari knew that wasn't much of an excuse.

Kiala shrugged, seeming to cast off her annoyance with the gesture, her frown easing. "Well, so much for getting the Aluiens to set the stone." She looked about at them, including Cooro, the Questri and even Mirimel's hawk in her gaze. "Let's all try not to do anything that will make them reconsider letting us stay, ban us, or generally dislike us. It's never good to insult an entire race of magic wielding beings, even if they are peaceful. Agreed?"

Ari nodded along with Cooro. Even Stew and the black mare dipped their heads. Behind him, the hawk let out a single cry.

Mirimel folded her arms across her chest, her expression hard. "I won't do anything to them that they don't do to me."

Kiala smiled. "Good enough. Now go find a place to set up your tent."

"You will stay at Dyne's?" Ari asked, his looking taking in Kiala and Cooro.

Kiala nodded, not bothering to ask Cooro, who offered Ari a shrug. "Though you may want to ask Dyne's express permission if you plan to, Lord Aridian. Wherever you stay, be ready. We'll make an early start."

She turned on her heels and walked away. Cooro looked at Ari, then at Kiala, and hurried after her. With a shake of his mane, Stew turned and trotted off, the black mare a step behind him on the narrow path he took.

"I guess she's in charge, then," Mirimel said.

Taking in the anger in her tone, Ari considered her words before answering. "No. I am."

"Really?" The sarcasm in her tone wasn't subtle.

"Really, but she's a princess. They're used to giving orders. Actually, as a princess, she can give me orders and expect me to obey, so long as they don't go against my vows to Lggothland, the royal family, Sorga and Sir Cadwel."

"And Ispiria."

"No one can give me orders that harm Ispiria in any way and expect them to be carried out," he agreed. "Does it really matter who's in charge of our journey?"

Mirimel shrugged. "I don't like her."

"You don't like anyone," Ari reminded her. "I'm not sure you even like the people you do like."

That earned him a scowl. "I'm going to go set my tent up near the giant oak. I like it."

"Sure, a tree you can like," he said, trying not to smile.

271

"A tree is a better companion than most people I know."

Ari shrugged, feeling there might be some truth to that. "May I camp there as well?"

"You don't want to ask permission to stay with Princess Kiala's friend?"

Ari shook his head. He didn't feel quite safe with the True Ones. They were too rigid in their views. People who were unbending had a way of forcing the world to fit with them, instead of the other way around. He wasn't quite over his anger at Castin attempting to imprison him in the valley, either. It left a taste of mistrust in his mouth that Dyne's words hadn't dispelled. He didn't want to tell Mirimel that, though. She was causing enough trouble without knowing he'd been threatened. "Come on. Let's get our packs."

He led the way back to Dyne's home, feeling the term only loosely applied. Without discussing it, they skirted the kitchen area, where Ari could hear Cooro and Kiala speaking in low voices. Securing their possessions, Ari set off for the oak, Mirimel matching his stride. Her hawk glided along above, a dark shadow among the fireflies.

The branches of the massive oak reached out over the land outside its small island, and they found plenty of room under its sheltering arms to set up their tents. Camping under the massive tree, stars visible far above and fireflies swirling through its branches, was pleasant. The streams around them gurgled cheerfully, and night insects played a lulling tune. Ari felt the peace there, and let it carry him to sleep.

He woke the next morning refreshed. He and Mirimel made quick work of readying for the day and packing up, setting a rapid pace toward Dyne's abode. Ari was pleased to fine the others assembled, including Stew and the black mare.

Only Mirimel's hawk was absent, as she'd sent it ahead at first light.

Dyne stepped forward when they arrived, offering the ritual greeting of the day before. Ari was unsurprised to see she now wore the writhing green stone necklace he assumed marked the council head. He wondered if they'd kicked Castin out completely, but didn't ask. He wanted to be on his way. He was too impatient to foster conversation.

"It was an interesting thing to meet you, Thrice Born," Dyne said, stepping back.

Ari shrugged, unsure if that was good or bad. "Thank you for your hospitality. I'm sorry for the strife we caused you."

"You have brought only a needed change, though disagreeably through strife." She smiled, but the warmth of it didn't reach her eyes. She turned to Kiala. "And you brought figs, for which I thank you." Kiala received a kiss on each cheek, as did Cooro. To Stew and the mare, Dyne only nodded.

"Right," Ari said, turning to Stew. "Let's be on our way."

Dyne didn't stay to watch them tack up their mounts and ride out. They left the valley in strange silence. Though they did pass some True Ones moving about the loosely scattered village, the southern Aluiens averted their eyes. It seemed Ari and his friends had been marked as being unfit to socialize with.

Ari didn't mind. As much as riding into the valley the day before had been a balm, riding out again was a relief. Peaceful as the True Ones claimed to be, one of them had already tried to detain him. Ari had no doubt that, if united, they could make a stronger effort.

His only real regret in leaving the valley behind was that the third stone still wasn't set. He searched his brain for a new plan to alleviate that circumstance, but could think of nothing.

He glanced back more than once at the camels, recalling Kiala's offer to kill several animals to pool enough Orlenia, in the way of the witches of old, but dismissed the idea each time it came to him.

There was something inherently evil about the notion of killing to harvest the spark of life. Unfortunately, his feelings on the morality of it meant he rode toward his meeting with the Lady without any means of countering her should he need to. He was armed only with the hope she was as good as he once believed, not as evil as some of her recent actions seemed to suggest.

Shaking off such grim thoughts, Ari raised his face to the new day. They were traveling south, rocky valley walls on either side and tall peaks high above. The sun was somewhere behind them, over Ari's left shoulder, and still low enough in the sky to cast most of the world into shadow. The morning air was cool in the mountains.

"Ari," Mirimel called from behind him. She rode second, followed by Cooro on his camel and Kiala on hers, leading the others.

Stew stopped, Ari twisting to look over his shoulder. The path away from the valley of the True Ones was as narrow as the one leading up to it had grown. Stew could turn, but it would be work for the camels to do so, not that Mirimel's tone suggested they would need to.

"My hawk sees something," Mirimel said, pointing upward. "Something beyond the mountains, near the shore."

Ari hadn't realized they were so near the ocean, but then, the mountains made it difficult to tell and they reached all of the way to the coast. He looked south to where Mirimel pointed. Her hawk was a barely discernable speck on the horizon, flying away from them.

"Something we need to worry about?" he asked.

"I don't know yet. She hasn't seen enough. She came back to warn me first. Now she returns to learn more."

Ari looked past Mirimel to Kiala. "Are we far from the coast?"

"Over a day's ride."

"Then we carry on," he decided, nudging Stew forward. The narrow pass would be defensible, but he'd prefer some distance between them and the True Ones. There was no reason to suspect that what the hawk had spotted was a threat, or had anything much to do with them. Ari wasn't about to give up a day's travel waiting to see if whatever was on the coast came to them. There would be other parts of the rocky terrain to offer natural defense, if needed.

Ari tried to put the news Mirimel's hawk had given them out of his mind as they rode through a series of widening valleys. Around midmorning, Mirimel reported the hawk was pleased by whatever she'd found on the coast, allaying their fears. The hawk was too far away to communicate more than emotions, but that was enough. The mood of their group lightened considerably and they ate a pleasant midday meal. The sun swung round in a steady arc, brightening the world as they pressed on southward. When they mounted up again, Ari went forward with hope for whatever it was that awaited them.

Chapter 24

Shortly after they set out the following morning, Mirimel's hawk returned with news that Sir Cadwel and Lord Kenmar awaited them on the beach. Eager to see them, and learn what their hunt for Mrakenson had unearthed, Ari and Stew set a swift pace. The peaks were still tall, even so near the ocean, offering no glimpse of the sea, but soon Ari could smell the soft salt air. When they reached it, the neck of the final valley all but spilled them out onto the seashore.

Ari could see his mentor and Lord Kenmar waiting to their east, Goldwin standing beside them. Stew must have seen them as well, because he angled in their direction, breaking into a run. His hooves kicked up sand, churning the soft footing. Overhead, Mirimel's hawk issued a cry of greeting, winging in a slow circle high above.

Though sunlight sparkled off the crashing blue-green waves to Ari's right, adding to the exuberance of the run, he had the presence of mind to rein Stew in before they reached their friends. Happy as he was to see Sir Cadwel and Kenmar, Ari knew that skidding to a halt in front of them and spraying sand in their faces would not be wise. Sir Cadwel was not only undisputedly the greatest knight. He was the grouchiest.

Stopping a safe distance away, Ari slid from the saddle, crossing the remaining sand on foot, Stew by his side. "Sir Cadwel, Lord Kenmar, Goldwin" he greeted, grinning.

"I'm surprised you aren't in K'Orge by now, lad," Sir Cadwel said, but his tone was warm. He held out an arm and Ari clasped it in greeting before offering Kenmar a bow.

"Well met, young Lord Aridian," Kenmar said. He was thinner than ever, his clothing so rumpled his trousers and shirt sleeves looked too short. His gray streaked brown hair stuck up in somewhat random directions. "I'm pleased to have placed us so directly in your path."

Ari looked around. "How do you come to be here? Did you find your son?" He could hear the others drawing closer, the camels making their odd braying sounds.

"Camels," Kenmar exclaimed. He offered a smile. "Perhaps now that she has seen them, young Mirimel believes they exist?"

"I suppose she must," Ari agreed, glancing back.

"You have a new friend." Sir Cadwel's warmth was instantly quenched by suspicion.

"Yes." Ari reached into his tunic, retrieving the stone. "And this," he added. He dumped the stone out on his palm, watching Sir Cadwel's brow crease in surprise.

"The third stone," Kenmar breathed, all levity leaving him. He lifted his eyes from it to look at Ari. "You've done it. You've brought all three together as they haven't been in thousands of years." Far from seeming happy, Kenmar shuddered.

"Not completely," Ari said, putting the stone away. "It's not set into Fwellian's hilt yet."

The others reached them, Mirimel, Cooro and Kiala dismounting.

"Swordmaster, Mirimel," Sir Cadwel greeted before bringing his mistrustful gaze to rest on Kiala.

Even before Ari spoke, Sir Cadwel's expression shifted to one of curiosity. Knowing his mentor could see the familial resemblance as plainly as he could, Ari didn't see any need to prevaricate. "This is Princess Kiala, Queen Reudi's second daughter. Lady Kiala, this is Sir Cadwel, Lord Kenmar and Goldwin."

"Lady Kiala," Sir Cadwel said, bowing. "It is an honor and a pleasure to meet you."

Kiala offered a regal nod, but her smile was warm. "I am honored as well, Sir Cadwel, to meet the world's greatest knight and his most noble partner." This last she addressed to Goldwin, nodding with more deference than she'd shown Sir Cadwel.

The dun destrier shook his mane. It was the most acknowledgment Ari had seen Goldwin give anyone aside from Sir Cadwel.

Kiala turned to Kenmar, her smile slipping. "Father of the Empty Ones. I knew a day would come when we would meet. I must admit, I thought the occasion would hold greater terror for me."

Kenmar ran a hand through his hair, causing more of it to stick up. He tugged at his tunic, pulling it off kilter in the opposite direction it had been. "I am happy to meet you, Princess of Wheylia, and pleased I don't inspire terror. I'd, um, that is, all things considered and whatnot, I'd prefer not to be called Father of Empty Ones." Kenmar's voice was pleading.

"But you are." Kiala shrugged. "Few are those who can unmake their sins."

Kenmar sighed, his gaze dropping to the sand.

"How is it you three are here waiting for us?" Ari asked, shooting Kiala a look of reprimand. It seemed cruel to torment Kenmar.

"We've been tracking Mrakenson," Sir Cadwel said. "We began at his keep and followed the trail here. By the time we landed and started along the coast, we'd become relatively sure he was headed for K'Orge. It's either there, or somewhere not on a map. There aren't any other habitations along this stretch of coast."

"So you're on his trail now?" Ari asked in growing excitement. "Can you tell if Ispiria and Siara are with him?" Beside him, Mirimel turned in a slow circle, her eyes scanning the beach.

"No, we cannot tell." Kenmar shook his head. "I do not think, though, that they are. I believe Suyla has them. You have followed their trail to K'Orge, I gather?"

"As best we can," Ari said.

Mirimel walked up the beach as they spoke, peering at the sand. Ari saw her go down to the high tide mark, then up again, to where the foot of the mountains rested. She went down on one knee, examining something. Ari hoped she'd found some clue.

"If Cooro may ask, how did you come to the shore so long before us?" Cooro asked. "We have not been idle in our travel."

Ari turned back to see Sir Cadwel wince. "On a raft."

"What?" Ari asked, startled. He cast his gaze toward the seemingly endless expanse of bright blue ocean on his right. "A raft?"

Goldwin shook himself from head to tail, an even more telling reaction than Sir Cadwel's.

"There were spells," Kenmar said. "We weren't in any real danger on the raft. You ca--"

"It was a less than pleasant voyage," Sir Cadwel said, cutting in. His gaze strayed to Cooro and Ari realized Kenmar had been about to comment on magic Sir Cadwel himself had worked. Mirimel and Cooro still didn't know he'd become an Aluien a few years past. Sir Cadwel wasn't very free with the information. He turned, cupping his hands to his mouth. "Mirimel, report."

She'd wandered a moderate distance down the beach. Instead of returning, she gestured for them to come to her. Ari supposed that was reasonable, as they were headed that way. "We can likely speak and walk," he said aloud. They were squandering time, standing about.

Sir Cadwel nodded. Reins were retrieved for the camels and they set off walking down the beach. Though the water there was the brightest Ari had yet seen, almost more green than blue, the sand was a strange dark gray, not light like along the southern coast of Lggothland. Behind them, Stew, Goldwin and the black mare remained in place, their heads together as they conversed in the way of the Questri. Ari was sure they would catch up soon enough.

As they walked, Ari did his best to impart everything that had happened. Ari spoke with sorrow about his cousins, reliving the shock of losing Cyanna so soon after meeting her. He tried to show no emotion when he spoke of the treachery of some of the Lggothian nobles, his own cousins included. It was easy to read the anger on Sir Cadwel's face.

About Parrentine's state Ari said little, focusing instead on getting the stone and meeting Quinless and Kanja. He moved on to Princess Kiala's part in the tale and the clues they'd gathered in the port city of Jondor. As quickly as he tried to speak, he didn't reach their time in the True Ones' valley before they drew abreast Mirimel.

"Two people and two horses have come through here, recently enough that traces linger," she said without preamble. "I would say within the past few days, for it looks to me as if the sea air and wind scours evidence of those who have passed with a fierceness we don't see in the northlands."

"We are nearer than I dared hope, then," Kenmar said, sounding both pleased and fearful.

"Can you tell if Ispiria is with them?" Ari asked. He wasn't quite sure where they'd come out of the mountains in relation to K'Orge, but he had the sudden hope of overtaking Ispiria and Siara before they even reached the city.

Mirimel shook her head. "Only two have passed, from what I can see, both with the boots men wear, not the slippers ladies use at court. One weighs much more than Ispiria or Siara could. The other, when they dismount to rest their horses, walks with a shuffling gate, like an old or lame man."

"That must be Mrakenson," Ari said, recalling the time he, Sir Cadwel and Larke had gone to Kenmar's former keep. "He was little more than a skeleton when we met him."

Sir Cadwel shook his head, exchanging a look with Kenmar. "Not any more, lad," Sir Cadwel said.

"He was weak, and shambling, when Suyla set him free." Kenmar wrung his hands as he spoke, pulling the skin tight. "But we've been following his trail. I'm afraid he's been . . . feeding. He will be strong now, his physical form recovered. It is his steward who is weak. His body was already broken when my son took him from life, and he isn't permitted anything but . . . scraps."

"Feeding?" Mirimel asked, a hard edge in her voice.

"Cooro does not wish to know," Cooro said. The slight gray tinge to his skin bespoke of someone who was already familiar with how an Empty One might feast.

"If we're that close behind them, we should get moving," Kiala said.

Sir Cadwel cast her a slightly surprised look.

"Yes, we should," Ari said, hoping to head off any discussion of who was in charge. It wasn't as if they had important decisions to make. They were following Mrakenson and heading to K'Orge. Those seemed to be one in the same and their route set.

"Would I be able to ride one of the camels?" Kenmar asked, looking between Ari and Kiala. "I think it might be wise to regather my strength, not squander it taking flight."

"Taking flight?" Kiala asked. She held up a hand. "Tell me later. Ride a camel now. There will be time for talk as we travel."

The Questri were called and packs on one of the camels redistributed. Kenmar seemed nearly gleeful over getting to ride one. Ari supposed it wasn't often the ancient lord had the chance to experience something new. He was glad Kenmar was semi-immortal, for he looked precarious perched on top of a camel. Ari wasn't certain he would maintain his seat.

They passed around bags of dried fruit and nuts as they rode, for the sun had climbed to its zenith while they talked on the beach. A steady wind blew in off the waves, nearly as cool as the mountain air had been. The sun was very bright, but already behind them in the sky as they headed eastward along the coast.

Ari rode in silence, half-listening to Kenmar's and Kiala's discussion on different types of magic and the art of transformation. Mirimel rode at the front of their group, her eyes on the ground and her hawk overhead. Cooro trailed behind, a glance showing he wasn't quite pleased to have his place at Kiala's side taken by Kenmar. For once, Kiala was permitting Cooro to lead the pack camels.

For his part, Ari was content to wait to finish his tale of their journey, able to find a modicum of peace in riding down the beach at Sir Cadwel's side. Now that Sir Cadwel was there, they were sure to succeed. Who could stand against so great a knight?

Ari did wish, though, that Larke would reappear. Now that they had the third stone, Larke's mission to find where the Lady was searching for it was pointless, but they had no way to let the bard know that, or where they were. Ari held hope he would appear soon. Larke's investigations must have led him to K'Orge as well, for all signs pointed to it. He tried not to worry, reminding himself Larke always turned up eventually.

Ari was aware Sir Cadwel could affix the stone into Fwellian's hilt, but didn't know how to ask. He knew his mentor didn't like to share that he was no longer a mortal man, but surely Mirimel and Cooro could be trusted. Ari felt Kiala could be as well. He also suspected she already knew.

"One for flight and one for fight, then?" Kiala's amused voice broke into Ari's thoughts.

"You could look at it that way," Kenmar said. "I very much wanted to fly, you see. The hawk gives me that joy, and can travel great distances and seek out knowledge. The other form is, well, as you said."

"Why would you wish to turn into a giant feline?"

"Partly, I wished to preserve them. They were fading even in my time. The world was colder, then, you realize? Or you do not. Most don't."

"No, I did not," Kiala said. "Though I'm not certain why it matters."

"I am not either, I admit," Kenmar said. "I know only that, when the world was colder, many creatures were larger than they are now. The great felines of the north were fearsome creatures. Larger than the giant bears you see in the pinewood now. Their fangs protruded, large as a strong man's forearm and sharp as blades. They were not to be taken lightly, even as their race fell away."

"We have, in one of our places of learning, bones from such creatures," Kiala said. "I think I never quite believed they were real."

Her words recalled the same knowledge to Ari's mind, for he'd visited the schools in Wheylia. With a shudder, he remembered the largest bones in their collection. Ones they attributed to a dragon.

"You trust the princess?" Sir Cadwel's rumbling voice barely reached Ari's ears. If he didn't possess extraordinary hearing, a gift from the Aluiens, he wouldn't have heard anything more than a sigh leave his mentor's mouth, if that. Fortunately, Sir Cadwel had similarly enhanced hearing.

"I trust that she is who she says she is," Ari whispered back. "She has been waiting here for me, for years."

"Why?"

Ari smiled slightly. Sir Cadwel was never verbose. "She says her sight told her this is the way to save Wheylia. She believes the Lady plans to visit death and destruction and that I will do something in K'Orge to prevent this."

Sir Cadwel didn't reply. Ari glanced at him, taking in the hard lines of his countenance.

"Does the princess know about me?" Sir Cadwel asked after a long silence.

"I haven't told her, but she is a Princess of Whey. She has the sight, and other magic."

Sir Cadwel gave a barely perceptible nod.

"You don't think she's right?" Ari whispered. "About the Lady, that is." This time, no answer came at all. Finally, Ari gave up waiting for one and changed the subject. "Will you set the stone for me?"

"If Larkesong doesn't find us before we reach K'Orge."

Now it was Ari's turn to be silent, his worries for Larke returning. Surely, Larke's research into where the Lady was would direct him to the same place it was leading Ari and Sir Cadwel. It seemed odd he hadn't joined them yet. Sir Cadwel and Kenmar had been trailing Mrakenson, a task which could have led them in many directions, so Ari hadn't been confident of seeing them so soon. Larke had only to go into the Aluien caves, look into the pool, pick up his favorite possessions and leave.

Ari frowned, the sun hot on his back. Before them, Mirimel rode with easy grace, obviously sure of their path. Ari had the unsettling feeling Larke would have joined them by now, if he could.

Chapter 25

When they set up camp for the night, a necessity that obviously chafed Sir Cadwel and Lord Kenmar, Ari finished his tale of their journey while they passed around food. Mirimel kept offering various bags of nuts and dried fruit to Sir Cadwel, who finally gave up and ate some, though he didn't seem to pay attention to which. Taking in the suspicion in Mirimel's blue eyes, Ari wondered if he should mention to Sir Cadwel that his behavior was less than convincingly human.

As they traveled, the terrain they crossed was striking but barren and windswept. Often, the foot of the mountains reached out to touch the water, creating sloping stone walls they were forced to climb. It was only brute strength on the part of Ari, Cooro and Sir Cadwel that got the camels up some of the steeper paths. Once, the Questri disappeared altogether.

This happened after they encountered an embankment so steep the camels had to be tied in makeshift slings, one at a time, and hauled up a short cliff. When the last camel was at the top and Sir Cadwel turned to Goldwin with the ropes, the dun destrier gave him a scathing look, nodded to Stew and the mare, and left. Stew looked about sheepishly, until the mare shook her mane at him and followed Goldwin. Casting Ari an apologetic glance, his destrier followed the other two. Though Stew, Goldwin and the black mare reappeared later, on the path ahead, their progress was poor that day.

That night, Cooro ventured the question of how Mrakenson had gotten his mounts up the low cliff.

"Oh, I suspect he used magic," Kenmar said.

"We could have used magic?" Cooro held up his rope-burned hands. "Cooro cannot be at his best in a fight with hands such as these."

"Well, you see," Kenmar hedged, casting a look at Sir Cadwel. "That is, it would take nearly as much effort with magic, you know, just of a different sort, and I'm afraid I am trying to store mine up, as it were, in case . . . rather, for the upcoming . . ." Kenmar grimaced.

Ari knew how he felt. He didn't like to think on exactly who it was they journeyed to confront either.

"Here, I will heal them for you," Kiala said, holding out her hands to Cooro. "We can't have our swordmaster at anything less than his best."

Cooro proffered his hands. Ari watched in fascination as Kiala drew blue runes in the air, murmuring in the lyrical language of Ancient Wheylian. At a gesture, the runes settled onto Cooro's palms, the rawness of his wounds receding to a mere redness, looking a week healed. Cooro sighed, the look he gave Kiala tinged with adoration.

Lord Kenmar leaned forward, peering at Cooro's palms. "That's well done. Now, I would have . . ."

Ari stopped listening, not interested in more unintelligible talk of the various magical forces the mind could be trained to call on. He noted the closed look Cooro's face took on as he all but glared at Kenmar, forgotten by Kiala while she debated with the aging lord. Shrugging, for Cooro's and Kiala's relationship wasn't a trouble for him to take on, Ari reached for more fruit. Not long after, he turned in for the night, knowing Sir Cadwel, who didn't need to sleep, would stand guard.

Sometimes as they traveled, instead of rocks and cliff-like barricades, they found themselves on sandy beaches, the hooves of both Questri and camel, and Ari's boots if he walked, leaving water filled pools in their wake. Depending on the tide, these places were as much as knee deep in seawater. After crossing beaches like that, Mirimel would spend extra time on the other side, ensuring they still followed the trail.

"We aren't making up any time," she said after one such beach, retaking her saddle. She glanced back at Ari, looking annoyed. "We gain in the day, for they must rest their mounts more often, but they keep on for much of the night and we do not."

"It's not a race." Ari shrugged. "We all know where we're going."

"It would be better to kill Mrakenson first, before he can join the Lady."

Ari winced. He knew he had to kill Mrakenson. In truth, he wanted something that evil scoured from the land. Still, he wasn't comfortable talking about it as coldly as the others could. Defending himself, his home, those he loved and the innocent, were all things Ari could do without hesitation. Plotting out someone's demise was not.

Mirimel squinted upward, at her hawk. "She says there is a stream coming down the mountain one beach over. We can refill our water there."

Ari nodded, relieved. They were getting low. Their provisions were dwindling a bit as well. Sir Cadwel had either noticed this or was weary of pretending he needed food, for he'd stopped eating any. Ari looked to his right, at the sparkling blue of the ocean, which had grown increasingly warm, bright and clear as they traveled. Likely there was something there they could catch. He shuddered, recalling the slimy fish globs he'd been forced to eat at a state dinner. Hopefully they could stick to nuts and fruit.

Behind them, Sir Cadwel, Kenmar and Kiala were engaged in a discussion of the workings of magic too arcane for Ari to follow. Sir Cadwel's increasing participation in these debates was another sign he was through hiding his nature from Mirimel and Cooro. For his part, Cooro trailed the others, leading the pack camels and looking rather sullen.

After they reached the stream, refilled their water and resumed riding, Ari let his attention wander back to the sea. He liked how bright it was, an ever more striking shade of blue-green. When he could press his worries from his mind, he enjoyed thinking that Ispiria, though imprisoned, might be looking out on the same ocean.

She would think it beautiful, with its glittering waves and swooping white gulls. Often, he could even spot fish frolicking in leaping arcs, or giant turtles just beneath the surface. He hoped Ispiria had seen a turtle, and was safe enough to find it in her heart to smile at the leaping fish. Reaching into his tunic pocket, he ran her hair ribbon, the one from the note Parrentine's men found, through his fingers.

"Ari, pay attention," Mirimel snapped. "Have you heard a word I said?"

Ari blinked several times. Mirimel had stopped and dismounted. She stood now at the edge of the beach, beside the foot of the mountains. Ari took in the long shadow stretching out across the rippled sand in front of him, originating at Stew's hooves. Somewhere in his daydreaming about Ispiria, her red curls swirling in the sea breeze without any hair ribbon to contain them, he'd lost track of where and when he was. "I beg your pardon?"

"I said, their trail leaves the beach here."

"For how long? Do they return to it?"

Mirimel gave him an exasperated look. "I also said, I'm going into the mountains to follow them and find out if and where they return to the shoreline."

"Absolutely not." There was no way Mirimel, skilled though she was, was going into the mountains following Mrakenson.

"Absolutely not?" she echoed, the words snapping in the air between them like a whip cracking.

"That is, not alone," Ari amended.

"I didn't say I would go alone. Do I look like a fool?"

She looked like a hawk guardian, and an angry one at that. Ari could see the strain in her. He knew she was at least as worried as he was about Ispiria, and Larke. He'd overheard her speaking to her hawk, asking the little brown raptor if she could sense any other Sorga Hawks near. That had only increased Ari's fear for Larke, for he'd forgotten the bird Mirimel sent with the bard. If Larke and the little brown hawk were anywhere around, surely Mirimel would hear the hawk and it her.

"You're taking an awful long time to answer," Mirimel said, but her tone held less anger. Beside her, the black mare pawed at the ground, gouging the sand.

"I didn't think you actually needed me to."

"What are you two arguing over now?" Kiala asked as she, Sir Cadwel and Kenmar reached them. As usual, Cooro trailed behind.

"They left the beach here and headed into the mountains," Mirimel said.

Kiala squinted into the sun. "We near K'Orge." She turned to Kenmar. "Do you think they've gone to the ruins of the old city, on the edge of the volcano, instead of to the new one on the shore?"

Ari looked between the two. "What, exactly, is a volcano?"

"It's when a mountain is full of fire," Kenmar said. "So full, in fact, the top is thrown off. I did not realize there was one near the fabled city of K'Orge until Lady Kiala spoke to me of it. I believe now, and she agrees, that it was this explosion of fire from the mountain that long ago shook the city loose and sent is sliding down to the shore."

Kenmar spoke with a certain amount of excitement, but Ari could see the worry he felt mirrored on Mirimel's face. He recalled Quinless telling them much the same thing. Fire had spewed from the mountain the day K'Orge fell into the sea.

"There is a painting of a fire mountain in the gallery at the school of arts," Cooro said, finally joining them. He craned his neck, looking up at the mountains to their left. "A spectacular image, but not one Cooro would care to live."

Kiala slid down from her camel, not bothering to have it kneel. With enough ease to show how automatic the gesture was, she unsheathed the curved sword she wore. Using it, she began to draw in the sand. Ari and the others dismounted as well, forming a loose circle around her.

"This is where we are, and this is the shoreline." Kiala accompanied the words with strong strokes through the sand. "Here, on the water, is the city of K'Orge. Here, in the mountains, is the peak the city once wrapped around. When the top of the mountain came off, hot liquid went this way, away from the water, burning, killing and burying all in its wake."

"A quick death for most who suffered it, at least," Kenmar murmured.

"There was little room for what spewed from the mountain, so it filled the shallow valley. As it cooled, it formed what is nearly a level plateau on one side of the missing peak. You can stand there and look down into the fire inside the mountain. Six times a year, the people of K'Orge hold a ceremony there and throw offerings into the fire."

Ari nodded. That made sense. It was obviously important to keep the gods inside the fire mountain appeased.

"Offerings?" Mirimel asked sharply. "Quinless spoke of offerings as well. You aren't going to tell us they throw children in there, are you?"

Sir Cadwel leaned down to study the rough map.

"Silks, pearls, gold, but no children." Kiala shrugged. "Much of what they trade for is purchased to offer to the mountain. The Dinji don't trade in flesh."

Ari realized Kiala's words implied there were others who did.

"On the peak's ocean side?" Sir Cadwel asked into the silence.

"Not all of the old city slid down the mountain to the seashore. What didn't remains as crumbled ruins. The people of K'Orge call them cursed. None who were stuck there when the mountain erupted were granted a quick death or the chance to live, like those who survived the fall to the ocean. Instead, they choked to death on the foul gas the mountain spewed forth in the wake of the fire. No one goes there."

"Does any gas remain?" Cooro asked, also studying the map.

Kiala shook her head. "I do not know how long it lasted, but there is none now. I searched for the stone there, years ago. It is as any abandoned city, ripe with forgotten treasure and tragedy."

"Surely you didn't take anything?" Mirimel asked, sounding slightly shocked by the idea.

"Nothing there was the treasure I sought."

"So, you think the Lady is up there?" Ari asked. "With Ispiria and Siara?"

"And Mrakenson," Sir Cadwel added.

Kiala frowned. "I would have expected Suyla to be near the shore, as she brought Lord Aridian here to search for the stone."

"You searched in the ruined city," Mirimel pointed out.

"Only as an act of desperation, as for a time I thought I'd exhausted my search of the bay. All know the stone was held in the sea. The home of the race guarding it was said to be in the bay below K'Orge. The city destroyed the sea folks when it fell. They say the taint of all the gold hoarded by the rich poisoned the water. I doubt that, but something did. Most likely all of the dead bodies."

Ari grimaced, trying not to draw too vivid of an image of that in his mind.

"Maybe the Aluien lady is desperate too, and so searches the city?" Cooro said. "We know she cannot have found the stone in the waters of the bay."

Kiala frowned. Sir Cadwel kept studying the map. Mirimel paced away, bending again to scrutinize the trail, as if it might hold more than the tracks she'd already found.

Kenmar scratched at his head, his expression thoughtful. "We've been assuming Suyla doesn't know you found the stone, or that Ari has it."

Ari nodded. "She's bringing me here, and using Ispiria and Siara, to force me to find it."

"So we deduced, but with all of her power, does it seem possible?" Kenmar frowned. "Could she have another reason for choosing this place?"

"I don't see what," Kiala said. "Why here if not for the stone?"

"Well, there's the fire mountain," Ari supplied. "That makes K'Orge unique. Unless there are others?"

"I've heard of others, far into the empty lands in the south or out to sea." Kiala looked to Sir Cadwel, then Cooro.

Shrugging, Cooro held out both hands. "We have none in the mountains of Wheylia, though they say once, long ago, there were."

"None in Lggothland," Sir Cadwel said.

"So, there are other fire mountains," Ari concluded. The Lady would have a reason for choosing K'Orge. "It must be because she thinks the stone is here. Why else bring us all this way?"

"Does the power of this Overgod truly reside here?" Cooro asked. "Mayhap the Aluien can use it?"

"I've seen no evidence of such," Kiala said.

Something stirred at the back of Ari's mind, but he couldn't yank it forward into the light. "Is K'Orge a large city?" Perhaps the Lady had fostered allies there.

"Very," Kiala replied. "It's the only city of the Dinji race. Though they travel for trade, they feel that to live anywhere else, as your friend Kanja does, is to betray the Overgod."

"A city doesn't seem like the place for a battle of magic," Sir Cadwel said.

"Perhaps this is why the Aluien chooses the mountaintop?" Cooro said.

"How large of a city?" Ari asked. Given enough people, the Lady could find ready allies. In a whole race, there were bound to be some of questionable morality.

"We gain nothing by guessing." Mirimel's tone was hard, her steps purposeful as she returned to where they clustered around the map. "We have two choices. We can follow Mrakenson's trail or go directly to the city." Her blue eyes pinned Ari. "What will it be, Thrice Born?"

Chapter 26

While Ari didn't appreciate being called Thrice Born, he did appreciate Mirimel's not too subtle reminder this was his mission. "We follow the trail. We were going to K'Orge because we thought Ispiria and Siara were there. I think it's more likely Mrakenson will lead us directly to them."

"Or into a trap," Kenmar said, wringing his hands.

"If it's a trap, we'll fight," Ari said with a calmness he didn't quite feel.

"Get out the stone, lad," Sir Cadwel said. "It's time."

Ari nodded, retrieving the pouch from his doublet.

"Time for what?" Mirimel asked, her eyes narrowing in suspicion.

"To set the stone." Sir Cadwel looked between Kenmar and Kiala. "Does anyone know the words to the spell?"

"I knew it." Mirimel marched up to Sir Cadwel, hands on her hips. "I knew you were an Aluien. You don't eat. You don't sleep. You and Kenmar aren't even traveling with any packs, just that rangy old horse of yours."

Goldwin let out a snort. The black mare whinnied.

"My apologies, Goldwin," Mirimel said, addressing the Questri before turning back to Sir Cadwel. "How long has this been the case?"

Sir Cadwel placed his large calloused hands on Mirimel's shoulders. "I'm still me."

Some of the tension went out of her frame. "I know, Uncle Cadwel, but you've been lying to me." There was the slightest tremble in her voice as she spoke those words. From where he stood, Ari couldn't see her face to read it.

To Ari's astonishment, Sir Cadwel pulled Mirimel into a hug, patting her hair with an awkward hand. It wasn't a long embrace, for he soon set her away from him. "All right?"

Mirimel nodded, swiping at her face with her hands.

Ari never really thought of Mirimel as Sir Cadwel's niece. Yes, Ispiria was, and they were cousins. Sir Cadwel had married into their family years ago. Mirimel never spoke of the knight in those terms, though. She'd grown up in Hawkers, likely seeing Sir Cadwel rarely. His rank and unsociable tendencies didn't make him any less family, though, especially when all three had so little family left.

Sir Cadwel turned from Mirimel. "The stone, sword and words."

The command in his tone spurred Ari back into motion. Drawing Fwellian, he awkwardly dumped out the stone and fitted it into the hilt. "I don't know the words."

"I do," Kenmar said. "I recall the spell Larkesong used." He cast a wincing glance Mirimel's way, as if regretting bringing Larke up. "You'll need a knife."

Mirimel pulled out her hunting knife, handing it over hilt first.

"It only takes a drop," Kenmar cautioned.

Kiala leaned close, her dark eyes intent. Her hair fell forward into her face. With quick hands, she swept it back, twisting it into a quick knot at the base of her skull. "Do you want me to cut you?" she asked Sir Cadwel.

"I was waiting for you to be ready."

Someone gasped slightly as Sir Cadwel plunged the knife into his finger, but Ari didn't know which of them it was. The knight reached out, holding his hand over the hilt of Ari's sword, where the third stone rested loose in its fitting. Kenmar murmured words in the language of magic the Aluiens used. Sir Cadwel squeezed his already healing finger, spilling a glowing blue drop of Orlenia onto the stone. He repeated the words Kenmar offered.

A blue-white glow engulfed the stone, brightening until it was almost too difficult to look on before fading away. All three of the milky white stones seemed to shimmer. Fwellian's hilt grew warm in Ari's hand.

"It is done?" Cooro whispered where he stood beside Kiala.

Ari shook the sword slightly. The stones seemed firmly affixed. He looked around at the ring of faces. "Now what?"

"No idea." Sir Cadwel straightened, wiping Mirimel's knife on his breeches before handing it to her, though the blade appeared unsoiled. "Princess?"

"I don't really know." Kiala sounded uncertain for perhaps the first time since Ari met her. "Once completed, the sword is supposed to be a powerful weapon."

"Maybe he needs to hit someone with it." Mirimel turned to Cooro. "Whey?"

"A fight with Cooro?" Cooro looking Ari up and down. "Only if Cooro may fight back."

"I'm not hitting anyone with it," Ari said. Reversing Fwellian, he sheathed the blade. "Least of all my friends."

"Kenmar?" Sir Cadwel said.

"Lord Kenmar is my friend as well," Ari protested, startled Sir Cadwel would suggest it.

"Do you know anything, Kenmar?" Sir Cadwel said, giving Ari a reprimanding look.

The graying lord shook his head. "I've never see anyone use it. In the stories, it sounds as if it works, well, like a sword."

"So he does have to hit someone with it," Mirimel said.

"I suppose he does," Kenmar agreed.

"Let's go find someone for me to hit, then," Ari suggested, taking in the lowering sun. "Mirimel, you lead. Let me know when it gets too dark to follow the trail."

Mirimel nodded and they mounted up, both Questri and the camels well rested. They followed Mirimel single file, Ari and Stew keeping close in case the prints leading into the mountain were a trap. Sir Cadwel came next, then Kenmar, Kiala and Cooro. No one spoke, an alert silence settling over the group.

Their tension proved unfounded that day, and the following one. They climbed ever higher, though the trail they were on was passable. The camels had to be unloaded twice to fit through narrow gaps, each occasion setting Ari's teeth on edge. Steep walled, narrow gorges were perfect locations for an ambush.

In the evenings, before trying to sleep while Sir Cadwel and Kenmar guarded, Ari studied Fwellian. The sword seemed different, somehow. It weighed less. The hilt, where the stones rested, was always warm. When Ari closed his eyes, he could almost sense a questioning in the blade, as if Fwellian sought to know his mind. Ari sat with the sword for long moments, considering Larke's long ago words. The stones would link body, mind and intention.

Several days after leaving the shore, Cooro came to sit beside Ari once they'd eaten, the two of them the only ones in their small camp. Though the sun had set, Mirimel was hunting in an attempt to add to their dwindling food supply. She said she wouldn't find anything with Sir Cadwel accompanying her, but Ari couldn't consent to any of them wandering the mountains alone. Mirimel claimed the knight blundered about like a blind bear. Ari knew Sir Cadwel could move quietly when he wished.

Kiala and Lord Kenmar were taking their turns refilling their water supply at a nearby stream, so Ari was a touch surprised by Cooro's appearance. Normally, he all but haunted his future queen. Ari met the swordmaster's approach with a smile, though.

"It's a magnificent blade," Cooro said as he sat on the rocky outcropping with Ari. "Cooro has never seen finer."

Ari reversed Fwellian, offering the sword hilt first. Cooro took it. His eyebrows went up in surprise. Clasping the hilt of the massive blade in one hand, he held it out parallel to the ground, studying it.

"Nearly all the weight of it is gone." Cooro sounded slightly amazed. "The third stone did this?"

Ari shrugged. "I don't know if it was that stone, or having them all together."

Cooro handed Fwellian to Ari. He angled his head back, his eyes on the stars. The constellations they could see now were almost completely unfamiliar to Ari. Those southernmost in Sorga were nowhere to be seen. Only ones that appeared in Poromont remained as familiar friends.

"Cooro is in misery," Cooro said, breaking the silence.

"Misery?" Ari repeated, surprised.

"Do you keep in your mind the times you and Cooro have spoken of fair maidens and love?"

Ari nodded. "I suppose I can remember them."

Cooro rested his elbows on his knees, dropping his head into his hands. "Cooro did not want love, does not wish it. Love is not freedom. Love is jealousy and spite, especially when it comes to one who does not return it."

"Are you saying you're in love?" Ari looked around, as if the words might summon whoever had claimed the swordmaster's heart. "Who with?"

Cooro's head jerked up and he looked at Ari. "Princess Kiala. Who else would Cooro love?"

"Oh." Ari thought about that. "That's good, though, right? I mean, since you have to marry her."

"She does not love me. Never will she. A queen cannot afford to thaw her heart. The Curse of Whey would claim her, and jeopardize her and the realm."

"Why?" Ari asked. "I mean, would it be so bad if she let herself love you?" Ari still had no idea how someone could accomplish walling off their heart. He suspected magic was involved, for he knew he couldn't do it.

"If a queen loves, she dies without her lover, just as any other Wheylian woman with power would. Someone could make threats on Cooro to force her actions, or Cooro could die. Our kingdom must be put first." His tone was glum.

"Who is going to make threats? Kiala doesn't strike me as the sort to let anyone get away with that. It isn't as if Wheylia is at war."

Cooro shook his head before dropping his chin into his palms once more. "Cooro never asked to be loved, for the responsibility is great, but to love without its return is to know pain."

"I'm sure all will be well. Kiala said she saw a bright future for you two."

Cooro didn't reply. Not knowing what else to say, Ari left his friend to his thoughts. From the look on Cooro's face, they weren't happy ones.

Two days later found them at an intersecting trail. It was larger than the one they followed, and joined with where they stood, the augmented path widening as it led upward. Even Ari could see the broader path was used, and pick out signs of passage. Mirimel called a halt, not letting any of them onto the new trail. Leaving her mare behind, she went forward on foot to examine it. Ari and the others dismounted as well, stretching their legs and letting their mounts rest.

"The tracks we follow lead upward," Mirimel said, returning to the trail they were on.

"We're not far from the remains of the ruined city." Kiala glanced at the sun, still low in its ascent for the day. "If we go up, we'll reach it not too long into the afternoon."

Ari swallowed the dryness in this throat. Today. They would find Mrakenson up there, today. Would Ispiria and Siara be with him?

"We should send my hawk to scout," Mirimel said.

Ari didn't need to look up to know the raptor was executing a slow spiral high above. "If they see her, they'll know we're near."

"They already know we're near," Kenmar said, wringing his hands. The graying lord radiated nervousness. "They've

303

likely been watching us, one way or another. There is no hope for surprise."

"I'd send the hawk, lad," Sir Cadwel said. "We can't surprise them. No need to let them surprise us."

Ari looked at Cooro.

The swordmaster shrugged, his face folded into what had become typical lines of moroseness. "Cooro knows little of such things."

"Send her, but warn her to take care not to get too near," Ari said, turning back to Mirimel. "I worry what they might do to her."

"She knows the risks." Mirimel raised her face to the sky, the sunlight glinting off her orange curls.

High above, the hawk let out a cry, breaking off her lazy spiral to wing eastward, higher into the mountains. Ari quickly lost her against the sun. He hoped it wouldn't be the last they saw of her.

"Do we wait or ride?" Mirimel asked.

"Ride," Ari said, at the same time as Sir Cadwel and Kiala spoke the same word.

Kiala gave Ari a tight smile. "No sense in putting off the inevitable, after all."

They mounted up, Ari moving to the front, in spite of Mirimel's protests. She had her bow out, an arrow held loosely in her other hand. It reassured Ari somewhat. He knew how quickly Mirimel could let fly an arrow, and with what deadly accuracy.

Time seemed to slow as they crept up the mountain. Ari watched the trail ahead intently, taking in every movement, every sound. Stew had his head up, his ears swiveling constantly, letting Ari know he was doing the same. Each step felt as if it brought them nearer to some unknown doom. The feeling became so oppressive, Ari didn't even notice at first that his amulet was ice cold.

He held up his hand, stopping their progress. Glancing back, he took in the strained faces of the others, their darting glances. They turned questioning eyes on him. Even Sir Cadwel looked worried.

Ari dismounted, stretching to unshackle himself from the magic-induced tension attempting to immobilize him. "Can one of you do something about this?"

Sir Cadwel gave his head a hard shake, his features moving from nearly fearful to annoyed. "Kenmar? Your type of spell?"

Lord Kenmar blinked rapidly, wringing his hands so hard Ari wondered that he didn't pull the skin off. Mirimel was looking around now, too, as was Cooro. Kiala gave her own head a shake.

"Oh dear, it's my son, isn't it?" Sliding from his camel, Kenmar crossed to the edge of the trail. He searched around, bending to pick up a large, flat stone. He held it in his fingertips, as if reluctant to have it touching his skin. "I should have realized sooner." He turned the stone, and Ari could see the scrawling runes etched into it.

"We all should have," Kiala said, her tone disgusted. "I haven't been so afraid in years."

Cooro let out a relieved sounding sigh. "Cooro feared he was a coward."

Kenmar was studying the stone. "Yes, yes, I taught him this." His features contorted into a strained grimace. "Yes, I think, a rune for each of us."

"A rune for each of us?" Mirimel snapped. Her hand went to the amulet she wore, the small stone hawk Larke had carved for her. Ari wondered if it offered as much protection from the influence of magic as his amulet did.

Kenmar tossed the stone aside, walking over to Ari and Stew. "Well, no, not really each of us. Would you care for one my Questri friend?"

Stew shook his mane.

Kenmar nodded. "No, I thought not. Now that you know, you will counter the effects yourself." He turned to Ari. "As will you, and you, Mirimel. You have an amulet to guard you." Kenmar turned to the others. His face took on an apologetic look. "Actually, I think just the camels must be warded and, um, you, Swordmaster."

"Cooro and the camels?" Cooro's expression conveyed the offense he took. "Only Cooro and the beasts must be warded?"

"It's only because Mirimel and I already have amulets," Ari pointed out.

Cooro answered that with a glare.

His expression still contrite, Kenmar walked around their group, warding Cooro first and then the camels. Though Ari was sure Cooro wouldn't admit it, he could see some of the tension leave the swordmaster as Kenmar applied his spell. When he finished, Kenmar asked his camel to kneel, nodding to Ari to continue.

"She's returning," Mirimel said, before Kenmar could mount. Mirimel held up her arms, her hawk winging down to land on her leather-clad wrist.

"What does she say?" So much anxiety washed through Ari as he asked the question, he almost suspected magic again.

"She says she found Larke."

Chapter 27

"Alive?" Ari asked, his voice cracking.

Mirimel pressed her lips together, blue eyes intent on her hawk. "He's on the flat plateau, on the high side of a large crater full of fire."

"The volcano," Kiala supplied.

"She's picturing him . . . restrained somehow. It's difficult to understand." Mirimel bit her lip. "I should be better at this."

"May I?" Kenmar asked, his tone gentle.

Mirimel nodded. She gave a flip of her wrist and the hawk flew over to Kenmar, landing on the still-kneeling camel's saddle. Mirimel blotted her eyes. Seemingly unbidden, the black mare turned, angling away to hide Mirimel's face.

"Larkesong is alive," Kenmar said, but his voice held sorrow. "She says he is changed. He cannot speak to her." Kenmar looked about at them. "I think . . . I think she means he has lost his power. I do not think Larkesong is an Aluien any longer."

Ari gaped at Kenmar. Larke not an Aluien? It was at the core of who the bard was. He loved magic. He was an artist when it came to crafting certain spells, better even than the Lady. Ari felt something harden inside him. How could the Aluiens do such a thing to Larke?

Kenmar cleared his throat. "She says he is bound and collared." His voice shook slightly as he spoke. "There are runes on the ground, and Larkesong is inside them. The other hawk, he is there too, in a cage of some sort. She says the cage keeps his voice trapped inside with him." Kenmar closed his eyes, all trace of color leaving his face. "My son is there."

"Is Ispiria there?" Ari asked when Kenmar fell silent. He directed his words to the hawk.

She made a light chirping sound, a strange noise for a hawk.

Kenmar had his eyes closed still, deep lines marring his brow. Ari turned to Mirimel.

"She did not see Ispiria, or anyone else." Mirimel's face was composed into a total lack of expression. "Only Larke, her fellow hawk and Mrakenson."

"He waits for us, as suspected," Sir Cadwel said, sliding from his saddle. "We need a plan."

Ari nodded, dismounting as well. Soon they clustered in a loose circle on the road. Kiala took out her sword again, quickly sketching another map.

"The volcano is nearly round," she said, drawing a circle. "The ruins of old K'Orge are here. This is the path we're on, with another going up the other side. Both skirt the edges of the ruins on their way to the top, and both go down to K'Orge, which is directly below. You can see it laid out before you when you stand on the upper plateau. The plateau where they are is flat and open. He can see everything for miles."

"Two ways up. No element of surprise." Sir Cadwel scowled.

"The last bit on both sides is a staircase," Kiala said. "Too steep for Questri or camels."

Ari eyed the map for a long moment. When he looked up, everyone was watching him. He turned first to Stew, the mare and Goldwin. "I'm sorry to ask it, but I think the three of you should go back to the smaller trail to wait. I'd ask that you take the camels with you and guard them."

The black mare shook her mane, clearly displeased. Stew and Goldwin both turned to look at her. Ari could sense more than see the argument the three engaged in. Finally, the mare whirled away, huffing, trotting back down the trail. Stew turned back to Ari and nodded. He walked over to the camels, most of which were laying down now, and began prodding them into motion. Mirimel's hawk left her perch, each flap of her wings taking her higher into the deep blue sky above.

"Stew," Ari called.

Stew looked back at him.

"Stay safe. I'll see you when this is done."

Stew dipped his head, his expression grave. He returned to moving the camels.

Ari turned to Cooro, opening his mouth to continue explaining his plan.

"Do not dare to send Cooro with the steeds," the swordmaster said before Ari could speak.

"Why would I do that? Is something wrong with your legs?"

"Cooro is fit as always."

"Good, because I need you, Kiala and Sir Cadwel to continue up this trail. You're the quietest on your feet, so I want you to take point."

309

Cooro nodded, appearing pleased.

Ari looked at Mirimel, then Kenmar. "The three of us will cut through the ruins and come up the other side. If we can't surprise him, we can at least surround him."

"Are we sure we should go up there?" Kiala ventured. Four sets of eyes turned to her. "Suyla isn't up there, or the prisoners. It's either a diversion or a trap."

"A madman has Larke tied up on the edge of a giant pit of fire," Mirimel said. "I don't care what his plan is. Mine is to get Larke back."

"And I must confront my son," Kenmar added, his voice quiet.

"I know your goal is to stop Suyla," Ari said, addressing Kiala. "And yes, this is a trap of some sort. It must be. We cannot pass on a chance to confront Mrakenson, though, or give up on Larke. He would never leave one of us up there." Ari glanced at Sir Cadwel to gauge his thoughts.

"We confront the enemy." The knight's tone was firm. "We are united. To stage their plan, our enemies seem to have divided. If that turns out not to be true, we're no worse off than we thought we'd be, fighting both at once"

"If we even have to fight both," Ari said. "Maybe Mrakenson and the Lady have parted ways." He ignored their slightly pitying looks. Ari was unwilling to consign the Lady to the role of enemy without incontrovertible proof. "Are we agreed with the plan?"

"How will we know you have reached your place?" Cooro asked. "We shall be swifter, with no broken city to pass through."

"Simple," Ari said. "I'll attack him."

"That works." Sir Cadwel stepped back from the map. "How far to old K'Orge?"

310

"Not far now." Kiala looked up the trail.

"Alright, then." Ari squared his shoulder, leading the way. He kept one hand on Fwellian's hilt, reassured by the warmth of the stones against his icy palm.

Kiala's estimate was correct, for it didn't take long before the slope cut away to Ari's right, capped by a narrow strip of land. The trail leveled off with it, at least until it reached a set of narrow, rocky steps ahead, but Ari stopped. He glanced back once, seeing the others crowding the trail behind him.

The remains of the first city of K'Orge stood in crumbled splendor on a slender ribbon of even ground. Seaward, the mountain broke away into harsh, jumbled cliffs that cascaded downward. Landward, another cliff rose, a nearly sheer wall of rock rising up toward a peak that wasn't there. Ari couldn't see the pool of fire, or the higher plateau, but Kiala's drawing made greater sense to him now that they'd reached the ruins.

The hewn off peak curved away before him, shaped like the outside of a massive bowl. The stone steps carved into it to reach the upper plateau were curved as well, wrapping around the outside of the bowl and disappearing from sight. Before him sprawled the broken walls and paved streets of a city, it too reaching around the mountain, twisting back on itself somewhere ahead.

"Why would anyone think that place is cursed?" Mirimel muttered, her tone sarcastic. "Thank you for volunteering me to go in there, Ari."

"I'm going, too," he said. He took in the thick layer of black dust coating the skeletons of buildings. "I don't think it's cursed, only sad and ruined."

"I've been in there," Kiala said. "It isn't cursed."

Mirimel opened her mouth, but Ari cast her a quelling look. Whatever she planned to say about the quality of Princess Kiala's life, now wasn't the time.

"It doesn't feel cursed." Kenmar held his hands out to the city, like someone warming their fingers on a fire.

"How long are the stairs?" Sir Cadwel asked Kiala.

"It's not a quick climb. Nearly a hundred steps."

"And how long should it take them to reach the other side?"

"No more than half of an hour."

"Right." Sir Cadwel nodded, turning to Ari. "We'll spot you most of that. No sense getting there ahead of time."

Cooro held out his hand to Ari. Ari clasped it.

"A safe crossing, my young friend, and a swift and valiant battle."

Ari nodded. He turned to Sir Cadwel, while Cooro repeated the gesture, one of equals, with Mirimel. Sir Cadwel, though Ari stood slightly taller than the knight now, placed a calloused hand on his shoulder.

"Gods' speed, Ari."

Again, Ari nodded, unsure what to say. He turned to Kiala, to wish her well, receiving something that resembled a salute. Ari paused for a moment, to make sure everyone had said their goodbyes, then strolled into the city.

Old K'Orge, spared the flow of molten stone but not the ash, was an odd collection of tumbled and standing. It was as if, when the mountain shook long-ago, some buildings were left unscathed while others fell. Even the cobblestones lining the streets replicated this capricious whim of the gods. There were stretches where each and every stone was overturned and others where a whole street seemed untouched.

Consistent, though, was the coating of black dust thick over everything. It obscured homes and shops, waterless wells and monuments alike. It outlined half crumbled tables and chairs seen through glassless windows and gaping doorways. It covered piles of what Ari could only assume were dishes and choked alleyways. It also, he discovered as his foot sent a small object skittering ahead of him, stood as a blessed layer of concealment over the bones.

Once he saw the first, Ari couldn't help but pick out more. Most of the dust covered ruins were easy to place. A wardrobe, tipped over and smashed. A rotted out wooden chest, its contents long since disintegrated. Vases, small statues and other remnants of civilization. The unidentifiable piles, though, were ash covered bone.

They were everywhere. Inside the buildings, and out. Clustered on the streets. In corners, in the open and, sometimes, forming massive piles blocking roads leading down the mountain. Countless moldering piles of bone.

Ari suppressed a shudder. The ruined city might not be cursed, but it may as well be. He would never dispel the sight from his mind. If Mirimel and Kenmar hadn't been following him, looking to him as leader, he would have abandoned all pretense of stealth and run through the city. At least then, he would sooner be out the other side.

As it was, they reached the second staircase in good time. Mirroring the one Sir Cadwel, Cooro and Kiala had taken, it curved up the outer edge of the hewn off peak, twisting out of sight. With a look to Mirimel and Kenmar to make sure they were ready, Ari started up.

He climbed at a steady pace, not really eager to reach the top. In spite of the many hours Ari put into sword work and the study of war, he was never excited to deal out death. Nor could he count on doing so. Mrakenson was a terrible foe. When last they met, it had taken Larke and the Lady together to stave him off long enough to simply escape. That was in his keep, full of spells to increase his power. Likely, the runes the hawk reported were of that ilk.

When they neared the top, Ari halted. The stone of the mountain was to his left, nothing but open space to his right. Before him, he could see the wall of the above plateau stretching toward the next peak in the chain. It stood less tall than the one they climbed, across a shrub studded valley. One more step, and Ari's head would be visible to anyone standing on the plateau above, for there was no shelter.

"I know you're there, Father, Thrice Born. I can smell you."

The voice was grating, but not loud. Mrakenson would know how well they could hear. There was nothing to be gained in shouting.

"And something more. I smell a flower of the north," the voice continued. "And on the other side, the stench of an Aluien, a witch and a mortal man. How nice of you to bring me snacks. A flower and a Whey. I shall use them to replenish myself once I've killed you."

Ari looked back, taking in Kenmar's pale face, so white even his lips lacked color. The older lord seemed almost to tremble, though in anger or fear, Ari couldn't tell. Behind him, Mirimel peered up the staircase through narrowed blue eyes, her bow out and an arrow fitted. Drawing Fwellian, Ari headed up the final steps.

He could see why the Dinji thought the plateau was a sacred place. It stretched out before him, disturbingly flat, glossy black stone. It was as if someone had made a liquid of black glass and poured it into the valley that was once there,

314

letting it cool smooth. Who else but a god could accomplish such a thing?

To Ari's left was the pool of liquid fire, but it wasn't what he expected. Instead of bright flames, it was coated in a black crust. The surface moved and churned, minute cracks offering glimpses of the fire below. If asked, Ari would have likened it to a charred log, all dark on the outside, but bright within. Both the black glass-like plateau and the pit of charred fire were a stark, disturbing contrast to the bright blue sky above and the high afternoon sun. A distant speck, Mirimel's hawk soared overhead.

Ari's surroundings took little of his attention, though, beyond establishing where the edges of sure footing lay. Their enemy, Lord Mrakenson, stood in the center of an elaborate array of runes, drawn on the ground in dull, rusted red. Ari's nostrils confirmed what his eyes suspected, for the reek of dried blood was discernable even through the burnt, sulfur-tinged air.

His enemy was no longer the emaciated skeleton Ari had met so long ago, in the mountains of Sorga. He stood tall and straight, taller than Kenmar. He looked disturbingly like his father, though younger, without a touch of gray in his hair or a stoop to his shoulders. They even wore similar unassuming trousers and tunic, though Mrakenson was unrumpled and had a blade at his waist. The resemblance would have been greater, however, if Mrakenson's expression didn't radiate endless cruelty.

Larkesong lay at his feet. He was bound with black ropes, his hands tied behind him, legs hobbled and a cord about his neck. Mrakenson held that cord loosely in one hand, though Larkesong appeared unconscious. Across from Ari, where Sir Cadwel was coming into view, the hawk Mirimel had sent with

315

Larke stood awkwardly on the black surface of the plateau, a cage of some dull iron-like metal over him. He opened his mouth, but no sound emerged.

"We've been waiting for you, Father." Mrakenson's face contorted with vicious hatred as he spoke. "My new friends and I."

Kiala and Cooro filed up the steps opposite Ari, following Sir Cadwel. All three had swords drawn. The air about them thrummed with the potential for violence.

Mrakenson turned slowly, taking them all in. He smiled a slow, spiteful smile. "So many of you, just for me? I must be mighty indeed."

"What are these runes?" Kenmar's voice was ragged. "Whose blood is this?"

"Thinking of the pretty ladies?" Mrakenson's smile grew.

Ari felt his heart halt its beat. It hadn't occurred to him the blood might be Ispiria's.

"Never fear, father mine. The pretty ones are there, in a lovely tower in the sea, with my steward to see to their every need." He pointed.

Ari's heart resumed beating. He followed the gesture, taking in the view beyond the plateau for the first time. At the foot of the mountain sprawled K'Orge, a city of broad avenues and high stone towers. It was a gray city, for the stone there was gray, but lovely nonetheless. A line of towers stood in the sea as well, as if in silent watch.

"It is horse blood," Mrakenson continued, drawing Ari's eyes back. "I had no more need of mounts, so I dined on one and gave the other to Suyla. It is she who drew these runes." He looked down at them, his expression loving. "They are too elaborate for me, I'm afraid. I was always an indifferent student of the Wheylian arts, and these are Aluien besides." His eyes snapped back up, going to Ari. "I do know what they'll do, though, and how to wake them."

"What will they do?" Ari asked, aiming the words at Kenmar, though he didn't take his eyes from Mrakenson.

"I'm not sure. I can't sort them all out." Panic edged Kenmar's voice. "It is Suyla's work. I recognize her hand. I've never seen anything like it."

Ari looked across to Sir Cadwel and Kiala, but both shook their heads. "What will the runes do?" he asked Mrakenson.

Mrakenson lowered his lids, looking at Ari through hooded eyes. "They will punish you if you do not take the bargain I offer."

Ari waited. It was obvious their enemy wanted him to ask. Baiting Mrakenson was likely dangerous, but Ari knew an opponent ruled by emotion was more apt to make mistakes.

Mrakenson glowered. He shook the black cord that was wrapped around Larke's neck. "It's a simple bargain, Thrice Born. Help me kill my father or this one dies. His death will activate Suyla's runes, and your punishment."

Ari looked across the square to Sir Cadwel. There was no way they were taking that offer. "I think not."

"Let's wake the bard up and ask him, shall we?" Mrakenson began murmuring in the guttural tongue Ari had heard Kenmar use for spells.

Beside Ari, Kenmar stiffened, raising his hands, fingers spread wide, as if readying himself to cast a counter spell. Mrakenson smirked at his father, but turned and made a gesture over Larke. Ari could see Mirimel from the corner of his eye, her bow held at the ready.

Larke jerked, blinking. He craned his head, looking about with bloodshot eyes. Seeing Ari, Mirimel and Kenmar, he struggled into a kneeling position. His blond hair hung in dingy strands. His clothing was stained with blood.

"Well, bard, do you think they should take my bargain and spare your life?" Mrakenson asked, giving the black rope a shake.

Chapter 28

Larke shook his head, his eyes meeting Ari's. "Ari, don't kill any--"

Larke's blurted words were cut off as Mrakenson yanked on the rope, closing the noose tighter about the bard's neck. "I warned you what would happen if you didn't say yes."

Larke toppled over, his face turning red. With his arms bound behind him, he was powerless to cushion his fall, or free himself to breath. Before Ari could act, an arrow sped through the air, hitting the rope. Instead of breaking it, the arrow bounced off.

Mrakenson, still pulling the cord tight, turned a twisted grin on Mirimel. "It is a magic rope, prett--"

His words broke off as a second arrow hit his hand, the tip going clear through, leaving only the feathers sticking out on one side. Mrakenson screamed, dropping the rope. A third arrow flew directly for his heart, but he batted it away with a snarled word of magic.

Ari was already running when Mirimel loosed the third arrow. Sir Cadwel charged in from the other side, Cooro and Kiala on his heels. They met at Mrakenson. Before Ari's raised swords could land, a wall of undulating blackness came up before him. He skidded to a halt, unwilling to swing blindly into the darkness.

Mirimel darted around him, diving into the haze, toward where Larke lay. A sword whipped passed Ari's face and he jumped back. It was difficult to tell, but he thought it was Sir Cadwel's. Ari circled, trying to get around the barrier of darkness, which seemed to condense before his eyes. He could hear swords clashing, and Cooro cursing. Kiala let loose a scream of rage.

Giving up on circling, Ari dove toward the darkness, as Mirimel had. It repulsed him, sending him flying back. He landed hard, shaking his head to clear it. It felt like he'd run headlong into a wall. He looked over his shoulder. "Kenmar," he roared. "Get me in there."

His face set in grim lines, Kenmar began weaving a spell.

Ari hauled himself to his feet, running back toward the haze enveloping the others. Just before he reached it, it erupted forth. Tentacle-like arms of darkness reached out. They wrapped about Ari, pulling him in.

He saw Cooro sail past, his face bloodied and stunned as he was expelled from the darkness. The tentacles released Ari. He stayed on his feet, dropping low to catch his balance. Fwellian lit up, blue-white witch fire dancing along the blade.

In the center of the runes, Mirimel crouched beside Larke. Her hands clawed at the rope strangling the bard. Her face was a cloud of desperation. Larke was purple. He no longer moved.

320

Mrakenson charged toward Ari, sword in hand. He recognized it as Sir Cadwel's blade. The knight and Kiala were nowhere to be seen.

Ari snapped Fwellian up, blocking. Blue sparks flew from the blade. Mrakenson swept out a foot. Ari jumped, avoiding the attempt to trip him. He blocked a swing aimed at his middle, exposed as he leapt. Spinning faster than a normal man could hope to, Ari disengaged Fwellian, bringing the massive blade around to strike Mrakenson from the other side.

An Empty One, Mrakenson was fast too. He parried, dodging back. "Take my offer, Thrice Born. No one but my father needs to die."

Ari didn't bother to answer, unleashing a flurry of blows.

Mrakenson met them, sword hilt clutched in both hands, but he was pushed back. The ring of darkness engulfing them went too, Larke and Mirimel disappearing outside it. Ari realized he could hear the others, though muted. He pushed the sounds away, intent on his enemy. With each swing, he drove the Empty One backward across the plateau.

The darkness pulsed around them, tearing open. Kiala, Cooro and Lord Kenmar dove inside, the rift closing behind them. Mrakenson whipped Sir Cadwel's blade around, sending them diving to the ground. Before Ari could capitalize on the Empty One's exposed side, Mrakenson whirled back.

Ari struck, aiming for Mrakenson's neck. The Empty One parried, greatsword in one hand. The other snaked out. Grit filled Ari's eyes. He jumped back, bringing Fwellian up.

Ari blinked furiously. He could tell the harsh sand wasn't natural. It nearly welded his eyes shut. He could hear the others fighting.

Kenmar's voice rose, though Ari didn't know the words. The binding sand fell from Ari's eyes. He blinked again, trying to see.

Mrakenson had dropped Sir Cadwel's sword. Even as sight returned to Ari, the Empty One launched a dark dart of magic from each hand. One toward Kenmar, the other Cooro.

Kiala, between them, launched herself in front of Cooro. The streak of dark magic slammed into her chest, sending her flying backward into the swordmaster. Both were knocked from the undulating ring of shadow Mrakenson had thrown up around them.

Ari dove forward at the same time Kiala leapt. He was too far away to stop the second dart. It took Kenmar in the chest. He crumpled. Mrakenson threw his head back, howling with glee. Ari kicked Sir Cadwel's sword, sending it skittering from the darkness.

Seeming to ignore Ari, Mrakenson pulled free the sword at his waist. He lunged toward his father. Ari jumped between them, Fwellian deflecting the Empty One's blade. He wasn't sure if Kenmar lived, but he drove Mrakenson backward.

Mrakenson snarled, foam flecking his lips. He launched into an attack of his own, trying to reach his prone father. Ari was forced to defend, blue light skittering off Fwellian with each parry. They moved back across the runes.

"You have no reason to love him. He murdered your parents." Mrakenson's voice held strain.

Ari took back the attack, willing himself to be faster. He pushed the Empty One back until Kenmar was outside the circle of darkness. Mrakenson dropped a hand from his sword hilt. A word and a gesture sent darts of black magic at Ari's chest. A swing of Fwellian swept them away.

"You have all to gain in siding with me. Siding with Suyla. Rule with us." Even as he spoke, Mrakenson unleashed another wave of magic.

A web of darkness dropped over Ari. He jerked Fwellian up. The sword easily cut the web away, but the magic clung to the blade, weighing it down. Mrakenson slashed out. The sword he wielded bit deeply into Ari's arm before he could pull free of the broken web.

"Join me or I will kill you, Thrice Born."

Hot blood streamed down Ari's sword arm. He switched Fwellian to his off hand. The wound would heal, but Ari didn't have the time that would take. He brought Fwellian up to parry another blow.

A slow smile curved Mrakenson's lips. "You do not know how to use the blade."

Ari fought not to scowl, not to let the truth show on his face. Mrakenson attacked again. He seemed renewed. He danced around Ari, raining down blows. Ari felt like a bear encircled by a band of hunters, though Mrakenson was alone.

Parrying as many of the blows as he could, though several shallow gashes landed, Ari strove for some understanding of the blade he wielded. Fwellian should link mind and heart with intent. What did that mean? What was the key?

"Ari," Larke's broken voice cried, somewhere outside the darkness.

The bard dissolved into a fit of coughing. Multicolored light flickered at the edges of Ari's vision. He realized there was other magic trying to break through the undulating inky enclosure.

Mrakenson's leg darted out. This time, Ari was too slow. He tried to jump, but the blow caught him. He crashed to his knees, cursing himself for letting Larke and the flickering magic distract him.

Mrakenson's blade came down. Ari brought Fwellian up, blocking. Crushed by the weight of the Empty One pressing down with all his strength, Ari tried to force himself to his feet.

Fwellian, blue-white light flashing along its length to fill Ari's vision, crept ever closer. Mrakenson's face was split by a vicious grin as he pressed Ari's own sword down on him. Ari gritted his teeth, calling on all of his strength. He brought his sword arm up, the wound nearly healed, both hands once again wielding the blade.

Fwellian touched his forehead, the sharp edge cutting a thin line. Ari felt anger flash through him. He didn't want to die by his own blade.

Heat shot through the sword. It seemed to jerk away from Ari's head. He blinked, blood tricking into his left eye. Panic flashed across Mrakenson's face.

It was his enemies fear that drove home for Ari what he'd done. He didn't want Fwellian to kill him, and the sword complied. Finding strength in hope, Ari surged upward.

Mrakenson danced back. He crouched low, defensive, no longer grinning. Terror flickered in his gaze.

"I've been wanting to parry, wanting to fight," Ari said, his voice low. "Now, what I want is to end you."

Ari leapt forward. He brought Fwellian down in a massive overhand blow. He filled his mind and heart with the desire to see Mrakenson dead.

Mrakenson tried to parry. Fwellian flared a blinding blue, cleaving clear through the Empty One's blade. Not pausing, his swing, Ari sliced Mrakenson down the middle, sending one bloodless half of his body toppling to each side. His two eyes, falling away from each other, were round pools of shock.

"Ari." Larke stumbled through the dissipating darkness, batting at it. "Don't kill him," he rasped out, his throat so broken the words were nearly unintelligible.

Ari stepped back. Larke's eyes fell on the rapidly disintegrating form at Ari's feet. The bard's face drained of all color. He fell to his knees, squeezing his eyes shut.

Mirimel rushed forward through the ever-thinning clouds of dark magic. She dropped into a crouch beside Larke, looking up at Ari with angry eyes. "What did you do to him?"

Ari sheathed Fwellian, the sword's light extinguished now that the battle was won. Behind Mirimel, Ari spotted the overturned cage where the little brown Sorga Hawk had been. "Nothing. He told me not to kill Mrakenson, but it is done."

Tears were streaming from the bard's eyes. Ari stared at him, unsure what he'd done wrong. Kenmar and Sir Cadwel hurried over to the piles of dust that marked where Mrakenson had been. Sir Cadwel let out a curse, sheathing his reclaimed greatsword.

Kenmar slid to the ground, his face crumbling in sorrow. He ran his fingers through the dust "My son," he whispered.

Cooro and Kiala stood to the side, supporting each other. The swordmaster had a broad gash in his tunic. Through it, Ari could see a half-healed wound, gouging Cooro from shoulder to hip. At his side, Kiala looked exhausted, a large hole burned in the center of her shirt.

A tremor went through Ari. It took him a moment to realize it was the ground shaking, not his limbs. He looked around, seeing on their faces that the others had felt it too. Larke let out a choking sob.

The bard's neck was obviously healing, though the blood would need to be wiped away. Ari realized that, though Larke had been stripped of the Orlenia, they must have returned him to a human state, like Ari. If they'd only reclaimed the magic from his veins, he'd be an Empty One now. He wouldn't bleed. Ari hoped Larke could live that way. They said taking the Orlenia from an Aluien drove them mad.

"Why didn't you want me to kill him?" Ari asked, crossing to Larke.

Mirimel tugged the bard to his feet. He let her, but tears made trails in the grime coating his face. She ducked under his arm, wrapping it firmly about her shoulder so she was holding him up. The ground shook beneath them, harder this time.

"Suyla's spell," Larke whispered. His voice was broken still, but now more by tears than the damage to his neck. "Mrakenson couldn't, but I could read Suyla's spell."

Ari's eyes went to the dried blood scrawled across the shiny black ground. "What does it do? I thought killing you would set it off?"

Sir Cadwel came to stand beside Ari. Cooro and Kiala limped closer. Kenmar stayed where he was, his tears dripping on the ashes of his son.

Larke grimaced as the ground shook again. "She lied to him. Not my death. Any death. Mine, yours, his. Any death."

"So the spell is working?" Ari asked. He glanced about quickly, trying to spot any new danger.

The earth beneath them gave a heaving lurch. A thunderous cracking sound echoed through the mountains. Cooro and Kaila fell, trying to catch themselves on each other.

Ari turned in a slow circle in the stillness that followed. Hot steam belched from the fire-pool. A thin line rent the plateau, bright orange light shining up from it. The earth began to tremble again.

"What did the spell do?" Ari repeated, aware his voice was loud with fear.

"The unthinkable," Larke whispered.

The world exploded around them. Ari was thrown through the air, Sir Cadwel beside him. Steam shot up from the ground, spewing razor sharp shards of black rock everywhere.

Ari rolled onto his hands and knees. He was aware of a terrible roaring sound. Smoldering stones showered down around him. He staggered to his feet.

A glance showed Sir Cadwel running toward Kenmar, who lay sprawled not far away. Ari ran seaward, where last he'd seen Cooro and Kiala, the shaking ground making every step a battle. He caught sight of Larke, quickly realizing the bard was sheltering Mirimel with his body. Seeing them both look toward him with scared, but rational, eyes, Ari ran past.

Sir Cadwel, Larke and Kenmar would all heal, as would Ari. Nothing short of death or dismemberment would truly harm them. Cooro and Kiala, though, they were human. A Wheylian Witch she might be, but Ari had no idea if Kiala's magic could protect them from the chaos of fire and debris raining down. Besides, if he was any judge, she's spent most of her energy healing herself and Cooro.

They came stumbling toward Ari, emerging from a billowing cloud of black ash. He ran to them, wedging himself between them so he could support them both. Together, they struggled back the way Ari had come.

"Ari." Sir Cadwel's roar cut through the ash and falling rock. "This way."

Unable to see his mentor, Ari followed the sound of his calls. He, Cooro and Kiala stumbled forward over the broken, shaking ground. The sound of rock splitting ricocheted around them. At one point, they had to cross a deep fissure, filled with liquid fire. Cooro jumped first. Ari all but threw Kiala to him before following.

Finally, they came out the back side of the plateau, crawling up the slope of the next peak toward the others. Sir Cadwel was there, watching for them. Larke and Mirimel clutched each other, their eyes wide with horror. Kenmar sat on the ground, his hands clutching his head. All four were burned and bloodied, as Ari, Cooro and Kiala were.

As they clawed their way up the mountain, Ari realized the terror on his friends' faces was directed below. He didn't look, needing all of his concentration to climb. He came last, in case Cooro or Kiala slipped. Both were agile, though, even wounded and weary as they were. Neither needed Ari's help.

The shaking subsided while Ari climbed. A harsh wind blew in off the sea, scouring them with ash, smoke and fiery shards of stone. Once they reached the others, Ari slumped down beside Kenmar, needing a moment to catch his breath before standing.

Reluctantly, he raised his gaze from the rocks at his feet. At first, too much smoke swirled through the air for Ari to see what was causing the sickened looks on his friends' faces, or Kenmar's sobs. He kept his eyes trained toward the ocean, as theirs were, waiting in sinking dread.

The sea wind gusted. In a swirl of darkness, a gap opened in the obscuring wall of ash. Through it, Ari glimpsed the shoreline. He saw K'Orge.

Hot, liquid fire streamed down the side of the mountain. Blackening on top, near them, it was a bright wave where it hit the city walls. It washed around buildings, melting them as Ari watched. The streets were flooded orange. Heat shimmered above K'Orge. The flow of destruction only ended where it hit the sea, forming a black wall sizzling with steam. Beyond that wall, the ocean towers still stood. Ari counted it a blessing from the gods he was too far away to hear the screams, if indeed those trapped in K'Orge had lungs left to loose any.

He sat beside Kenmar and stared, slack jawed. Ari's mind seemed slowed, his thoughts stuttering. He couldn't understand, was unable to comprehend, the extent of the destruction below. The sky swirled. A curtain of ash closed off the glimpse of K'Orge, but Ari couldn't wrench his gaze away.

"Why?" The single word was all he could muster.

"Suyla," Kenmar whispered. "She found a way to claim her thousand lives."

"Thousand lives?" Ari echoed. He couldn't make his mind work. He couldn't drag his thoughts past what was happening to the city. "Where are the other Aluiens? How can they permit this?"

"They won't stop her." Larke's voice shook. "I saw the mountain in the pool. I studied her books, guessed her plan. They refused to stop her, but they . . . they took the Orlenia from me. Made me like you. As a kindness they said, but I think to make it impossible for me to stop her."

For as an Empty One, Ari realized, stripped of Orlenia and left hollow, Larke would still have had magic. Making him mortal again had robbed him of that. "Why would she do this to the city?" Ari asked again, numbness slowing his thoughts.

No one answered him. Ari tried to make his mind work. The Lady created the runes. Mrakenson's death triggered them, but letting him kill Kenmar would have as well.

A hollow rumbling sound rolled through the mountains, sounding almost like laughter. The smoke before them swirled. A harsh wind drove into Ari's face. It took him a moment to realize there were twin, matching points of churning ash, one far to his left, the other to his right. Twin red lights appeared, hovering high above.

"It's a beast," Mirimel's voice trembled. She clutched her bow, though the string was burned. Her hand fumbled with the pouch where she kept spares. "The hawks are above. They say a beast rose from the city. It is here."

Ari shook his head. The swirls in the ash grew. The wind buffeting them became increasingly violent. Beside him, Kenmar stood.

The graying lord raised his hands, words of magic spilling from his mouth. He made a sweeping gesture, his voice growing louder. He slashed his hands downward. "Reveal yourself," he boomed in Ancient Wheylian.

Ash rained down about them, falling from the sky to leave it a startling, almost luminescent blue. Out across the sea, the day was dying, the sky streaked a sinister red. Ari hardly noted that, though, for something massive shielded their direct view of the sun. He surged to his feet, drawing Fwellian once more.

It was a winged beast, lithe in body and covered in black scales. A long neck snaked out, ending in a wedge-shaped head and jaws filled with teeth. The giant leathery wings swept back and forth, holding it in the sky above them, swirling the air. Clawed talons clenched. Twin red eyes looked down on them, and the beast, what Ari could only name as a dragon, seemed almost to smile.

Chapter 29

"I offer but once more." The voice of the dragon was smooth, flowing about them like honey. It was the Lady's voice, yet also more. It was as if the strength of the form she'd taken added power to her words. "Kill my ancient enemy now, and I shall let you live. You are precious to me, my Aridian. I have spent years crafting you."

She folded her wings, dropping down. Ari stepped in front of the others, sword held low. The dragon settled on the cracked rim of the volcano, seeming not to mind that the tip of her tail swished back and forth through the molten fire. She was vast, bigger than the king's stable or a large inn. A black trail of hardened, melted rock cut a channel down the mountainside behind her, ending in a dark stain covering the smoking ruins of K'Orge. Far out to sea, the lowering sun reflected off the ocean.

"You think to protect your friends from me?" the dragon asked. Her head snaked back and forth, the weaving pattern nearly mesmerizing. "Give me your answer, my Aridian."

"You killed the people of K'Orge." Ari's voice was harsh, the betrayal of the Lady's cruelty ripping through him. "For what?"

"To ensure my revenge, and harvest their power. Nothing shall stand before me now. Not you and that little sword. Not my most ancient foe. Nothing. I shall put an end to all who have crossed me, and take my place as Queen of Wheylia."

"Our people will not stand for that," Kiala said. If she was afraid, her voice didn't reveal it.

"My people will have no choice." The dragon's forked tongue flicked out, as if tasting the air. "I would have kept you, my pet, as a human figurehead, but you have sided against me. There is nothing left for you but to die."

Ari could feel the others shifting behind them. He knew he needed to act, to prevent them from throwing away their lives attacking her. Sir Cadwel and Kenmar might stand some chance, though even the great knight seemed small compared to the vastness of the dragon. Mirimel, Cooro and Kiala were mortal. Larke could heal, but was unskilled in any form of war.

"My Lady," Larke called, stepping forward. "Please, what is this madness that has taken you? Where is your finer nature?"

"My Larke," the dragon all but purred. "I have kept you for one purpose, to sing of my glory. I truly was sorry to have the Orlenia stripped from you. They say the pain is unbearable, that the wound of its loss never heals." She lowered her head to eye level with them. "It was to keep you safe, my Larke. Now, you cannot fight me. With no fight in you, you won't need to die."

Stepping up beside Ari, Sir Cadwel drew his sword.

The dragon let out a breathy sigh. Flames flickered about her muzzle. "I grow weary of waiting for an answer, my Aridian." Her head snaked toward him. "You should know, I think, that my enemies old steward is with your pretty womenfolk. If the sun sets without your answer, the correct answer, it is by his hands they will die."

"Ari," Mirimel said, her voice low.

Ari stared at the beast before them. She was the Lady no more, if she ever had been. She was Suyla, a vast, black-scaled dragon who wished to kill Ari and his friends and seize an entire kingdom. Somehow, he didn't think one kingdom would satisfy her.

Ari closed his eyes for a long moment. He'd never wanted it to come to this, but he must kill the Lady. "I want you all to stay out of this," he whispered, opening his eyes.

There was no reply. He risked a quick glance away from the dragon. His friends' expressions were as hard as his heart felt. He shrugged. He'd tried.

Turning back to the dragon, he made one final attempt. "My Lady, please reconsider this course. How can vengeance mean so much? Look what you have done. Think on what you are about to do."

"Vengeance?" The giant wings flapped, showering Ari and his friends with hot stones. "It is not only vengeance I seek, my Aridian. It is justice. It is dominion. Long ago, I failed to win Wheylia or put an end to my enemies, but my time has come again. Who succeeds first is nothing. Who remains standing last is all. That is the way of war. I shall never be one of the fallen again."

She swept her wings in great arcs as she spoke, rising into the air. Fire sputtered from her muzzle like spittle. "I shall do what must be done to right this world. I have the strength to kill when killing is the only course. My homeland shall be scorched free of the idle and weak. All the lands shall be cleansed of Empty Ones. My rule will be absolute, and I will never die."

Ari watched her sail in a wide circle above them, her shadow falling on him in a curtain of darkness. Sorrow washed through him. Once, he'd loved the Lady. He'd ascribed to her all that was good in the world.

He clenched his jaw, pressing sorrow away. The time for remorse had long since passed. The sun was dipping ever lower. So many lives had been lost that day that the pain of their passing spread through Ari like numbness, but only one more needed to die.

She was laughing to herself now, spiraling above them. Mirimel's hawks winged away. Even Ari could sense their terror. She shot a gout of flame at them, but they were already too far from her.

"Do any of you have a way to get to that tower before the sun sets?" Ari asked his friends, his voice low.

"I can," Kiala said. "Cooro and I can. We'll save my niece, and your lady."

"Try not to kill the steward," Kenmar said. "He isn't evil. Tell him I sent you. He should listen."

Kiala shrugged. "I'll do what I can. This way," she added to Cooro. With a nod to them, Kiala started scrambling along the peak, angling toward the ruins of the northernmost staircase.

"Fight well," Cooro said, setting off after her.

Ari turned to the others. "Larke, Kenmar, you should probably hide."

Lord Kenmar shook his head. "We can make a shield, to hold back some of the heat. Larkesong, you must know the runes. Help me draw them, before she comes down. I'll add the magic."

"Right." Larke squared his shoulders. The two of them started sliding down the hillside.

"Ari, she's spotted Cooro and Kiala." Mirimel's tone was urgent.

Ari looked up. No longer circling, the dragon's course straightened. Her back was to them, her long tail a streamer behind her. "Shoot her," he barked, for Suyla was already moving out of range. It would be easy enough for her to destroy Cooro and Kiala, and then come back for Ari and the others.

Mirimel had her bow up before Ari even finished the command. Arrows sped through the air in rapid succession. The first two bounced off the dragon's scales. The following two stabbed into the leathery membrane of her wings.

The dragon banked, hovering midair while she craned her neck to look at her wings. She turned back, red eyes narrow. With a screeching cry, she dove toward where Ari, Mirimel and Sir Cadwel stood. Ari grabbed Mirimel by the arm, pulling her one way while Sir Cadwel ran the other. Mirimel was still trying to shoot. Shrugging Ari off, she sent an arrow into the softer flesh lining the dragon's nose, and another into her eye.

Suyla roared. She dropped to the ground, clawing at the bolts. Both came free, appearing to have done little damage.

"Ari, Mirimel, quick," Larke yelled, gesturing them toward him.

Larke crouched behind a boulder. In front of it, Ari could see hastily scrawled symbols. Dragging Mirimel with him, Ari dove behind the rock. A stream of fire hit. It broke in front of the rock, not melting it as magic kept the heat at bay.

"Where's Kenmar?" Ari yelled over the roar of flames. He clutched Fwellian in one hand, wondering how he would get close enough to use the blade, and if even it had the power to stop a dragon.

"Finishing a second fire block," Larke said.

Fire crackled around them, the rocks to either side of their small shelter melting. The air shimmered with heat. The smell of charred earth seared the inside of Ari's nose.

The fire abruptly stopped, replaced by a howl of pain. Ari stuck his head around the rock. Sir Cadwel was at the dragon's tail, hacking at it with his greatsword like a man chopping firewood.

The dragon snaked her neck around, her razor-like teeth speeding toward the knight, her mouth wide. Ari cried out, leaving the shelter of the rock to run toward her. In his hand, Fwellian brightened with blue-white flame.

Sir Cadwel jumped back. The dragon's teeth snapped in mid-air. She sucked in a deep breath. The knight ran toward another rock, with the same markings before it as the one Ari had been hiding behind.

Before Suyla could loose a stream of flame on Sir Cadwel, there was another roar. An enormous feline barreled passed Ari, its four legs outdistancing his two. It launched itself at the dragon's throat, giant tusks and white fur gleaming. Ari faltered, shock making him clumsy as he realized it was Kenmar.

The dragon bellowed in pain. She writhed, twisting her neck to throw Kenmar off. He dropped to the ground, landing on his feet. Dark blood painted the cat's fangs and dripped from the dragon's neck. She let loose a gout of flame. The great cat that was Kenmar leapt away.

Ari charged forward, knowing he was too slow. The dragon angled her head, flame following Kenmar. Dodging it, the cat launched himself at her neck once more. Suyla brought her wedge-shaped head whipping around, slamming it into Kenmar. The giant feline sailed through the air, bouncing off the side of the mountain. He struggled up, swaying on his feet.

More arrows flew in, peppering the dragon's face as Ari reached her. He could see Sir Cadwel charging back toward her tail. Ari's sword bit deeply into the scales of her chest. She slashed at him with one taloned foot. He caught two of the massive claws on his blade, but the third gouged his chest. Hot blood bubbled forth, soaking his tunic.

Her head whipped around, away from him. Before Ari realized her goal, she bathed Sir Cadwel in fire. Ari yelled, swinging again. He cut a deep gouge in the scales on her chest. She reared back in pain. He dodged away, trying to see Sir Cadwel.

Ari couldn't distinguish the knight from the blackened ground. He let loose another cry. Taking Fwellian in both hands, he ran forward to drive the sword into her chest. She dropped back to the ground as he reached her. Ari braced himself, lunging. Slipping in his own blood as he drove the blade forward, he stumbled, dropping to one knee.

He pushed himself to his feet, aware of a tight clump of arrows dangling from the dragon's right eye. She raised her head, sending fire spewing past him, toward Larke and Mirimel. Ari caught sight of the giant feline, his white fur dark with blood. He was dragging a charcoaled form, angling toward the other fire block.

Ari slashed at her throat, his sword cutting a long gouge through her scales. She dropped her head down, almost crushing him with it as he dove away. Coming to his feet again, he spun, slashing open one of her nostrils as she darted her head forward to bite him.

She heaved back onto her hind legs. With two great downward sweeps of her wings, she lifted herself from the ground. Her unscored eye burned into Ari.

"Enough," she hissed as she rose above him, beyond his reach. "I shall end this now."

Flecks of blood spewed forth with her words, raining down from her wounds. She sucked in a deep breath, readying her flame.

"No," Ari yelled. He would not let her get away. She would not be permitted to rain down fire on them from above.

Ari drew back his arm, Fwellian's pommel clenched like a javelin in his hand. Blue-white fire danced along the blade. Putting every ounce of intent he could muster into the throw, he launched his sword.

She dropped her head down as he did it, opening her mouth. Flame shot toward Ari. He saw the blue-white light of the blade disappear inside the fire. He dove away, rolling across the ground as flame buffeted it. The fires igniting on him were alternately lit and extinguished as he rolled away.

The fire stopped. The earth shook with a loud crash. Ari pulled himself to his hands and knees. His face was burned. He couldn't see. What was left of his tunic was a blood-soaked, tattered, smoldering rag flapping against his skin. He shook his head to clear it, his hands scrambling for a rock. Anything to use as a weapon. The pain began to recede from his face. His eyes started to clear.

The dragon's nose was only a handbreadth away. Ari fell backward as it came into focus, shock surging through him. He tried to calm his breath, the smell of scorched flesh assailing him with each inhalation. He took in the stillness of the dragon, the dimness of the arrow-studded eye. No life flickered there.

Fwellian, the blade dull and coated in blood, protruded point-first from the dragon's skull. Ari came up on his knees, rubbing at the still seeping wound in his chest. The hilt of his sword was somewhere inside the dragon, down her throat from the looks of it.

A noise brought Ari to his feet, whirling to face it. Mirimel and Larke crept from behind the rune-warded rock, gingerly crossing the swaths of charred ground alongside it. Both were covered in ash. They looked battered, a large bruise coloring one side of Mirimel's chin, but fairly unharmed.

His eyes going wide, Ari turned away from them, stumbling around the dragon. He found Sir Cadwel on his back, sprawled flat. His clothing was mostly burned away, but his skin was nearly healed. His greatsword lay darkened and warped nearby.

Kenmar lay on his side, curled in a ball, unmoving. Passing Ari, Larke knelt by Kenmar, gently turning him on his back. The bard put an ear to Kenmar's chest. Ari could see Larke hold his breath. Mirimel came to kneel beside him. After a long moment, Larke let out a sigh of relief.

He looked up at Ari. "I don't know why I was worried. I suppose if he died, he'd disintegrate."

Ari nodded, having forgotten that himself. For all he was their friend, Kenmar was still an Empty One. He would die as any Empty One died.

Ari turned to the dragon again. It sprawled across the plateau. He stared at it for a long moment, feeling dazed. The red of the setting sun glinted off the black scales.

"Ispiria," he cried, spinning back to Larke and Mirimel, terror shooting through him.

A hawk cried out above. Two little brown raptors dove toward them, from the direction of the sea. They landed on

Kenmar's unconscious form, making excited, unintelligible noises at Mirimel.

She lifted her face to Ari, her smile brighter than the sun. "Cooro and Kiala have them. Ispiria is safe." Mirimel burst into tears.

Larke pulled her into his arms, burying his face in her hair. The hawks made their strange chattering sounds. Beneath their talons, Kenmar groaned.

Ari sat down in the rocks and ash. He was exhausted. He shot the dead dragon a scathing look, filled with grief for all she'd done. "I would have stopped it, if I could," he whispered. "I would have done anything to save them all."

"I know you would have, lad," Sir Cadwel said. He sat up, looking about. "Sometimes, all we can seek for the innocent is vengeance." The knight looked down at himself, his eyebrows shooting up. "Where are my clothes?"

"They burned in the dragon fire. You're going to have to have your sword repaired."

"Right." Sir Cadwel glanced at his greatsword. He blinked once, eyes flying wide in alarm. His hand shot up, checking his drooping mustache.

"I think your magic protected that," Ari said. He wanted to smile, but he could still see the smoke rising from the ruins of K'Orge.

"You did all you could, lad," Sir Cadwel said. He stood, his skin almost completely healed, and scanned the dragon carcass. "Get your sword, wake up Kenmar, find me some pants, and we'll go look for the others."

Chapter 30

They did wake up Kenmar, although he had a huge lump on his head and was noticeably groggy. Ari knew Kenmar would heal quickly enough, as would he, Sir Cadwel and Larke. Luckily, Mirimel hadn't been injured in any serious way, as she was the only true human who'd stayed on the plateau with the dragon.

Ari retrieved his sword, a gruesome act, and they headed down the mountain. To Ari's surprise, the camels waited where the Questri had been told to leave them, laying about chewing their cuds. Ari had expected to find they'd bolted. They made quick work of finding clothing in their packs for Sir Cadwel, and Ari washed up and found a new tunic. There was no sign of the Questri, but Ari wasn't very worried about them. Stew, the black mare and Goldwin knew what they were about.

Taking the camels with them, they started the trek down to the ocean. Ari did his best to keep his eyes averted from the swath of cooling black rock, a veritable river of destruction. A deep ache settled in his chest, a nearly physical pain, though with no corporal cause.

As they neared the shore, Ari's keen eyes picked out people. Many people. They were dark skinned and wearing bright sashes, the men bare chested like Kanja. They stood clustered alongside the ruins of K'Orge, now mostly half-melted gray stone remnants sticking up from the cooling black rock. There were thousands of them. Peering through the smoke, Ari saw a like number gathered on the opposite side of the city.

As they drew nearer, the mass of people below noticed Ari and his companions. People began turning toward them, looking up. Many pointed. They started shouting, and clapping.

It took Ari a long moment to realize the people of K'Orge were cheering. He shot a glance at Sir Cadwel, but the knight looked equally confused. There was a movement in the crowd as it split. Stew, the black mare, Goldwin and Larke's silver steed came forward through the crowd. People reached out to touch them as they passed.

Following them came Cooro and Kiala, and, to Ari's relief, Siara and . . .

Ari dropped the reins of the camel he led, breaking into a run. He knew Ispiria saw him, for she grabbed up her skirts, obviously soaked through, and started running up the mountainside toward him. She passed the three Wheys, and the Questri.

Her red hair curls were in complete disarray, streaming out behind her as she ran. She appeared half-drenched, likely by sea water. She was the most beautiful sight Ari had ever seen.

As soon as she was within reach, Ari swept her up, spinning them both to break their headlong forward motion.

Ispiria wrapped her arms around him, kissing him so fiercely he stopped spinning. Stopped thinking. His whole world was her.

Finally, she leaned back, smiling up at him. "I missed you."

Ari pulled her back close, burying his face in her curls. His throat was too tight for words. He squeezed his eyes shut. He'd just slain a dragon. Knights who slew dragons did not cry.

Ispiria wiggled and he forced himself to loosen his arms. She slid down, her feet returning to the ground. She made an effort to push her wayward locks from her eyes.

Ari reached into his tunic, retrieving the ribbon he carried. "Here," he said, managing to get that single word out.

Ispiria's smile was a balm against the pain in Ari's soul. She took the ribbon, tying back her hair. "Thank you."

Wrapping one arm about him, she turned, snuggling herself under his shoulder. He put his arm about her, silently vowing to keep her there. He never wanted to be without her again.

"I told you he would come for me," Ispiria said.

Looking up from his study of her, he saw she was addressing Siara, who stood talking in a low voice with her aunt and Cooro. The princess looked bedraggled, and worn, but unharmed. Ari tried to see if he could discern her state, but her dress hid any signs she was with child.

"For the five hundredth time, Ispiria, I never doubted he would," Siara said, looking up at them. She sounded exasperated.

Ispiria wrapped both arms about Ari again. "I told her you would come," she whispered, smiling up at him.

Ari stared down at her. Nothing in the world could be as beautiful as Ispiria's smile.

A shifting in the crowd brought his attention up. A man came forward from the watching mass. He, like them all, was soot-stained. A bit of his hair appeared burned away as well. He bowed to Ari and his companions.

"You have slain the dragon. We saw it," the man said, his words thickly accented. He pointed.

Turning, Ari looked back up the mountain. His eyes traced the black river up to the plateau, where the giant scaled carcass lay. He looked back, taking in their ruined village. He couldn't quite bring himself to feel he was to blame, for this was the Lady's work. Still, he somehow felt responsible for the death and destruction about him. He took in the gathered people, men, women and children. He was happy so many survived, though he knew the number of dead must exceed one thousand. "How did you know to leave the city?"

"The magi steeds came," the man said. "These three came again and again. They took up our children by their sashes and carried them from the town." He pointed to Stew, the black mare and Goldwin. "The silver one, he ran through the city. He made no sound, but all who saw him knew we must flee. In this way, many of us ran from our home, finding safety outside K'Orge." The eyes he turned on his city as he spoke were dark with pain.

Ari looked at the Questri, giving them a nod he hoped would suffice until he had time to better thank them for what they'd done. "I'm sorry about your home," he said to the man, taking in the destruction once more. Where would they go? What would they eat? Ispiria snuggled against him, looking between him and the man.

A woman came up to stand beside the man. She spoke rapidly in a language Ari didn't comprehend.

"She says it is mostly those who forgot the teachings of our god who perished. She says the Overgod has blessed us again, reminding us of his will."

Ari raised his eyebrows. That seemed like an odd way to take the death of so many and the almost absolute destruction of their city. "I don't understand."

"When the witch came, we knew her for a witch. She brought these two, who all could see did not wish to be brought," the man said, gesturing to Ispiria and Siara. "She gave some in the city bright gold and gems, prevailing on the council to allow your women to be kept in our watchtower. All know greed is forbidden by the Overgod."

Ari nodded, recalling like ideas expressed in the scrolls he'd read in the water baron's library. The woman spoke again, her words so rapid Ari wondered how even someone who spoke her tongue could comprehend her. Ari was aware of his friends gathered in a semicircle around him and Ispiria. Most were silent, but Kiala was whispering to Siara. Ari guessed from the joy that came over Siara's face that the news had been shared. Kiala was her aunt, who would next be queen of Wheylia, and baby Tiana could return home to Lggothland.

The woman stopped speaking and the man turned back to Ari. "She is correct. The magi steeds gave good warning. When the first tremor came, we did not know what to think, but the steeds showed us. Mostly, those who perished did not flee when warned. They returned to their homes and shops to gather items. This is against the teachings of the Overgod. Possessions, things, are an evil our god will not tolerate. It is to remind us of this lesson he opened the volcano."

Ari knew that wasn't true, but he was too exhausted to argue. Let them believe their god had done this thing to them. Assuming the Overgod was real, he supposed it was even true. A god could have stopped Suyla, or put the idea of coming to K'Orge and transforming herself into a dragon in her mind. Who was Ari to say that wasn't the truth of it?

345

"What can we do?" Ari asked, looking around. They couldn't leave a city full of people with no homes, their food and water supplies destroyed.

Sir Cadwel cleared his throat. "Larkesong, Kenmar and I will go rally the Aluiens. They will come fix this, as they did with Sorga. This is on their heads."

"I'm going too," Mirimel said. Above, her hawks cried out their agreement.

"That bard friend of yours is Larkesong?" Ispiria whispered.

"Yes." Ari wondered if the name meant anything to her.

"Only, that terrible lady, the one who took us and who we saw turn into a dragon, she tried to use magic on me, I swear it. The necklace you gave me for our betrothal got so cold, I thought the stone would shatter. Then, she pulled it out of my dress. It sort of shocked her, I could tell. She said Larkesong, in a very terrible voice, and started cursing, mostly in Wheylia."

"You know Wheylian curses?" Ari couldn't picture his beautiful Ispiria cursing in any language.

She pulled away from him a bit, looking up at him through narrow eyes. "I do, and I may use them on you yet. It occurs to me, Lord Aridian, that you have a lot of explaining to do. I'll forgive you for not telling me Princess Siara kissed you, but you must promise to come clean on the rest."

Ari swallowed. Ispiria looked a bit daunting, the way her green eyes flashed. Before he could answer, she turned away, casting her glare around the ring of people. "That goes for you as well, Mirimel, Uncle Cadwel."

"This is a conversation for later," Sir Cadwel said.

"Yes it is." Ispiria's tone held iron.

"I promise," Ari said, pulling her back against him. He turned to Sir Cadwel. "What can we do for these people in the meantime? It won't be today that the Aluiens come to repair their city, and even once they do, I imagine much of their foodstuffs have burned."

"We shall feed them." The voice came from behind Ari. He turned, his jaw going slack with surprise. Dyne stood behind him. Willowy True Ones poured down the mountain. They streamed passed Ari and his friends, melding into the mass of townsfolk. They carried sacks and urns, from which they began distributing food and water.

"Dyne," Kiala said, coming forward, Cooro and Siara following her. "You are most welcome here."

"It is not your place to welcome us, Princess of Wheylia," Dyne said. She shrugged then, her expression softening. "We have been too long from the world. It is forbidden to sow strife, yes, but that should not prevent us from doing good. We saw what happened here. We shall feed these people. When our kin come, we will learn to know them. The city of K'Orge will be rebuilt, as will be the alliance of the Aluiens. It may be we can help them find their way once more."

"I'm happy to hear that," Kiala said, with a deep nod that was not quite a bow.

Dyne nodded back, including Ari and the others in the gesture, and glided away.

"Well then, I see things are in hand here," Larke said, watching the True Ones with mild envy clear on his face. "My mighty steed has arrived, though I don't how he comes to be on this side of the ocean or if he is still my companion, now that we cannot speak." Larke grimaced. He cleared his throat. "Regardless, we need a way back to Lggothland."

"Are you ever going to tell us his name?" Mirimel asked, looking over her shoulder at the silver-toned prince of the Questri. The people of K'Orge clustered about all four Questri, thanking them and holding up their children to touch their brows.

"I can't ask him if I may," Larke said, his tone pained.

Kenmar and Sir Cadwel both looked toward the Questri. The silver-toned stead lifted his gaze, turning to them. Sir Cadwel laughed, shaking his head.

"What?" Ari asked.

"He said he told Larke to share his name years ago, but the bard prefers to be mysterious."

Larke coughed, looking down. "Fine," he muttered. "Thalysar. His name is Prince Thalysar. Now shall we find a way to return to Lggothland?"

"We can't leave yet," Ispiria said.

Ari looked down at her, surprised. "We can't?" For his part, he longed for home, with Ispiria beside him, and their wedding to look forward to, so he would never be parted from her again.

"First we need the head."

"The head?" Ari looked about, at a loss as to what she spoke of.

"Of the dragon you killed. We all saw you throw your sword into her mouth." Ispiria sounded quite enthusiastic about the event. Sometimes, Ari forgot how bloodthirsty she was. "It was magnificent. I want her head. I'm going to put it in the great hall."

"No," Ari said, horrified by the idea. Much evil as she'd done, the dragon was the Lady. He couldn't have her head mounted on the wall.

"Yes." Ispiria's tone was firm. "She kidnapped me. She buried a whole city in fire. She tried to kill you, Mirimel and Uncle Cadwel. I am having her head on the wall, Ari, and that is final."

"Look," Larke said, pointing.

As Ari turned, Larke caught his eye and winked, but there truly was something to see out on the water. Sailing into the bay came a magnificent, four-masted ship. The figurehead on her prow was an elegantly carved white seabird. The vessel cut through the waves like she had wings.

Ari let out a happy cry. "The Albatross."

"Where?" Siara cried. She stood on her toes, but it was obvious the diminutive Wheylian Princess still couldn't see. "Is Parrentine aboard?"

Her voice held such hope, it was nearly pain. Ari looked about. Catching sight of Stew, he waved to the Questri. Stew dipped his head to the townsfolk still gathered about him and trotted over.

"Siara," Ari called.

The princess turned from where she still tried to peer out to sea. Seeing Stew, her face lit with understanding. She gathered her damp skirts and hurried over.

"Let me assist you, my lady," Ari said, releasing Ispiria to lift Siara onto Stew.

Her smile was radiant, but she hardly looked at Ari. Her eyes were turned toward the sea. Wrapping her hands in Stew's mane, she leaned low over his ears, whispering to him. Turning, the two headed for the shore.

Ispiria ducked back under Ari's arm, wrapping it firmly about her shoulder. "Is the prince here? I know she is becoming ill without him. I worry for the baby."

Ari squinted at the ever nearing ship. He didn't think it was just hope that made him think he could see Parrentine standing on the forecastle deck. "He is. The prince is here." He squeezed his arm tighter about her shoulders. "I have you back. We can go home."

"That sounds wonderful. Home." Ispiria sighed. She turned, wrapping her arms around him and pulling his head down for a kiss that left him dazed. A smile turned up her lips and brightened her eyes. "But first, I want the head of that dragon."

Epilogue

Ari looked up from Sorga's books at the sound of running feet. Just outside his office, they stopped, and whispering ensued. He set down his quill with a smile as his seven-year-old twin daughters entered the room. They had their chins up and moved with graceful steps, not realizing their father could hear well enough to know they'd been running about like banshees only moments ago.

"Father," they said in unison, curtsying.

"Alliria, Cyanna," he greeted. "To what do I owe the joy of your company?"

"Mama said you're planning our spring trip," Alliria said.

Cyanna, the better reader of the two, inched closer, trying to peek at his ledger. Ari didn't close it, knowing the numbers meant little to his daughter. He did turn over a letter he'd been writing to King Cooro earlier, talking about the state of Lggothland's and Wheylia's relationship. Most of the missive related to pleasantries exchanged about their families, for the two nations were at peace, but there was some state business within. His daughter's keen mind didn't need to be worrying over politics.

"I am." Ari hid a smile, already knowing what each would ask for.

"Are we going to the capital for the spring tourney?" Cyanna asked.

"Yes. I promised your little brother we would go this year. He wants to see his father act, as he puts it, like a real knight." Not to mention, Stew's younger brother, Gaust, was chafing for another go at jousting. Apparently, when Stew convinced his brother to be Ari's stead, he'd promised Gaust it would be entertaining.

Alliria let out a dramatic sigh. "All you and Arden care about is knight stuff," she groused. "We don't want to go to the capital."

"Don't you want to see Princess Tiana and Prince Serretine?"

"Serretine's nice enough, but people are always watching him so none of us can have any fun if he's around," Cyanna said.

"And Tiana is such a lady," Alliria added, rolling her eyes. She huffed out a breath to blow her orange curls out of her face.

"Well, I'm afraid we are going to the capital. Might I remind you, your father is King's Champion. On occasion, I must visit the ruling monarchs."

His daughters exchanged a look. He knew they were silently communicating, as only twins could do. They turned back to him with sweet smiles.

"What about after that?" Alliria said. "Where are we going after we leave the capital?"

352

"You're coming back here, and I'm traveling to some of the southern towns in Sorga. It's been three years since I made a tour of that region."

"Or, you could go on your boring tour and we could go visit Papa Cadwel and Papa Kenmar," Cyanna said.

Alliria turned to her, scowling. "No, we said we would ask to go visit Aunt Mirimel and Uncle Larke."

"You said that." Cyanna stomped her foot. "I want to go to the school and learn more about magic from Papa Cadwel and Papa Kenmar, and see Mialar and the dragon head. Even Arden likes the dragon head."

Ari grimaced. He didn't care for the dragon head, though his children, and everyone else who'd ever mentioned it, seemed fascinated. The head of a real dragon. One Ari had slain. It was legendary. People would visit Sir Cadwel's and Lord Kenmar's school of the magic arts just for a look at Suyla's head. Natan, who'd gone to be their steward there, said it was good for enrollment. Ari found it worse than macabre.

Visiting Mialar, on the other hand, was a reasonable request from Cyanna. Mialar was the daughter of Ari's friend from the Tybrunn Plains, Tewlar. He was the first to send a child to study with Sir Cadwel and Lord Kenmar. Mialar was a good student, and had proven the Questri didn't need the Orate Tree's magic. Still, it had taken Prince Thalysar overthrowing his father, the old Herdmaster, to end the practice of sacrificing the first born of the plainspeople and turning their children into voiceless. Mialar spent half of each year in study now, at the school.

"Now you've done it," Alliria whispered at her sister. "You know Father hates the dragon head." She turned to Ari with a smile. "We should go visit Aunt Mirimel and Uncle Larke instead. Aunt Mirimel said I need more lessons. She said I'm to be as good a shot as she is, someday."

"But Mialar is almost done studying and I want to say goodbye. She's my best friend," Cyanna wailed.

"I'm your best friend," Alliria snapped.

"She's my other best friend."

"You only get one, and it's me."

Ari cleared his throat. "Alliria, your aunt and uncle aren't in Hawkers. They're in the village in Tybrunn meeting Stew's new son." In addition to welcoming Stew and the black mare's newest colt, they were working with the voiceless, trying to return free will to them, but Ari declined to tell his daughters that. Explaining about the voiceless would give Cyanna nightmares, and provide Alliria with a way to torment her more sensitive sister.

Alliria's face fell, but Cyanna's split in a grin. "You see? We must go visit Papa Cadwel and Papa Kenmar. And Arden will be happy. Papa Cadwel can give him sword lessons."

"Father gives him sword lessons already," Alliria muttered.

"Yes, but we want to go on another trip," Cyanna said, elbowing her sister.

"To a boring magic school," Alliria said.

"I'll tell you what, I'll give you some shooting lessons," Ari offered.

Alliria shook her head. "Aunt Mirimel says you'll teach me bad habits. She says there's no good can come from learning from a . . ." His daughter frowned, obviously trying to recall her aunt's exact words. "A second-rate marksman who never bothers to put the time into shooting he needs to in order to be good."

Ari would have to remember to thank Mirimel for that one.

Cyanna looked back and forth between them. "But we can go to the school, right Father?"

Ari shook his head, but he smiled. "I'll tell you what, if you get Steward Peine to agree, we can go. You know it's more work for him when we all leave him here to manage on his own."

"He says all you and mama do is make work for him," Alliria said, putting her hands on her hips.

"Does he? Well, it shouldn't be difficult to get him to agree, then, should it?"

Together, his daughters shook their heads, orange curls dancing.

"Good, then let your poor, trouble making father finish his work. You can tell me Master Peine's answer at dinnertime."

"Yes, Father," they said. Cyanna dropped a curtsy, elbowing Alliria to do the same. They went to the door.

"Thank you, Father," Alliria said on her way out, grinning. He could hear them skip down the hall.

Ari leaned back in his chair stretching his legs out under the desk. They were spoiled, his beautiful daughters. He knew as much. Not as spoiled as Princess Tiana, but surely used to getting their way.

The door opened again and Ispiria slipped in. "So, where are we headed when we leave the capital?" she asked, coming around his desk with a smile on her face.

Ari pushed back his chair, holding out his arms to his wife. She slipped into his lap, resting her head on his shoulder. "I am going on a tour of the southern region. You, the girls and Arden may be going to visit Sir Cadwel. Or nowhere. I left it up to our chief steward. Peine could always say no to them."

Ispiria laughed. "True. Or you could fail to win the tourney. Or Uncle Cadwel could shave off his mustache. These are all things that could, possibly, in some way, happen."

Ari hugged her to him, joining in her laughter.

The End

ABOUT THE AUTHOR

Summer Hanford is primarily a fantasy author, but also enjoys science fiction, Regency and adventure. The first four books in her five book Thrice Born series are: *Gift of the Aluien*, *Hawks of Sorga*, *Throne of Wheylia* and *Plains of Tybrunn*. The final novel in the series is *Shores of K'Orge*. Summer's first full-length solo Regency Romance, *The Archaeologist's Daughter*, was released by Scarsdale Publishing in the summer or 2017. Shorter works include two Scarsdale Half Hour Reads series; *Ladies Always Shoot First* and *A Lord's Kiss*. Summer's work can also be found in various magazines and anthologies, including *Aoife's Kiss*, *Something Wicked Anthology Vol. II*, *Daughters of Icarus*, *The Ampersand Review* and *Nightmare Walkers and Dream Stalkers Vol. II*, as well as in her *Thrice Born Chronicles*, a collection of short stories designed to augment her Thrice Born series.

Starting in 2014, Summer was offered the privilege of partnering with fan fiction author Renata McMann on her well-loved *Pride and Prejudice* variations. To date, they have over twenty popular *Pride & Prejudice Fan Fiction* stories currently available, including four national and international Amazon Classic Romance Best Sellers, with more variations to come. McMann's original and diverse interpretations of this classic love story, combined with Hanford's descriptive skills, create new and exciting versions of everyone's favorite tale that readers all over the world can't put down. More information on these works is available at **www.renatamcmann.com**.

Summer is currently writing with McMann, working on her own Regency and Fantasy titles, providing content for, creating and managing websites, and is the fantasy and science fiction faculty member at AllWriters' Workplace and Workshop, LLC., an international creative writing studio. She lives in Michigan with her husband and compulsory, deliberately spoiled, cats. For more about Summer, visit **www.summerhanford.com**.

www.ingramcontent.com/pod-product-compliance
Lightning Source LLC
Chambersburg PA
CBHW071305200626
46813CB00015B/96